THE
NIGHTSHADE
GOD

By Hannah Whitten

THE NIGHTSHADE CROWN

The Foxglove King

The Hemlock Queen

The Nightshade God

THE WILDERWOOD

For the Wolf

For the Throne

THE NIGHTSHADE GOD

The Nightshade Crown: Book Three

HANNAH WHITTEN

orbitbooks.net

Copyright © 2025 by Hannah Whitten

Cover design by Lisa Marie Pompilio
Cover illustration by Mike Heath | Magnus Creative
Cover copyright © 2025 by Hachette Book Group, Inc.
Map by Charis Loke

Orbit
Hachette Book Group
1290 Avenue of the Americas
New York, NY 10104
orbitbooks.net

First Edition: July 2025
Simultaneously published in Great Britain by Orbit

Orbit is an imprint of Hachette Book Group.
The Orbit name and logo are registered trademarks of Little, Brown Book Group Limited.

The publisher is not responsible for websites (or their content) that are not owned by the publisher.

The Hachette Speakers Bureau provides a wide range of authors for speaking events. To find out more, go to hachettespeakersbureau.com or email HachetteSpeakers@hbgusa.com.

Orbit books may be purchased in bulk for business, educational, or promotional use. For information, please contact your local bookseller or the Hachette Book Group Special Markets Department at special.markets@hbgusa.com.

Library of Congress Cataloging-in-Publication Data
Names: Whitten, Hannah, author.
Title: The Nightshade God / Hannah Whitten.
Description: First edition. | New York, NY : Orbit, 2025. | Series: The Nightshade Crown ; book 3
Identifiers: LCCN 2024050185 | ISBN 9780316435598 (hardcover) | ISBN 9780316435796 (ebook)
Subjects: LCGFT: Fantasy fiction. | Novels.
Classification: LCC PS3623.H5864 N54 2025 | DDC 813/.6—dc23/eng/20241025
LC record available at https://lccn.loc.gov/2024050185

ISBNs: 9780316435598 (hardcover), 9780316595674 (signed edition), 9780316595704 (BarnesAndNoble.com signed edition), 9780316435796 (ebook)

Printed in the United States of America

LSC-C

Printing 1, 2025

For anyone who has found a beginning in an ending.
And for me.

And also for Miss Rachel, without whom I would not have had the time to edit this book. You're a real one, Rach.

APO

LA VIE ET LE JOUR

CALDIEN

BURNT
ISLES

RATHARC

GOLDEN
MOUNT

Kettleburgh

LA MORT ET LA NUIT

CALDIENAN-CLAIMED
TERRITORY

Farramark

OURISH PASS

Huverraine

ROUSKA

Dellaire

BALGIA

KALIACH

EROCCA

KIRYTHEA

Laerdas

MYROSH

MALFOUR

KADMAR

NUX

MAP BY CHARIS LOKE

CONTENT WARNINGS

Sexual violence (implied, not on page), religious abuse, graphic violence, and sexual content. Read safe!

I am the fiery life of divine substance, I blaze above the beauty of the fields, I shine in the waters, I burn in sun, moon, and stars.

—Hildegard of Bingen

THE
NIGHTSHADE
GOD

The surface always seemed only a breath away. He couldn't catch that breath.

There was only gold, as if he were trapped in the center of the sun or an ocean on the perpetual edge of morning. Power all around him, but he could never use it. He could only feel it, concentrated in the god who'd overtaken him, jealously hoarded and drowning him out.

Though lately, he'd been feeling a strange sort of pull. Something gently tugging on that power, like a bit in a horse's mouth.

It took too much energy to think, most of the time. Too much energy to try taking over the body that was rightfully his. Bastian had never considered himself someone who excelled at persevering, really; the things he was good at he did, and everything else he left alone. The easiest thing to do now was float. Enjoy the gold when he was conscious enough to do so, and seep back into the dark when he wasn't. He'd lost. Might as well accept it.

But then he'd think of Lore.

Then he'd think of Gabe.

And Bastian would try to hang on, just a little longer. Fight a little harder.

For as long as he could, at least.

CHAPTER ONE

LORE

Let all my abasements be used for glory, for the uplifting of my betters.

–The Book of Prayer, Tract 367

L ore was exceedingly bad at being a convict.

Maybe if she'd been left to languish in a prison, draped dramatically over a cot in a bare stone cell and not required to do anything but wallow, she could have excelled in her newfound position. She wasn't as good at brooding as Gabe—gods, no one was—but she thought she could have given it a solid go. At least then she wouldn't have perpetually watering eyes from the ash in the air, and always-open blisters on her hands, and a crick in her neck that at this point she assumed was permanent.

No, Lore was not good at this at all.

But she tried her best not to show it, because the guards on the Burnt Isles all wanted to make her as miserable as possible. And if there was one thing Lore hated more than her current circumstances, it was letting someone else win.

She straightened as much as her sore back would let her and wiped her wrist across her brow. The ridged skin at her temple was still a surprise every time she felt it. A scar from that day in the North Sanctuary when she'd brought the whole thing down, tried to kill herself enough to banish the gods in her and Bastian's heads.

Thinking of him hurt. Thinking of Gabe hurt, too. She tried to do both as little as possible. Thankfully, there were many other things to think of, like how in every hell she was going to get off this damn island. How in even more hells she was going to get to Apollius's body on the Golden Mount.

How she was going to kill Him.

But even though she thought of those things constantly, she wasn't any closer to actually knowing how to accomplish them.

And in all that thinking, she still had to find at least three pieces of gems or gold if she wanted a meal and a place to sleep tonight.

Lore wiped at her temple again. It was hard to get a good look at her new scar—mirrors were scarce on the Burnt Isles—but she'd managed to glimpse her reflection in the trough where they were allowed to scoop water into tin cups four times a day for five-minute intervals, drinking as much as they could before the seconds ran dry and their cups did, too. Red lines wavering from the corner of her eye up to her hairline and down to her cheekbone. It wasn't terrible, but Lore was vain, and it still made her want to cry.

She didn't. Couldn't spare the water.

The pickax had a splintery handle, and she took a furtive moment to rewrap the cloth around her bleeding palms before picking it up again. Bastian's old trick from the boxing ring served her well. None of the pickaxes were in especially good shape, but some were in worse shape than others, and the better ones were on unspoken reserve for the most senior inmates.

Though Lore was sure she'd have to use a shitty pickax even if she was here for fifty years.

She lifted the pickax again, brought it down on the rock in front of her. It bounced off, barely making a dent. A faint gleam of gold seamed the scratch the blade had made.

"Guess we're eating tonight," Lore muttered, resenting her own inner leap of enthusiasm. Sleeping on the ground was no particular horror after the life she'd led, but hunger was. Her first few days here, when she'd barely managed to find anything and gone without dinner most nights, her stomach had felt like a feral animal trying to claw its way out of her throat. Desperation had claws, too, and when she saw inmates attacking each other for pieces to turn into rations, she understood.

There wasn't much here—the Second Isle had been mined to death already—but she managed to find at least one piece a day. Mostly because she didn't want to think about how far she could push that understanding before it became a plan.

The main mine on the Second Isle was mostly just a hole in the ground, dizzyingly deep. Concentric rings lined the hole, different levels where prisoners hacked the chasm ever deeper in search of jewels and gold made by Apollius's and Nyxara's blood, dripping to the ground in the Godsfall, growing treasure like seeds. The deeper you went, the more there was to find.

There were paltry railings to keep prisoners from falling to their deaths, but they were as splintery as the pickax handles. It wasn't unusual for someone to pitch over the edge, whether by accident or with a push. Or by a solemn decision.

The railings on the First Isle were better, apparently. That was where the prisoners with money went, those who had a few years to serve instead of a lifetime. The Second Isle was for poison runners, back-alley murderers, and petty thieves. You only ended up here if the Sainted King didn't care about you or was very, very angry.

So Lore's arrival was bound to be a topic of amusement.

Something slammed into the small of her back, nearly sending her headfirst into the open pit. "*Fuck!*" Lore dropped her pickax, cloth unraveling from her bleeding hands as she gripped a rock beside her to keep from pitching over. The sharp edges she'd made earlier this morning bit into her palms, thin blood obscuring the seam of uncovered gold.

Below, jagged stones, winking with the occasional gem; prisoners winding around them like ants headed for the hill. It all shimmered in her vision, dehydration and exhaustion turning the belly of the mine into a kaleidoscope.

"Apologies, Your Majesty." Gods, they all got a kick out of that. Lore had hoped that maybe her identity could be kept under wraps, but that proved exceptionally foolish of her. Every convict on the Second Isle knew who she was, and every one of them hated her for it. "I thought your balance would be better, being honed in ballrooms."

"You do know that I spent maybe six months of my life in ballrooms, right, Jilly?" Lore turned, her balance regained, and scowled at the woman behind her. "The rest of it was spent poison running. Just like you."

Jilly scowled right back. She was probably forty, but years in the mines had put a hunch in her back, and her skin looked sun-leathered despite the coating of ash and fog in the air. Her own pickax, with a handle that looked silky smooth to Lore's eyes, waved in her direction again. "You were never just like me."

Truer than the other woman could know.

"And now you're here, with your big death-power," Jilly continued, "and you won't even use it to get us out. Fat lot of good you are, Your Majesty."

Lore's fingers twitched involuntarily against the linen wraps. Searching for Mortem threads, trying to call them. She could feel the filaments of death running through everything here, the rock and the dirt, closer to the surface in the people than they should be.

But they wouldn't come. Mortem wouldn't obey her.

Lore couldn't tell Jilly that, either. "How exactly do you think that would work? I turn all the guards to stone and we take the ships, only to be executed when we get to the mainland? I know dust inhalation is bad for your brain, but surely you still have one."

The older woman's lip lifted, a sneer that showed her nightshade-stained teeth. "It'd be something," she said quietly, with a lace of desperation. "Something other than this. Hope is enough, even when it doesn't make sense."

"Get moving!"

The guards on the Burnt Isles were somehow even worse than the bloodcoats in the Citadel. Just as self-important, with an extra helping of stupidity and brute strength. This one, Fulbert, was as tall as Gabe and probably twice his weight, with what seemed to be the common sense of a dazed cow.

"You're up farther than you should be, Jilly; get back down to your tier and leave the Queen alone." Fulbert leered at Lore, waving Jilly on with a hand built for fistfights. "Are you trying to hold court, Your Majesty? Miss having a whole Citadel pay attention to you?"

"You people desperately need a different bit," Lore muttered, rewrapping her hands and retrieving her pickax.

Fulbert wagged his finger and grabbed it from her. "No more mines for you today, Queenie. You're on dock duty. Martin's orders."

Ah. Time to make a bad day even worse.

❦

The sun was covered in a gray miasma, but Lore still squinted as she stepped out of the rickety lift between the central mine and the beach—the sunlight reflected off the particles in the air, making it bright but not really *sunny*, which didn't seem fair. She paused, trying to get her bearings, but Fulbert was impatient and pushed her out, sending her stumbling onto the rocky sand.

"The beach is no marble floor, huh?" He grinned, poking her

again. The end of his bayonet was blunt, but it still hurt. "Not like the Citadel. Can't walk without iron bars under your feet?"

Lore kept her mouth shut. It was the one skill she'd honed on the Burnt Isles. If she had any hope of escaping, of finding a way to the Golden Mount so she could finish the job Nyxara had left undone, she had to let them tire of her. Become one more unwatched face in the crowd.

With no response to his needling, Fulbert grew bored quickly, as men of his intelligence were wont to do. "Martin's at the lighthouse," he grumbled, turning back to the lift. "Go straight there and get a mop."

She was sure a mop was not the only thing Martin would try to give her. Fists already clenched, Lore stumbled her way across the beach in her flimsy prisoner-issue boots, blisters screaming across her arches.

At first, she'd been shocked by how little the guards here... well, guarded. But after a week or so, it made sense. For the few miles directly around the Isles, the sea was nigh unnavigable, the ash so thick in the air that you could barely see a yard in front of your face. The only way the prison barges were able to make it was by following the steel lines in the water, anchored to the Auverrani shore and the island's beach, laid by the first generation of prisoners. Every once in a while an inmate would disappear, but it was chalked up to either suicide or murder. If you were on the Second Isle, those were the only two ways to get off it.

Lore walked slowly across the beach, since there was no guard to prod her on. She wanted to spend as little time at the lighthouse as she could and already felt the first pangs of hunger. It'd be bad tonight. When you worked dock duty, Martin decided if you got your rations or not.

The Burnt Isles' harbor hardly deserved the name. Five sun-bleached docks jutting out into the surf and a barnacle-encrusted lighthouse a few yards out, barely visible before the curtains of fog and ash closed over it, both thickening over open water. Depending on the tide, you had to either climb over sharp rocks to reach the lighthouse or wade through the ocean and hope you didn't trip over them.

Today was a wading day. Lore hitched up the baggy trousers she'd been given upon her arrival—too long in the leg, too tight in the waist—and made her way to the lighthouse. The current pulled at her from the moment she stepped into the sea, forceful as hands on her ankles.

Martin was waiting. The lighthouse keeper lounged in the doorway and watched her approach, his tall, thin frame giving the impression of a spider lingering in a web. A sly smile revealed blindingly white teeth in a sunburnt white face, his cut-short hair turned the same grayish not-color as the sky. His neck was tanned, but his arms were nearly as pale as his teeth, as if he covered them up when he went outdoors. "If it isn't the Queen."

Lore stopped on the rock closest to the lighthouse, blessedly flat and mostly out of the water, locking her legs against the wind. "You called?"

He pushed off from the door, hands in his pockets, eyes flickering lazily up and down her form. She'd been wrong before. He wasn't like a spider; he was like a snake, eyes slitted against the ashy light, body primed for striking.

"I have work for you." Where most of the other guards on the Isles spoke roughly, Martin always had a superciliously polite air about him, carefully articulate. "Both inside and outside. Which will it be, Your Majesty?"

A seemingly benign question. But Lore had an advantage, the one kindness her fellow prisoners had shown her.

Space in the communal bunkhouse was reserved for prisoners who found at least five valuable pieces a day, and Lore never had. Her first night, she found a shallow cave with a relatively soft sandy floor, one that already held a few others who'd had the same idea. One of them was a girl who'd been on the Isles for weeks, and she gave them all a rundown of the guards.

"Gellert is an ass, but he'll let you get an extra drink from the trough if you're quick about it and no captains are watching. Don't try to go down a tier in the mine, or the seniors will jump you, and the guards won't do shit about it. And if Martin calls you to the lighthouse, never tell him you want inside work." She'd narrowed reddened eyes, pointed with a broken-nailed finger at no one in particular. "Or do—I'm certainly not above sticky work for a favor—but be smart about it. He's the kind who doesn't just want that."

The bruises on her cheekbone had told the rest of the story.

The girl had been gone in the next couple days. No one looked for her. Martin started calling up new girls for the lighthouse afterward.

And it hadn't taken long for him to ask for Lore by name. This was the third time he'd called her here, given her the choice of inside or outside work. They both knew what he was really asking.

And they both knew a time was coming when she wouldn't get the luxury of choice.

"Outside," Lore answered, same as she always did.

The smile on his face turned sharp at the corners. Martin advanced a step, out onto the flat rock where Lore stood. She fought the urge to step back, knowing it'd just send her toppling into the water—onto the rocks. The tide was going out.

"You think you're too good for me?" He still spoke with that polite tone, and it made gooseflesh ripple up Lore's arms. She'd had similar things spat at her before when she rebuffed an advance in a tavern or alleyway, but none of those catcallers had been in a position of power over her. "You think that because you were a Queen for two minutes, I can't have you whenever I want? I keep asking because I like them willing, but I'll be having some of what the King was having, deathwitch."

Gods, she hated feeling afraid. She'd fielded many unpleasant emotions recently, but fear was always the worst, the most helpless. Lore's fingers worked back and forth, metaphysically clawing at the rock below her, the dead driftwood on the beach, the stone of the lighthouse.

"Outside work," Lore said again. Then, choking on it, "Please."

Martin stood right in front of her, now. Still smiling, he shook his head. "No. I think you need some inside work today, Hemlock Queen."

"What about a trade?" she said, quickly, the words racing her disgust so they couldn't be overtaken. "I'll do something for you if you do something for me."

"*Something*," Martin scoffed. "Say it. I want to hear it."

The back of her throat tasted sour. "I'll choose inside work if you get me a boat."

Martin stared at her, near-colorless eyebrow raised to near-colorless hairline. Then he brayed a laugh. "You think you're in a position to bargain?" His leathery hand closed around her wrist. Instinctually, Lore jerked backward, losing her balance—he used the moment to pull her to his chest, his breath in her face, hot and harsh and smelling like cheap alcohol. "Even if I gave you a ship all to yourself, you wouldn't be able to get off this island. The prison galleys can barely navigate through the ash even with the steel guidelines. What makes you think you can?"

Nothing did, but she was desperate. Lore's fingers worked and worked as she tried to pull away from Martin, weaving at magic that was no longer there.

She'd held all of it, every drop of Mortem left in the world. And now there was nothing.

It'd happened right as the barge approached the shoreline of the Second Isle, a deep *ripping* feeling, something vital as an organ torn out. Lore had gasped, pressing a hand against her middle. *Nyxara?*

Something happened, the goddess had murmured, a thrum of anxiety in the back of Lore's mind.

She knew even before she reached for magic that it was gone, her grasping hands gripping nothing. No darkness, no death, just the stale, smoggy air of the Isles.

What do I do? Panic made her heart race and her breath come heavy.

I don't know, the goddess said, sounding as helpless as Lore felt. *I don't know.*

The next morning, the gray stars on Lore's palms had faded. She could feel Mortem, but she still couldn't wield it. And though that was something she'd always wanted, now it felt like a punishment. One she couldn't figure out what she'd done to deserve.

Especially since the damn Buried Goddess was still in her head.

Not now, though, as the sun burned high behind the ash, this awful man trying to haul her toward the door and not caring about anything but showing his own power. Now Nyxara was silent. Cowed once again by a man who looked at a woman and saw nothing but a vessel for his violence, a tool for his use. Lore's feet fought for purchase on the rock, her hands pressing fruitlessly at Martin's chest, trying to keep him away.

"Stop fighting," Martin said, slapping the side of her face, the barely healed lines of her new scar. "I own you, Lore Arceneaux."

And something about that—how it reminded her of Apollius, reminded her of how she was married to Bastian when Bastian had been locked inside his own mind—made Lore's fear alchemize into rage.

She tore away from Martin, letting the momentum force her off the rock and into the churn of the sea. The currents pulled at her ankles, but she didn't topple. "Don't touch me."

"Have you forgotten where you are?" He crowded her again, his face mere inches from her own, gaining extra height from his position on the rock. "I can do whatever I like, and then I can throw you in the sea, and no one will care. No one will come looking for you." He smiled again, sour wine fuming into her face. "I'll make you call me Your Majesty while you're choking on—"

Maybe it was the reminders of Bastian. Maybe it was something that had been brewing ever since she set foot on the Isles, so near to the Golden Mount and the Fount the gods had broken.

Or maybe it was just plain desperation making her try something she wasn't sure would work.

Part of her didn't expect that she could use Spiritum anymore. Mortem had been pulled from her grasp when she arrived here; she assumed the same thing had happened to the power of life, especially now that she was separated from Bastian, their Law of Opposites sundered. Using magic didn't really fit into her tentative plan to become an irrelevant face in the crowd, unmarked enough to someday, somehow slip away.

But when she reached for the threads of Spiritum lurking in Martin's skin and bone and blood, they jumped to her like they'd been waiting.

Lore channeled it through her, second nature. She tugged on a strand, and Martin's heart sped, galloping behind his ribs. He dropped back, hands pressed to his chest, his face turning red and his veins swelling like leeches.

Martin stumbled on the rock, gasping, crawling toward the lighthouse door. When he reached it, he pulled himself up, his face an alarming shade of purple.

She let the thread go, slowly. Let it wind its way out of her, let his heart regain its rhythm, his veins return to their usual dimensions.

"Be careful, Martin," Lore said quietly. "Seems like your heart isn't doing so well. You probably don't want to get too excited for the next few days."

Martin said nothing, still gasping, the doorframe the only

thing keeping him upright. Watching her like she was the spider now, and he the fly.

Stupid of her to try bargaining with him. But her chances of success were already thin and getting thinner.

Martin closed the door, apparently content to leave her be for now.

That was all well and good, but she still needed a mop.

Sighing, Lore picked her way around the lighthouse, headed for the back entrance. The incoming tide swept over her boots and soaked the too-long hem of her trousers.

Mops and buckets for swabbing the prison ships were right inside the back door. Lore stepped into the lighthouse and grabbed one, enjoying the momentary coolness and a break for her eyes from the constant itch and glare.

Something moved in the shadows. One of the other prisoners, probably; one who'd taken the risks of Martin's attentions along with the easier labor. Lore opened her eyes, sure she'd be shooed out.

A familiar face stared at her from the spiral stairs that led farther up into the lighthouse. Blond hair. Blue eyes. Beautiful.

For a minute, Lore thought it was Amelia, come back to haunt her.

No, not Amelia. Her sister.

"Dani?" Lore breathed, but the other woman was already gone.

CHAPTER TWO

GABE

If you can't find love, start looking for a fight.
—Caldienan proverb

He was getting better at taking a punch.

His opponent was shorter, but broader, and had clearly been fighting far longer than Gabe had. Gabe hunched over, the back of his wrist against his bloodied nose, and knew that taking a moment to regain his bearings was a mistake even before the massive Caldienan man kicked him in the gut.

Heat at the tips of his fingers as he fell, his back cracking against a stone floor softened by dirty straw. Flame flickering in the corners of his vision.

No, Gabe snarled inside his head. *Stop*.

It did.

Briefly, he considered getting up, refusing through sheer spite to let the bout end. But his eyes were watering, and his stomach hurt, and he was already going to be sore as every hell tomorrow, when he'd have to either come back here or find work in the market somewhere. Rent was due.

He closed his eyes, ears ringing as the referee shouted the

countdown. The crowd roared, stomping onto the straw, rallying around the man who'd won.

Good for you, Gabe thought. He pushed himself up, wincing. *Be thankful I didn't use every tool at my disposal.*

A singed smell in his nostrils, like burning wood.

The crowd mostly left him alone. That was something different between the fighting rings here and those in Auverraine. There wasn't much jeering in Caldien. They were content to celebrate their winners without heaping misery on the loser.

It was an odd dichotomy, since the fighting was so much more brutal. There was no genteel pretense of boxing, with wrapped hands and defined rules. In Caldien, people just beat the shit out of each other.

That suited his mood fine. Gabe felt like he probably deserved to get the shit beat out of him.

It was not lost on him, the irony that he was coping the same way Bastian had, back when Bastian was...well, was Bastian. Gabe tried not to think of the implications, of why he felt better when he was subjecting himself to the same humbling. A twisted kind of closeness.

He wished he could find something that made him feel even marginally closer to Lore.

Now upright, Gabe limped to the edge of the ring, holding on to a wooden post for balance. Most fights here took place in repurposed barns, since outside it was always either raining or about to be. Gabe supposed that was a good thing, for him. The weather in Caldien was not conducive to fire.

The referee approached holding a small bag, clinking coins. He handed it to Gabe with an almost-pitying look before turning back to the next fight. Gabe stuck it in his pocket without counting the winnings. He didn't necessarily want to draw attention to the fact that he was betting against himself. His dignity had taken enough hits as it was, no pun intended.

After arriving in Caldien two weeks ago, following a week on the sea, Val had found them a few rooms in a hovel near the harbor. She knew the landlord from running poisons, but smugglers were not a warm bunch, and even their acquaintance didn't equal out to free rent. Malcolm's friend at the university, a librarian named Adrian, had offered to help them with accommodations, but there were no cheaper rooms to be found, and Adrian's own apartment was far too small for all of them.

And there were the Citadel guards crawling all over the city that made staying near an escape route seem like a good idea.

So they earned money however they could. Mari had sold off one pistol, though she still wore a bandolier with enough ammunition for two. Malcolm did the landlord's accounting.

And Gabe bet against himself in the fighting rings.

"Again, Gabe?"

Michal. He'd known the other man was here; he always came to watch the fights. Gabe supposed it was a nostalgia thing, Michal remembering who he'd been before he got caught up in god-schemes.

"You only have the one eye," Michal said, leaning against one of the barn's support beams. "You should really take better care of it."

The aforementioned eye was already swelling, smarting to the touch. "I'll sacrifice my eye so that we don't have to sleep in Caldienan weather."

Michal glanced at the sky beyond the door. Rainy, as always, and threatening to blow into a full storm. "There are other ways to earn coin."

"Nothing I'm good at."

There were other reasons, reasons Gabe probably wasn't hiding half as well as he wanted to be. Getting beaten to a pulp every day gave him something to think about that wasn't the complete mess they found themselves in. His body being one constant ache made other thoughts, if not disappear, at least recede into background noise.

Thoughts like Bastian being Apollius. That the return of the benevolent god their entire religion—Gabe's entire life—was predicated on was actually the precursor to an Empire that would smash everything beneath a holy fist.

As if in response to the thought, the perpetually threatening storm finally arrived, thunder crashing as endless rain poured from the clouds. A spear of lightning split the sky.

"You're making a spectacle of yourself," Michal said quietly. "You're someone they'll all remember."

A risk, certainly. Gabe hadn't heard any murmurs of whether the Citadel was looking for them, but the bloodcoats lurking in every corner of Farramark made it seem likely. He and Malcolm had taken to wearing fingerless gloves to hide their palm tattoos, but there was nothing to be done for his eye patch.

He nodded. "Point taken."

But he wasn't going to stop, and Michal's pinched expression said he knew it.

The punishment of fighting felt right. Penance for the ones he couldn't save, for his betrayals. He wasn't worthy of the love he held, and though no one could beat it out of him, he could at least feel the pain of it and be reminded of all the ways he'd failed, so maybe, hopefully, he wouldn't again.

"Myriad hells." A winner from a previous bout approached the barn door, hands on her hips, bruises blooming on her shoulders. The broad brogue of her accent made the profanity somehow softer. "The weather in autumn has never been good, but storms like this are usually reserved for summertime."

"We have cloaks," pointed out her friend, presumably antsy to leave the barn. "We can brave it."

The fighter snorted. "Raincoats are as useless as the Rotunda when it's this bad."

Her friend smirked. "Maybe they'll put the weather to a vote next session. It'd be just as effective as the shit they actually vote on."

The fighter laughed, then the two of them wandered back into the barn, supposedly to wait out the storm.

"Malcolm wants you to meet him at the boardinghouse," Michal said when the fighters were far enough away not to overhear. "He's found something."

Water from the trough dripped off Gabe's bruised nose. "In one of those books from Adrian?"

Michal shrugged and didn't answer, canting his eyes toward the milling crowd. "Something that shouldn't be discussed in mixed company."

Gabe ran another handful of water through his hair. It was longer than he liked; he'd have to get Mari to cut it again. "Lead the way, then."

"You don't want to do something about that nose first?"

"What's the point?"

Michal sighed, headed for the door, shoulders already hunching in expectation of rain. "Sometimes I can't believe you were the Priest Exalted."

Sometimes Gabe couldn't, either.

The storm had mostly stopped by the time they reached the boardinghouse. Calling it such was kind; it was more like a shed with bedrooms. It wasn't as dilapidated as some of the row houses in the Auverrani Harbor District, but it was close.

Val waited just inside the door, perched on a stool, picking at her nails with a knife. She looked up as they entered, water from the erstwhile rain streaming off their shoulders and puddling on the floor. She raised a brow at Gabe. "Did you lose another fight?"

"Maybe."

"You might earn more if you won once in a while."

But Gabe was not prone to betting on himself. Not in anything.

A small room right off the main entrance served as Malcolm's office, cluttered with stacks of water-spotted paper. Apparently, the landlord's accounts had been neglected for quite a while before Malcolm came along. He sat at the table, dark circles under his eyes. "Took you long enough."

"He was getting beat within an inch of his life again," Michal said, going to sit next to Malcolm. The two of them were always in close proximity when they were in the same room.

But Gabe was not interested in defending his extracurriculars. He was far more interested in the man standing in front of Malcolm's desk.

He was dressed too well for the slums, though not so well that it immediately stood out. Handsome, well-groomed, with short dark hair and a trimmed beard to match, green eyes with a glint that said he would be a good friend to have at a bar and a bad enemy to have in a dark alley. The bare outline of a dark tattoo showed beneath the white linen of his shirt, and he stood with a lazy grace that reminded Gabe of Bastian.

The mysterious man looked to Gabe's eye, which must be fully purple by now. He raised a brow.

"I wish you'd..." But Malcolm didn't finish the thought, just shook his head instead. He didn't stand up, but waved a hand at the newcomer. "This is Finn Lucais."

"And?" Whatever manners Gabe's nobility had bred into him had bled out by now.

Finn didn't look offended. He looked delighted, in fact. "And," he said, "I believe I can help you with your bloodcoat problem."

The name clicked into place, recognition dawning even as Gabe's muscles tensed for yet another fight. Finn Lucais, the former pirate. The Caldienan naval officer.

The only inroad into Caldien that the Kirythean Empire had ever almost made was through the Ourish Pass in the mountains. That was due, in large part, to Finn Lucais. He'd been an outlaw then, back when Ouran was the Emperor of Kirythea and slowly conquering the whole continent. Finn's crew had targeted mostly Kirythean ships, and they'd done such a good job at it that the ships had never made it to the Caldienan shore, leaving Ouran stranded at the pass without reinforcements or supplies. After the battle, Finn had been pardoned on all charges of piracy and made an honorary officer. By all counts, the rest of the navy loved him. The way he managed to leak charisma even in this tiny room with a tired, hostile audience made it easy to see why.

But Gabe had little patience for charisma, and he was across the small room with his hand on Finn's throat in two strides.

"Our bloodcoat problem?" he said, sneering. "Currently, we don't have one, but I assume you're here to make one if we don't pay up?"

"Gabriel!" Malcolm shouted, standing so quickly his chair toppled over. "Hear him out—"

"Fuck that," Gabe snarled, but the low words were nearly drowned by Finn's chuckle.

The fact that the man chuckled when Gabe was seconds away from crushing his windpipe just made his fingers tighten.

"While we can certainly discuss payment," Finn wheezed, "I was actually thinking more along the lines of getting you under the Prime Minister's protection."

Gabe's hand relaxed by increments. If looks could kill, Malcolm's glare would be a bullet, and Michal and Val both looked less than pleased with him, too. With a stormy frown, he stepped back and crossed his arms. "I'm listening."

Finn grinned and made a show of straightening his pristine shirt. "In the course of my service to Caldien, the Prime Minister became my lover. Pillow talk suggestions tend to go over fairly easy. Though I'm not surprised you don't know that, given your station." He cocked his head. "I've heard interesting rumors in that regard."

Gabe had never been one to play the subtle insult game. He sat heavily in one of the chairs at the table.

"Finn," Malcolm said, rubbing wearily at his eyes. "If you could tell Gabe what you told me, please? I know he's an ass. We're working on it."

"Oh, don't try to fix it." Finn flopped in another chair, still grinning. "I like it."

"Gods dead and dying," Val muttered.

"Now." Finn knit his long, pale fingers together and set them on top of a stack of rent records. Nearly every finger wore a ring, the most ostentatious an emerald glinting on his thumb. "Eoin— the Prime Minister—was an ally to King August, but ever since his son took the throne, he's been…rethinking some things."

Gabe's jaw clenched. Malcolm sent him a warning look. "And why is that?"

"Mostly, the new King's strict attitude about religion."

"I thought Caldien wasn't religious?" Michal said. "So why would they care?"

"We aren't, at least not compared with Auverraine. But that doesn't mean Eoin isn't fascinated by the gods," Finn continued. "He and a handful of others are very invested in…alternative paths, I suppose you could say."

"So he doesn't like Apollius," Gabe said bluntly.

Finn tipped his head. "I wouldn't say he doesn't like Him. Just that he's skeptical, and more interested in the rest of the pantheon. Which the new King in Auverraine doesn't much appreciate."

Across the table, Malcolm stared intently at Gabe, as if compelling him to listen closely.

"He's particularly taken with the elemental gods," Finn concluded.

Gabe kept his face composed, though his hand twitched. Going further down that path would raise questions he didn't want to answer; he changed subjects. "And how, exactly, does this information help with our bloodcoat problem?"

"They're looking for you." Finn sat back, tapped one of those rings on a watery ink-bloom in a neglected ledger. "Reportedly because you have the same fascination."

That was one way to put it.

"At this juncture," Finn continued, "I believe if you asked Eoin for religious asylum, he'd be inclined to give it to you."

Gabe and Malcolm slid each other calculating looks across the desk. Their entire escape here had been predicated on finding help to stop Apollius, to warn Caldien that Auverraine would invade sooner or later. If they could get an audience with the Prime Minister, warn him while ensuring his protection...

"Why are you helping us?" Val asked, still glowering by the door. "How did you even know we needed help?"

"Like I said, I've heard interesting rumors about this one." Finn gestured to Gabe. "The eye patch and palm tattoos are rather distinctive. He matches a description that should be making its way around town soon, once Auverraine officially puts out warrants for your arrest."

A frisson of dread coursed around the room, straightening every spine.

"Eoin's protection would keep you from being extradited," Finn said. "And it seems you're going to need it."

"So what do we do?" Michal's voice was quiet, his eyes wide. He was no stranger to running away from the law, but the prospect of the law catching up made him sound half strangled. "To get his protection?"

"I can take you there." Finn shrugged. "Probably only two of you, to be safe." He gestured to Gabe and then Malcolm. "You two would be sufficient. You could petition for everyone in your party."

"When?" Gabe asked.

"Let's say tomorrow night." Finn stood and stretched, as if all this talking had put an ache in his back. "I'll knock four times. That's your signal." He grinned. "Wear something with a hood."

Then he left, strolling out the door as if on his way to a party.

They all sat in silence, waiting to hear his footsteps recede. "Well," Val said. "That's suspicious. I can't be the only person who finds that suspicious?"

"You aren't," Gabe replied. "But it seems we have little choice. We'll meet him."

"And if he's lying?" Michal asked.

Gabe sighed. "Then at least it's only two of us. The rest of you, run."

Michal reached over and grabbed Malcolm's hand. "I'll go with you."

"No, you won't," Malcolm said, though he didn't remove the other man's hand. "Worst case, it'll be blackmail. Gabe and I can handle that."

Gabe's fingertips warmed. Oh yes, he could handle that.

"If we aren't back by the next morning," Malcolm continued, looking to Val, "you, Michal, and Mari take the ship."

Val's lips were a bloodless line, but she nodded.

And that was that.

A book sat on the desk, one smuggled to Malcolm from the library at Farramark University. Gabe jerked his chin toward it, eager to change the subject. "Find anything in there?"

"Possibly." Malcolm waved his hand at the notes. "Something about pieces of the Fount, bringing them back together. Could be something, could be nothing."

That singed scent was in Gabe's nostrils again. He eyed Malcolm's notes, flames flickering at the edges—three pieces, marked with a moon and a sun and elemental carvings. Hidden, the notes said, both in plain sight and in deep places...

"I need a drink," Malcolm murmured.

Gabe shut the book, closing the notes inside. "On that, we agree. Come on; if there's one thing this city has, it's an abundance of taverns."

CHAPTER THREE

ALIE

Keep your lovers close at hand
And your enemies near your heart.
They both hold knives.
                —Excerpt from *Mother Says* by Honora Torlius,
                                        Kirythean poet

A lie."

She ignored him. She had gotten very good at ignoring him. Especially when he used her shortened name, as if they were friends. As if this engagement were anything more than a punishment.

"Alienor."

No. Still ignoring. Even though there was a pleading edge to his voice now, and even though they were in mixed company. Once, she'd cared what this court thought of her. She'd done her best to play her part perfectly. A good daughter, even if she and her father barely spoke. A witty socialite, hosting the best parties for the right people. A loyal friend.

Now she was the fiancée of the Kirythean Emperor, half sister of the Sainted King. Alie didn't know how to play those parts. She was stumbling around on the same stage without cues or lines.

Jax sat next to her, face expectant and anxious. It still unnerved her, how *anxious* he always looked when he was trying to engage her in conversation. When he was trying to make it seem like this was real.

It was easier to believe that he was playing a part, just like she was. Alie didn't want to consider the alternatives. But he was undoubtedly a better actor.

She finally tore her gaze away from her half-full wineglass and focused her attention on the Emperor. He was attractive, unfortunately. Not in the way she usually preferred, rugged and brooding, but in a clean, meticulous way. His blond hair was always tied back just so. His spine was always straight.

"Yes?" Alie said, realizing she'd completely missed whatever it was he wanted her to comment on.

He relaxed, just a bit. Every call and response between them seemed like a game, points kept in a croquet match. "Lady Villiers was wondering if your afternoon walk was disrupted by the high winds today."

"They were dreadful." The aforementioned lady shivered theatrically in her seat, making sure the reaction could be seen. The long table in the rose-choked atrium was full of courtiers today, and she was clearly relishing being sat so close to the head. So close to the King.

"It's been such a nice autumn," Lady Villiers continued, picking at the roasted pheasant on her plate, "so lovely and warm, I'd forgotten that winter was on the way." A high, tinkling laugh. "Those winds surely reminded me."

Alie's hand tightened around her goblet, so much so that she was sure her engagement ring would shriek against the crystal. It was a pretty, simple thing, a square-cut diamond on a golden band. Too big, so it was always twisting toward her palm. "I suppose I missed them," she said. "I don't recall any winds when I took my walk."

None that were natural, anyway. None that she hadn't conjured herself. She'd have to be more careful now, since it'd been so unseasonably warm. The deep heat of this past summer had abated, somewhat, but it certainly didn't feel like fall.

Her eyes flicked toward the head of the table, the man sitting there. Flicked away.

"Well, count yourself lucky," Lady Villiers breezily replied. "I nearly broke out the furs!"

The surrounding courtiers tittered, louder than necessary so that those at the foot of the table would hear and hopefully think they'd shared an inside joke with the King. Alie didn't join in. She polished off her wine, ardently wishing for something stronger.

His eyes were on her. She could feel them, the burnished gold of a starving wolf, Bastian's dark irises banished. If any of the courtiers had noticed the change, they didn't comment.

Alie had managed not to look at the Sainted King through the entirety of this cursed dinner, but she would have to eventually. Might as well be now.

She looked up. Met those gold eyes. Refused to cower.

Apollius grinned.

The god's assimilation into Bastian's place had been seamless, even as He dismantled the citizen payments, as He bought or bullied back the art pieces Bastian had auctioned off to build up the treasury. All the courtiers loved Him again, even those who'd been angry before. He'd stopped trying to change tax laws, stopped trying to change anything.

At least, as far as they knew.

Behind the scenes, the entire Kirythean Empire was slowly being handed over to Him, a bit more power relinquished from Jax day by day. In the usual, pedestrian way: money and paperwork, the way wars were really won once the battles were over. Or if they'd never happened.

The plan was to wait and unveil the Sainted King as the

Emperor on the day of Jax and Alie's wedding, when Jax would essentially become the regent of Auverraine.

Alie, whose royal blood made that possible, wouldn't get any extra power at all.

But she wasn't supposed to know any of that. Those were the whispers her winds brought her, on those long afternoon walks when she ranged around the edge of the Citadel green, one hand on the cool stone wall, the fingers of the other twitching as she wound iridescent threads of air.

There'd been an argument between Jax and Apollius today. Probably the reason Jax was focused so much on Alie rather than his King, his god.

"It isn't time yet," Jax had said. "I promise You will get the worship You are owed, Holy One. This entire continent will bow to You in Your fullness, not just to effigies. You will direct them to venerate You as You see fit—"

"Yes, I'm aware," Apollius had hissed, every syllable enunciated. "What I'm telling you, *Emperor*, is that I am going to tell them who I am now. Not when it's all over. Not when every country is won."

"I don't think it's a good idea." There was no waver in Jax's voice, and Alie had to give him that: He held tight to his convictions in the face of a god, and that counted for something. Even if those convictions were dead wrong. "You'll be opening Yourself to assassination—"

Apollius's laugh hurt Alie's ears, nearly made her pull back on her threads of wind. "They'd be welcome to try."

"You are immortal, Holy One. The body You inhabit is not. And though You can heal Yourself, there could come a point when the damage is too great."

One lie and one truth. Apollius wasn't immortal, and that was the inconvenient fact that had spawned this whole nightmare.

But Bastian could die, easily.

She couldn't see the god from her place by the Citadel Wall, but she could imagine His face, the thoughts racing through His silence. "I take your meaning."

He'd said nothing else, no promises made. But they'd gotten all the way through this dinner without Him standing on the table and declaring His divinity, so Alie supposed Jax's meaning had, indeed, been taken.

It was risky. She knew that. Not just that she was eavesdropping, but how she was doing it. Right now, it seemed that Apollius didn't know she'd inherited the power of Lereal, though Alie couldn't really figure out how that was true—He'd known about the others, somehow. But if Apollius knew about her, He hadn't yet done anything about it, for reasons Alie couldn't fathom.

There were rumors in the court about the day Gabe and Malcolm left, how Alie had defended herself with…something. Scraps of elemental magic was the prevailing thought, though none of the courtiers were brave enough to actually ask her about it.

Maybe Apollius thought her betrothal to Jax was more important than an admittedly paltry power, putting her at the bottom of His priority list. The lies He'd concocted about Gabe kidnapping her made it seem likely. That part she'd played for so long came in handy here; Alie was a fixture of the Citadel, and it would take massive effort to make them accept her execution or banishment even if she was proven to have used lost, illegal magic. Especially now that she was an Arceneaux.

However she'd managed to get lucky, it didn't make her complacent. Apollius had killed Amelia for her god-power; whatever plan had stayed His hand wouldn't last forever.

But she had to do *something*, and magic was the only tool at her disposal. Surely, she couldn't be expected to sit around and attend parties and wait.

So she experimented. Read everything about her god-power and how it might be used that she could find in the books Malcolm

had sourced before his hasty departure. Listening on the wind
was one thing. There were others she'd tried.

But she was the only one of the five of them using her magic,
apparently, so walking in their dreams was proving difficult.

She kept trying, though. Every night for the past two weeks,
when they'd been scattered to the corners of the continent.

Maybe the fact that the others weren't accessing their power
should have made her reconsider her own willingness to do so.
But, Alie felt, if it would make a difference, she would be selfish
not to use it.

"Hopefully the weather will hold for your ceremony, Your High-
ness." Another sycophant, Lady Beaumont. She'd tried to seduce Jax
on more than one occasion. Alie heard it while she was listening to
the wind. Jax had never given in, though Alie wasn't sure if that was
because he didn't realize he was being propositioned, or from some
misguided sense of loyalty to their engagement. "It's soon, is it not?"

"Two months," Jax replied. Alie couldn't parse his tone. He sat
up a little straighter, the austere planes of his face unreadable.

"If you choose to wait that long." Finally, Apollius, butting
into the conversation from His place at the head of the table. He
leaned forward, speared a potato off Jax's plate, and popped it in
His mouth. "I've told Jax that I can move the ceremony up, if he
prefers. I know how hard it can be to wait for your bride." He
raised a brow. "Though before her betrayal, My own bride didn't
make Me wait for the perks of matrimony."

Laughter at the table again, uproarious this time. A blush heated
Alie's cheeks. One would think that a jilted husband wouldn't
want to dwell on his absent wife, but Apollius brought up Lore—
and Nyxara, in subtle ways that only Alie would understand—
every chance He got.

It annoyed the new lovers He'd taken. Alie heard that on the
wind, too. Everyone Apollius had brought to bed dreamed of taking Lore's place, but He wasn't looking for a new consort. There

was only one person He would deign to share a throne with, and She was locked in Lore's head in the Burnt Isles.

Color stained Jax's pale cheeks. "I am content to wait as long as I need to," he said stiffly.

Apollius waved a dismissive hand. "Where's that indomitable spirit I heard so much about, Jax? I'd think a man who built an Empire would have no problem changing situations to take what he wanted."

More laughter, though some gave Alie slantwise looks, those married to powerful nobles. They were familiar with being treated like objects, art pieces to be moved and gazed upon and owned.

That was another reason she used her magic. All her life, she'd seen what happened to the powerless.

"Land and people are very different matters." Jax's voice was low. There was a gleam in his eye, almost dangerous. "I find that patience is rewarding."

Alie clenched her fists beneath the table.

Golden eyes narrowed, as if Apollius wanted to stoke the flames of the latent fight she'd overheard. But He shrugged instead, sat back. "I suppose I'm used to indulging My impatience. Terrible habit."

"Who would make you wait, Bastian?" Beaumont smiled, only the glint in her eyes showing her nerves at using the Sainted King's given name. It still jarred Alie to hear it, knowing Bastian was long gone. "I'm sure you've never had to wait for anything."

Apollius grinned with Bastian's mouth. He'd only slept with Beaumont once, a fact she lamented at her weekly tea with her friends. Alie had stopped listening in on those; it upset her too much to think of Apollius using Bastian's body like that.

"Not often," He said. "And when I do, it's always worth it."

Something low in His voice, contemplative. Alie stared at her empty plate.

"So I suppose I agree with you, Jax," the god said. "Some things are worth the wait."

No change in Jax's expression, but the tension in his body dissipated.

"I grow tired." Apollius stood and stretched His arms over His head. "Go to your chambers, all of you."

And with that, dinner was dismissed.

The courtiers tried to linger, some from the end of the table coming closer to where Apollius had sat, hoping to catch Him in conversation. But the Sainted King was already out the door, headed to His own chamber.

Outside the window, the sky darkened.

It gave Alie the smallest spark of hope. Apollius didn't seem to fade fully away at night—at least, He hadn't at first. Alie had listened, carefully manipulating threads of air from her own apartments, tapping at the door of the Sainted King's suite for clues. Nothing interesting, other than sounds of the King enjoying Himself with whomever He'd summoned that evening. That was enough to tell Alie it wasn't Bastian. Bastian would never, not anymore.

But the past few nights, Alie had heard crashing. Cursing. The sounds of a brawl, but with only one physical participant.

"Jax." Apollius turned around in the doorframe. There were circles beneath His eyes, as if He'd grown exhausted in the thirty seconds since standing up. "Come to My apartments when you can. We have things to discuss."

Jax's mouth thinned. He nodded.

Hope, that tiny spark flaring in Alie's chest.

Alie stood from the table and went to the door without saying goodbye to anyone. Her part was played for the evening; she had no further energy to expend.

"Alie, wait." Her fiancé caught up with her, holding out his elbow.

She looked at it as if he were offering her an insect. She said nothing.

With a sigh, Jax dropped his arm. The only time she ever saw him look anything but completely self-possessed was in moments like these, when he tried to act like her betrothed and there was no incentive for her to match his performance. It almost made her think that, for him, it wasn't all a farce.

That was a dangerous line of thought.

"May I walk you to your apartments?" he asked, stiff and formal.

And there were enough people still in the atrium that it would look odd if she refused.

"Yes," she said.

He smiled at her. Just the barest corner of one.

Jax didn't offer his arm again, instead ambling beside her as Alie made her way out of the atrium and toward the turret stairs. They walked in silence, and while it wasn't exactly comfortable, it didn't make Alie feel like she was on the verge of a full-blown panic, either. Small mercies.

But when they reached her door, Jax reached out and touched her arm. Anxiety bloomed just below her breastbone, her stomach hollowing.

"Alie, I . . ." It was strange to see him lost for words. Jax stopped touching her, as if suddenly aware that it wasn't welcome, and tucked his hands behind his back. "I understand that our circumstances are not ideal."

"That," she said primly, "is an understatement."

He lifted a shoulder and let it fall, conceding. "But I truly want to have a partnership," he continued. He didn't meet her eye, instead looking at the pothos vine curling over her door. That nervousness, again, making him strangely vulnerable. "I want us to be friends. I wouldn't presume to ask for anything more, but I hope we can cultivate that."

"A friend wouldn't lie," Alie said. "A friend wouldn't chase all of my other, true friends out of the damn country. A friend wouldn't use me for power." She looked up at him, resolutely set her chin. "I don't know you, Jax Andronicus. And I do not care to."

She stepped into her room without looking at him and closed the door. She didn't need to tap into air threads to hear his sigh or the soft pad of his boots down the corridor.

Alie slumped once she was alone in the dark, blowing out a harsh breath and making one white curl flutter on her forehead. She stripped out of her gown and left it on the floor, collapsing on the unmade bed in her chemise.

She had things to do.

It was easy to fall asleep. Alie had never been someone who struggled with it; her body let her rest without much fanfare. But this kind of dreaming took precision, keeping a handle on her mind even as it slipped into sleep. She'd perfected the technique with the same determination she'd used to hone her croquet swing and the steps of a complicated minuet. There was no skill she could not acquire, given proper time.

An island. That's where this kind of dreaming took her. A beach, white sand beneath her feet, cliffs at her back, and foaming blue water before her, meeting the equally blue sky in a blurred horizon line. The beach was silent, even the waves soundless.

There was no one here. That didn't surprise her. There never was. According to the books, dreamwalking could be done by any two people with power from the Fount, and the more you had, the easier it was. But Alie assumed that in order to truly dream-walk, you had to be using that power.

And she was, apparently, the only one foolish enough for that.

Something flickered in the corner of her eye. Short and softly curved, long brown-gold hair, the runnels of a new scar.

Alie shot to her feet. "Lore?"

And there she was, just for a moment. Long enough to turn and look at her, long enough for her eyes to go wide.

But then she vanished, and Alie was all alone on the beach again.

CHAPTER FOUR

LORE

Abandon not your fellow faithful.
                    —The Book of Mortal Law, Tract 90

Every day on the Burnt Isles was mostly the same, which was comforting, in a way. Wake up at least an hour before dawn, wipe at streaming, reddened eyes. Eat the tasteless porridge slopped into the same tin cups you used for your allotted water breaks, the only meal you didn't pay for. Covering your mouth to filter the ash, wrapping your hands if you had the cloth to spare, grabbing a pickax, heading to the mine.

Lore had spent last night thinking about trying to use Spiritum again, somehow finessing the power into a mode of escape. But the only idea that came was to overwork the heart of every guard on the island, and Lore wasn't sure she was capable of that. Besides, what would she do afterward? Even if she took a prison barge and followed the steel guidelines, she'd just end up back in Dellaire, surely caught before she could escape elsewhere. Useless, just like she'd told Jilly.

And she was pretty sure that Apollius would notice if she kept using Spiritum, anyway. She'd like to keep Him as far away from her as she could.

So instead, Lore thought about her dream.

Alie was there. She'd reiterated this fact to the goddess in her head at least ten times by now. *So she's using her power, right? That's how dreamwalking works.*

So it would seem. Nyxara's voice was always thin and faded in waking hours, weakening as the sun grew brighter. Sometimes, Lore could still hear Her in the sunlight, a fact that should have sparked intense worry but instead felt like security. Something to do with her proximity to the Golden Mount, probably. *I do hope she's being careful.*

Alie is always careful. Lore adjusted her grip on her pickax and brought it down on a chunk of rock. Nothing. She kicked the pieces aside and moved on.

Nyxara paused, an apprehensive lull in the conversation Lore could feel even if she couldn't see. *If you dreamwalked,* Nyxara said, *then it means you're using power now, too.*

They hadn't talked about Lore using Spiritum. They had barely talked about her losing Mortem. Sure, when Lore first arrived on the Isles, first reached out in a panic and tried to wind death around her fingers, she'd asked the goddess why it was gone. Why Nyxara remained when Her magic had fled.

The Fount, Nyxara had said, sounding just as fearful as Lore felt. *It must have gone back to the Fount. You relinquished it, somehow. Wanted it gone.*

On the boat, when she'd slammed her mental door on Nyxara. When she'd rebuked Her power. Lore hadn't expected it to actually work. It seemed too simple, that the solution they'd spent frantic weeks searching for was just to...wish the power away.

Though that wasn't quite right. It only worked when you were close to the Fount, apparently.

But the Fount left You here? Lore had pressed her hands against her temples, like she could force the goddess out, make Her follow Her power back into its source. Her new scar had felt rough on her fingers, spiderwebbing over her temple.

I suppose, Nyxara said, *that we're holding on to each other a bit tighter than we thought.*

Now Lore mulled over what Nyxara had mentioned before. About her wanting Mortem gone, her rejection sending it away once she was close enough for the Fount to take it. Her whole life, Lore had wanted to be free of her innate magic. Even in the Citadel, where it'd brought her a measure of safety, Mortem had never been a thing she wanted. It was a millstone around her neck. Something she'd built the muscle to live with but could never really welcome.

Spiritum, though...yes, the eclipse ritual that gave it to her had been awful, violating. But Spiritum felt *good.* Life, health, vitality. Apollius might be a power-hungry asshole, but His magic was something Lore couldn't help but crave now that she had the distance to think of it objectively.

Or thought she'd had the distance. For all that her Mortem had apparently been relinquished back to the Fount, it seemed she hadn't let go of Spiritum so easily. Some part of her had wanted to keep it.

The ash was thick on the air today. Lore coughed into her sleeve before moving on. *So what do I do about it? It looks like dreamwalking is my only way to communicate with the others. And we have to make some kind of plan. We can't keep just—* She paused and brought her pickax down again, harder than necessary, shattering yet another useless rock. *—waiting around. Even if using magic makes Apollius pay attention.*

In her head, Nyxara gave a wry-sounding sigh. *It is foolish to think you don't already draw His attention, Lore. With or without using His power.*

Lore didn't want to think about that.

The sun finally rose, cutting weakly through the miasma. Lore could never figure out how it was so gods-damned hot here when sunlight barely broke through the ash.

Nyxara faded from her head, a dark presence at the back of her skull.

Logically, Lore knew Apollius was somehow watching her. Their connection was still in place while she was this close to the Fount. Now that she realized how entrenched Nyxara was in her mind, Lore was half convinced that the only escape from feeding His power was her own death. Permanent, this time, not the half measure she'd taken when she brought the North Sanctuary down. A path she still refused to take, after everything.

Seed of the apocalypse, indeed.

Still, her brief bout of dreamwalking brought a rush of relief. For weeks, she'd rotted here, with no way to check on Bastian or Gabe or any of her friends. She tried to listen to the guards, but their gossip rarely turned to the mainland. More prisoners arrived every day, but very few of them seemed interested in what was happening in the upper echelons of Auverrani society. None of them had any real information, other than whispers about Alie being Bastian's half sister, now engaged to the Emperor of Kirythea. Nothing new.

What could you do with it, even if you did hear something new? she asked herself as she broke another rock. A sliver of gold; she licked her finger to pick it up and put it in the worn pouch at her waist. *It's over. He won.*

But just like she couldn't resign herself to dying, neither could she resign herself to letting the God of Everything take over... everything.

Lore's grip tightened on her pickax. If she had to use Spiritum so that she could walk in her friends' dreams, go back to making some kind of difference, she'd do it. Damn the consequences.

Shouting drew her attention. Over by the lift down to the mine, Jilly was towering over someone down on the sand, an extra tin cup held in her fist. "You won't need it now. Not when you get a pass to the third tier where the good shit is. How many of them did you have to fuck for that? Did they at least let you rest in between?"

The person on the ground—whose cup Jilly was apparently holding—said nothing. A woman Lore recognized, a face in the crowd that stood out. Rosie, she remembered, a prisoner who'd arrived shortly after Lore. She'd slept in the same cave a handful of times.

Rosie made a swipe for her cup, but Jilly kicked her hand away. "If you get thirsty, I'm sure one of the guards will give you something to suck—"

Jilly stopped, her voice strangled out into nothing. Having your heart race like a runaway horse would do that.

Lore calmly took the cup from Jilly's spasming grip, the fingers of her other hand crooking as she twisted strands of the woman's Spiritum around them. She didn't say anything as she gave it back to Rosie.

Slowly, Lore let the strands go, releasing Jilly's heart to shudder back into regular rhythm. Jilly gaped at her, gasping, the fear of a cornered animal glinting in her eyes.

"Go ahead, Rosie," Lore said calmly. "Hope you find something good down there."

Rosie scrambled up from the sand. She looked from Jilly to Lore, decided against getting involved further, and scurried to the lift.

Jilly just stared. Lore stared back, waiting to see if this would escalate into a brawl, trying to ignore the exhilaration that sang down her veins at this use of her power.

Trying to ignore the sense of being observed. Marked by something larger.

With a final shudder, Jilly turned away, hurried back to her own forgotten pickax.

For the first time since she'd been on the Isles, Lore grinned.

The day passed quickly, sweaty and largely fruitless, though she did find enough to turn in for a pallet. At the end, Lore gave the guards her pickax and submitted to the pat-down to make sure she hadn't smuggled out any particularly sharp rocks. She wasn't sure why they bothered; the guards were more likely to bet on inmate fights than break them up. When the guard was satisfied she had no contraband, Lore handed over a chip of ruby and two gold slivers for a pallet and a plate of limp potatoes and headed for the cave at the base of the cliffs, her paltry dinner finished before she was across the beach.

There was never a fight for space, and the other people who frequented the cave left her mostly alone. It wasn't roomy, but it was the only place where Lore felt safe enough to really sleep.

And if she was going to dreamwalk, she needed to really sleep.

Lore twitched her fingers, pulling at the bare threads of life she found in the sand. Mites, tiny insects. Their golden threads were thin, not rope-thick like Jilly's. Easier to grasp, to twist and snap.

They didn't have hearts, not like humans did, but she sped up their processes, channeling so much life through them that their microscopic bodies gave out. Cruel, maybe, but she was nearly past caring about that. The only strengths she had here were her vices.

Her breath came harder, filling her lungs; her face flushed with pumping blood. Gods, it'd been so long since she'd felt this alive. Since she'd felt anything but downtrodden and helpless and afraid.

Lore *hated* feeling afraid.

Using her power on Jilly today had felt...right. A good deed, even. Gods knew she needed to add some to her ledger.

Ducking into the cave, Lore placed her pallet over by the damp stone wall. No one else was in the cave yet, which was unusual, but maybe she'd just gotten here early.

Wincing against the pain in her back, Lore stretched out on the thin pallet. Her eyes drifted closed, her mouth held in a determined clench, focused on that beach where she'd seen Alie.

"There she is."

Her eyes popped open.

It took a moment for them to adjust to the gloom. Three men, looming over her. All of them scarred.

Lore's heart jackknifed against her ribs.

"Jilly told us you slept here. You were never good at making friends." One of the men crouched next to her. A spark in his hand—a lighter, illuminating his face. It was gaunt, his eyes wild. "Recognize me, Your Majesty?"

She did, almost. Like someone you often passed on the street, whose face became a familiar part of the scenery.

But Lore was still flush with power, from Jilly and her experiment on the beach, and it made her overly confident. Her fingers bent. "Can't say I do."

"You ruined us." He was their spokesperson, apparently; the other two men behind him said nothing. "We were only following orders. Doing as the King and Priest Exalted willed. What our *god* willed."

Ah. So they were Presque Mort, then. Or had been. As if to drive the point home, one of the other men turned his palm to face her in the lighter-light, a flash of inked candle.

A slow grin spread across Lore's face. "Oh, I remember you now. Has it been hard, adjusting to no magic? Sorry about that. Didn't mean to take it all."

Stupid, to taunt three angry men when she was all alone. But that flare of power burned through her, beacon-bright.

"You poisonous bitch." The hand not holding the lighter moved upward, something else in it. A rock, sharp.

It happened quickly. Lore's hand shot out as she rolled aside, barely missing the blow, the sharp rock coming down where her head had been. Her fingers twitched, tugging at Spiritum, the golden threads in the former monk twisting around her hand.

Or they would, if the damn things didn't keep slipping from her grip. The other times she'd used Spiritum, it'd jumped to her easily, but now trying to grasp the strands felt like trying to hold on to an oiled rope. They pulled away, as if her power were a tide pool that someone else was draining.

And who else could that be but Apollius? Knowing she was trying to use their shared power. Keeping it from her.

Lore snarled, an animal sound. She thrust out her hands, grabbed the strands, and pulled with every ounce of determination she'd ever had.

They came to her this time, overcoming Apollius's hold.

She didn't finesse it. She just twisted and twisted, the only application of her will the desire to make him stop, make him leave her alone. The Mort's heartbeat sped in his chest, almost audible; she felt his veins pop as too much blood crowded them, saw them swell in the confines of his skin. His eyeballs bulged from their sockets, his muscles twitching.

The monk fell to the ground. Blood leaked slowly from his ears, pink foam from his open mouth.

Lore stared at him. Mortem couldn't be used to cause outright death; all it could do was encase someone in stone, like she'd done with Milo long ago in that alley. Stop life in its tracks, but not obliterate it.

It was almost funny, that the power of life was the one you could use to kill.

The other two monks stared at her. She could do the same to them; her fingers itched for it, the golden lines of their lives begging her to snatch and pull.

But whether from a desire not to draw undue attention, or a latent wish for goodness, she didn't. "Get out of here," she whispered. "And tell your friends to leave me alone."

They nearly fell over each other trying to leave the cave. Just outside, Lore heard an *oof,* the sound of one body smacking another before two pairs of Isles-issue boots pounded sand down the beach.

At first, Lore assumed they'd run into one of the other women who normally slept here, her conscience pricked by leaving Lore alone for whatever the Mort had planned. But then the figure stepped into the cave, close enough for Lore to make out her face.

"I was going to help you get rid of them," Dani said. "But it looks like you did just fine on your own."

CHAPTER FIVE

LORE

Mutual enemies make for powerful allies.
                                    –Kadmaran proverb

Power still sang in Lore's fingertips, still pulsed down her veins with every golden beat of her heart. It would be so easy to gather up the threads of Dani's life, wind them into herself, and leave the other woman as broken and empty as the Presque Mort on the ground. Her fingers twitched to do it without her conscious direction, a sneer on her mouth.

Dani raised her hands in surrender. "Lore. I'm not trying to hurt you."

"Of course not," Lore snarled. "That would be overkill at this point."

It was Dani's fault she was here at all. Leading her down Anton's path, dropping the bread crumbs that Lore had followed so faithfully, drowning before she knew she was in far over her head.

Her hands were still raised, but Dani's shoulders relaxed. "I *am* sorry about that. Mostly. I was just doing what I thought I had to at the time." Her eyes narrowed, turning her beauty to calculating angles. "You're familiar with that, surely."

Lore gnawed her lip. The righteous anger that had suffused her just a moment ago—the unassailable knowledge that she was right, her violence justified—bled out, just a little.

"We've hurt each other enough." Dani made a rueful sound. "We're both stuck here, and you already have one body to dispose of."

She had a point. Lore let her hands drop. The rush of power subsided, though her awareness of Spiritum all around her didn't fade. Gold flecked the corners of her vision, spangling like starfields when she moved.

With a sigh, Lore leaned against the rough wall of the cave. "What do you want, Dani?"

"Do I have to want something?" Dani shrugged, turning her attention from Lore to the body on the floor. "Damn. You did a number on him. Is that from Mortem?"

"No." Immediately after she spoke, Lore clenched her teeth, as if she could bite the words in half. She shouldn't be telling anyone that she couldn't channel Mortem anymore. She wasn't sure *why* she shouldn't tell them, but the instinct to hold the secret coiled deep.

That, Nyxara said, *is the first rational thought you've had today.*

Lore didn't respond. Though she did wonder at the fact that this was the first time Nyxara had spoken to her since the sun went down. Usually, the goddess was chatty after nightfall.

Dani's eyes cut over to her, though her exact expression was hidden in the gloom. She didn't press further, nudging the dead Presque Mort with her toe. "So. Do we bury him, burn him, or throw him in the ocean?"

🦋

The ocean won, mostly for convenience's sake. Lore wrapped the body in her pallet, and together, she and Dani hauled it out of the cave, sticking to the shadows of the cliff face as they made their way to an empty stretch of beach. The Mort swung between them like a macabre pendulum, blessedly slight. Ash coated the air, reducing visibility to a few feet in front of her, but right now, Lore was grateful for the extra cover.

The guards were busy either having lackluster sex or playing cards, and almost all the other prisoners were deeply asleep or joining them, so there wasn't much worry about being seen anyway. Still, Lore was jumpy, flinching at every sound.

"Don't worry," Dani said, voice strained. The monk's dead-weight might have been less than anticipated, but hauling him this far was still quite the task, especially on Burnt Isles rations. "It's not like anyone will come looking for him. The guards don't give a shit, and the other Mort are cowards. I'm surprised any of them approached you. They're usually all talk."

"You seem to know a lot about them," Lore grumbled, stepping carefully to find purchase on the sand.

"We stayed together when we first arrived. For obvious reasons." Dani shrugged, as much as she could with her hands full of dead man. "But now we've all gone our separate ways."

She didn't elaborate.

Are you sure that following the sister of a woman you're blamed for murdering into the night is a good idea? Nyxara sounded snippy.

Absolutely not, Lore replied. *But I can defend myself just fine.*

As long as He doesn't try to pull it away from you again, Nyxara said, but then She fell into pensive silence.

Finally, they'd gone far enough that they were unlikely to step on a sleeping prisoner. The moonlight reflected on the particles in the air as they made their way down the beach. Dani nodded toward the surf when they were close enough to see it. "There's a sandbar that ends a few feet out. If we take him to the end, wrap him up with a few rocks, no one will find him." She snorted. "Not like anyone will care, even if he does wash up. Prisoners walk into the ocean all the time."

Lore found some rocks by the cliffs and tucked them into her pallet. She'd be sad to lose it; when she didn't turn one in come morning, the guards wouldn't give her another, no matter how many gold flecks she found.

When he was wrapped, they hauled the dead man into the sea. The pull of the tide against her ankles made Lore think of Caeliar. Of Amelia, killed by Bastian because she threatened Lore. Amelia, who'd just wanted to please her god.

The end of the sandbar was easy to identify, the water darker and colder as it abruptly deepened. With a heave, Lore and Dani pushed the body out beyond its edge. The Mort sank easily as the water soaked into his clothes, blood still leaking from his ears and nose and eyes. It pooled beneath his skin, making it lumpen and splotch dark.

They stood there until he was out of sight, Lore with her arms crossed against a shiver, Dani with her hands on her hips. "How'd you end up here?" Lore asked after a beat of uncomfortable silence. "Figured you and yours would have enough money to stay with the rest of the nobles on the First Isle."

"We did," Dani answered. "But the King really, really hated us."

Lore pressed her lips together to keep from turning them to a feral smile, her second of the day. Deciding to use her power had done wonders for her mood.

"So," Dani said after a moment. "Did you do it?"

There was only one *it* she could be referring to. Lore tensed, her awareness of the Spiritum around them jumping to attention, ready to be called. "I didn't kill Amelia."

Dani nodded once. "I thought so. Not that you don't have it in you. You do, clearly. But the idea that a jealous rage would turn you murderous seems out of character. You need more reason to kill someone."

"I do prefer to keep my murders well justified," Lore said.

Dani snorted. There were specks of blood from the Mort's

ears on her hands; she bent and washed them in the churning surf. "Now, killing Amelia for being the second coming
of Caeliar...that could be a reason. Depending on whose side
you're on."

Lore's stomach fell to somewhere near her ankles.

Dani straightened, her gaze steady and even. "But if you're on
Apollius's side, I don't think you would have ended up here. Since
it seems like He's winning."

A million questions poured through Lore's head, but the only
one that came out was "How did you know?"

"I was part of Anton's cult, remember?" Dani's tone said this
should be obvious. "We all knew what would happen if you didn't
die on the night of the eclipse. That the power of the other gods
would find new vessels. The Presque Mort who were sent here,
the ones in Anton's inner circle, comforted themselves with the
fact that even if you weren't dead, at least Apollius had His new
body. Once it became clear Bastian wasn't Bastian anymore—
imprisoning people for minor infractions, sending orders not to
antagonize the Kirythean ships on the Sapphire Sea—it wasn't a
logical leap that the rest of it was happening, too."

She turned, started slogging toward the shore. Lore followed
at a safe distance, still wary. "As for how I knew Amelia had
become Caeliar's avatar," Dani continued, "Apollius sent the phy-
sician who did her autopsy to the Isles the day after it happened.
He fell in with the Presque Mort and told them about her cause of
death. About the puddle that came out of her mouth."

Caeliar's swallow of the Fount, fully surrendered. Lore still
remembered the taste of Nyxara's drink, clear and cold, before she
gulped it back down and took the power again.

For a little while, at least.

Amelia didn't have to die for Apollius to take Caeliar's magic.
She'd given it up willingly. Bastian had killed her anyway.

"It was easy to put together." Dani stopped just shy of the

beach, staying in the water, the tide billowing her trousers in ebb and flow. "And that's when I stopped believing."

Still half convinced that this might be the kind of confession that preceded a revenge killing, Lore kept her distance, stepping around Dani and up onto the sand. She'd rather have the cliffs at her back than the sea. "Stopped believing in what?"

"All of it." Through this whole speech, Dani had been dispassionate. But now there was a spark in her eye, the tendons in her neck going tight. "That mortals matter. That there's any point to all of this when our gods are selfish and the world is twisted."

Lore had spent plenty of time in the last year around every extreme, from zealots to hedonists. But this casual nihilism was far more unsettling to her than even Anton's crazed piety.

"Maybe there could be something better." Dani finally climbed out of the surf. If she noticed that Lore stepped back, keeping the same amount of distance between them, she didn't comment on it. "But in order for that to happen, everything—*everything*—would have to change."

She looked at Lore expectantly, as if she thought she had made some point perfectly clear. As if this were a game, and Lore had the next move.

Lore's mouth worked a moment, unsure of how to respond. "That's... certainly a philosophy."

"Spend long enough thinking about it, and the entire bedrock of civilization unravels," Dani said, warming to her topic. "Once you get into the *just becauses*—mortals deserve to have a habitable world just because we think we do, the gods should be revered just because they're gods—you've already lost."

This woman, Nyxara said, *truly loves to hear herself talk.*

The goddess wasn't wrong. Lore could see some of the logic in Dani's declaration, but she couldn't buy into the whole of it. She wasn't a sentimental person—at least, she tried very hard not to be—especially not about human nature. But she had to believe that the world was mostly good. That there was something about it worth saving.

Dani sounded like she'd just as soon annihilate it and start anew.

"All that to say," Dani concluded, trudging up toward the cliffs, "if you want to finally get to the Golden Mount and kill Apollius, I think I can help."

Lore froze. "What?"

"His body. His second death." Dani turned, gave a tight smile. "Cult, remember?"

His first death, technically. But Dani didn't know that. And even once she got to the Mount and killed the body, Apollius would still be in Bastian's head, a problem she hadn't yet figured out how to solve.

You should keep that to yourself, Nyxara said.

Lore wholeheartedly agreed. "That's not going to be easy."

"Sure it is." Dani's tight smile expanded, became a convincing simulacrum of the real thing. "We just have to get to the Golden Mount. And I know how to do it."

He could tell time now. Well, sort of. He could tell when it was passing. He could feel its tiny ravages.

He could see more now, too. More and more often, his eyes would open on the Citadel instead of endless gold; he could see the world, hazy as it was. But there was no control over it, try as he might. He was still just a passenger, floating in a void.

He could feel the other getting angry about it, though. Recognizing that Bastian was growing stronger, here in the sunlit sea. That His hold was faltering.

One night, Bastian had almost managed to break free. It'd been surreal, moving without moving, flailing in all this gold and knowing that his movements were tracked by his body but having no way to monitor them. Like fighting in the dark.

Apollius had pushed him farther under, after that. Where the gold almost became black, where life held on by its fingernails.

But there was a slow leak, still. Something, somewhere, siphoning power, making the god weaker.

Bastian just had to bide his time.

Chapter Six

GABE

Desperation and dignity never hold hands.
—From a letter written by Fergus Almont,
Rotunda delegate

He was not himself, and he was watching Apollius.

Gabe felt his shoulder lean against a tree, the bark rough against skin that he knew was not his own. It felt stretched in the wrong direction, too short, broader and more muscled. And that should have made him panic—panic lurked in the very back of his head, relegated to animal instinct—but he was distracted by the man in front of him.

It was Apollius—he knew it was Apollius—but much as knowing that he was not in his own body should have been a source of panic and was not, the sight of his former god working a forge in the greenest forest he'd ever seen didn't alarm him. Instead, he was warm all over, content. Happy. What a foreign feeling.

The forge was open-air, in a small clearing. The stones that made it were of a piece, like they'd been manipulated into shape rather than built. Apollius was stripped to the waist, his brown hair matted against his skull with sweat, skin gleaming. Golden phosphorescence hovered around him like a halo. He was the most beautiful man Hestraon had ever seen.

The back of Gabe's mind—the part that was still him—jolted when he thought the name of the fire god as if it were his own.

This wasn't a dream. It was a memory.

Apollius whacked at whatever he was creating with a steel hammer, turning it in the fire. Gold and silver, melted together into the shape of a dagger. He looked up at Hestraon, grinned. "I think I'm getting the hang of this."

"I still can't believe I let you take first crack at forging something with the ore on the island. That's quite an inaugural project."

"I can believe it." He turned the blade again, showering embers. His smile lit up the whole island. "You let me do whatever I want."

The first shade of a dark thought in the alien consciousness that trapped Gabe's own. It was true.

Hestraon pushed off from the tree and approached the forge. For a first attempt, Apollius's dagger was better than good. The pommel was a bit crooked, and the blade a bit thin, but he had no doubt the weapon would hold up to use. He hadn't experimented with anything mined from the Mount, but it stood to reason that it would be stronger stuff than he used to work with.

Back when he was human.

Apollius picked up the dagger with tongs and dunked it into a bucket of water. Steam roiled over him, turning his body momentarily ghostly. "There."

Hestraon gave the blade a moment to cool before plucking it from the water. It shone bright in his hand. "Well done."

"Had a good teacher." Apollius stood close, the heat of him warming Hestraon's arm. He pushed forward until they touched, and the burn in Hestraon's chest had nothing to do with his power.

"Imagine how much we could sell that for on the mainland," Apollius said.

"You're a god now, and you're still thinking of money?"

"I have retained my practicality."

When Hestraon turned, Apollius's face was close enough to feel his breath. Hestraon's eyes closed, almost of their own accord. His mouth parted slightly.

Apollius leaned in. It wouldn't be the first time they'd kissed, but with him, it always felt like it.

No kiss came. When Hestraon opened his eyes, confused and slightly hurt, Apollius was grinning, his eyes bright as a child's who'd just pulled off a trick.

"Why not?" Hestraon breathed, no dignity in the plea. He was past that with Apollius. Always used to begging.

The god of light and life smiled, leaned in closer, so his lips brushed Hestraon's cheek. "Because you haven't earned it. Go on. Try again."

This was a joke, and a cruel one. Ever since the Fount, Apollius had amused himself by asking Hestraon to try channeling Spiritum, the power that now came to Apollius as easily as calling a well-trained dog. It was impossible—when Hestraon concentrated, he could barely see the glimmers of gold, and they wouldn't obey him.

Still, he tried. Closing his eyes, focusing so hard he swayed on his feet. Sunlight threads, weaving through everything alive, but no matter how he coaxed them, they wouldn't respond.

Failure landed like a rock in his ribs, sinking low, settling. Familiar, by now.

"No kisses for the weak." Apollius grinned. "Come on. Let's go show Nyxara. See if she thinks my work is as good as yours."

Gabe opened his eyes.

His breathing came ragged as he reoriented himself to the correct dimensions, got used to filling the whole of his head again. This was what had happened to Lore, back when Nyxara first burrowed into her mind—dreams that were memories, the goddess's life played out behind her eyes.

I didn't mean to do that.

A voice that was not his. Low and rough, warm, like the graze of hot smoke when you drew too close to a candle.

"Fuck." Gabe grabbed his head. "Gods damn it."

Apt.

They weren't supposed to do this. They weren't supposed to be this strong. But hadn't he known something was happening? The singe in his nostrils, the heat in his hands. It'd been growing stronger for weeks.

"You can't do this," Gabe murmured into the dark. "We thought You couldn't do this."

When Hestraon's voice came, it was apologetic. *You were wrong.*

❧

Gabe's next day was spent in a flurry of aching stomach and jittery hands, trying not to think of what had happened in the night. Finn wasn't coming to collect them until dark, so he set out before dawn lightened the sky, ranging along the beach until the sun was high enough that he could probably find a fight. Off to the barn, then, where he had his ass handed to him three times before his body told him in no uncertain terms that he'd taken enough beatings for one day. He pulled up his hood as he left, avoiding the bloodcoats that seemed to linger on every corner, and headed back to the boardinghouse, where Malcolm was still poring over the latest book Adrian had sent him.

For a moment, he considered telling Malcolm. Asking about his dreams. He didn't. If it was happening to Malcolm, too, they were well and truly fucked.

And if it was only happening to Gabe...

He didn't want to think about that.

His knee bounced nervously as he sat down, arms braced on his knees. Malcolm calmly turned pages and made rows of neat notes. The ledgers he was supposed to be working on had been shoved aside, a drift of paper falling off the edge of the desk.

"Find anything else?" Gabe asked.

"Not really." Malcolm sighed and leaned back, rubbing at his eyes as if they ached. "The Fount is broken, and It can't hold all of Its power until someone repairs It. Which means that if we want to get rid of our god-power problem without handing it over to Apollius, the Fount has to get cobbled back together first."

"I assume the books have no clues about where the pieces are."

"Of course not. That would actually be helpful." Malcolm shut the book with uncharacteristic force. "But it seems like our only option is to try looking for them. Myriad hells."

"If what Finn said is true about the Prime Minister's interests, maybe he'll have an idea." The words sounded hollow. Neither one of them had much faith in this new venture with Eoin Iomare.

His friend raised a brow. "You think it will be that easy? Just ask him, and he tells us? Even if he knows where the pieces are and by some miracle gives us asylum, the chances of him turning over what are undoubtedly some of the most valuable things on the continent—on the damn globe—are next to zero."

"Maybe if we tell him what's happening to Bastian—"

"Then he'll just want to kill Bastian, Gabe. He won't care that Bastian isn't in control."

He was right. Dammit. "So we keep it secret. What's happening to Bastian, and what we're looking for. And just hope it somehow drops into our laps."

"Stranger things have happened." Malcolm's jaw worked, his eyes canted to the side like he didn't want to meet Gabe's gaze. "Or we tell him anyway."

The unspoken consequence was clear. Tell Eoin. Let the war start.

Let him try to kill Bastian.

His hands felt like they were on fire. Gabe closed his fists, hard, half expecting smoke to leak between his fingers. "No. That's not an option."

"It might have to be," Malcolm murmured.

"But it doesn't have to be right now." Gabe looked up, flame-shadows spinning in the corners of his vision. "Please."

I was never too proud to beg, said a voice in the back of his head. *Not for His sake.*

Gabe gritted his teeth.

Malcolm sighed, leaning back in his chair until it creaked ominously, fingertips on his temples. When he spoke, it wasn't about Bastian. "I lied to Michal. Blackmail isn't the worst possibility. The worst possibility is that there's a reward attached to our upcoming warrants and Finn is trying to get it first."

"Michal was a poison runner. He knows." Gabe thought about asking why Malcolm would feel the need to assuage the other man's feelings, but he bit down on the question. He'd seen the sidelong looks they gave each other, how they always wanted to be within touching distance. He was happy for his friend, though the circumstances were far from ideal. But jealousy was a thorn in his side: That the person Malcolm cared for was with him. That he could at least attempt to keep Michal safe.

"If he tries anything," Gabe said quietly, giving words to what they both knew, "we kill him."

Slowly, Malcolm's chair balanced on all four legs again. He knit his fingers on the table, addressed them instead of Gabe. "Is it hard?"

Gabe had killed before. Malcolm hadn't. His position as the head librarian kept him from the usual violence of the Presque Mort, from the arrests gone wrong and the revenants put out of their misery.

"No," Gabe said, standing. "It's not hard at all."

The day passed, finally. He managed to sleep a little, but by the time night fell, Gabe and Malcolm both loitered by the door, their nervous energy cracking like sparks in the small room. Val and Mari had gone to bed, but Michal lingered in the office, picking up papers and putting them down again just for something to do with his hands. "Did he give a time?"

"Night." Malcolm shifted on his feet, wearing a long, dark cloak. He kept fiddling with the hem. "Just night."

And then—four knocks on the door.

Gabe strode toward it, ready to wrench it open, but Michal stopped him. "Wait." He walked over to Malcolm and took his hand. "Please, please be careful."

Malcolm just nodded. He laced his fingers with the other man's, squeezed.

Gabe looked away.

After a moment, giving Michal time to let go, he opened the door.

Finn stood on the other side, hands in his pockets and a small smile on his face. "Ready to plead for asylum?"

Gabe didn't respond, pushing past the pirate and into the night. He didn't wait for Finn or Malcolm, striding purposefully down the street, his hood up over his face.

So when the blow came to the side of his head, he didn't even see who struck it.

♥

Stupid.

He wasn't sure if the voice was Hestraon's or his own. Both, maybe.

So fucking stupid.

He should have known this was a trap. Nothing had ever been easy, and everything that was only led them deeper into the tangled web of the gods—of course this wouldn't be any different. He should have shot Finn the moment he appeared in Malcolm's slum office. Desperation made him blind, grasping at increasingly thin straws.

There hadn't even been a chance for him to fight back, to kill Finn or his accomplices like he and Malcolm had planned. It happened too quickly. For a moment, he entertained the possibility that Malcolm had escaped, but when he opened his aching eye, the former head librarian was right beside him, shackles around his wrists.

Surrounded by bloodcoats.

Gabe blinked, trying to orient himself. His head still smarted from the blow, his vision swimmy, but it appeared they stood on a dais at the bottom of an amphitheater, rings of seats working their way down, a square of light from a door at the top of the stairs. A lectern stood before them, empty.

He turned his head slightly. Behind the stone-faced bloodcoats, a statue stood, one that looked familiar. Apollius Avenging, one hand stretched out to the side holding a moon-marked rock, the other over His head. But the rock He held in that hand was different, not the sun-carved piece like in the same statue back at the Church. The stone here had other markings—a wave, a wind gust, a leaf.

No flame.

In his head, a sense of something turning away, as if ashamed.

Gods dead and dying. Well, they'd found a Fount piece.

Figured it would be right before they were shipped back to Apollius to die.

"Gentlemen." A new voice, crisp and polite, its owner coming into Gabe's still-blurred vision. "What brings you here at this hour?"

The bloodcoat behind Gabe jerked at his shackles, pulling him upright. "We found who the Sainted King is looking for, but since they were in Caldien, we need dispensation for them to be extradited. It's simple paperwork; once we have your signature, we can be on our way."

Slowly, Gabe's vision cleared as the man before them dipped his chin. Tall but spare, with salt-and-pepper hair and a short beard just showing the first laces of gray. He pursed his lips thoughtfully. "And how did you come to find your fugitives so quickly?"

"Finn Lucais," the guard answered, saying the name with a bit of pride. Talking to the pirate-turned-naval-officer had probably been one of the highlights of his life.

"Ah." The man—whom Gabe assumed was Eoin Iomare—smiled. "He does have an uncanny ability for giving gifts."

Next to Gabe, Malcolm hung limp in the bloodcoat's grip. He'd always traveled with a dagger since they left Auverraine, but it'd been taken, the sheath hanging empty. Not that it'd do them much good.

You have other weapons.

No, Gabe snarled at Hestraon. *No*.

Eoin Iomare's eyes turned to him, sharp and searching, like a hawk spotting a mouse. He grinned. "Now, about that extradition. I must say, I am conflicted on the matter."

The leader of the bloodcoats jerked Gabe again. "Beg pardon?"

"I believe I was clear." Eoin shrugged gracefully. "Though, honestly, it's not up to either of us. It's up to *them*."

Gabe looked up, brow furrowed. Malcolm's mouth hung in a confused gape.

Eoin, nonplussed, gestured expansively and stepped back. "Gabriel," he said, nodding. "Malcolm. Who are you, really?"

It took Gabe a moment to realize it was actually a question and not some trick. "What do you mean?"

"Shut *up*." The bloodcoat behind him dug the heel of his boot into the back of Gabe's calf; Gabe fell to one knee, biting his lip bloody but refusing to cry out. "This is a matter of Auverrani justice, Iomare. No games will be played—"

The Prime Minister twitched a finger.

Behind the Citadel guards, figures melted out of the shadows. A sea of dark cloaks, all holding pistols.

All pointing those pistols at the bloodcoats.

The guard holding Gabe slackened his grip, reaching for his own gun, but Eoin wagged a finger. "Touch your weapon and you're dead. Now, as I was saying." He turned his attention back to Gabe, and then Malcolm, as if they were the only men in the room. "Who are you? Or, should I say, who have you become?"

The question made sense now. Between the double ambush and Finn's information about Eoin's fascination with the elemental gods—that's what he wanted to know. Somehow, he'd put together the dregs of the truth from rumors out of Auverraine, and wanted to hear it from the source.

Malcolm spoke first, his voice hoarse and defeated. "Braxtos."

The guard holding him backed up a step, his grip loosening as if he wanted to drop Malcolm to the ground. He didn't, but it was a close thing.

"Excellent." Eoin looked to Gabe. "And you?"

"Hestraon." The name scoured his mouth. He didn't want to play this sick game, but once again, he found himself with little choice. It was becoming a pattern.

"Ah." The Prime Minister's eyes glinted. "Of course."

He gestured once more, a wave of his hand as if beckoning on a reluctant child.

It happened fast. The cloaked figures fell on the bloodcoats, outnumbering them two to one. Most were shot in the head in seconds, some uncanny device attached to the muzzles muffling the sound. Gabe fell backward when his guard was shot before letting go of his shackles, pulled over into a pile of still-warm corpses.

Panicking, he tried to wrench out of his bonds, cutting his wrists against metal. Then, a hand on his arm, a soothing voice. "Gabriel. Gabriel, calm down."

Malcolm, somehow freed, pulling him up from the dead men. He'd gotten the key to the chains; with shivering hands, he unlocked them, helped Gabe shake them off his wrists.

They both faced the Prime Minister.

He smiled at them, warm as a father. "Finn truly knows his way around a gift. Come now, we have much to discuss, and the Brothers have much to clean up."

CHAPTER SEVEN

GABE

Unexpected help always comes with strings.
                                    –Caldienan proverb

As they followed the Prime Minister up the stairs, Gabe caught Malcolm's eye, jerked his head toward the dais. Malcolm nodded, his mouth pressed tightly shut. He'd seen the statue, the stone. He knew what it was.

Maybe they could ask Eoin for the piece? Though the mass murder that had just taken place made Gabe wary of asking the man for anything.

Or maybe they could just steal it.

Assuming they made it out of this alive.

Eoin led them up to the top of the amphitheater. It wasn't until they were in the foyer of the building that Gabe realized it was the Rotunda, where the governing body of Caldien was located. He'd seen the structure from the street—round, with a golden domed roof that had been a gift from one of Bastian's ancestors.

The Prime Minister was the only delegate of the Rotunda who had an office in the building. The delegates were voted on every three years by the citizens of Caldien, and allegedly anyone could run. But it took money to finance a campaign, so those who made it in were generally from wealthy families who already boasted many politicians, and there was very little turnover. Eoin's father had been Prime Minister before him. For all their talk of democracy, it seemed to operate very similarly to the monarchies Gabe had grown up with.

Eoin led them to a wooden door, opened it without knocking. A well-appointed room with a large oak desk and a few green houseplants crowding a glass-paned window.

"Tea?" Eoin asked as he took his seat behind the desk, gesturing to two other chairs for Gabe and Malcolm. "It's the middle of the night, but politicians pull odd hours, and there's still staff around." He didn't wait for an answer, ringing a small brass bell on the desk. A moment later, a servant with dark, tired bags beneath their eyes appeared and took his order.

Gabe twisted his wrists back and forth, still numb and red from the shackles. "So Finn set us up?"

Eoin didn't even look away from the servant, holding up a single finger, telling him to wait. Gabe was too taken aback to argue.

When the servant left, Eoin turned back and steepled his fingers beneath his chin. "Finn did you a great favor, actually. He told me his suspicions of who you really were, and that he thought it would serve Caldien better to work with you than with the Sainted King. He knew every Citadel guard in the city would come running if he said he found you."

"So now every Citadel guard in the city is dead," Malcolm said quietly. "Killed by the...you called them Brothers?"

"I did." Eoin grinned. "The Brotherhood of the Waters. It's a...a study group, I suppose you could say. I hesitate to call it a church, but our areas of interest certainly tend toward the spiritual." His eyes went shrewd. "Toward the elemental gods."

"We can't help you with that." Malcolm sounded exhausted. "Yes, we're...we've become...we're tangled with Them, somehow, but we don't understand how Their power works. We can't help you use it."

"Oh, no, you misunderstand me." The door opened, the servant bringing in tea; Eoin doused his in cream from a tiny saucer and took a sip. "We are purely motivated by study. We simply wish to speak with you about the power, perhaps see it demonstrated."

"What do we get, then?" Gabe's voice was dark. "For being your circus animals?"

Eoin's grin sharpened. "Saving you from certain execution seems like quite the repayment. Though other things could be discussed."

It was as good an opening as they were likely to get.

"The statue," Gabe said, haltingly. "It holds a stone..."

"Oh," Eoin said over the lip of his teacup. "You want the Fount piece." He waved a hand. "Yes, perhaps we can come to an agreement on that."

Across the table, Malcolm gaped. Gabe shut his own mouth with a snap of teeth.

Eoin cocked a brow through the steam off his tea. "Anything else?"

"The Queen." No more halting words; Gabe spoke strong. "She's on the Burnt Isles; we have to rescue her. And Alienor Bellegarde, in Dellaire—we need to bring her here, keep her safe from Jax Andronicus and... and the King."

The Prime Minister's expression went grim. "You want me to start a war for you."

"A war is coming," Malcolm said quietly. "Who starts it is irrelevant at this point. The Sainted King and the Kirythean Empire will come for Caldien, probably sooner rather than later."

"I'm aware," Eoin said, setting down his cup. He went to a sideboard and rummaged in a drawer, coming up with a bottle of whiskey and generously dosing his tea.

"You're aware?" Gabe asked. "And doing nothing?"

"Finn has kept me abreast of the situation in Auverraine. At the moment, it's more prudent to bide our time." He sat back down. "We're all spying on one another. You know that. And Finn is the best of the best. He's been in and out of Auverraine for years, working the docks. More than one Citadel courtier sneaks down to rub shoulders with the rabble. They have loose lips when they do."

"So he's your spy," Gabe said. "Not your lover."

"Oh, he's both. A man of many talents." Eoin shrugged. "All those rumors a few months ago—a courtier dead in the King's apartments, the puddle of water around her body, then, finally, the conviction of the freshly minted Queen—would have been too chaotic for anyone who hadn't been paying attention to put together. Anyone who didn't know the myths, and anyone who was too blinded by religion to believe.

"Now, Finn knows his subterfuge, and he knows his myths, so it was fairly easy for him to figure out. The King wanted that courtier—Demillier? Devaux? Something like that—dead, because she was the avatar of one of the elemental gods." Eoin circled his wrist as if hurrying himself along. "And then, once you lot left Auverraine and came here, with wanted notices soon after, it wasn't a stretch to think that you perhaps had the same affliction."

"You're incredibly nonchalant about it," Gabe murmured.

Eoin shrugged. "Our gods were men who wanted more power. There's not much to be awed by, really. Who among us wouldn't do the same, given the opportunity?"

"Me," Malcolm said quietly. "I wouldn't."

"Well, your King is of a different mind, it seems. I'd long had my suspicions about that Tract, the one about the chosen Arceneaux. Seems Apollius finally found the one He wanted."

They didn't have to worry about telling Eoin what had happened to Bastian. It seemed he already knew.

"You know the kind of danger we're in, then," Gabe said. "All of us."

"And that is why I prefer not to act rashly." Eoin sat back in his chair, once again steepling his fingers. "You want my piece of the Fount, you want a rescue for the Queen of Auverraine and another one for an Arceneaux half sister currently betrothed to the Emperor. That's quite a lot of favors to ask. It almost outweighs political asylum."

"What more do you want?" There was a haunted look in Malcolm's eye, one Gabe couldn't quite pin on their current circumstances.

"Nothing much," Eoin said. "Just what I mentioned before. For you to demonstrate your power for me, let the other Brothers witness the miracle of it with their own eyes." His smile widened. "No scientific experiments, promise. The most we'll ask is for you to talk us through the particulars."

Gods dead and dying, they didn't know the particulars. The Prime Minister was treating this like some grand illusion, a natural curiosity rather than evidence of the apocalypse.

"That's all you want?" Gabe asked incredulously. "A demonstration of power?"

"It's a good place to start," Eoin replied.

In his head, Hestraon was silent. For that, Gabe was grateful.

The god was talking to him. He was seeing Hestraon's memories. The last thing he should be doing, no pun intended, was playing with fire.

But if it could save Lore and Alie, he had to try.

And maybe, somehow, he could find a way to save Bastian, too.

Malcolm looked at him, gave a slight nod. They'd never fallen into the deference proper for the Priest Exalted and one of his Presque Mort, but here, for this, the decision was deferred to Gabe. Malcolm would follow his lead.

"Fine," Gabe said. "We'll do it."

"Excellent." Eoin stood. "I'll begin working on saving your Queen and your friend, and you can have the Fount piece once I decide your debt is paid." He snapped his fingers. "And before I forget, there's a boardinghouse in the city that we allow guests of the Rotunda to use. Rooms could be ready for you tomorrow?"

"Please." The Fount piece, asylum, and no longer being a punching bag for rent. The whole evening was a miracle.

But Gabe had grown very, very wary of miracles.

The Prime Minister led them from the room to the front of the atrium. "Our next meeting is tomorrow night, here at the Rotunda. We'll be expecting you."

He left them on the wide wrapped porch, aglow in gas lamplight.

"That..." Gabe shook his head. "Well. That was something."

"It certainly was," Malcolm agreed, eyes still distant.

Thunder rolled through the sky, and the heavens opened in a downpour.

CHAPTER EIGHT

ALIE

Chance is just fate biding its time.
                    —Malfouran proverb

She'd never been one of those courtiers who sneaked out into Dellaire, at least not often. Her friends would go once a fortnight, it seemed, either in their covered carriages or dressed as they thought commoners did, to *experience the city*. Alie had never had much interest in that endeavor. Not out of any sort of snobbery—in fact, the opposite: She knew she was in a privileged position, and pretending otherwise never sat well. Especially when the outfits her friends put together made it so obvious they were merely sightseeing, trying on poverty like a costume.

But, desperate times.

Ever since Gabe and Malcolm had made it onto that ship— ever since she hadn't—Alie had been looking for a way out of Auverraine. She was well aware that staging an escape on her own would be nearly impossible, but still, she sneaked into Dellaire as often as she could. Every time, going out a little farther, making it a bit closer to the city's border. Making plans.

Jax knew she did this. She assumed Apollius did, too. But

neither of them stopped her, and she made it a point to act secretive when she came back into the Citadel, pretending that she didn't know she'd been found out the moment she set foot outside. If they thought she was inept and would always come back, they'd be less likely to come after her the one time she didn't.

If she could ever get up the nerve. She'd come close to actually packing today, filling her satchel with provisions and money instead of an old dress and the clean lengths of linen she used when she bled to make the bag look full. But Alie had left with the same decoy pack she always did; today was not the day she would escape.

Alie wandered around one of the markets in the Southeast Ward. She wore a plain dress, fine enough that no one would mistake her for poor, but not so ostentatious that she'd look like a noble voyeur. A scarf covered her distinctive hair.

The energy of the Wards invigorated her. She'd grown up a fixture of the Citadel, one of the people whom others looked to, emblematic of the perfect noble. Her visibility had only increased since she'd been engaged to Jax, since her true parentage had been revealed.

Here she was one of many. Anonymous. It felt nice.

And here she could practice using Lereal's power without worrying she'd be caught. She still didn't use much—a flutter to run through a child's streaming hair, a whisper of wind to soothe the farmer at his fruit stand—but it was enough to hone the magic. To wrestle it further under her control.

There was an ease to her thoughts when she used it, a soft lightness, like this was something she was supposed to be doing. But Lereal never spoke to her, never made Their presence known in more than a feeling. Alie could live with that.

She only hoped the others could, too.

Alie approached the fruit stand, the farmer looking much more pleasant after her manufactured breeze. As she inspected apples, she flickered the fingers of her other hand, drawing whispers from the farthest corners of the market to her ears.

The payments dried up almost as soon as they started.

Once he got a feel for all that gold, he didn't want to part with it.

Useless. He's just as bad as his father. Just as bad as every other Arceneaux.

Worse, I'd say. No other Arceneaux invited a neighboring dictator to marry his half sister.

It was the same everywhere. Whispers about Bastian that ranged from irritated to seditious. Alie couldn't blame them, really, though it only added one more layer to her anger—Bastian was taking the public fall for what Apollius had done. A revolution right now would be disastrous, but what was one more disaster at this point?

She wouldn't fare well if the citizens of Auverraine decided to upend the monarchy. But monarchy was starting to make less and less sense. The Arceneaux line claimed to rule by divine right, and Alie had seen just what a farce divinity was.

Alie let go of the threads of wind carrying the whispered conversations. One problem at a time, and she already had a full ledger of them.

"I recognize you."

Oh, excellent. Here was one more.

Alie considered ignoring the speaker, pretending she couldn't hear. But she couldn't guarantee that whoever it was wouldn't make a scene, and the only thing worse than one person in the Southeast Ward knowing she was nobility was for everyone to know.

Slowly, she turned around.

The woman behind her wasn't someone she recognized, though that wasn't really surprising. What was surprising was the air of familiarity around her—she looked like someone Alie *should* recognize, a slightly off reflection of a person she knew.

The woman narrowed hazel eyes in a spare, white-skinned face. Her blond hair was held back in a drab scarf, and her black dress had seen better days. "It's not here. What you're looking for."

"Pardon me?" Alie didn't try to obscure the Citadel-polish of her voice. If she was caught, she was caught. Though it seemed like this woman might be a few drops shy of a wineglass.

"The thing you're looking for." The woman looked at Alie as if she were the cracked one. "The piece?"

"I'm sorry." Nerves pricked their way down Alie's spine; if the woman got agitated, she could get violent, and Alie had no weapons other than a dagger slipped in the top of her boot that she barely knew how to use. "I can't say I know what you're talking about."

The woman rolled her not-quite-familiar eyes. Then she grabbed Alie's arm and hauled her toward an alley.

Her boots skidded in the dust of the Ward; Alie tried to struggle away without making too much of a scene, but the woman's grip was iron. As a last resort, Alie looked around desperately for the bloodcoat she was sure dogged her steps. There was no one. Maybe Jax and Apollius weren't watching her as closely as she thought, at least not today.

Figured.

The woman pulled her into the shadows of the alley, old wooden crates stacked against stone walls, rotting through with rain. She turned and glared at Alie. "Are you going to run, or are you going to listen?"

The dagger glittering in the woman's hand made running seem like a bad choice.

Her own dagger was itching in her boot. But all Alie knew was that the pointy end should be turned toward your enemy, and the woman in the black dress seemed like she was more knowledgeable than that. The best thing to do was to play along.

Alie nodded smoothly. "I'll listen."

"Good." The woman tucked her own knife back into the ratty cloth at her waist. As she did, her palm turned toward the light. White scars scored the bottom edge where her hand met her wrist, the rough approximations of the phases of the moon.

The nerves in Alie's spine went from pinpricks to near-painful gooseflesh.

"I know who you are," the woman said. "You don't know who I am, and that's fine. I'm Lilia, and I want to help you."

Another nod, still smooth, still courtly.

"If you aren't looking for the piece of the Fount yet, I assume it's because you didn't know you should be." Lilia crossed her arms, but the movement seemed more like she was trying to hold herself up than meant to convey any particular emotion. She looked tired, as if it had been ages since she felt safe enough to sleep. "I guess I'm not surprised. All the pretty ethereal things made it into the Tracts; the gritty parts were only for those of us in too deep already."

In too deep, with moon scars on her hands. "You're one of the Buried Watch."

"Worse than that." Lilia barked a short, painful laugh. "I was the gods-damned Night Priestess."

The Night Priestess. Lore's mother.

A pale brow arched over a hazel eye, one the exact color of Lore's, now that Alie knew what to look for. "Are you going to run now?" Lore's mother asked.

"No." Alie shook her head. "If you know something that can help us, I want to hear it."

"You're far more willing to listen than my daughter," Lilia said, trying to smile and succeeding only in twitching her lip. "Though I suppose that shouldn't be a surprise." She leaned her shoulder against the wall. "You're all trying to kill Apollius, then?"

Hearing it said so baldly made Alie's eyes widen. She was still a courtier at heart, far more used to dancing around ugly subjects than addressing them outright.

"Of course you are," Lilia said. "You're in league with Lore, and she doesn't do half measures." A distant look came into her eyes. "Maybe if I'd told her all this, she would have asked for my help sooner. Though I can't really blame her."

Alie didn't respond. She wasn't sure if Lilia wanted her to. It sounded like she was talking mostly to herself, a conversation retread over and over.

Lilia shook herself, as if casting off a sudden chill. "Too late for that," she said briskly. "I made my bed. So I'll tell you, and I'll trust that you have a way to get the information to the rest of the reborn avatars. We in the Buried Watch knew about dreamwalking, even if we couldn't do it. Some of the Presque Mort used to, back when Nyxara was newly dead and Her power was everywhere. They can't anymore, but I'm sure you can manage it."

That, Alie should probably respond to. "I'm not sure what you mean," she said, trying to sound nonchalant despite the panic clawing into her chest. "But if you have helpful information—"

"Save it." Lilia's voice was threadbare, like this gruff, to-the-point persona was something she'd slipped into out of necessity, and it was wearing down fast. "You're Lereal. I could feel you manipulating the magic across the Ward. How else do you think I knew to approach you?"

Shit. Shit shit shit. She thought she'd been so careful, so clever. "If you could feel it, then..."

"Apollius absolutely knows," Lilia said, answering before Alie could finish, stating the obvious she hadn't let herself think about. "And we should both be very concerned why He hasn't done something about it."

And of course she'd known that, but hearing it said so plainly made her shoulders tense.

"Which means," Lilia said, "that we should move quickly.

If you want to kill Apollius, you'll have to first make the Fount whole again. It can't hold everything, not while It's broken."

"Then we're fucked," Alie said simply. Her language had gotten so much worse since she made friends with Lore. "Seeing as the Fount is on the Golden Mount, and the Golden Mount is hidden in ash so thick that you could choke on it."

"There are ways to get there. Especially now that Lore is on the Burnt Isles." Lilia's eyes clouded at the mention of her daughter. "I may not know her well, but I know she can find her way to the Mount. Especially if you tell her to."

By dreamwalking. Alie sighed, shaking her head. "I can only see the others with power in dreams if they're using it, right?"

"They'll use it," Lilia said. "They may try not to, but eventually, they'll give in."

Wasn't Alie proof of that herself?

"Now." Lilia straightened. "There are three pieces of the Fount missing. One was never accounted for, but Apollius had the other two hidden by His followers, in the hope that the Fount could never be made whole again. We know one is in Auverraine somewhere, because the Priest Exalted was tasked with keeping it safe." She arched a brow. "Though I don't think Gabriel ever got that particular instruction."

"I doubt Apollius would have told him, no." Alie was fairly certain Apollius had started His influence right after the ritual, but the decision to make Gabe the Priest Exalted was all Bastian, wanting to keep the other man close. "So we have one. Where are the others?"

"That's the only one we have an exact location for. After the Godsfall, when all the pilgrims were fleeing the Isles, there was quite a bit of confusion, and the second one is probably in some rich family's art collection. No one knows where the third ended up." Lilia had deflated somewhat, as if realizing that this revelation didn't help them all that much. "But if we can find the one here, we can tell the others what to look for, at least."

"So we don't even know what it looks like?"

"I assume," Lilia said, slightly icy, "that it looks like a broken piece of a fountain."

In that moment, she was undeniably Lore's mother.

Alie sighed. "Fine. It's better than nothing. What do you need me to do?"

"It's likely that I'll need to get inside the Citadel to search," Lilia said. "That seems the most obvious place for it to be. If we can't find it there, we may need to try the catacombs again, though I've looked through as many tunnels as I can get to."

The idea of scurrying around down there made Alie shiver. "I can arrange that. How will I know when?"

The other woman thought for a moment. "A rose," she said finally, quietly. "I'll leave a rose in the door."

Alie nodded. "I'll be looking."

"Good." Then, with no further instruction, Lore's mother ducked out of the alley and into the falling light.

Alie sneaked back into the Citadel the same way she left, through the storm drain that led to the manicured forest at the edge of the grounds. She'd hidden a change of clothes in the hollow of a tree, a ruse that would look like someone was trysting if anyone came across it. Alie changed back into a court dress quickly, shivering in the chill. Summer had been punishing, and it seemed winter would be, too, once it finally got here.

She paused a moment, twisting air in her fingers. It had become second nature to check for whispers when she returned from Dellaire. Usually, she heard nothing interesting, and she let the murmurs of courtiers who thought their conversations were private wash over her without much thought.

But one voice gave her pause.

"You think far too highly of your damn Empire, Jax," Apollius sneered. "You of all people should know that I have more important things to attend to."

"I'm aware." Jax's voice was stiff and resigned, as if this was the tail end of an argument he'd long accepted losing. "But while You are caught up in heavenly pursuits, there is still ruling to do. Our forces in Kadmar are subsisting on starvation rations—"

"So let them." Apollius sounded bored. "We have the troops to spare."

"Holy One, I cannot in good conscience—"

Apollius laughed, harsh and brassy. Alie winced. "Since when have you done anything in good conscience? Taking over the continent? Pulling out Gabriel Remaut's eye?" A pause, and the next words sounded sly. "Killing your father?"

It was an open secret, but it still made Alie start.

Silence. Jax's next words were quiet. "I did that for You."

"Whatever you have to tell yourself. You were a weak, stupid boy, willing to do whatever it took to feel less weak and less stupid. You didn't do it for Me, you did it for yourself." The slight sound of a wineglass clinking against rings, a swallow. "I don't care about your fucking Empire, Jax Andronicus, and I certainly don't care about your troops in Kadmar. I care about getting back the power owed to Me. And you are going to marry Bastian's bastard half sister, and have lots of weak, stupid babies, and shut up about an empire that won't be yours for long, anyway."

Alie let go the strands of air. Her heart thumped painfully in her chest, unwelcome sympathy.

Bundling her other clothes into her bag, Alie affixed the grate to the drain entrance again and hurried toward the Citadel.

Two bloodcoats stood at either side of the doors, looking bored. Alie was halfway up the stairs before they acknowledged her, and when they did, they stood up straighter. "His Holy Majesty has asked for a word with you, Lady Bellegarde."

She froze on the steps, one foot awkwardly raised. "Pardon?"

"The King." The bloodcoat looked at her as if she were wearing a live peacock on her head. "He asked you to meet him in his chambers."

Shit shit *shit*.

Alie nodded graciously, managing to make it the rest of the way up the stairs and into a secluded alcove beside the foyer before her fear made her double at the waist. Deep breaths, in and out, her mind already tripping over excuses, deals she could make, how she could salvage this.

A cool breeze slid across the back of her mind, gentle and reassuring. Kind. She felt a survivor's guilt, sometimes, that the power she'd inherited was kind.

At Bastian's apartment, Alie took another deep breath, did her best to calm her heart. Then she pushed open the doors and strode inside.

She expected Apollius Avenging, just like that awful statue in Courdigne, standing in a spill of light and sneering at her.

But instead of standing straight and strong, sharp and cruel as she'd heard Him moments before, Apollius was hunched over, nearly on His knees. His back heaved like He might vomit; sweat dropped from His forehead to the floor.

And when He looked up, it was Bastian staring out of his own eyes.

"Alie." Her name was a rasp. "I don't have much time."

She froze only a moment before rushing to him, trying to grip his shoulders and pull him up, but Bastian waved her off. "Something is happening. He's weakening. I can…" He trailed off, grimacing, as if fighting back a cramp. It subsided, and he started again. "I can see, sometimes. And I think I can hear His thoughts, look into them. It's like the power is being pulled elsewhere." His head wrenched to the side, teeth bared in a snarl as he tried to hold on. "I don't fucking want it. I did, at first. Wanted the power, the security. But not anymore. I just want it *gone*."

Alie had always been a quick study. "Can you see His thoughts?"

"Sometimes." He winced. "Sort of."

"Then there's something you need to look for. A location, one He thinks is important. A place He's hidden something." She kept it vague. The ways Apollius's and Bastian's minds came together now were alien to her, but she knew that in the months before the god fully took over, Bastian wasn't able to hide much from Him. If she kept things to broad strokes, maybe the god wouldn't know exactly what Bastian was searching for.

Bastian seemed to understand what she was doing. He nodded, once, painful. "I'll do my best. Now go—"

He fell fully to the floor, finally, his forehead pressed against the marble, his breath hissing between his teeth. One hand flailed toward the door, urging her away. She understood, backing up but not quite able to make herself leave.

Bastian thrashed. His body convulsed over the tiles, contorting into shapes that hurt to look at. He made a choked, gasping sound, a drowning moan.

Then He looked up, golden-eyed and all god.

"Sister," Apollius said, standing gracefully and straightening His shirt. "To what do I owe the pleasure?"

"I was looking for Jax," Alie said, the lie coming easily. "I was told he was attending You." She almost asked if He was well, but that would be a step too far. Apollius knew she didn't care.

"He's not here." Apollius smiled. "Though I am pleased to see you coming around to your betrothal." He cocked His head. "They're not so bad, the plans I have for you. You'll come around to them, too, I think. You won't have much choice."

So calm as He threatened her. Sure He had won, and the only thing left was hemming up the ragged edges.

Alie didn't respond. She just pulled her skirt into a quick curtsy and slipped out the door, those golden eyes burning into her back.

CHAPTER NINE

LORE

King Lucius Arceneaux once tasked the Burnt Isles guards with taking a census at the beginning and end of the year, to see how many prisoners on the Second Isle survived. There were nearly five hundred fewer inmates when the final census was taken.

No investigation was deemed necessary.

      –Fabien Triou, *Gods and Guards: A History of the Burnt Isles*, 478 AGF

It figured that when Lore actually wanted to dream, she couldn't. Ever since seeing that glimpse of Alie, she'd tried to make herself end up on that beach every time she closed her eyes. But her mind kept sending her mundane dreams instead, anxiety scenes of being naked in a city Ward or quizzed by Val in some nonsense language. Lore was on the verge of trying to knock herself unconscious with her pickax, just to see if that would make a difference.

But tonight, finally, she ended up on the beach.

It was the Burnt Isles; she recognized it now. Before they were burnt, before the catastrophe of the Godsfall left them in perpetual ruin. This was the beach as she'd seen it in Nyxara's memories, all white sand and blue sky, gray cliffs and silence.

And no Alie.

"Shit." She sat down on the sand, staring out at the endless ocean.

Any ideas? She prodded at the back of her mind, where Nyxara slept. But the goddess was quiet. In fact, the goddess seemed nearly gone, just a dark space left behind.

Apparently Nyxara couldn't speak in these dreams. Interesting.

A moment, then Lore lay back, mindless of the sand working its way into her hair. Her eyes drifted closed. At least she hadn't actually knocked herself out.

"Lore?"

Finally.

Lore scrambled up from the sand, already running as soon as she got her feet beneath her. Alie wasn't a mirage, wasn't some filmy ghost; she looked as real and solid as Lore did, standing at the tide line in a white gown with a relieved look on her face. She had to fight to keep her balance when Lore slammed into her, hugging her like she was an anchor in a storm.

"Gods, Alie," Lore stammered, "I've been so worried about you, I can't believe I left you there—"

"Not like you could have done anything different." Alie patted her hair. "You were rather incapacitated when they shipped you off." She pushed Lore gently away, feathering her fingers over the scar on Lore's temple. "Looks like you healed up just fine."

"How are you?" Lore didn't want to talk about her scar. "Are you safe? Have you gotten away?"

"Yes, I'm safe; no, I haven't gotten away." Alie gave her a weak smile. "I have a lot to tell you, and I don't know how long we have. So listen closely."

Lore did. Lore listened to Alie tell her what this place was—the Isles pre-Godsfall, like she'd thought, but mostly just a constructed place where they could dreamwalk—and how Bastian was able to break free of Apollius, sometimes. Alie told her of the shards of the Fount, how they had to find them and make them whole again, how she was certain one was in the Burnt Isles and another in Auverraine, and then a third somewhere else on the continent.

Lore listened quietly all the way up until Alie mentioned Lilia.

"Wait." She waved a hand, as if Lilia were something she could reach out and grab. "You met my mother?"

Alie shifted on her feet. "She wants to help us, Lore. She's the one who told me to find the shards of the Fount, make It whole before we can restore Its power."

"She could be lying." The idea that her mother would suddenly want to help her was almost laughable. Yes, she'd had a change of heart, telling Lore to run rather than let herself be killed, but Lore still couldn't think of her as an ally. It would hurt too much when she was once again proven wrong.

"Why would she?" Alie shook her head. "No, don't answer that, I know why you think so. But Lore...she doesn't want Apollius to be the God of Everything. She doesn't want the world He's bringing."

Seasons scrambled, dying crops, churning storms. All the little ways the earth had been dying since the gods stole the power of the Fount, some Lore had seen with her own eyes, others she'd only heard of secondhand.

Lore looked away from Alie, toward the ocean. "Fine. Say you're right, and Lilia does want to help. How in all the hells are we supposed to find this Fount piece? And even if we can, how do we get it to the Golden Mount?"

"Bastian thinks he can break into Apollius's mind, the same way Apollius did to him," Alie answered. "If he can search Apollius's thoughts, he can find where the piece is hidden."

"That would be a stroke of luck," Lore muttered. "Almost too much luck."

Alie shrugged. "We'll take what we can get, at this point."

Lore chewed at the inside of her cheek. "How is he?" An ache in her voice, too acute to hide. She'd tried very hard not to think too much of Bastian, how he had to be suffering. It hurt too much, to know his pain and be unable to do anything about it. At least she knew Gabe was in charge of his own body.

"Not well," Alie answered. "But he's broken through Apollius's hold more than once."

Bastian was strong-willed. Maybe he could beat the god back once and for all.

Hope was an improbable seed, rooting without soil, without water.

"So if everything goes well, Bastian can find the location of the shard in Auverraine, and I'll bring it to the Mount," Alie continued. "Somehow."

"And I find the one on the Isles." Ideally without having to tell Dani what she was looking for. The other woman might be a temporary ally, but Lore still didn't trust her. "And Gabe looks for the one still on the continent, I'm guessing. Can you talk to him like this?"

"You can, too," Alie said softly. "This space is shared by all of us, as long as we're using power from the Fount. If Gabe is channeling fire at all, he'll show up here eventually."

"And we just have to hope we're all dreaming at the same time?" Two steps forward, one step back.

"It's certainly not an exact science." Alie was fading. Lore could see the cliffs through her torso, her friend turning ghost. Waking up. "You'll see him," Alie promised as she disappeared. "And if you do before me, tell him to find the shard."

Then she was gone.

Ridiculous, how much lighter Lore felt with a plan, even one as far-fetched and unlikely as this. Part of her thought they were deluding themselves, thinking they could find the shards of the

Fount scattered all over, somehow bring them to the Mount. But it was better than nothing. Better than helplessness.

Lore lay back on the sand, the warm water washing up over her ankles. She waited to wake.

💮

The next day, Lore got up long before the dawn. She had no pallet to bundle up, having used hers as a burial shroud for a dead monk, so she had a few minutes before it was time to head to the mine. She used them to stand at the shoreline, the water washing up over her still-bare feet, the anemic light of morning a thin scrim over the horizon. The guards up by the barracks kept a wary eye on her but didn't say anything. She was almost certain they had orders to keep her alive, but as long as she didn't walk into the sea, they'd leave her alone.

So she had to find a piece of the Fount, then get to the Golden Mount. At least one of those things seemed slightly doable, now that Dani was her ally. The closest thing she had to one, anyway, and that connection was nearly as anemic as the sunlight. It didn't sound like they had the same end goal—hells, it sounded like Dani's end goal was the annihilation of everything—but Lore could use her. If Dani truly had a way to get off this island, a way to find the Golden Mount, Lore would play along with her nihilism.

You have more patience than I, Nyxara said in response to the thought.

Lore ignored that. *You wouldn't happen to know where the shard of the Fount is, would You?*

The goddess paused. *I know it's somewhere on the Isles. But I don't remember which one I hid it on.*

You hid it? Lore supposed that shouldn't be a surprise.

During the Godsfall, Nyxara said. *When I had ... had a moment.*

And You didn't think that was something You should tell me?

One piece of the Fount is useless. It cannot hold the whole of Its power again unless all of them are found. I didn't want to give you false hope.

As if that wasn't the only kind Lore had.

The sun was starting to rise, a weak glow filtering through the ash. Without its constant cover, the heat would have been punishing. *You've been quiet lately,* Lore said, hurrying before the full light of day pushed the goddess too far back in her head to speak. *This is the most I've heard from You in days.*

I've tried to speak to you. Nyxara already sounded distant. *It's... harder, lately.*

What is that supposed to mean? But Nyxara was already gone, hunched into the darkness behind her thoughts.

"I know You can still hear me," she said grumpily, but she didn't try to further engage her parasitic goddess. Lore rubbed at her tired eyes. Then she turned and walked up the beach, grabbing her boots from the cave before heading to where a queue of prisoners already gathered, waiting to choose their pickaxes for the day. She pulled the cloth from her pocket and started wrapping her preemptively stinging palms.

"No need for that." A familiar slender figure appeared at her side, almost as if she'd conjured herself out of the fog. Dani, pulling the cloth from Lore's hands. "You aren't mining today."

"How do you figure?" Lore snatched her bandages back. "We work or we get beaten."

Dani rolled her eyes. "We're still working, Your Majesty." She gripped Lore's arm and steered her away from the crowd. "But we're working in the lighthouse."

"Absolutely not." Lore dug her heels into the sand. "I don't want to get within ten feet of Martin." And she should start her search for the Fount piece. The chances of it being in the mine, or anywhere on this island, were small but not zero.

"You won't have to," Dani replied, grabbing Lore's hand and

dragging her down the beach, out of earshot. "He and I have an understanding. If I tell him to leave you alone, he will."

Lore didn't trust any sentence that contained both *Martin* and *understanding*. "I'd rather stick with the mines."

Dani stepped up until she was bare inches from Lore's face. They were of a height, both shorter than average. The person before her now bore very little resemblance to the person she'd met in Bastian's atrium so long ago, sipping tea and eating macarons. Her face had been turned from delicate to gaunt by imprisonment, filed to sharp edges. Her nails dug into Lore's forearm.

"Do you want to kill Him," Dani said, cold and even, "or don't you? Because you won't be able to pull it off without my help, I can promise you that. You might think yourself street-smart, Lore, but here, you're nothing more than a walking target. You think those Presque Mort were the only ones who want to come after you?"

"I can take care of myself," Lore said, jerking her arm backward and wishing she believed it like she once had.

"Can you?" Dani cocked a brow. "Are you just going to keep using Spiritum, sucking it out of everyone who crosses you? I understand that it's really the only thing you can do with it, but it might become suspicious after a while. And it will certainly draw His attention. Mortem would be more useful, but that's not an option anymore, is it?"

Lore clenched her teeth. Stupid of her to think Dani hadn't noticed that.

"Simply put," Dani said, "I know more than you. I know how to get off this island." She smiled, tight and spare. "So you can either keep floundering around and doing nothing, unless you finally decide to die like everyone wants you to, or you can trust me."

If the piece was on the Second Isle, surely Nyxara would feel it. If it was on any island with a mine, though, chances were it had already been found and either taken back to Apollius or smashed apart by a prisoner's pickax.

If Dani could truly keep Martin off her back, a break from the mines might be nice.

"Why do you care?" Lore asked, rubbing at the skin of her arm where Dani's nails had gouged. "You don't think the world is worth saving."

"It's not. But I also don't want to see Apollius in charge of it." Dani shrugged. "He's the reason I'm here, really. And I'm petty."

Not the best answer, but probably the only one she was going to get.

So Lore gave her one firm nod. "Fine. Let's go."

"Excellent." Dani turned and started down the sand. "I hope you're a good hand with a mop."

They arrived at the lighthouse at the same time as a handful of other convicts, all of them young, pretty, and femme. The others cast curious looks at Lore, but none of them would even make eye contact with Dani, slithering aside when the other woman strode up to the door and pounded on it with her fist.

"Open up, Martin, don't make us wait!"

The door opened, Martin standing in the darkness on the other side. He said nothing, though his eyes widened when he saw Lore, then narrowed in hateful wariness. A moment, then he looked to Dani, jerking his head toward the staircase before wordlessly heading up to the higher reaches of the lighthouse.

The other prisoners filtered inside, but Dani hung back until Lore caught up with her. "I have business to take care of, but in half an hour, meet me in the shipping office."

The shipping office was back at shore, at least half a mile away. "How exactly am I supposed to get that far without being shot? The guards here are lax, but none of them are just going to let me wander down the beach."

"They will if you're carrying a mop and have a suitably hangdog expression." Dani stepped into the lighthouse, gesturing for Lore to follow. "They'll be thrilled that Martin finally broke you."

That felt uncomfortably close to the truth. "Until Martin disabuses them of that notion."

"I have that handled, remember?" Dani squared her shoulders. "If he wants to keep the good thing he has going, he won't tell them shit. Now, speaking of, I have to go. Get a mop, get there in thirty minutes."

She disappeared up the dark stairs after Martin.

The others had all dispersed, too, each of them headed to their usual jobs. Lore didn't miss the relieved looks that followed Dani up the stairs, the way shoulders softened and fists unclenched. It made Lore indignant; they were fine with Dani taking the brunt of Martin's perversity as long as it meant they weren't bothered.

But wasn't Lore doing the same thing? Life here was survival, and survival didn't leave much room for taking high roads.

Still, she thought Dani deserved better. Some gratitude, or at least not to be vilified.

One of the prisoners looked more relieved than the others, her arm bent across her chest, delicately holding her wrist. Another girl bumped into her, and she hissed, her face paling as she pulled her arm in closer.

Cautiously, Lore stepped toward her. The girl didn't move away—the bottom floor of the lighthouse didn't have much room to do so, even if she wanted to—but her expression was full of apprehension.

"Are you all right?" Lore asked.

"It's nothing." The girl adjusted her hold on her arm. "Just sore from . . . from last time."

Either she was lying, or she had an incredible pain tolerance. This close, Lore could see that her wrist was slightly bent out of shape, hanging limply. Probably broken.

And here, at least, was something she could fix. "Let me see."

At first, it seemed the woman would refuse. But either because of some latent respect for her former station, or just because she'd grown used to following orders, she tentatively held out her arm.

Lore held it gently, slipping into channeling-space. Healing was easy. It simply involved seeing what was wrong—where those golden lines of life went crooked—and straightening them. She channeled the girl's life through her fingers, imbuing it with her will. Strength. Stability.

A soft gasp. The girl jerked her arm away, but not before her wrist had straightened.

She looked at Lore with wide, fearful eyes, rubbing at her healed bones. Then she turned and fled farther into the lighthouse.

"You're welcome," Lore murmured.

Sighing, she took a mop and bucket from the closet under the stairs and made her way back out into the ash, following another group of convicts who were apparently headed to clean the few barges at the dock. Lore peeled off in the opposite direction, the squat building of the shipping office standing sentry on the shore.

The sun was bright enough to have reddened her skin even through the ash-veil by the time Lore reached the office. *Office* was a stretch, really. The place was one room, a rickety desk in the center covered in schedules for which ships needed repairs, which ones would be going to the mainland to ferry back another load of prisoners. One of the desk's drawers yawned open, emitting a flutter of old maps.

Martin was the only person Lore knew of who ever worked in here, and only when he had to. He preferred to stay in his lighthouse. Lore supposed if another guard showed up, she could say Martin told her to meet him.

It only took five minutes to clean the floor of the small room. Lore discarded her mop and flopped into the chair at the desk, tipping back her head. Resting in the middle of the day was nigh unheard of. After a moment, she went over to the bucket, dipped in her hand, and took a drink. The water in there was just as good as what they were given at the trough, and she'd missed her chance at it this morning. The twisting in her gut reminded her that she'd missed her chance at breakfast, too. She sat in the chair and put her head on the desk.

Lore didn't realize she'd fallen asleep until the sound of the door slamming jarred her awake. She jumped up, searching desperately for her mop.

"Calm down." Dani dropped a heel of bread in front of her, in the middle of all those shipping schedules. "It's just me." She grinned, a flat one that stopped short of her eyes. "Myriad hells, this place has done a number on you. You were never this jumpy before, even when you should have been."

She wanted to retort, but there was no point. Dani was right. The Lore who would indolently lounge when she was supposed to be working, who would relish being caught flouting the rules, had been slowly dredged out on the Isles. She was left like this, a half-starved shell perpetually on the edge of panic.

"Eat," Dani said, jerking her chin at the bread. "Then we'll start looking." She sat down in Lore's recently vacated chair, wincing slightly. When she shuffled through the schedules, Lore caught the purple blooms of bruises on her forearms.

"Are those from him?" she asked quietly.

Dani flexed her wrist back and forth. "Don't worry about me," she said in answer. "I give as good as I get. That's why Martin likes me. He wants them to have some fight."

The bread tasted ashy. Lore wasn't sure if it was due to Dani's words or actual ash. "I'm sorry."

"We take power where we can get it." But the other woman's flippant tone was brittle. "Not all of us have the option of fucking the King."

That was fair.

Dani thumbed through schedules until she found the one she was looking for, laid it out flat. "A week from now," she murmured, "the Blue is headed to port, the Green stays, and Red and Gold are due for repairs and moving to the southern dock." She nodded curtly. "Two ships out of commission, so most guards will be at the arrival port to help with overflow. He'll come then."

All the prison ships were named after colors. No great creative thinkers, were the guards of the Burnt Isles. "Who is *he*?"

"The Ferryman," Dani said, pulling a handful of maps from the drawer. "The man who's going to get us off the island."

"I'm sorry, who?"

"Did you really think every person who disappears from the Second Isle either killed themselves or was murdered?" Dani scoffed, digging another schedule from the drawer to cross-reference. "Some of them, sure, but lots go to the Ferryman. He can't get you to Auverraine—you'd get lost forever in the ash if you tried—but he can get you to the Harbor. Assuming you can pay."

Lore's head was spinning, and not just from hunger and dehydration. "What's the Harbor? And it doesn't matter anyway, because we have nothing to pay with—"

Without looking up from her papers, Dani dug in her pocket, pulling out a small silver instrument that looked like a needle balanced on top of a pyramid. It wobbled back and forth, loose on its hinges. "Stole it from Martin," she said, tucking the instrument back in her pocket once Lore's silence made it clear her point was taken. "The Ferryman likes those kinds of things. Balances, compass pieces, anything that can be salvaged for science. Most people just steal something from the mine, though, or anything that looks like it could be pre-Godsfall. You have to bring *something* to make it worth his while, but he isn't picky."

The fact that a solution to at least one of Lore's problems had been right under her nose this entire time was galling. "So there's been a way to escape the Isles all along. One that, apparently, most inmates know about." And hadn't shared with her. That shouldn't sting. By design, this place didn't foster camaraderie.

"Not most," Dani countered. "Only a few, and they're cagey. I've been here awhile, remember?"

The slantwise reminder of how they'd first met, what Dani was here for, made Lore's eyes narrow.

That only made Dani's smile go brighter. "You have every right to hate me," she said, cutting straight to the heart, not bothering with lesser wounds along the way. "Do you?"

The question was unexpected enough that Lore actually took a moment to think on it. "No," she said finally. "I feel sorry for you."

The feral gleam in Dani's eyes flickered. Her hands arched on either side of the map.

But she didn't do anything but laugh. "Good," she said. "That makes two of us." She shook her head, continued. "Believe it or not, even among the prisoners who know, most of them would rather stay here than risk a trip to the Harbor. Half of the inmates have lived on the Second Isle since they were children. This is hell, but it's home. It's hard to let go of the familiar."

Lore shifted uncomfortably, leaning on her mop. "What exactly is the Harbor?"

"The Third Isle, technically. One of the ones hidden in all this shit from the Godsfall." She waved a hand, indicating the ash and fog beyond the office walls. "There's an entire community of escapees there. The ash won't let them leave the archipelago, but they don't have to stay in prison, at least."

"And this Ferryman will take us there, but not all the way to the Golden Mount."

"Small steps are better than none." Satisfied that she'd confirmed the shipping schedule, Dani shoved the papers back into the drawer and pushed it closed. "Once we're at the Harbor, we can make plans to keep going. Find a boat."

"Finding the boat isn't the problem. Navigating through the ash is."

"As if you haven't been thinking on a way to manage that since you got here." Dani gave her a sardonic look. "Don't sell yourself short, Lore. I'm sure you can find some way to use that power of yours to get us to the Mount, even if you can't do anything else with it."

The mention of Spiritum sparked her awareness of it, made the air around Dani glimmer golden.

"Why haven't you used it?" Dani continued, sitting back in the chair and crossing her arms. "Surely it could help you in some way."

"How?" Lore barked a dry laugh. "The only thing I've come up with is killing all the guards, but that's not going to get me off the island. More likely, all the prisoners would form their own tribunal and kill *me*."

"Yeah, probably." Dani didn't seem interested in discussing how people who'd had the humanity bled out of them were more apt to emulate their jailers than band together for some greater good. "Watch for me in a week. We'll meet at night, slip away like we did when we got rid of that body. If we go inland and make our way across the cliffs to the southern dock, no one will see us." She grinned. "I hope you don't get seasick."

CHAPTER TEN

GABE

When you meet together to worship Me, know that I can hear, even in the Shining Realm. And when you meet together to disparage Me, know that I mark your name.
                    –The Book of Holy Law, Tract 622

A nother dream that wasn't. Another memory.

Gabe was in that wrong body, alien angles, pushed to the back of an unfamiliar mind. Hestraon stood at the Fount, the wide sky above cloudless and perfect blue. He stared at the ground, at the three pieces of the broken Fount lying in the grass.

They didn't look right. One of them didn't, at least. There was the sun, the moon, the leaf and wind gust.

But on the end of the stone with the elemental carvings, there was another. A small lick of flame, the shape and size making it easy to mistake for a natural cleft in the rock.

Gabe could tell that this memory was old, not long after Hestraon's ascent to godhood. Magic still felt foreign in the god's body, sparks and embers flickering painfully along his veins, not yet settled. An earlier memory than the first one he'd seen, Apollius and Hestraon at the forge.

The ache in Hestraon's heart wasn't so great, not yet. There was still a shine of hope that he could become something Apollius and Nyxara could love the way they loved each other.

Hestraon weighed something in his fist. A hammer, handle sweat-slicked. He picked up the third piece and laid it carefully on the edge of the Fount.

Then He brought down the hammer.

His accuracy was impeccable. A crack appeared between the flame and the rest of the carvings; picking it up, Hestraon gently worked at it until the flame-carved piece broke off in his hand.

And what did you think that would accomplish?

A new voice, weak and distant, floating through the air.

Hestraon clenched his fist around the stone.

You are not like them, the voice continued. **No matter what stones you split. They are a thing apart. More powerful. They drank twice, and offered you only a mouthful.**

The god took in a shaky breath. He dropped the stone to the ground. He turned and walked away.

See? Hestraon's voice came close, as if He whispered in Gabe's ear. Present, not in memory, like He was watching this just as Gabe did. *Loving Them is useless.*

It doesn't matter, Gabe answered. *I can't stop.*

Hestraon sighed. *Neither can I.*

Slowly, Gabe woke up.

He'd never wondered why there was no flame on the elemental stone. Maybe because somehow, he knew, by virtue of the god burrowing into his head. Did that mean he would have to find it in order to surrender his power to the Fount? One more impossible errand in a list of them. He closed his eye, pressed the heels of his hands against his forehead.

Surrendering is not so easy, Hestraon said.

"I don't have a choice," Gabe murmured aloud.

You have more choices than you think you do.
Gabe didn't reply.

❦

"We should never have agreed to this."

Caldien's wealth of taverns made finding one to kill time in before their first meeting of the Brotherhood of the Waters an easy task. This one was dirtier than most, on the outskirts of Farramark. Everyone here was too drunk to remember their faces, which seemed prudent even with Eoin's protection.

Gabe was half tempted to join them. But he mostly just stared into his beer, his stomach too unsettled to do more than sip it halfheartedly. "And you used to be an optimist."

"All my optimism is gone." Malcolm was on his second drink, his eyes going glassy. "Who knows if Eoin can actually help Lore and Alie? Or if he'll give us the Fount piece?"

"There's a chance," Gabe said. "And we have to take it."

Malcolm threw back the rest of his ale. His hands had stopped trembling, but there was still a faraway look on his face. The same one he'd had since they were captured, the one that seemed to be about more than their present circumstances. Gabe had known Malcolm for most of his life. He could tell something was badly wrong.

"What happened last night, Malcolm?"

"Other than being chloroformed in an alleyway like a non-sanctioned channeler?"

"You know what I mean."

Malcolm shook his head, just slightly. He sat back, staring down at the table, and for nearly a full minute, he was silent. When he finally started talking, his voice was low.

"I was scared," he said. "I think that's why it happened. I was looking for a way out, after they got you, any way out. I panicked, and then..." He waved his hand, trying to conjure words from the air. "I changed. I could feel earth all around us, every particle of it, and I . . . went into it. Disappeared, became something else. I could have gotten away like that, I think. Followed the earth elsewhere, traveled through it. But I didn't."

So he wasn't the only one beleaguered by the god in his head. Gabe's relief felt mean-spirited.

He clenched the handle of his tankard. "Why?" If there was a way they could use this power to travel undetected, to get back to Auverraine, to the Isles . . .

"Because Braxtos was there," Malcolm spat. "Like He was waiting. I thought They couldn't do that, Gabe."

Blame, fire-hot and just as easy to see. Not because it was Gabe's fault, but because there had to be someone to blame for this.

"We were wrong," Gabe said, staring into his beer. "I've been having strange dreams. Memories." A pause. "I heard Him."

He hoped that Malcolm didn't ask what Hestraon had to say.

Malcolm breathed harshly, raising his hands to press at his forehead, elbows on the table. A moment, then he lowered them carefully and set them on either side of his cup, and continued speaking as if Gabe hadn't interrupted. "I could feel Him taking over. And I knew if I stayed like that, used it like that, whoever came out on the other side wouldn't be me." He finally looked up. "It isn't worth it. Especially if you're *hearing* Him."

Surrender is not so easy, the god had said in the dark predawn. Power was a hard thing to ignore, for someone whose power had always been at the whim of another, easy to take away.

Gabe's fingers curled on the table. "But if we—"

"No." He'd never heard the word said with such vehemence. Malcolm glared, all the glassiness of drink gone in a blaze of determination.

Gabe stared at his friend, mouth pressed tight. Then he nodded.

They sat in silence, the patrons of the tavern getting steadily drunker around them. When Gabe spoke again, it was on a completely different subject, since the more pertinent one was clearly off limits. "How do you think this is going to go?"

"Any group that calls themselves the Brotherhood of the Waters seems like a hotbed for drama." Malcolm sat back, relieved that they'd moved on. "I'm thinking cloaks and chanting, at the very least."

"Excellent." Gabe drained the last of his lackluster beer. "Sun's going down. We should head that way."

They paid their tab and started across Farramark, toward the Rotunda. The golden dome glittered between the plain stone and wood buildings of the rest of the city, calling them on like a beacon.

"If there's any sort of bloodletting, I'm leaving," Malcolm said, looking squeamish. "Everyone cutting their hands, or something. Do you know how many diseases you can get from that?"

"I'd say we're locked in, no matter what happens," Gabe said grimly. "If we want the Fount piece and safety for Lore and Alie."

Malcolm sighed.

Thinking of cutting hands brought Bastian's Consecration to mind, when Anton carved half of a bloody eclipse into his palm. Gabe had been shocked then, though sure that whatever Anton was doing had some greater purpose, meant for good. How naive he'd been.

But, gods, Bastian had looked beautiful that day. Between him and Lore at his side, Gabe's head had been spinning like bubbles in a glass of champagne.

The Rotunda was dark, the countless windows ringing the building shuttered. A lone man stood to the side of the grand staircase, a dark hood pulled up over his face. When he saw Gabe and Malcolm, he bowed slightly, gestured for them to follow.

"Oh, look," Malcolm muttered. "Cloaks."

"Point for you," Gabe replied.

The cloaked man led them to a side entrance, opened the door.

Beyond, darkness, cut through with the smoky light of sconces. A tiny landing before a steep staircase.

As they passed through the door, the man bowed again. "Honored ones." He came in behind them, giving them space.

Malcolm shifted uncomfortably.

The staircase ended in a round room. Gabe had heard of this— the bottom level of the Rotunda was a shelter for Farramark citizens when the weather turned particularly nasty. Usually, when the skies were what passed for pleasant in Caldien, the area was used for storage. Whatever had been stored here had now been moved out to make space for a gathering of nearly fifty people, all wearing black robes with the hoods pulled up, hiding their faces.

To make room for the Brotherhood, but also for the wide stone fountain in the center of the floor.

The sides of the fountain were smooth, rising to about knee height, made of stones stacked and mortared together. The mortar had been gilded, and thin lines of gold paint ran over the stones, making it shimmer in the low light. Water burbled in the fountain, a clever mechanism making a spout rise in the middle though the rest of it remained placid. It must be fed by some underground spring.

Clearly, this was meant to be a replication of the Fount.

"This seems like slight blasphemy," Malcolm murmured, his voice hidden in the susurrus of other Brotherhood members visiting with one another.

"More than slight," Gabe replied. "I'd say this is far more accurate blasphemy than we're used to."

One figure broke from the crowd and stepped up to the fountain, throwing back his hood. Eoin, grinning wide. "Welcome, Brothers," he intoned, his arms spread benevolently. "If you are here, you are a seeker of truth, a mind uncontained by tradition. You do not follow scriptures; you follow power."

"We follow power and see where it leads," the rest of the group replied.

"And now for the chanting," Malcolm whispered.

Gabe barely kept his face stoic beneath his own hood.

One of the Brothers stepped up to Eoin, handing him a silver goblet. Eoin took it and dipped it into the false Fount, holding it up in the dim light as water streamed down his arm and wet his cloak. "To knowledge, and the making of a better world."

The rest of the Brotherhood repeated the sentiment. Gabe stayed quiet.

Eyes alight with holy fervor, Eoin brought the goblet to his mouth and drank.

The Brotherhood member took it back and did the same, pulling down his hood to reveal his face as he did. Gabe didn't know his name, but he recognized him from the Rotunda, one of the elected representatives. The man passed the goblet, and the next Brother took his own sip.

"Are we doing that?" Malcolm asked as they watched the water make its way around the room. "I feel like we shouldn't do that."

"We have to." The goblet was close now. Five more Brothers and it'd be their turn. "I don't see a refusal going over well."

The Brother closest to them drank. He passed the goblet to Malcolm.

There was only a tiny bit of water left in the bottom. With a sigh, Malcolm pulled back his hood and drank.

If the other Brothers were surprised to see a new member, and one wanted by Auverraine, they didn't make it obvious. Gabe pulled down his hood and took the cup from Malcolm, taking his own tiny sip. The water tasted cold and mineral. He half expected it to knock him out, for this to be part of some greater ploy. But it was just water. One more bit of exaggerated theater, making mortals feel closer to gods.

Across the room, Eoin watched him, that same eager smile on his face.

Minutes later, the goblet was back in the Prime Minister's hands. With great reverence, he set it on the lip of the fountain.

"Brothers," he announced, spreading his hands, "this is a momentous day indeed. Long we have studied the elemental gods, those powers forgotten by the larger world, made irrelevant in the face of Apollius. But today, we see that we were right. That Their magic is still here, and still powerful." He gestured to Gabe and Malcolm. "Today, we see those gods made flesh in human avatars. The inheritors of lost magic."

The Brothers turned to them, awe on their faces. Gabe fought the ridiculous urge to wave.

"Gabriel. Malcolm." Eoin stepped aside and waved them up to the front of the group. "A demonstration, if you would."

He'd known this was the deal, but Gabe suddenly felt at a loss, completely unsure of how to proceed.

You know.

Hestraon, His voice low, a banked fire in the back of his mind.

Find the heat and make a spark.

Instinctually, wordlessly, Gabe held out his hand. His vision immediately went black and white, save for the red-orange threads glimmering in the air, more concentrated around the dark shapes of bodies. He grasped one of those threads hovering right above his palm, pulled it through himself.

A tiny spark of flame floated above his hand.

The Brothers gasped, stepping back. Curious murmurs filtered through the crowd. A few braver ones overcame their initial fear and stepped closer, as if they'd examine the fire. A circus act, just like he'd said in Eoin's office.

Gabe closed his hand, smothering the flame.

Eoin watched avidly, one finger tapping at his mouth. "Fascinating." He grinned. "And how, exactly, did Hestraon's power come to you?"

He knew already, if his words the night of their capture were to be believed. More theater. Gabe wasn't sure if Eoin wanted them to lie or tell the truth.

"It just happened." Malcolm spat it like an accusation. "We didn't do anything."

Eoin just nodded, nonplussed by his tone. "And have you experimented with it? Seen what else you can do?"

"We have not." Malcolm's arms were tightly crossed. "We don't want it."

"Is that so?" Eoin's eyes slid to Gabe.

Gabe swallowed. His voice sounded hoarse, as if he'd channeled that fire directly through his vocal cords. "Yes."

Liar, Hestraon said.

CHAPTER ELEVEN

LORE

One will hold any hand in the dark.
                                        –Kadmaran proverb

The week passed in a foggy blur, much like every week before it. Dani offered to keep her on dock duty for the few days it would take for the Ferryman to arrive, cleaning glass and swabbing ship decks instead of hacking apart rocks in the mine, but Lore didn't take her up on it. If she didn't have backbreaking work to keep her occupied during the day, she would go insane, and she was already close enough that it felt like hubris to tempt a further fall.

So she was in the middle of whacking at a clod of dirt in hopes for gold when she saw Jean-Paul.

Back when she lived in the Citadel, for the brief months she was nearly the Queen, Lore had dreaded seeing anyone she'd known in her former life as a poison runner. The two stations were grossly incompatible, and she didn't know how to live in the space between them, much less perform it for others. But now she was as far from a Queen as she could get, in station if not official title. Selfishly, seeing a familiar face was a relief.

Jean-Paul was still chained to the same line as the other newbies—they kept you on it for three days, usually, to make sure you knew your place. The days were up, and a guard marched down the line, freeing the new prisoners from their shackles. Jean-Paul had been arrested the day she raised Horse in the Ward market, but apparently he'd managed to escape then. For a while, at least.

She cleared her throat to say something as she passed, but the words died prematurely. Lore lingered behind the line for the lift, blinking ridiculous tears from her eyes. Dammit. She hated crying, always pushed it down when she felt it coming on, but that usually just meant it would come out unexpectedly.

It'd come easier since that day at Courdigne, when she broke down in the hall. Good for her, probably, but extremely inconvenient when one had so much to cry over.

"Taking a break, Your Majesty?" Fulbert stopped too close behind her, his humid breath on the back of her neck. "Expecting someone to bring you tea?"

It wasn't worth the fight. Lore moved forward, pickax held in her limp hand.

"I'm talking to you, Queenie." A sharp shove between her shoulder blades. Lore lost her balance, her knee hitting the sand. Golden lines wavered in her vision. "Maybe you could have ignored me in the Citadel, but here, I'm your better—"

"Lore?"

Jean-Paul. He'd come up close, his bulk crowding out Fulbert, whose small eyes swung from one of them to the other, clearly assessing his chances in a brawl. One hand gripped his pistol, so even if it did come down to a brawl, he clearly had no intentions of playing fair.

"A new one," Fulbert sneered, even as he stepped back from Jean-Paul. "Too new to know that you shouldn't get mixed up into things that don't concern you." A split-second decision, his pistol coming free of the holster.

Lore grabbed his Spiritum and tugged.

Not enough to kill him. Just enough to speed his heart, like she'd done to Martin, sending him stumbling back.

The momentary brush with mortality was enough to convince Fulbert that this wasn't worth it. With one more halfhearted kick at Lore, he wandered away, rubbing at his chest.

Jean-Paul offered his hand. Lore took it, let him pull her up. When she was upright, she threw herself at him.

He let her hug him, though the baffled way he returned the embrace only reminded her of how she'd kept her distance during her time as a poison runner, how aloof she'd been all those years she hid from what she was.

"You're all right," Jean-Paul rumbled. "You're all right."

Those damn tears threatening again. She was the furthest thing from all right.

She let go, gave him a weak smile. "I would ask how you're doing, but I'd wager the answer is bad."

"Spot on." Jean-Paul snorted. "I assume the same could be said for you?"

"You assume correctly." She steeled herself for questions, a barrage of curiosities about her life in the Citadel and how it had ended here, but Jean-Paul just nodded. That was one of the things she'd always liked about him. He had a calm, easy manner, going his own way and letting others go theirs.

Another guard walked past, looking too harried to harass them, headed toward the beach. Two ships were being repaired, Lore knew. The arriving prison barges were overfull, necessitating all hands on the proverbial deck.

So far, Dani's plan was going seamlessly.

Jean-Paul looked slightly dazed, taking in the crowd and the mine. All jewelry was confiscated when you reached the Isles, but his thumb kept tapping against his ring finger, as if he was looking for something.

"Is Henri all right?" Lore asked, remembering his husband's name. "Etienne?"

"They're safe," Jean-Paul said quietly. "When the Sainted King started going after everyone who'd ever run poisons for Val, I sent them both to Henri's mother, over in Ratharc. It was too risky for me to travel with them."

Ice prickled down Lore's spine, followed by intense gratitude that Val and Mari had been on that ship to Caldien. Part of her had anticipated Apollius taking some sort of revenge—something more than sending her here—but going after everyone who'd known her, everyone who'd ever had the opportunity to show her kindness, was a level of cruelty she hadn't anticipated.

Stupid of her. Apollius loved being cruel.

She couldn't think too hard about how he was using Bastian's body to enact those cruelties, or she would lose it.

"How'd you escape the first time?" she asked.

"Slipped from the bloodcoats' hold while they were preoccupied with looking for you," he said. "You offered a hell of a distraction. Laid low for a bit afterward. Mari had me doing paperwork."

"She always hated that," Lore murmured, thinking of her mother. "But she had a better head for numbers than Val."

"Didn't do much good in the end." Jean-Paul sighed. "When the King came calling, he knew right where to look."

Bastian knew the way to the warehouse. Back then, he couldn't guard his thoughts from Apollius.

Oblivious to her rapidly deteriorating emotional state, Jean-Paul gave her a wearily amused smile, like a man might wear at the gallows when he knew there was no escape. "You must have really done a number on him."

Lore laughed, a ragged sound.

"But really," Jean-Paul went on, achingly sincere. "You went from engaged to the Sainted King to a prisoner on the Burnt Isles. What *happened*, Lore?"

And how in all the myriad hells was she supposed to answer that?

She was all out of lies. She'd never been that great a spy, at least not at this level, doing anything more than petty subterfuge for warring criminal enterprises; she could see that now. And gods, she was so tired.

So she told him the truth. Kind of. "He...isn't himself."

"I suppose I'll take your word for it." He shook his head. "Though he's certainly acting like an Arceneaux."

"I guess none of us got far from where we started," Lore said quietly.

"You did."

Her brow knit.

Jean-Paul shrugged. "After that business with the horse—I still have nightmares about that thing, by the way—Val told me about you. Where you came from, what you were meant for." He put a hand on her shoulder. "And you rose from that to become a Queen."

"And yet here I am."

"For now." He nodded. "But if there's one thing about you, Lore, it's that you always land on your feet."

She could only hope he was right.

"Well." Jean Paul patted her shoulder with a bemused smile. "At least there's no horses here for you to accidentally reanimate. That was a bit of a shock. Didn't know you could channel Mortem until that day, and it was a hell of a way to learn."

"Horse," Lore said, thinking of the animal, how she'd always wanted his affection. How Bastian had gotten it, albeit after the beast was dead. Nuzzling the Sun Prince's shoulder, his neck hanging open, still sweet even in death. Animals were less complicated than humans. They could come back.

Bleeding *God*, how she wanted to go back.

She didn't realize she was finally crying until she felt Jean-Paul's hand on her shoulder again, drawing her attention away from thoughts of the past and to the wet slide of tears down her neck. And she was too far gone to swallow it back now; when she tried, she just sobbed, a grating sound that tasted like seawater.

Lore sat on the sand, burying her face in her hands. Jean-Paul lowered himself beside her, a solid arm over her shoulders. And she cried and cried and cried, while the other prisoners filtered around them, uninteresting rocks in a rapidly drying stream, hiding them from the eyes of the guards.

She only cried for about five minutes, but it was more than long enough to feel absolutely mortified once the storm of emotion abated. When she apologized to Jean-Paul, jumping up from the beach like something in the sand had stabbed her, he just waved a hand. "I'm used to parenting an eight-year-old. This is nothing."

"I don't think that's a flattering comparison." Lore wiped at her eyes. "But thank you, anyway."

He glanced around them, a line of prisoners still waiting for the lifts. "I was under the impression we were supposed to mine while we're here?"

"Stick with me," Lore said. "If we find anything, we'll share."

And he did, staying by her side as they spent hours breaking apart rocks, collecting enough for them both to get dinner and for Jean-Paul, at least, to get a pallet. They didn't speak, but his presence near her was bolstering. And no one approached to taunt her, which was a nice change.

When the day was done, they walked down to the barracks. Lore showed Jean-Paul where to pick up a pallet, explained the haphazard way sleeping arrangements worked. "I sleep in a cave. You're welcome there, if you want."

It might make sneaking away tonight harder, but Lore didn't care. She'd wondered if she should tell Jean-Paul about the plan, about how she'd be gone in the morning. But she didn't want to make him lie if he was questioned. The less Jean-Paul knew, the safer he would be.

She half thought about asking him to come tonight, taking him to the Ferryman with her and Dani. But Lore still didn't trust the other woman, and part of her half expected this Ferryman situation to be an elaborate revenge scheme. If it was, he'd be safer here.

"I'll stay outside," Jean-Paul said, making a face at a large stain on his pallet. "Small spaces make me nervous."

So by the time Lore was staring at the dark ceiling of the cave, listening to the soft snores of the other people around her who also called it home, Jean-Paul was on the sand outside, curled up against the rock.

Help him be safe, she thought. *Help him see Henri and Etienne again.*

Are you talking to Me? Nyxara asked.

I guess. Lore hadn't meant to be talking to anyone, just wishing into the dark.

I'm afraid I'm not in the position to be answering prayers, Nyxara said wryly. *Not that I ever was, really.*

Lore didn't reply. She knew nothing was listening when she prayed. She just hoped the wish itself was enough, fed into the world, becoming tangible with her will.

All this, and she still hoped the universe had the capacity for kindness.

Dani hadn't given her an exact time for their escape, just said to meet her on the dunes when she could get away after nightfall. Lore waited until the breath of everyone else in the cave was long and even, then slowly sat up and slipped into her flimsy boots.

"Where are you going?"

The thinnest whisper from across the cave. Lore froze.

A rustle, and someone sat up. Rosie, hair tousled, eyes wide in the dark. The woman she'd defended from Jilly, given back her stolen cup.

Rosie kept her voice down, barely enough to hear. "Are you going to the Ferryman?"

Briefly, Lore considered lying. But before she could come up with one, Rosie nodded, as if answering her own question. "Of course you are. You don't belong here."

Lore didn't know what to say. She could threaten the other woman, or beg, or offer for her to come, too. Though if Rosie already knew about the Ferryman, surely she'd had an opportunity to meet him before now?

"Be careful," Rosie said. "He knows how to navigate well enough, but it's still a dangerous journey. Easy to get off course."

"I'll be careful." Empty words for empty sentiment. Lore had never been careful.

Rosie nodded. "If the guards ask where you went, I'll tell them you walked into the ocean."

Jarring, to hear it said so plainly. But Lore nodded. "Thank you, Rosie."

Lore headed for the cave entrance. Right before she stepped out into the night, Rosie spoke again. "What was it like, being Queen?" Wistful and almost embarrassed, like she'd long wondered, finally asking now because she wouldn't get another chance.

The stone was cold beneath Lore's fingertips as her hands tensed. "The Queen part was awful," she said quietly. "But him... he was kind. None of this is his fault."

She didn't look behind her as she left the cave, not wanting to see the skepticism on Rosie's face.

Outside, Lore stepped gingerly around Jean-Paul. After deciding it wasn't safe to bring him, she'd considered leaving a note, but that would necessitate finding paper and pen, and she didn't have time.

Lore gave Jean-Paul one last look and hurried into the fog.

The dunes were between the barracks and the lighthouse, a stretch of empty beach populated by nothing but the sand mites. In the dark and perpetual ash, it was hard to see more than a few feet in front of you.

Which was why she didn't see the Mort until she was right on them.

A fist in her stomach, first, clipping the bottom of her ribs and doubling her over. The rest of the monk melted out of the fog like a ghost, shoving her sideways. Lore skidded on the sand, tried to get up, but another Mort was behind her now and planted a boot on her shoulder, pressing down until the cartilage bent dangerously.

The first one who'd punched her crouched, level with her eyes. Lore was prepared for some villain monologue—gods knew she'd endured enough of those in the past few months—but he just shook his head. A long scar snaked down the side of his face, disappeared into the collar of his shirt. She recognized him from the other night, one of the ones who'd run when she killed their leader.

"We can't let you escape," he said, and to his credit, he sounded almost regretful. "The world demands your death."

She was so, *so* tired of hearing about how she had to die.

Lore tried to roll out from under the Mort's boot, but she only managed to dig herself farther into the sand. Another Mort wound his hand into her hair and pushed her head forward, driving it down in the grit. Some of it got in her mouth; Lore gagged.

The threads of Spiritum were slippery, try as she might to grasp them. The same as on the night with their leader, magic tugged from beneath her like a rug. She couldn't concentrate, and every time she dropped into channeling-space, the golden strands slithered away, blinking in and out.

Apollius pulling it back, away from her. Surely, He couldn't know just how badly she needed it right now; the god had put her through every hell, but He didn't want her dead.

Lore snarled into the sand.

The snatches of moonlight that fought through the ash gleamed along a knife blade, clutched in the first Presque Mort's fist. He knelt, almost reverently, and brought it close to Lore's neck. "We kill you and the world is saved."

A crack. The Mort's head, struck by a rock. His eyes rolled back as he fell over on top of Lore, a vague shape behind him raising the rock again.

Jean-Paul. He must have seen her leaving, followed her.

Fulbert had gotten off easy earlier; the old poison runner hadn't forgotten how to fight. He twisted sideways, lashing out with the rock again, but now he'd lost the element of surprise. Another of the Presque Mort grabbed the knife from their fallen leader and spun to Jean-Paul, scoring him across the shoulder.

"Hey!" An inane thing to scream, but it was all that came to Lore's tongue. She pushed up, lashing out at the nearest Mort, punching him in the knee in a move that hurt her as much as it did him. The knee went sideways, bringing the Mort to the ground, but he didn't stay there long, limping up again to go after Jean-Paul. Jean-Paul, who was fading fast, another bleeding mark opened across his stomach.

"Lore!" His shout was thin. He lunged with the rock again, but the Presque Mort dodged him easily. "Lore, run!"

They were going to kill him. He'd come after her out of some remaining dreg of affection for the girl she'd been, and now he was going to die for it. Henri and Etienne would be left alone, across the sea in Ratharc, always wondering.

Lore reached for her power again. Spiritum, flickering gold. It tried to slip away, water dragged toward a drain, but she didn't let it, not this time.

"Fuck you, Apollius," she growled, and grabbed the threads in tight fists, not letting them slither from her grasp.

She dropped into channeling-space with teeth-clenching

effort, the world going black and white except for the bright stars of Spiritum at the center of every living thing. The cosmos of the Presque Mort glowed, Jean-Paul a constellation. The smaller sparks of sand mites, the tiny flecks of plankton in the ocean beyond them.

There wasn't time for finesse, but Lore didn't need it, not anymore. She could make this power do whatever she wanted, and now, she wanted desolation. She wanted apocalypse.

Her fingers curled. And Lore pulled.

This was different from the night she'd killed the other Mort. Her will was different, and thus the magic reacted to it—she didn't just want to use Spiritum, to force it into allowing an escape. She wanted it to be *hers*, wanted to grab it all and undeniably stake her claim. Lore was afraid, and her fear made her reckless, made her willing to do whatever she had to.

Spiritum responded. It slid into her, curling up like a golden serpent. It set fire to everything else, shone in all the dark places. Lore felt like a star, wreathed in bright light. She felt like the sun.

Every shadow washed out of her, every darkness, the moon scoured away by the daytime, death defeated by unfettered, wild *life*. All of it, hers, because she claimed it, because this power could belong to nothing else in her vicinity.

A ponderous shift, the world readjusting its axis. Something taking notice. A decision being made, somewhere out there, a path rewritten.

Lore didn't realize just what it was she'd done until every last drop of that light was gone from the space around her, contained inside instead.

Gasping, Lore fell to her knees. And so did the bodies, before slumping forward onto the sand.

She threw her head back, staring at the sky, pulling in great lungfuls of ash-tinged air through her teeth and smiling a wide, sharp-edged smile.

Myriad hells, Mortem had never felt like this. So much *power*, crowding her out of herself. Making her empty and invincible.

With a short laugh, Lore looked down at the dead Presque Mort fallen around her. Their bodies were dry and desiccated, every bit of life wrung from them like wet rags on a laundry line. Three bodies, one for each of the Mort—

Wait. Four bodies.

Jean-Paul.

Her mind wouldn't string the information together, not at first. It shied away. Lore had killed people before, and probably some of them hadn't deserved it. But Jean-Paul *certainly* didn't. Jean-Paul whom she was trying to save, with his husband and his son in Ratharc, with his life still stretched ahead of him—

She'd killed other things, too, grasped the lives of everything close enough for her to reach, but this was the only one she cared about. The mites were dead in the dirt, the fish were dead in the waves, but Lore couldn't bring herself to give a single shit.

She walked slowly past the bodies of the Mort, approached Jean-Paul limp on the ground. Lore lowered herself down, slowly, careful not to touch any part of him.

There were no tears. She'd spent all of hers earlier. She settled, pulled her knees into her chest.

Lore was still sitting there when Dani appeared.

The other woman didn't speak. She slowed her hurried gait as she approached Lore on the dunes, her eyes widening as she took in the bodies. "Run into trouble?"

"Presque Mort." Lore's voice sounded like she'd swallowed sand. "And my friend."

Dani didn't make her explain. The bodies were explanation enough. "When this friend asked to come, did you tell him it wasn't a rescue operation?"

"No," Lore said listlessly. "He didn't ask. He was just here. Trying to help."

"Ah." Dani stood at a distance from Lore, as if afraid she wasn't done tugging Spiritum out of anything living that might wander close. She offered no comfort.

Lore was grateful for that.

Sometime later—enough time that her legs were numb, that the air had grown frosted with deeper night—Lore stood and moved away from Jean-Paul's body, a little farther down the beach. She dug a shallow hole with her hands. Dani didn't offer to help.

Such a brief glimpse of the life she'd had before, an abrupt reminder of who she'd been, and now he was gone. It seemed fitting, almost. Killing Jean-Paul was like killing the last part of herself that existed before becoming Nyxara's avatar. She'd chosen to live, but she couldn't do that as the person she was before the Citadel, before the eclipse ritual that was her twisted Consecration. The prices were too high.

It didn't take much to roll Jean-Paul into the grave she'd made. No vault for him, no aboveground burial for the faithful—there was no need, now, and there was nothing to be faithful to.

When Lore was done, she straightened, brushing sand off on her knees. She wouldn't waste time burying the Presque Mort. They hated buried things. "Let's go."

Dani nodded. "He should be at the repair docks by now. Head down toward the shore. The tide will wash out our footprints."

Lore followed her, steady and blank as a sleepwalker. Dead fish littered the tide line. She stepped over them.

CHAPTER TWELVE

ALIE

Motherhood heals and wounds in ways that cannot
be fully spoken.

—Marya Addou, Malfouran poet

There was little Alie hated more than waiting.

But there was really nothing else she could do. Until
Bastian managed to break into Apollius's mind—a feat that still
seemed nigh impossible—and found the location of the Fount
piece, she was stuck in her Citadel routine.

Alie was first and foremost a diplomat. If Bastian was fighting
Apollius off, keeping Him occupied while he searched His mind
for the Fount's broken pieces, the god didn't have much attention
left for Alie. She could feed into that distraction by doing something to make Him happy, make Him think she was defeated.

Which was why she found herself at a romantic candlelit dinner with Jax.

It'd been her idea. She'd sent the handwritten invitation,
scented lightly with her perfume, at a time she knew Jax would be
in audience with Apollius. She'd gone to the kitchens herself to
collaborate on the menu. Dates and olives, lamb as a main course,

foods that were popular in Kirythea. She'd picked the bouquets of marigolds and arranged them in vases, she'd bought fresh white tapers, she'd sent for her mother's good plates from Courdigne and selected wine from her late father's personal casks.

In fact, the only part of this Alie hadn't meticulously planned was what in every single hell she was supposed to *say* to her fiancé once he was here.

The soup course passed in relative silence, with only murmured assurances that the room was lovely, the food smelled lovely, she looked lovely. If she didn't know that his Auverrani was flawless, Alie might think Jax only knew one complimentary adjective.

She managed to smile and nod, her stomach tangling with her liver as she sipped her wine and cast around desperately for something to talk about. She used to be good at this. But now, with her head a riot of worry and wind itching at her fingers and a cool, looming presence in the back of her thoughts, Alie had nothing to say.

She'd dismissed the servants, on the off chance she and Jax spoke of something that shouldn't be shared around the Citadel. On the off chance they *spoke*. So she refilled their wine, brought out the steaming lamb.

"This smells excellent," Jax said, smiling at her before his eyes dipped to his plate. There was some respite; he seemed just as nervous as she was, though Alie was sure their reasons were wildly different. And he'd managed to find another adjective.

He was always kind to her. She'd give him that.

"Perfect," Jax said after taking a bite, filling the silence Alie left alone. "My own kitchen couldn't have prepared it better."

"Thank you." Alie took her own bite. It *was* delicious. She was, apparently, still good at planning parties.

She clung to the thought, finally finding something she could turn to use. Alie brightened her smile, leaned forward with her elbows on the table and her hands clasped beneath her chin, the picture of rapt interest. "Are there other dishes from your home you'd like the kitchens to try? I'm sure we could source the ingredients locally—"

"Alie." He said her name so softly. She didn't like it, didn't like the familiarity it implied, though his voice was low and even in a way that hummed down her spine. "You didn't call me here to talk about food."

Shit. All her energy had been focused on distracting Apollius; she hadn't spared much thought to distracting Jax.

The Kirythean Emperor set down his knife, candlelight gleaming along the sharp edge. "You've made a valiant effort," he said, almost ruefully. "But I know you don't want this. And contrary to your obvious belief, I'm not such a monster as to force it on you."

She relaxed at the realization he was talking about their relationship, not the god puppeteering the King. Certainly the safer subject to argue over. Still, this wasn't necessarily a conversation she was prepared for, and that made her blunt. "So you're going to call off our engagement?"

He rubbed at his temple. Some of his pale hair had escaped its queue, catching the light like a halo. "I would if I could," he said. "Now that it's become clear you won't come around to the idea."

Was that hurt in his voice? She didn't care. She desperately wanted not to care. Alie wasn't very good at hurting people, even people who deserved it.

"But I'm afraid it's bigger than us," Jax continued. "Our marriage will begin Apollius's Holy Empire. It will be the culmination of everything we've worked for. Everything *He's* worked for. And I don't think He'll allow us to potentially ruin that."

A spark of irritation was hidden in his voice, in the way his eyes cut across the room when he said the god's name. So subtle Alie doubted Jax even knew it was there, but she filed it away, a string she could tune to her own melody.

She thought of that conversation she'd overheard when she

returned from Dellaire, Apollius taunting him for killing his father. Would something like that change Jax's convictions, or was he too far gone?

"And," Jax added quietly, "it's keeping you safe."

Cold nerves wound up her spine. "Keeping me safe from what?"

He didn't say. He just looked at her. He knew.

She'd tried to be so careful, so meticulous. But she'd known that Apollius wasn't in the dark about her power; she should have anticipated that Jax would know, too.

Alie curled her hand around her fork, like she'd use it as a weapon if needed. "And you still want to marry me?"

Jax eyed her grip but didn't move. "How can I blame you for something you can't control?"

"So you're going to let Him kill me for it after the wedding, is that it?"

"Would I have brought it up, if that were so?"

Point.

The Emperor sighed. "He has . . . gentler plans for you than He did for Amelia. He didn't kill her; Bastian did, to protect Lore. He won't harm you." His gaze sharpened, brighter than before. "But marrying me offers yet another layer of safety."

She didn't expect this. Didn't expect his insistence on their marriage to have anything to do with her own well-being.

Alie loosened her grip on the fork, just a bit. "He doesn't need me," she said quietly. "I'm just the means to a throne, but He's a god. He could give it to you with no one batting an eye."

"Keeping a mortal claim is still a good idea," Jax said. "Having a clear line of succession."

Succession, implying children. Alie drained the rest of her wine.

Jax noticed her discomfiture. He shifted in his seat, mouth opening and then closing again. With a sigh, he closed his eyes. "This isn't going how I thought it would."

"Our engagement?" She bit off the end of the word. "Or your general takeover of the continent?"

He barked a harsh laugh. "Neither."

Alie kept her silence. It was the surest way to make someone else talk.

Maybe that awful conversation she'd heard had changed him, after all.

Jax followed her lead at first. But his silence was weaker than hers. "I was raised to believe that Apollius was perfect," Jax said. Quietly, like he was afraid of being overheard. Ironic, considering her recent activities. "To believe that He had transcended His humanity. But over the last few weeks, He..." His finger tapped nervously on the table, making his knife ring faintly against Alie's mother's fine china. "He is capricious. Quick to anger. He is more focused on vengeance, on taking back power from the other avatars, than He is on creating His kingdom." His lip lifted, half sneer and half grimace. "He's leaving that part to me, apparently. And I'm weary of it."

Alie hid her hands in her lap. "Does He know where to look?" she asked casually. "For the other avatars, I mean. Other than me."

"He has an idea. Truth be told, I think Apollius is...overzealous in His pursuit."

"I'm surprised." Her tone was cutting; she didn't temper it, not for this. "It seems out of character for you to wish any clemency for them. Especially Gabe, after what you did."

His hand, still lying on the table, curled into a fist. "I," he said finally, "am a different person than I was at sixteen, Alienor. As are most of us."

She swallowed.

"I wish I weren't, sometimes." Jax sat back in his chair, his gaze directed unseeing to the far wall, as if picturing that sixteen-year-old self. "It would make it easier to live with the things I've done. It was a time of war. My father raised me in his image, and that image was cruel." He paused. "I would never venture to say I've become a good man. I am still cruel. I will still do whatever I have to. But I do not take joy in it."

He was a bad man. That wasn't changed by the fact that he sometimes felt remorse, or the fact that he thought he was protecting her. But Alie made her face soften, made herself nod. "There is always opportunity for change." Something she believed, even if she was only trying to keep him talking.

He just nodded, still staring at the middle distance. "I thought killing my father could be an atonement," he murmured. "But it was just one more weight."

Alie wasn't in a position to judge someone for wanting their father dead.

She retrieved dessert from her kitchenette, shaking off thoughts of patricide. Alie ate the flaky pastry and cream in moments; nerves made her crave sugar. Jax barely touched his.

A moment, staring at his pastry, then Jax rose from his place. He walked over to her, slowly, waiting for her to turn him away. Alie didn't, though the muscles in her shoulders tightened with every inch he gained.

He stopped an arm's length from her. They made eye contact, the flickering kind that seemed like an accident, but neither of them could look away.

"I hope," Jax began, "that we can find our way to a mutually beneficial arrangement. I can't release you from this engagement, Alie, but please know I would never force a closer relationship than you want. If you'd rather live separate lives once we're married, that's fine. I will do whatever I can to make you happy."

There was nothing to say to that, really. She wasn't Lore, with her biting remarks and acerbic wit; there was no way for Jax to make Alie happy, and they both knew it. Drawing attention to the fact would do nothing but make them both feel worse.

Jax offered his hand. A heartbeat of hesitation, and she placed hers in it. He had calluses, which she supposed was to be expected when you'd spent your formative years conquering most of a continent.

"We are at the tipping point of a whole new world," Jax said. "We can make the most of it, you and me. We could be something good. Good for us, good for Auverraine, good for the Holy Empire."

He kissed her hand. Then he left, closing the door softly behind him.

Alie chewed on her lip. Then she wiped the back of her hand on her wrinkled skirt and poured herself another glass of wine.

So they knew who she was. Jax and Apollius both. They knew, and were content to leave her be. Far from comforting, it made her even more fearful. There was some larger plan here, one she couldn't fathom.

She poured the rest of the bottle.

🍂

The rose was right where Lilia said she'd leave it. Stuck in the front door of the Citadel, woven between the hinges. By the time Alie saw it, it had been nearly shredded by the door's opening and closing, apparently unnoticed by anyone else. But she knew what it meant. The former Night Priestess was ready to search the Citadel for the missing Fount piece.

"Dammit," Alie muttered, picking up her skirt to stride out into the southern green.

If Lilia had managed to get inside the walls of the Citadel, Alie was fairly certain she could search it without her help. But an agreement was an agreement, and she didn't blame Lore's mother for wanting a measure of protection. An unknown woman alone in the Citadel would raise suspicion; an unknown woman with the King's half sister would be assumed new hired help.

Lilia had told her she would wait in the South Sanctuary.

It seemed like a risky place to be, given what she was, but Alie wasn't in a place to critique her plans. They were all doing the best they could, under the circumstances, and the circumstances were uniformly terrible.

Pushing open the Church doors, Alie gave a demure nod to the bloodcoat waiting just inside and walked toward the Sanctuary, trying not to run.

The former Night Priestess stood in front of the altar, as close as the velvet ropes blocking it from the pews would allow. There were no such ropes in the North Sanctuary—noble penitents could get as close to the lectern as they wanted. The braziers were already lit, clouding the air with fragrant smoke.

Alie stepped up to Lilia's side, followed her eyeline. The older woman stared at the small, circular stained-glass window set into the arch of the Sanctuary, one Alie hadn't paid much attention to before. A white-skinned hand, holding a knife. Jeweled blood dripped from its point.

"It's funny, really," Lilia murmured. "How we were ever convinced He was kind."

She wanted to say she'd never been convinced, but that wasn't exactly true, was it? Before all this, Alie had never given much thought to Apollius, but when she did, she assumed He was good, because that's what she'd been taught.

With a shake of her head, Lilia turned away from the window. "Come on." She set off for the doors.

Alie scampered behind. "There are hundreds of storerooms in the Citadel," she whispered. "You'll have to be specific about which one you mean to search."

"Whichever one the King was using to keep the art pieces he was selling before Apollius took over." Despite her quiet words, Lilia seemed to know exactly where she was going, and she walked with such purpose that the bloodcoat by the door didn't give them a second glance. Lilia waited to continue until they were outside on the green, bathed in morning sun. "I intercepted a letter that mentioned specific instructions to notify the King on arrival, and for the parcel indicated to go directly into storage without being opened. The letter mentioned the specific room."

"How did you manage that?"

"Did some paperwork for the postmaster—he wasn't picky about employment history, barely even asked my name. He didn't keep letters in a particularly safe place."

"And you think this parcel was the Fount piece?" It was plausible. If the piece had previously been kept away from the Citadel, Apollius might want to bring it closer.

"I don't know what else it might be." Lilia fell in behind Alie as they approached the Citadel doors, sparing only a glance for the shredded rose in the hinges. "It's the only lead we have."

"Seems to be a pattern," Alie muttered. "Keep your head down. If anyone asks, you're my new chambermaid."

The storerooms of the Citadel were a warren beneath the structure, much like the sealed prophecy rooms under the Church, and mostly used for things deemed too valuable to be kept within the Wall. Back in the summer, when Bastian was still Bastian and she didn't have any trace of magic, Alie had helped catalog some of the art pieces he'd wanted sold, grouping them all in one of the few rooms that was previously empty. According to Lilia's stolen mail, that's where this shipment was headed.

She turned left after they crossed the foyer, down one of the smaller, less-used hallways. Servants used these corridors around the edges of the Citadel far more often than the nobles did. Alie relaxed a bit, sure that they wouldn't run into anyone.

So when she saw Olivier, it was a bit of a shock.

It'd been ages since she'd seen her old friend. His sister Cecelia's sickness had worsened, and she'd gone back to their family's holdings in the countryside. Olivier had planned to go with her, but then their father had passed, and since their mother had been dead a long while, it fell to Olivier to fulfill their obligations at court.

None of which entailed wandering through the back passageways, as far as Alie knew.

She froze when she saw him coming, her hand instinctively snapping backward to stop Lilia. The other woman walked into it with a huff of air, loud enough to make Olivier look up from the floor. "Alienor?"

Her smile felt painted on, painfully false. "Olivier! How are you?"

"Fine," he said, an inane answer for an inane question, when she knew perfectly well it was a lie. His eyes were tired, shadows deep around the sockets. "Didn't expect to run into anyone back here."

Alie almost said she'd expected the same, but didn't want to make it seem like she was hiding something. Her false smile widened. She probably looked mad. "It's nice to find somewhere quiet," she said, continuing her inanity.

Behind her, Lilia stood close by the wall, head down. For Olivier, who was used to seeing servants as sentient furniture, she was as good as invisible.

"Indeed," he said softly. He raked his hair back, huffed a small laugh. "I find myself walking back here often, looking for somewhere quiet. I've found it, certainly, but I can't bring myself to stop moving." He tried to smile, but it didn't have enough scaffolding, and it fell from his face half formed. "So I walk."

"I'm thinking of Cecelia," Alie said. "She's...she's in my prayers."

Lilia shifted on her feet.

Olivier didn't pick up on the hesitation. "Thank you," he said sincerely. His fingers worried at something on his chest—a gold pendant. An Apollius medal. Most noble children received one upon their Consecration, but Alie hardly ever saw one worn.

"She'll be healed. I'm sure of it. Apollius will wipe away her sickness, all in His good time."

He smiled at the god's name, wide and beatific. He spoke with such conviction.

Alie smiled back, though she couldn't quite smooth the line between her brows. She'd never known Olivier to be pious. "I certainly hope so."

"I know so." He rubbed at the necklace again. "He always takes care of His most faithful. He always fulfills His promises."

"Of course." Her smile went strained.

With a nod, Olivier continued down the hall, still holding his pendant.

"Your prayers?" Lilia murmured when he was gone.

"I didn't know what else to say," Alie answered, not looking at the other woman.

A beat of quiet. "I understand," Lilia said.

They walked on in silence, finally reaching the stairs that led underground to the Church storerooms. At the bottom, long hallways lined in numbered doors, gilt-painted, because of course they were.

The room Alie remembered from the summer was painted with a *71*. Behind her, Lilia grimaced. "Seventy-one rooms filled with enough riches to feed the whole damn continent."

"The whole world, probably." The door was locked. Alie fished a pin out of her hair and wiggled it in the keyhole until the mechanism caught. "And there are over a hundred rooms, actually."

"Enough riches to feed the whole world, and they don't even have a dead bolt," Lilia muttered.

Opening the door was like opening a mausoleum. The only light was what managed to seep in from the dim hallway, barely illuminating giant shapes draped in white muslin. Gaudy statues, huge paintings. Most of them had a number pinned somewhere on the fabric.

A click; flame leapt from a lighter in Lilia's hand. "The letter said number two oh seven." She shielded the fire with her hand as she peered at the numbers on the ghost-lit shapes. "And I assume it's something small."

"It could take ages to find it in here."

"Then we'd better be fast. If Apollius catches wind that we want to restore the Fount, He'll probably swallow the piece before He lets us have it."

With a sigh, Alie started searching.

There were, unfortunately, lots of small things in the store-room, and also unfortunately, most of them appeared to be stacked together, making them difficult to search through. Alie found a pile of wrapped parcels wedged beneath a particularly ugly statue of a nymph and pulled a face. Clearly, whoever was in charge of this room now didn't care for organization like she did.

She crouched, reaching into the pile to pull out something that looked vaguely rock-shaped.

The whistle of wind was her only warning when the nymph statue toppled over.

It was instinct, movement without thought. Alie held up her hands, twisted threads, her thoughts gone to cloud and breeze. Air wove together, iridescent threads, stopping the statue right before the trident it held speared through her skull.

Alie stared up into the nymph's face, breathing hard. Her hands trembled as she kept hold of air, used it to gently lower the statue to the ground. She watched it wide-eyed as her vision bled back into color, magic seeping away from her fingers. They looked ghostly, nearly see-through, though that could have been the dim light and the way they trembled.

Close call, murmured a voice in her head, so quiet she barely heard it.

Alie froze. *Lereal?*

The voice was gone.

No. Couldn't be. Nyxara told Lore the minor gods were too diminished to speak, too weak to come back as anything more than Their power. It'd been a cold comfort, one Alie clung to.

But it wouldn't be the first time she and the others were wrong.

Cool breeze in her head, soothing. Lereal didn't speak again, but the feeling was a kind of reassurance. Even if the god could talk, They didn't want what Apollius did.

That was something.

For all that Lereal's presence was gentle, it still wound Alie tight as a bowstring.

Still shaky, Alie bent and unwrapped the parcel she'd nearly been impaled for. A collection of satyr figurines, just as ugly as the nymph.

Fitting.

Five minutes and a few more figurines later, she heard a small, guttural gasp.

"Lilia?" Her eyes had adjusted, but Alie still couldn't see much more than a few feet in front of her. "Did you find it?"

No answer. Alie followed the tiny flicker of flame from the other woman's lighter.

Lilia hadn't found the Fount piece. But she'd found something.

The Night Priestess stood in front of a huge painting, so large that the muslin cover still drooped from one corner where she wasn't tall enough to pull it all the way off. Alie could only see smudges of the subject until she stood directly in front of the canvas, and when she did, her mouth set in a grim line.

It was Lore. Lore dressed as the Queen of Auverraine, her generous body draped in white, a golden circlet in her brown-blond hair. A silver crescent moon was mounted in the center of the circlet, hovering over her hazel eyes. She wore a soft, demure smile, completely unlike any expression Alie had ever seen on her friend.

This was Lore as Apollius wanted her, Lore as a replacement for Nyxara, molded into the submissive wife the god had tried to force the goddess to be. It was almost like looking at a painting of a stranger.

"This was the piece the letter spoke of," Lilia said quietly. The flame of her lighter was precariously close to her fingers; she appeared not to feel it. "It had been sent back to the creator and then reshipped—I thought it was to confuse anyone who might be looking for the shard."

"It must have been sent back for artist revisions." The word seemed inadequate. Alie's mouth puckered around it. "Every Arceneaux ruler has a portrait. Bastian must have commissioned this one as soon as he asked Lore to marry him, if there was time for one to be completed and revised. I guess Apollius wanted it to look different."

A harsh swallow worked down Lilia's throat. She flipped the lighter closed, apparently feeling the burn of it on her fingertips, before opening it back up again.

Back in the fabric-swathed graveyard of old art, Alie heard the sound of a door closing.

Lilia reacted faster than Alie did. She ducked behind the painting, her lighter snapping shut; in the sudden dark, Alie flailed, unsure where to go. Light bloomed behind her from whoever approached, holding a candelabra of their own. "Alie?"

Of course it would be Jax.

Composing her face into gentle chagrin, Alie turned to face her fiancé. "I'm sure this looks odd." She huffed a rueful laugh. "I was just looking for an old painting I remembered my mother having when I was young—"

Behind the portrait of Lore, a crash.

Jax's eyes whipped from Alie to the portrait as he stepped in front of her, candelabra held like a sword. "Who's there?"

Lilia stepped out from behind the painting, eyes downcast, once again in the attitude of a servant. "I'm sorry, my lady." Even her accent was different, country-broad. Overkill, Alie thought, since most Citadel servants were from Dellaire, but she wasn't in the position to be giving notes. "I looked through to the back of the room, but I couldn't find it."

His brow rose, but the ruse seemed to work; Jax didn't waste time looking at Lilia once his mind categorized her as help. His face softened as he glanced at Alie. "Anything confiscated from noble houses will be in a different room," he said. "This is only for Citadel art."

"Of course," Alie said, smiling. But she couldn't help the way her eyes flickered sideways, drawn once again to that uncanny portrait of Lore.

Jax followed her gaze. He didn't grimace, but it was a close thing, a pull of distaste at the corner of his mouth. "Not much of a likeness, is it?"

Alie didn't respond.

She didn't really need to; he didn't look at her, instead frowning up at the giant portrait. "He's considering more revisions," he said. "The King wants her to appear triumphant. Fiercer." He shook his head. "It all seems like a waste of resources to me. I've never been one for portraits."

"I'm surprised that He would want her fierce," Alie said. "Seems more like He wanted her as broken as He could get her."

"I can't quite figure out His feelings on the matter," Jax murmured. "Whether He loves her or hates her or just wants to own her."

Next to the portrait, Lilia stiffened.

"Come." Jax turned back toward the door. "I'll show you the proper room to look in, for something from your mother's estate."

Alie and Lilia followed him out. Right before the door closed, Alie glanced back over her shoulder, looking at the portrait one more time.

In the dim light, the shape of Lore's face changed, angles sharpened and hollows deeper. It barely looked like her at all.

CHAPTER THIRTEEN

LORE

In all things, you will see My hand.
　　　　　　　　　　　　－The Book of Mortal Law, Tract 778

M orning, Your Majesty."
　　　Every part of Lore ached. Her head pounded, her eyes were gritty, and her back shrieked, stretched out on a thin layer of sand that barely cushioned against the shale of the cliff. They'd stayed worrisomely close to the edge last night, not quite near enough for Lore to reach out and touch empty air, but not far off. Safer that way, Dani said. Less likely for someone to come upon them by accident.

Not that anyone would be traveling on the cliffs, anyway. This part of the island, scrubby and nearly treeless, was mostly left alone.

The night before, they'd traveled halfway to the southern side of the island, where the repair dock was located. They'd stopped to sleep on the cliffs as the sun began to rise, where Lore anticipated being kept awake by nerves and guilt and the interruption of her natural rhythm. Instead, she'd dropped almost immediately into a deep sleep, ending up on the dreamwalking beach. No one else showed.

Still, she'd stayed there until she woke, not letting herself wander into another dream. On the off chance that someone would appear, yes, but also as a test of her mettle. The only other time she'd done this was when Anton was creeping into her dreams, unspooling her power to kill those villages, and dreamwalking still made her nervous. Making herself stay, forcing it to be on her own terms, helped heal that fear. Not all of it, but some.

She wished there were a way to reach out through the aether, make Gabe or Malcolm or Alie fall asleep at the same time. But like Alie said, it wasn't an exact science. They were all relying on chance, and chance had never seemed to be on their side.

Dani crouched next to Lore, holding a battered canteen. She sloshed it in her direction. "Be sparing. We won't get fresh water again until we're on the ship."

Lore sat up, squinting. She took a tiny sip of water—it tasted like dust.

The sun was on its way down, the light behind the fog tinged pink. Dani stood, brushing dirt off her knees. "Steel your stomach now if you're prone to seasickness." Dani stood and started picking her way over the cliff. "I'm not holding your hair while you vomit, and I doubt the Ferryman will, either."

An hour, walking silently through the falling dark, and they were at the edge of another cliff face. Lights gleamed on the beach below, sickly and yellow through the ash. The repair dock was little more than a shape in the shadows, hidden in shifting gray.

Lore slipped into channeling-space. Threads of gold glimmered in the sand and the sea, tiny life-forms close to the shore and larger animals out in the depths, but there was nothing human-shaped.

At least, not near the docks. But out on the water, a vague human form glowed golden.

"He's here," Lore said, blinking to banish the strands of magic. "Not docked yet."

"We'll signal him when we get down there." Dani stood,

walked over to a notch in the cliff face. A set of rough-hewn stairs, the middles worn slick with use, led down to the beach. "Now for the hard part."

I feel like there will be more than one hard part, Lore said to the goddess in the back of her mind. Nyxara had been quiet all day and into the night, a fact that she hadn't noticed until now. *It'd be terribly anticlimactic for me to slip on a step and die.*

No reply. Lore frowned, a slow bloom of panic setting into her middle as she mentally prodded at the space the Buried Goddess occupied, the deepest shadows of her subconscious. *Nyxara?*

Maybe Nyxara was just hiding, tucked so deeply into the back of her mind that She was invisible. Lore prodded harder, going deeper, reaching so far into her head that stars started swimming at the edges of her vision. *Nyxara, answer me.*

But the space was empty.

The goddess was gone.

"Don't tell me you're afraid of heights."

Dani's voice snapped her back, swaying on the cliff face as the other woman looked up from halfway down the stairs, her mouth set in irritation. "If you are, get over it."

Lore started down, her thoughts one huge scream of apprehension. Had she done something, accidentally cast Nyxara out? She supposed she should be grateful, if she had; wasn't freedom from the goddess exactly what she'd been working toward?

But instead she felt bereft, like something had been torn from her, just like she had when Mortem was gone. Nyxara had been a constant, the only person in hundreds of miles she could trust. Now Lore was truly alone.

Her foot almost slipped; Lore cursed, righting herself, focusing on the job of getting down the cliff without breaking her neck. Dani reached the beach long before Lore did; by the time Lore's boot touched sand, Dani was at the end of the dock, holding up a lighter. She waved it back and forth, then up and down.

The shadows out on the water moved, coalesced into a boat. More barge than ship, maybe forty feet across, roughly the same size as the vessel that ferried prisoners.

With an air of relief, Dani extinguished the lighter and dropped it into her pocket.

Neither of them spoke as the barge approached. As it grew closer, Lore could see that it was old, repaired in a series of patchwork jobs that left some boards on the hull looking new and others so sea-weathered she was surprised they held. When it bumped the dock, the sound made Lore jump.

A door at the prow, opening. A face peering over the side, light-brown skin and dark curling hair, eyes narrowed. The Ferryman spoke with a slight accent, one Lore thought might be Kadmaran. "Code word?"

Ah, fuck, Lore didn't know there was a code word. But Dani's smugly satisfied smile didn't change. "Tanzanite."

Some obscure stone, one that could be found in the Second Isle mine. The Ferryman nodded, his face disappearing.

"You could have told me there was a code word," Lore said.

"You have magic," Dani answered. "I get to have the damn code word."

A gangplank shuddered from the side of the boat, hit the dock with a muffled *thunk*.

"And now," Dani said, stepping up onto the gangplank, "we're officially fugitives."

Lore followed, embarking silently. When she reached the deck, she went starboard, staring out at the beach while the Ferryman brought the gangplank back in. There was nothing else to pick up; they were his only cargo. He went back to steering without a word, adjusting a sail, bringing them back out into open water without the benefit of guidelines.

The boat rocked, waves growing taller the moment they left shore, made more concerning by the lack of visibility. "You should go belowdeck," the Ferryman said, not looking at them. "It's going to get bumpy."

They did, Lore still drifting as if this were a dream. The hold was just as old and battered as the rest of the boat, the ceiling barely two feet above Lore's head. She sat by the wall, tucked her legs up beneath her.

"Well, that was easy," Dani said, sitting across from her. "Though maybe I shouldn't say so until we actually reach the Harbor."

"Why didn't you do this before?" Lore asked. "If it was so easy?"

A flutter of some unnamed emotion across Dani's face, but the other woman just shrugged. "Why would I? I had a fairly good deal going on the Second Isle. No mines, and three meals I didn't have to cook, which won't be the case once we get to the Harbor. I have no firsthand accounts, obviously, but we can assume it's all very community-oriented. Everyone pulling their own weight. That doesn't interest me."

She was lying. Lore knew it like she knew the scar on her hand. But she also knew that she was the last person Dani would share her secrets with.

"You'd be free," Lore said.

"I never have been," Dani responded. "So it wasn't really something to miss."

She and the former noblewoman were more alike than Lore cared to admit. Had their roles been reversed, if she had been the one sent here with no divine plan burrowed into her head and no real escape, she probably would have done the same as Dani had. She was endlessly, horribly adaptable.

Maybe in other circumstances, she and Dani could actually be friends.

"I killed him," Dani said casually.

The boat lurched. Lore grabbed at the boards to hold herself steady. "What?"

"Martin." Dani shrugged, but the tension in her body belied the blithe movement. "Before we left. I went into his room and slit his throat."

She couldn't tell if the other woman wanted her to be shocked, or if it was a simple statement of fact, an item on her list that she thought Lore should know.

But Lore wasn't shocked. She was, strangely, proud.

"Good," she said, leaning her head back against the side of the boat. It lurched again, almost like a cradle. She closed her eyes.

The next time Bastian found himself aware in the endless sea of gold, he was ready.

It was awkward to try to move when you technically did not have a body. He knew, intellectually, that everything here was a construct of his own brain. There was no golden sea; it was just what the remnants of his mind conjured to make sense of being held captive by the god of the sun. He had no physical form here that was separate from the one Apollius puppeted; he'd just gathered the dregs of his consciousness into a shape he remembered. Bastian was a man who enjoyed cerebral pursuits, but the exact parameters of his situation were enough to give him a headache if he spent too long dwelling on them.

Well, the construct of a headache, since he didn't technically have a head.

He shook his not-technically-a-head, clearing his mind of distractions. He had a job to do.

All around him, he felt Apollius tense, the sensation not unlike being slowly squeezed to death. The god was aware when Bastian woke up, for lack of a better term. He was used to being fought, now, and spent quite a lot of mental energy observing the piece of Bastian He couldn't snuff out, waiting for him to try to fight free.

That suited Bastian fine. The more energy Apollius wasted on keeping Bastian locked down, the less He had to spend on other things. Like conquering the world, for example.

And trying to stop the slow drain of power that was growing harder for both of them to ignore.

If being possessed by the god felt like being trapped in a golden sea, the leak of magic felt like a hole in the sea's bottom. The pool of the god's power draining, everything He held drawn elsewhere, like He was losing a game of tug-of-war. In the moments when Bastian paid attention to it, he saw more than gold flowing past him, into that leak. There were strands of shimmering blue-green, too, magic finding a new place to live.

Bastian didn't know where all that magic was going, or what it was going to. But he would take luck where he could find it.

For now, though, he wasn't concerned with the leak. He needed something more concrete.

He needed to get inside Apollius's mind, a locked room within his own.

This world that didn't really exist shaped itself around him, formed itself into functional pieces that made sense. Bastian was at the surface of the golden sea, just barely breaching the water. He stayed there, still and quiet, as if unaware that he'd come back up to the top.

Apollius watched him, waiting. For a centuries-old god, He had next to no patience, and His observance didn't last long.

The tense feeling ebbed away like a tide, the god confident that Bastian wouldn't make a move.

And Bastian didn't. When he tried to take over, to wrestle back some physical control, it felt like flailing up out of the sea, grabbing whatever might help him float. A dying man's last gasp.

But this time, Bastian dove deep. He kept his eyes open, his jaw clenched tight (not really, but his mind translated determination into parameters he knew), and arrowed through the gold. He wasn't sure what he was looking for, but with his trademark stupid confidence, he figured he would know it when he saw it.

And he did.

A door. Small and unassuming, easily missed, seen through the shifting glimmer.

He swam to it. He jerked it open.

And climbed out onto a beach.

His not-quite-body didn't care that it was just a mental construct, and Bastian braced his hands on his knees, gasping in air as if he'd actually been drowning. He fell forward, exhaustion catching him by the throat; his palms dug into white sand as he spat out mouthfuls of luminous water. Behind him, the door settled into the ground as if it had been there for centuries.

Bastian looked up.

White sand, blue sky, blue ocean, and gray cliffs. It wasn't a place he recognized.

Though he recognized the man standing at the tide line.

"Gabe." Bastian pushed himself up, his heart catching fire in his chest. "Gabe!"

The monk didn't hear him. Gabe stared out at the ocean, a furrow between his brows.

"Gabriel?" Bastian stumbled up to him, still pulling in air like it'd been denied him. "Listen, I know you're angry at me, but completely ignoring my existence seems rather shortsighted, given the circumstances."

Gabe still didn't respond, but the furrow between his brows went deeper.

Maybe this was a dream of some kind. A hallucination, Bastian's mind showing him what he wanted to see.

Slowly, he made his way around his Priest Exalted, until he stood in the surf and stared up at him, that two inches of height that annoyed him endlessly; the man was always *looming*.

"I never meant to hurt you," Bastian said, even though he knew the other man couldn't hear. Maybe because of it. "I know you don't believe that. I know you think everything I do is to hurt you, somehow. But it's not, and it never was." He paused, the next words coming on the end of a rueful laugh. "I hate it, actually."

No answer. Gabe sighed, tipped back his head, and closed his eye. A swallow worked its way down the long column of his throat, emphasizing tendons. The muscles in his shoulders were tense, his large hands held in fists. Gabriel Remaut had never relaxed a day in his life, and apparently he didn't when he was dreaming, either.

Bastian knew he was a handsome man—gods knew he'd been told often enough—and Gabe looked so different from him. But he was beautiful, too, a fact that came to him easily here, when they weren't locked in conflict, when they just...were. The line of his jaw stubbled red and gold, his eye clear and blue as the ocean they stood in. As long as Bastian had known him, Gabe always had a look of thoughtfulness on his face, as if everything needed to be analyzed and cataloged, as if everything was trying to trick him.

Gabe couldn't hear him, couldn't feel him, and there was no one here to see. Cautiously, Bastian raised his hand, gently traced Gabe's jaw.

The monk shuddered, just a bit, as if touched by a cold wind.

Bastian turned and trudged up the beach. His time was limited.

Another door, the mirror of the one he'd seen in the golden sea. Bastian pulled it open.

A long, dark hall, seemingly endless, lined with more identical doors. Bastian didn't care about Apollius's privacy—his own had been dragged out back and shot, after all—but he still hesitated a moment before tugging the first door open.

A burning house, seen from a distance. Small figures moved around it, throwing more fuel on the fire rather than trying to put it out. The sound of heavy breathing through tear-clogged lungs, the feeling of small, humid hands closing into fists.

Bastian shut the door, his own heart hammering. Memories. Moments in time burned into a god's brain.

He traveled down a few more doors before trying another, not wanting to see the rest of that childhood. One door opened on Apollius's memory of Nyxara and Hestraon, locked in a kiss. The feeling of a fast-beating heart, of heavy breathing, of ownership and knowledge that He was in control of the scene. Nyxara broke away from the fire god and reached out to Apollius in invitation, cheeks flushed and dark eyes bright. Bastian shut that door, too.

He passed a few more, picking at random now. More memories of Nyxara, playing and smiling and singing. A boat, gently rocking on the open ocean.

Behind one door, there was nothing but darkness, a sucking void of it that filled Bastian with a deep, unspeakable dread. He shut that one fast.

Time was running out. His vision feathered at the edges, his legs jellied. Apollius might have all these memories locked away, but there was no way to know if He could feel Bastian rifling through them.

He opened more doors, watched the memories just long enough to know if they were what he needed. A location, that's what Alie said, and she hadn't been able to trust him with more than that—

Another door, a room full of gold, voices in a low register. He went to slam the door shut.

"This will be the only clue," Apollius said. "So you'd better not lose it."

Bastian kept the door open.

Every memory was in Apollius's point of view, so the jewel He held up appeared huge to Bastian's eye, held close to the god's face. The perspective took a minute to resolve into something familiar.

Lore's engagement ring. The one he'd found in storage beneath the Church, the one he'd felt so compelled to give her, before he knew what was happening to him.

"Never," said another voice. The speaker came into view—dark-haired, dark-eyed. He bore a striking resemblance to August Arceneaux.

Gerard. Bastian's ancestor, the one to whom Apollius had dictated the Tracts. He looked at the ring with awe, barely brave
enough to touch it when Apollius dropped it in his hand. "It will
be kept hidden away, Holy One. Of that, You can be sure."

"Do whatever you want with it," Apollius said flippantly. A
feeling of satisfaction, a job finally done. "The only reason I'm
telling you is so you can keep it safe. I can trust you to do that,
can't I?"

"Yes, Holy One." Gerard looked at the ring with holy awe.
"The Arceneaux line is the most faithful of all You have chosen;
we will steward Your throne as we keep safe anything that could
harm You."

"If you ever need to move the piece," Apollius said, ignoring
Gerard's impassioned pronouncement, "hold the gem to the sunrise. It will tell you where it is."

Bastian closed the door, afraid to linger at this particular
memory in case it somehow alerted Apollius. Good timing, too—
the hallway swam and buckled, like a still-wet painting doused
in water, before dissolving into gold. Bastian's awareness of himself slowly faded, thrusting him back under the sea, back into
unconsciousness.

But he had a location. Or at least the clue to one.

And the next time he surfaced, Apollius wouldn't get off so
easily.

Chapter Fourteen

GABE

Power is like whiskey. It might burn at first, but eventually, you'll want more.

—Caldienan proverb

As it turned out, no longer being a fugitive was rather boring.

Gabe spent the next two days wandering the city. At first, from force of habit, he went to the fighting barns. But no one would fight him. He stood in the queue for a while with the other hopefuls after placing a fairly significant bet against himself, but the eyes of the referees kept roving over him, pausing only briefly before quickly moving along. Three matches later, one of them he recognized jerked his chin, gestured over to the wall. Fists clenching on nervous energy, Gabe followed.

The ref was a big man, blond and red-faced, nose blotchy with drink. He crossed his arms. "You might as well leave."

"Pardon?" Maybe he had retained his manners after all, though it seemed he could only access them when he was in danger of setting fire to the entire building.

"Rotunda orders." The fights here were technically legal, though

Gabe knew they played fast and loose with the law. "You aren't to be touched."

So. He was safe, but he was trapped. A familiar feeling.

Gabe didn't bother arguing. He nodded curtly and left the barn.

He could return to the boardinghouse that Eoin had so kindly placed them in, but it felt claustrophobic. Stupid, when it was so much bigger than the row house had been, but it wasn't so much the square footage as it was the emotional crowding. Val and Mari, happily married. And now Michal and Malcolm, their latent attraction finally given way to a relationship.

When they'd moved into Eoin's boardinghouse, Michal and Malcolm had decided to share a room. It wasn't unexpected, but Malcolm had drawn himself up as if it were when they were choosing accommodations. "I'll bunk with Michal."

Mari had shared a quick, warm look with Val before nodding smoothly. "I think that's an excellent idea."

Gabe had nodded, too. Apparently, this was not the reaction Malcolm expected.

His friend had sighed, scrubbing a hand over his hair. "Gabe, I didn't mean to leave you in the dark..."

"None of us were in the dark." He'd managed a smile. "I'm happy for you. Truly."

Malcolm smiled back, though it was tinged with something like pity. "I know it's hard. To see people with the person...the people...they care about, when you..."

"When I can't," Gabe said quietly. "With either of them."

It was the first time he'd admitted aloud that Lore wasn't the sole person he missed. But apparently, Malcolm wasn't the only one who was bad at hiding his feelings.

He'd clapped Gabe on the shoulder, not knowing what else to say.

Outside the barn, Gabe leaned against the wall, splinters scraggling into his hair.

His only options for the rest of the day before another meeting tonight were to wander the market square or go to a tavern. Despite his feelings toward Caldienan beer, the tavern won.

A fog of smoke hovered around the door as he pushed it open, seething from the ends of cigarettes held in rough fingers. The smell reminded him of Bastian.

Gabe sat down at a small table in the corner with his back to the wall. When the bar girl came, a pretty thing with brown eyes and a quick smile, he asked for beer, hopeful that this establishment had better brew than the one the other night.

When the bar girl moved aside, Finn was behind her.

The man sat down without waiting for an invitation, giving Gabe a halfhearted toast with his stein. "So you couldn't stomach another evening at the boardinghouse, either? I can't stand the place."

Finn lived in the same house where they did now. Yet another lovely surprise.

The other man took a drink. "Though I suppose you have somewhere to be tonight, so it would only be for a couple hours, anyway."

"You mean you don't?" He didn't recall seeing Finn when the Brothers removed their hoods at the last meeting, but he also hadn't been looking closely. It'd make sense for him to be a member.

"Hells no." Finn tossed back the rest of his pint and signaled to the girl at the bar for another. "Never been interested in religion, myself. Though you certainly make it hard for one to be an atheist, what with your"—he swirled his hand in Gabe's direction—"affliction."

The bar girl brought their orders. Gabe drained his stein and made a face. It seemed every tavern in Farramark carried the same kegs, and this draught had been pulled from the bottom.

Finn grinned. "So you know that I know. And you don't care?"

"Frankly, I don't care about anything having to do with you."

"Ouch." But Finn's smile only widened.

The barmaid brought him another. Gabe sipped it this time, rather than throwing it back. The taste did not improve. "And I assume you've known for a while. Eoin told us about your spying."

"I am rather good at it." Finn stretched his legs beneath the table and clasped his hands behind his head. "I could give you some pointers. I was told you and the erstwhile Queen made a pair of piss-poor spies."

Gabe gritted his teeth and took another sip of bad beer.

"I did want to apologize, though." The thorny grin was gone; Finn almost looked genuine. It made him look more like Bastian, and made Gabe's teeth grind harder. "I know you wanted to keep what you are a secret."

"And why, exactly, didn't you let us?" Heat built in Gabe's fingers again. If he lifted them from the table, he feared he might leave scorch marks.

"Because," Finn said, "it would be selfish of you."

Of all the answers he could have given, Gabe certainly hadn't expected that one.

Finn leaned forward, elbows on the table, demeanor sobering. "You have the power of a god. And from what I've gathered, you are only interested in getting rid of it. While another god does whatever the fuck He wants, the rest of the world be damned. You think armies can stand up to Him? Mortal men?" He shook his head. "No. If Apollius is going to be stopped, it's going to take something as powerful as He is."

"I'm not that powerful," Gabe said. "None of us are."

"Well, you're closer than anyone else." Finn sat back, took another drink. "And everything Eoin promised you in exchange for your little magic shows is sure to piss off Apollius, so you'd better be ready to use it."

"You seem awfully eager for war."

"I'm not eager for war," Finn corrected. "But I'm far less eager for what will happen if we pretend war isn't coming. Caldien has been the largest holdout against the Empire for decades. You think Jax will go easy on us, now that he literally has the most powerful god on his side?"

Beneath the patch, Gabe's empty eye socket itched.

Finn drained the rest of his beer. When the barmaid gave him a questioning look, asking without words if he wanted another, he waved her off. "You'll get your war, one way or another," Finn said as he stood to leave. "Make sure it counts." He rapped his knuckles on the table, then he was gone.

Gabe stared at the scratched tavern table. Deftly, cautiously, he let himself slip. Let the world go black and white, the same way he'd seen it back when he could only channel Mortem, when his grasp of power was so very weak. The difference now was subtle, a weaving of flame-colored threads among the monotone.

He tugged at those orange-red threads.

The beer left in his glass churned into a boil.

With a screech of his chair across the floor, Gabe threw a handful of coins on the table and stalked outside.

♦

When it was time for the meeting, Gabe met Malcolm by the boardinghouse. The gas streetlights came on as they made their way to the Rotunda, sparked to glow by young lamplighters who scurried up and down the poles in the fine mist of evening. The Rotunda was brightly lit, its columns casting shadows over the perpetually damp cobblestones.

"Have you thought about what trick you're going to perform?" Malcolm asked as they walked down the wet street. Sarcasm, but with an angry edge. "I imagine they won't let me off easy this time. Figured I'd grow a rose or some shit."

"I assume set something on fire." Gabe tugged up his hood. "Maybe Eoin, if he annoys me enough."

Malcolm snorted.

The guard at the door perked up when they approached. "Your...esteemed guests," he said, stumbling over proper honorifics. "Come with me."

Gabe stopped, his hand subconsciously stretching for the knife in his belt. "Where are we going?"

"The meeting tonight is elsewhere." The Brother dipped his head deferentially. "If you'll allow me to lead you there."

Malcolm looked at him, mouth grim.

Wearily, Gabe nodded, gesturing for the Brother to lead the way.

It was a long walk. The Brother led them through the back alleys of the city until they reached the outskirts, buildings tapering off, forests taking their place. It'd been an unusually dry stretch of days for Caldien, the mist never quite turning to rain, and the scent of the coniferous trees was heavy in the air.

A knot of black-cloaked figures waited at the edge of the woods. One figure broke away, pulling down his hood. Eoin, smiling widely. "The men of the hour."

"I don't like this," Malcolm muttered under his breath.

Neither did Gabe.

Eoin approached, clapping Gabe on the shoulder, then Malcolm in turn. Malcolm stood stiff as he did, body rebounding from the contact. "Delighted you could join us."

"A bargain is a bargain," Gabe said through his teeth.

Malcolm frowned. "Why are we here?"

"It seems we should use this opportunity to do something useful." Eoin gestured to the forest beside them. "This particular tract of land—one of my own, in the spirit of honesty—needs to be cleared for farming. The weather has not been cooperative. So you"—he pointed to Gabe—"are going to burn it down. And you"—now pointing to Malcolm—"are going to revitalize it."

They looked at each other, apprehension twinned. The first large-scale use of their power, and of course it had to be something that could go horribly wrong.

Heat built in Gabe's hands. Heat, and a horrible eagerness.

"I'm not sure if this is a good idea," Gabe hedged. "We have no practice..."

"Godhood doesn't need practice." Eoin's eyes glinted.

There was nothing else for it. With another guarded look at Malcolm, Gabe stepped forward, closer to the trees.

The Brotherhood hung back, making a half circle around them. It made Gabe feel like a caged animal. He fought not to bare his teeth as he raised his hands.

Ember threads appeared in the air around him, like cracks in the wall of a burning house. They twisted around his fingers, jewel-bright. He channeled all that fire through his body, imbued it with his will.

Burn.

The word was in his mind, his own inner voice. But another voice echoed it.

The forest burst into flame.

It was quick work, faster than a forest fire should be. The trees were immediately consumed, burning wildly, torches in the night-dark.

"Excellent," Eoin murmured, the flames reflecting on his face, hollowing out his features.

Within moments, the trees were ash. The forest was desolate, the plain beyond them clear to see. More a copse of trees, really. Nothing too impressive.

If he downplayed it in his mind, maybe it'd feel less momentous. Maybe his fingers wouldn't itch to do it again.

Malcolm came to his side, his jaw clenched tight. He knelt at the edge of the burnt woods, placed his hands to the ground. Green flickered at the corners of Gabe's vision as the grass of the fields beyond encroached on the cleared land, moss furring over the corpses of trees. A minute, and the field was lush, primed for sowing.

"I hate this," Malcolm murmured as he stood, backed away. "I *hate* this."

Eoin stared at what they'd done, openmouthed. Then, with a whoop of laughter far wilder than expected from a seasoned politician, he started applauding.

The rest of the Brotherhood picked it up, calling their praises into the night air.

Gabe barely listened. He just watched as steam rose into the darkness, the last dregs of smoke disappearing into the light of the full moon.

CHAPTER FIFTEEN

LORE

Every emotion is a tool.

–Kirythean proverb

There were ropes attached to the walls in the hold of the Ferryman's boat. Lore assumed they were for securing cargo, but after the second wave hit the side of the hull, she wrapped them around her waist and tied as tight a knot as she could, anchoring herself to the side. Across the hold, Dani followed her lead.

It kept them from being thrown across the room, but damn, the rope biting into her gut was almost as bad.

As it turned out, Dani was the seasick one. They sloshed back and forth, Dani going pale and sweaty before turning her head and losing what looked like the jerky and hard bread that had been dinner the night before. Lore watched her dispassionately. If she'd been free, she still wouldn't hold back Dani's hair.

A few minutes of furious rocking, the boat turning back and forth so steeply Lore was sure it was fully on its side. But the Ferryman knew his shit, and they never capsized.

Then it was over.

Lore sat still in her ropes, consciously holding her muscles loose to move with the ship, waiting for the next wave to hit. But a minute passed, then a minute more, and the waters outside seemed placid. She relaxed, marginally. Hopefully the rest of the journey stayed calm.

Dani still looked a little shaky as she untied her ropes and stood, casting a rueful glance at the puddle of sick on the floor. "I'm going up. It smells like vomit down here."

"Imagine that," Lore muttered as the other woman climbed the ladder.

Something glimmered in the top of Dani's boot right before she disappeared onto the deck. The hilt of a dagger. Lore supposed it was a good thing one of them was armed, but it wasn't lost on her that Dani hadn't been forthcoming about it. She tucked the information away.

Lore took a moment to get her bearings before standing on unsteady legs. She hadn't paid much attention to the rest of the hold when they first came down here, preoccupied with the loss of Nyxara in her head and an imminent trial-by-sea, but now she took the opportunity to look around. Other than the open area where she stood, the hold appeared to be divided into a few other rooms, with one door toward the stern and another to the prow. The stern door was open, revealing bare bunks and a chamber pot. The door at the prow was closed.

It was caution more than curiosity that drew her toward it. This was the last situation in which she wanted to be caught off guard. Lore searched around the floor of the hold until she found a splintery old chest with metal reinforcements at the corners that looked easy enough to pry off. The old metal piece had a sharp edge; a few minutes' work, and she had it in her hand, thin and narrow enough at one end to use as a lockpick.

It wasn't necessary. The door opened smoothly when she turned the handle. Still, Lore tucked the sharp implement into her boot. It wasn't a dagger, but it might do in a pinch.

The room was empty, other than a table in the center. A handful of silver instruments were placed at equidistant spaces around its surface. Some looked like pyramids, balancing delicate metal bars on their points. Others were arches with weights hanging from chains, preternaturally still. She thought of the thing Dani had brought the Ferryman, the silver balance to pay their way. It would fit right in here.

All the instruments were bolted to the table, presumably to keep them from being thrown around the room when the sea was raging. Brow furrowed, Lore stepped over the threshold, wanting a closer look.

Every instrument on the table spun in her direction.

The balancing pins whipped around on their silver pyramids. The hanging weights swung her way, held straight out on their chains, pointing right at her.

A moment later, a wave hit the side of the ship, almost sending her sprawling.

Lore scrambled out of the room, shutting the door behind her. Up on the deck, she heard Dani's surprised shout, followed by a muffled curse from an unfamiliar voice in a language she didn't know.

The ladder into the hold clattered as someone made their way down. The Ferryman, eyes narrowed, rushing for the room. He cast one dark look at Lore before shoving the door open.

Lore looked past him, at the table with all its delicate instruments. They were spinning, now, recalibrating, but only for a moment. They quickly settled back into a resting state, the pins balanced, the weights hanging still.

"Odd," the Ferryman muttered. He looked back at Lore. "Don't touch that. They're the only things keeping us on course. I have one up at the wheel, but we need the backup. If they malfunction, we'll be lost in ash for days."

"Sorry," Lore said, eyes downcast. "I got curious."

"Well, don't." The Ferryman checked on the instruments again before closing the door, then looked back at her. "We'll arrive in an hour." He went back up the ladder.

With one more glance at the room, Lore followed.

The Ferryman was true to his word. An hour later, Lore stood on the deck, peering through itching eyes at thick ash that made it look like they were sailing through a storm cloud, or through a puff of smoke from one of Bastian's cigarettes. Up ahead, the ash seemed to thin somewhat, let through a little more light, but it could just have been a trick of perception.

"I'd go below, if I were you."

Lore jumped. The Ferryman had come up behind her silently, giving her another of those searching looks. "The ash will get worse before it gets better."

"Your navigation is impressive," Lore said.

He stared at her long enough that she thought he might not respond. "I've studied." With that, he jerked his head to the ladder.

Lore followed the direction, Dani close behind. They waited in silence, both their eyes streaming from being abovedeck.

A few minutes later, she felt the telltale bump of the hull meeting a dock.

She and Dani climbed out of the bowels of the ship again, this time into thin, gray sunlight rather than the perpetual gloom of the open water. The Harbor dock was, strangely, in better repair than the ones on the Second Isle, with the same patchwork repair job as the Ferryman's ship. A stretch of rocky beach ended at a scrubby forest, the trees dark with centuries-old char. If it weren't for the lack of a mine, it would be almost identical to the island they'd just left.

It felt different, though. No, not felt…it *sounded* different, a fact Lore knew was true but couldn't quite put her finger on. A quiet hum, beneath the thrash of waves. One that almost resolved into a song, if she concentrated.

"Here," Dani said to the Ferryman, digging in her pocket. "You didn't take our payment before we left." She pulled out the silver instrument she'd stolen from Martin.

Lore tensed, half expecting the thing to swing her way, point at her like an accusing finger. But it didn't, swaying lazily with the force of Dani's movement and nothing else.

The Ferryman followed its motion, dark eyes narrowed.

But he took Dani's payment without comment, carefully, a contrast with the way she'd kept it stuck in her pocket. He nodded without a word and lowered the gangplank, disembarking before Lore and Dani had the chance, headed with purpose into the scrubby woods.

"A man of few words," Dani remarked, watching him go.

Lore's shoulders relaxed, a tension she hadn't known she was holding.

Someone came out of the woods at the same place the Ferryman entered them. A woman, dressed in nondescript clothing the not-color of something rough-spun and undyed. She and the Ferryman nodded to each other as they passed. "You need someone to take down the sails?"

"Please." The Ferryman glanced back. "I have...something to check on."

"Aye." The woman gave him a puzzled look as he slipped between the burnt trees, then turned back to Lore and Dani. "You're the newest escapees, then. I'm Sersha. Welcome to the Harbor."

Chapter Sixteen

ALIE

The heart is the hardest thing to guard.
　　　　　　　–Fragment of a poem found in a
　　　　　　　　　　Caldienan monastery

H e's doing it."
　　Alie hadn't had a chance to register the fact that Jax was in her apartments. Jax was in her apartments, and it was the earliest hours of morning, and she was wearing nothing but a dressing gown over her chemise, a fact that made her cheeks blaze. He'd knocked as if his own personal hell were on his heels, and Alie hadn't been awake enough to think it through; she'd let him in.

Now, mere seconds later, she was very awake and regretting that decision.

Jax looked more disheveled than she'd ever seen him. His hair was down, not constrained into its typical queue, falling ragged and golden around his shoulders. He wore plain trousers and a white shirt, with none of the Kirythean military insignia that usually marked his clothing. He looked, in short, like he'd gotten dressed and run here in as much of a panicked storm as Alie was feeling now.

She didn't like the way it set a twist into her middle to know that she was his destination when something was wrong.

It was too late to kick him out, and whatever had him in such a panic was probably important. Alie sat gingerly on the arm of her couch, wrapping her dressing gown tight. "Who is doing what?"

"Apollius." An unspoken *who else* lurked at the end of the name. "We agreed that keeping the King's true nature a secret for the time being was the best course of action. That showing our hand too quickly would do nothing but create chaos."

Alie was fairly certain that creating chaos was more a feature than a problem, in Apollius's eyes. But she remembered overhearing this argument on the wind, Jax telling the god to be cautious, Apollius agreeing. Apparently, He'd changed His mind.

"We need time for the situation here to stabilize. Time for you and me to take over the rule of Auverraine and cede control of the Empire to Apollius." He ran a hand down his face, apparently clueless to the way *you and me* sent an odd frisson all through Alie, made her sit up straighter. "Showing the world who He is now will do nothing but incite panic, when we have the opportunity to make conquering Caldien bloodless."

She sat up straighter, again, and this time it had nothing to do with thoughts of her and Jax as a unit. "What do you mean?"

He sighed, as if he hadn't actually meant to say that part aloud. Jax sank into one of the chairs next to her still-unlit fireplace. "We have been in contact with the Prime Minister," he said. "Relations between Caldien and Auverraine have been friendly for years, and Apollius reached out to Eoin to tell him how He's reached peace with us. Inviting him here, to meet with me and see a way forward." He gathered back his hair, as if he'd just realized it was still loose. "Our plan was to reveal His godhood in person to Eoin before we ever let the rest of the world know. Caldien may not be as religious as Auverraine, but being faced with a god would surely encourage him to see things our way."

Alie said nothing, chewing on her lip. She'd only met Eoin once, when he was newly elected to his position. She'd been a girl, barely in her teens, but Severin had offered to be Eoin's official guide in the Citadel, so she spent plenty of time with him. He'd looked at the icons and artifacts in the Church with more curiosity than anything, and spent quite a bit of time staring at the stained-glass windows that depicted the entire pantheon. She couldn't decide whether she agreed with Jax's assessment of him or not.

"So Apollius is planning to reveal Himself?" she asked.

Jax huffed a sound that was supposed to be a laugh, resting his elbows on his knees, his hands hanging loose between them. "Somehow, yes. I don't think He intended for me to find out before He did it. I only know because I overheard Him speaking with someone who called Him Holy One." He rubbed at his mouth. "So I suppose He's already told at least one person the truth."

Alie sat forward. "Do you know who?"

He shook his head. "I left before whoever it was exited His chamber. I don't think it would go well for me if I was discovered eavesdropping on a god."

A shiver pricked along her arms. Jax knew about her power, but she wasn't sure if he knew how she'd been using it, if he meant this as a warning. "What makes you think Apollius revealing Himself will make Caldien relations go badly?"

He arched a brow. Bruised circles stood out beneath his dark eyes. "Because people are full of fear. Human nature is to rebel, to be afraid of power when there is no means for you to seize it. True power can only be had over someone if you convince them they'll have a share."

She thought it might be a realization, Jax saying so plainly exactly what Apollius had done to him. But the Emperor of Kiry-thea just stared pensively into the middle distance, seemingly unaware that he'd just indicted himself.

Her fingers itched, threads of air calling her from the

atmosphere. "By that logic, it was never going to go well. Maybe it's better for Apollius to keep Himself hidden indefinitely."

"He's their god," Jax said plainly. "And once they're given something new to fear, something only He can stop, they'll rally behind Him. It's only this first revelation that's precarious."

"You have something to make everyone afraid, then."

"Apollius didn't keep the other elemental avatars alive out of the goodness of His heart," Jax replied. "We know they're in Caldien. He has His reasons for letting them live."

"Scapegoats," Alie murmured.

"Exactly."

Her heart kicked against the bottom of her throat, so hard she could nearly taste it. If Apollius could paint Himself not just as a god, but also as a savior, keeping the world from the harm the reawakened pantheon could cause, no one would stand against Him. "And yet He's keeping me here, with no apparent plans to use me as a scare tactic."

He glanced at her. "Because you're my betrothed. And an Arceneaux."

Saved by a cage.

Alie got up off the couch arm, turning to her kitchenette. "Do you want coffee?"

Jax seemed surprised. "Please."

The motions of gathering the supplies gave her time to collect herself. This certainly wasn't ideal, but as long as Apollius had need for Gabe and Malcolm, they were relatively safe. If one of them would fucking *dream*, she could warn them. The last two nights she'd been alone on that beach.

Alie brought the tray over to the fireplace, which Jax had graciously lit. She hung the pot over the glowing coals. "I assume trying to talk Apollius out of this is pointless."

"He doesn't listen to me," Jax muttered, sitting forward and resting his forearms on his knees. A strand of dark-gold hair fell over his forehead. "I suppose it's some kind of blasphemy, trying to direct a god."

She said nothing to that. Alie made the coffee, poured the milk. Sat back down on her couch like this was a perfectly normal thing.

"Do you have any idea of when?" she asked.

"No." Jax sat his cup—mostly untouched—on the table and watched the steam curl from its lip. "Though I can't imagine it will be long."

The silence that gathered around them wasn't comfortable, but neither was it awkward. Alie pulled her knees up into her chair and sipped at her coffee, painfully aware of Jax doing the same. Going back and forth on whether there was a crack here she could widen, a string she could pull.

"It seems Apollius isn't very interested in cooperating with you," she said finally. Quiet and introspective, as if she were just sharing an idle thought. "I suppose He didn't realize that becoming flesh meant He would have to listen to someone other than Himself."

That last part was risky. But Jax just shifted in his chair, staring at the embers in the fireplace. "When you're used to absolute power, having to temper it does not come easily."

She supposed he would know.

Jax stood. "I apologize for intruding on you so early. It was rude of me. I just...I didn't know where else to go."

Alie didn't say anything. She nodded.

With a stiff bow, Jax left the room.

She sat there for a long time, her second cup of coffee forgotten in her hand, watching the coals go cold.

Alienor Bellegarde had never missed a First Day prayer. Every day from her infancy, when her mother brought her to the Church while Severin glowered from another aisle, she'd been in the North Sanctuary just as the sun was beginning to blush the sky.

The day after Jax appeared at her door, she got there even earlier. Alie dressed herself in the dark, having told her lady's maids not to bother attending her today. It was an uphill battle to get them to agree; ever since Alie had been revealed as an Arceneaux, technically a princess, her staff had been overly attentive. She stepped into a midnight-blue gown, simple silk, and gathered the cloud of her white hair into a puff on top of her head, letting a few curls hang artfully against her temple. Then she was out the door, into the green, up the path to the Sanctuary.

The North Sanctuary had been rebuilt in a hurry after Lore tore it down. The resulting building looked enough like the old so as not to be obvious, but there were subtle differences. The archway over the door wasn't carved. The rosebushes by the pathway that had been flattened in the collapse had never been replanted. Inside, the braziers were clunky constructions, nothing like the sleek containers of before. It pleased her that the Sanctuary had been left marginally uglier.

Jax was already there, the only person present other than a couple Presque Mort. He always arrived early. The monks set up the platform for service: lighting the candles, sweeping the floor, coaxing the coals in the braziers to bloom red.

She recognized one of the Presque Mort. Alexis. They gave her a surreptitious look as they lit tapers, as if they wanted to speak to her but knew now wasn't the time.

Alie wasn't sure what to make of the Presque Mort who were still in the Citadel. After Bastian came to power, he'd banished all those who were loyal to Anton. But no such action was taken after Gabe left. Either Apollius didn't care to clean house, or all the monks left were faithful enough that He didn't think it would be a problem.

But the look Alexis gave her seemed heavy.

They disappeared into one of the side doors while the other

Presque Mort, a woman with a thick, runneled scar across her throat, carefully scattered perfuming herbs over the brazier coals. Alie couldn't see the braziers without thinking of Anton, his burn scars and his prophecy.

His murder had been chalked up to Gabe, when the second Arceneaux brother was found beheaded in the greenhouse. But she didn't believe it. She thought that violence much more likely to be Lore's.

Jax sat in the front pew. Silently, Alie sat down next to him.

"You couldn't sleep, either?" he asked quietly.

Alie had slept just fine, actually. Another night on the beach alone.

But she nodded, building one more tenuous bridge. Jax sighed and marginally slumped in his seat. The movement made his posture nearly match that of a normal man.

"I almost wish He would go ahead and get it over with," he murmured.

Other courtiers filed in shortly, all unusually quiet. Ever since Lore was banished, since Jax was welcomed into court, the nobles of the Citadel had treated morning prayers with more gravitas than before. They arranged themselves in their seats, waiting silently for services to begin, their clothing plain and subdued by court standards.

It made Alie nervous, how much more pious the nobles seemed even now. Made her wonder what the court would look like once Apollius revealed Himself.

Alexis had fulfilled the default role of Priest Exalted since Gabe left, even though they hadn't been officially given the title. But today, rather than standing behind the lectern and finding the day's Tracts, they sat next to Alie, boxing her between them and Jax. "Any idea what this is all about?" they murmured.

Jax turned to look at Alexis, anxiety in the shape of his mouth. "What *what* is all about?"

Alexis shrugged uncomfortably. "I received a note from the King this morning. Apparently, he wants to lead the prayers today."

Jax stiffened. With a truncated nod, he sat back, his hands curling to fists on his knees.

Apollius entered from the main doors at the back of the Sanctuary. He seemed frazzled, and it made Him look more like Bastian, enough that Alie's breath caught.

The god in Bastian's body didn't acknowledge the crowd. He went to the lectern and braced His hands on either side of it, the grip blanching His knuckles. One finger twitched.

Alie's skin rose in gooseflesh. He was channeling. She could almost see it, flecks of gold in the atmosphere. A slight tug in her center, the threads of her life grasped in a godly hand to be woven or spun or snapped.

For a moment, she wondered if He would channel all the Spiritum out of every living thing in this room, turn it all to His will. That would certainly send a message, to Caldien and everyone else. That would give them something to fear.

But the charge in the air softened, the divine hold on her life letting go. Alie let out an unsteady breath and wondered if anyone else had felt it.

A brief look of relief crossed Apollius's face. As if He'd been testing Himself.

Apollius flipped through the Compendium. Then He shut the book, lifted His head, and surveyed the room. "First Day prayers are generally about peace. Asking for a pleasant spate of days to follow and giving thanks for those that have come before. But the time for peace is past. Today we speak of war."

No sound, no movement. The Court of the Citadel watched their King like mice made aware of an owl.

"When I became your King," the god continued, "and I took up the holy mantle of the Arceneaux rule, I promised that I would protect us. Do My best to make the continent a place that pleases our god." He raised a hand, gesturing to Jax. "By uniting with the Kirythean Empire, I have brought us one step closer to making the world as it should be. But there are threats to our dream of global harmony. They must be snuffed out."

Slight rustling in the pews, sidelong looks.

Apollius dropped His hand and looked down, flipping through the Compendium to find the Tract He wanted. "When you are threatened by the unfaithful—"

"Warmonger!"

The cry came from the back of the Church. Alie's head whipped around.

Olivier. It was the first time Alie had seen him since she and Lilia searched the storeroom, and he looked worse for wear—gaunt, eyes sickly bright. He stood framed in the open double doors, the light of morning seeping in around him. His finger was raised, pointing at Apollius, his face flushed. Not with anger, though. The emotion looked closer to triumph.

"You were never fit to be King, Bastian Arceneaux." Olivier advanced down the aisle, finger still pointed like a bayonet. "You will lead us into ruin!"

Gasps rang through the sanctuary, nobles looking at one another with shocked faces, but none of them moved. None of them wanted to be involved in whatever this was.

Up on the dais, Apollius dispassionately watched Olivier walk toward him, still spouting accusations. He moved slowly away from the lectern so nothing stood between Him and the shouting courtier.

At the braziers, Olivier stopped, chest heaving. His hand was in his jacket, a fact none could see but the first row.

"Shit," Jax said, standing and tossing back his coat to reveal the handle of a pistol.

But he froze before he could draw it, a choked sound in his throat. Alie felt the frisson of channeling, the hum in the air, saw

Apollius's fingers twitching toward Jax. Holding his Spiritum, his life captured in a fist. Holding him still.

It was only then that Alie realized there were no bloodcoats in the Sanctuary. No Presque Mort, either, other than Alexis, sitting still as a prey animal beside her.

Apollius looked to Olivier. Gave a tiny, almost-imperceptible nod.

Olivier lurched toward Him, something shining in his fist. A dagger. A dagger that he plunged straight into the Sainted King's heart.

As he did, Apollius smiled.

The gasps of the courtiers turned to screams. Some of them rushed to the doors; others just stood in shock, watching their King bleed out.

Still standing upright, Apollius raised both hands to His chest, wetting them with Bastian's blood. Briefly, He touched Olivier's cheek, leaned in to whisper something in his ear.

With blood on his face, Olivier beamed.

The hum of channeling changed direction; Jax, freed from Apollius's hold, still didn't move. He stared at his god, jaw locked tight. He knew what this was now.

The big reveal.

Looking skyward, Apollius stretched out both hands, blood on His palms and on His chest, looking just like the statues of Him that dotted the Citadel. He held the position for a long moment, long enough for every eye in the North Sanctuary to mark the resemblance.

The hole in His chest began to close.

It only took a moment, the wound healing neatly, though crimson still stained His white shirt. The panicked cries of the nobles turned to murmurs, to shocked gasps.

But that wasn't enough. Bastian had been able to heal wounds, too; He had to do more to really convince them.

Outside, the sun brightened rapidly, enough for Alie to shield her eyes. The light came in through the stained-glass window behind the lectern, outlining Apollius in blazing glow. Making Him look like a god.

The hum of channeling was almost enough to drive her mad, now, an infernal buzz in her ears that itched like a mosquito bite. Wind howled in her head, a storm only she could hear, Apollius's power calling to her own.

He raised His hands. The sun kept shining, but the unmistakable sound of a thunderclap reverberated through the air, rattling the walls. Rain lashed against the windows, a sudden downpour that couldn't be mistaken for natural.

Displaying all the magic He had. Spiritum, and the power of Caeliar, stolen from Amelia.

"I did not mean to reveal Myself so early." His voice had an extra resonance, reverberating as much as the thunder. "I have not been honest with you, My faithful. I am not Bastian Arceneaux, blessed with the power of Apollius." He looked down from the vaulted ceiling, down to the cowering nobles. "I am a vessel for our god. I have become Him, in the flesh."

Beside her, Jax let out a long, slow breath.

Silence in the Sanctuary. There was a chance they wouldn't believe Him; they'd seen Him use this power while still pretending to be Bastian, if not so spectacularly.

Apollius seemed to know this. He turned to Olivier, bowing on the floor, his forehead pressed against the wood.

"And threats against Me cannot stand," He said, sounding almost sorrowful.

Olivier looked up, brows knit.

Apollius's hand closed to a fist. Immediately, Olivier convulsed, his veins standing out thick on his skin, eyes popping nearly free of their sockets. He rose toward the vaulted ceiling, carried by threads of Spiritum, the god's grip defying gravity.

Right in front of the window, Olivier dangled in midair, gasping, his heart beating so furiously it could be seen beneath his shirt. His arms stretched to the sides. His head dropped forward.

And his eyes exploded from his head, the pressure of his rapidly pumping heart pushing them out of his skull.

Blood sprayed the front rows of pews. Alie felt it lash against her cheek, hot and metallic.

Apollius dropped His hand. Olivier's body fell to the floor.

A show of power, and a threat. Apollius was not one to do things by halves.

He turned to the silent congregation, His face somehow both sorrowful and triumphant. "I am your King and your god," He said. "And together, we will make the Holy Kingdom."

No one spoke. No one breathed.

Gingerly, Apollius stepped over the mess of Olivier, closer to the congregation. "Danger is coming, and it is more than war," He said. "My wife should have died the night of the eclipse. I saved her, blinded by love. But her continued existence means the rest of the pantheon, those faithless gods who turned on Me and wrecked the world, have risen as well. I will protect you from Them. I will be a wall against Their wickedness." He raised His arms. "You only must believe."

Lord Villiers was the first to bow. He fell to his knees, pressing his head against the floor. Others followed, some crying, others mouthing prayers. The silence slipped into a clamor of awful, fearful joy, some hands raised, some beginning to sing.

Slowly, Alie lowered herself to the floor along with the rest of the nobles. Olivier's blood trickled down her cheekbone. She wiped it away.

Jax was the last to take to his knees. He stared at Apollius, fury in his face.

Apollius looked at him and smiled.

"Alie."

Barely sound—in the rising cacophony, she could hardly hear it. Alie turned, looked to Alexis.

The Presque Mort jerked their head eastward, toward the Citadel Wall dividing them from the Northeast Ward. *Tomorrow*, Alexis mouthed.

Alie nodded. Then she stared at the floor, at the pool of Olivier's blood just beginning to drip from the dais, as all around her the courtiers prayed to their god in His newfound flesh.

CHAPTER SEVENTEEN

LORE

When it rains in the Sapphire Sea, it feels like the world has turned upside down. I've never seen so much damn water.

−From the diary of a Myroshan pirate, 56 BGF

It didn't rain near the Isles often. But when it did, it was the kind that scoured and flooded.

The storm broke seemingly out of nowhere. Clouds gathered in the sky thick and dark as vultures on a new kill, erupting into pounding rain in seconds.

"Huh." Sersha didn't seem fazed, even as she quickened her pace, headed toward the edge of the forest. "That's odd."

The scrubby trees did little to block the rain, but it stopped within moments of them crossing the tree line. The clouds cleared, as much as Lore could tell behind the ash. The rain was gone as abruptly as it had come, leaving no trace but a few puddles on the ground.

"Very odd," Sersha said. Her accent was broad; she sounded Caldienan, though in order to be on the Isles, she had to have been arrested in Auverraine.

The rain seemed more than just odd to Lore. It seemed

portentous. A frisson of energy ribboned in the air, the same feeling she got standing close to someone channeling.

Though that might not have anything to do with the storm. The whole island felt infected with magic, strands of it churning in the air.

The piece of the Fount was somewhere on the Burnt Isles. It could be here. Lore was fairly certain she wouldn't have time to search the whole island, especially not while keeping Dani in the dark, but she'd have to at least try.

Sersha led them through the trees, following a well-worn path in the sandy dirt. "You two are from the Second Isle, right? Raihan's contact said there was a guard shortage. He'd been watching the lines out there for a while, saw the repair docks abandoned."

Raihan must be the Ferryman, but Lore couldn't make sense of the phrase *watching the lines*. As far as she knew, there were no steel cables connecting the rest of the archipelago like there were between Auverraine and the first two Isles. "What does that mean?"

"The lines?" Sersha snorted. "Your guess is as good as mine, girl. All I know is they're how he manages to navigate the sea. Something to do with all those silver doodads he has, how they interact with magic from the Golden Mount and what's left over from the Godsfall. They work as well as a compass to lead you through the ash." She shook her head. "He tried to explain it to me once. Was a scientist before he came here. But I was just a thief, and all of it went straight over my head."

Dani whipped around to look at Lore. Her hand arched toward the pocket where she'd kept the balance she'd given Raihan—the Ferryman—clearly regretting handing it over. If those silver instruments could guide them through the ash, they'd need one to sail to the Mount.

Up ahead, the charred trees parted, revealing a town.

Well. *Town* was overselling it. But it was certainly more civilization than Lore expected. Thatch-roofed huts ringed what looked almost like a Ward square, a patch of browning grass holding a few market stalls that actually seemed rather sturdy. Buildings made of rough-hewn timber marched up and down dirt roads, the bark still on their beams, and behind them, Lore could see well-tended garden patches, though there weren't any live-stock to speak of. The gardens were full of low-growing plants, root vegetables and mushrooms, things that could thrive even in these conditions. The ash here was somewhat thinner than on the Second Isle, but still enough to make the air taste burnt.

People of every color, gender, and nationality ranged about on their business, speaking to one another in a jumble of languages, all wearing clothes of the same undyed linen as Sersha. A few wore face coverings, but most of them seemed used to the ash. There were even children playing on the green, moving wooden pieces around a painted board in some game Lore had never seen before, not that she spent much time with children.

The kids were what finally drove home what the kind-of town meant, the permanence of it. "You've been here awhile."

"Some of us." Sersha, she was learning, was not loquacious. "A few of the buildings have been standing near forever, though. Might even be pre-Godsfall."

The memories she'd seen of Nyxara's life as a living goddess, the ships full of pilgrims coming to dwell within the pantheon's light. Lore remembered the cities she'd seen them build on the Golden Mount, the houses and towers, gilt-painted with the gods' names. She supposed it stood to reason that some of the penitents might build on other islands, though it looked like whoever had settled here hadn't been nearly as wealthy as those on the Mount.

Some things always stayed the same.

Sersha marched them down one of the dirt roads to a thatch-roofed cottage and opened the door. Other than a bare cot and a table with two chairs, the cottage was empty. "Somewhere for newcomers," she said. "We do shifts in the gardens; yours can start tomorrow. Once you get accustomed, you can see about either trading for one of the empty houses or building your own—"

"We aren't staying," Dani said primly.

Lore was too far away to kick her ankle. But, gods, did she want to kick her ankle.

Sersha raised a brow, her perpetually downturned mouth pursing. "How you figure?"

"The Ferryman—Raihan—seems to get off the Isles just fine." Dani shrugged. "Stands to reason he could teach someone else."

The look on Sersha's face said she thought Dani had an inflated view of her own intelligence. "You're welcome to ask him, I guess. His hut is just down the way."

"I certainly will." Dani walked farther into the hut, arranged herself at the table in a clear dismissal. "Thank you, Sersha."

With one more withering look, the older woman left.

Lore crossed her arms. "Hate to break it to you, but I don't foresee Raihan spilling extremely valuable navigation secrets just because we ask. Do you know how much the Empire would pay for easy passage near the Isles?"

"He doesn't have to tell us," Dani said. "You can control Spiritum, Lore. If anyone should be able to use an instrument calibrated to the magic of the Fount, it's you. All we have to do is get our hands on one." Her teeth ground, a near-feral look crossing her face. "If I'd fucking known, we wouldn't have handed over the one we had. Martin had a thousand other things in his room I could have stolen for payment. I grabbed the first thing I saw, after I slit his throat."

When Dani took the instrument out of her pocket, it hadn't spun to Lore. Hadn't done anything at all. And if it had been attuned to the lines of magic still emanating from the Fount, wouldn't it have reacted like the ones on the ship? Surely Dani would have noticed.

"I don't think the one we had worked, anyway," Lore said.

A sharp cut of Dani's eyes her direction. But the other woman just shrugged again. "I suppose you can sense that shit."

"When are we going to steal one, then?" Lore had no moral compunctions about it. She'd done far worse.

Sometimes, when she closed her eyes, the memory of Anton sneaked up on her. His bloody face overgrown with roses. The sound his bones and cartilage had made as she sawed through his neck with the rusty garden shears.

"*We* aren't doing anything." Dani crossed to the one unmade cot and stretched out with a sigh. "You're the criminal. You're doing the stealing. You'll be much better at it than me."

Lore had to agree there.

"But I'd wait until it gets dark." Dani shifted on the tiny cot, grimacing as she tried to get comfortable. "And do your best not to get killed. Though I guess I don't have to tell you that, do I?" She yawned. "Thus far, you've put quite a lot of effort into staying alive."

Clearly, Dani was taking the bed, but Lore's weariness was great enough that she didn't really care. She stretched out on the floor, her back to the wall, facing the closed door of the cottage. It probably wasn't safe enough for both of them to sleep. She resolved just to rest her eyes for a moment.

Less than a minute later, she was on the beach.

It wasn't empty this time. Malcolm stood on the shore, looking pensively out at the false horizon.

Lore rushed to him, afraid that he might turn ghost and fade away before they could speak. Even though this was a dream, she was still out of breath when she reached the tide line. "I was starting to think you weren't using your power."

Malcolm's mouth twitched. "Not willingly."

There was much to unpack in those two words. "So you channeled it just for this? How did you know about the beach?"

"I didn't. Though I'm not surprised, really." He glanced around at the white sand and blue ocean as if expecting it all to disappear at any moment, and half hoping it would. "I suppose we can all dreamwalk now?"

"As long as we're channeling."

His eyes closed. "That's something, at least."

Lore sat down in the sand. After a moment, Malcolm followed suit.

"So you said you aren't using it willingly," Lore said. "Is it just...happening?"

"Once," he answered, brushing sand off his knee. "Sometimes I hear Him."

Her mouth dropped open, dread running cold fingers up her back. "That's not supposed to happen."

"None of this is."

He had her there. Lore drew her knees up to her chest. So they'd been wrong. The elemental gods weren't too weak to speak, to come back as nothing but magic. They'd just needed more time.

The noose around their necks was tightening.

"Maybe you can stop, then. Since you know what to watch out for—"

"Due to a deal we made with the Prime Minister of Caldien, refusing to channel is unfortunately not an option."

"Why in every hell would you make a deal with the Prime Minister?"

"Because he has one of the pieces of the Fount." He sighed. "And he promised to rescue you and Alie."

Well, there was an easy solution. Kind of. "I don't need rescuing. I'm almost to the Mount."

"Somehow, I don't think that will convince Gabe."

His name struck something in her, like she'd been punched in the stomach. "How is he?"

"Taking to this better than I am." But Malcolm didn't sound like he thought that was a positive development.

The outline of the cliffs showed through his middle. He was fading, waking up; soon he would be gone.

"Tell him not to do it." It came in a rush, and it hurt to say, killing any chance she'd had at seeing him. "If using the power is making the gods stronger, tell him not to use it."

"I don't think that's going to work, Lore." Nearly mournful as he faded away. "I think we're past that."

She opened her eyes.

Night had fallen on the Harbor while she was sleeping. The scant sunlight was gone, though the darkness wasn't as profound here as the Second Isle, where ash nearly covered the moon. When Lore crept to the paneless window, she could just make out the glow of stars. Out on the water, the ash grew thicker the closer you drew to the Mount, but it seemed the islands themselves got a reprieve. She wondered if it had something to do with the mines on the First and Second, stirring up dust and latent magic.

On the cot, Dani was fast asleep, her arms flung up over her head, her mouth open. Her face was softer than Lore had ever seen it, even at the tea with Alie. All the malice drained out of her, all the anger and determination.

Lore slipped out the door.

Sersha hadn't been forthcoming with actual directions, just saying that Raihan's hut was *down the way*; Lore assumed that meant on the same dirt street as their own. She'd just have to peer in the windows of every hut until she saw one that looked like it could belong to the Ferryman. But as she exited their rough cabin, a sound rose on the breeze.

Singing.

It was subtle, a gentle lilting right at the edge of her hearing, almost too soft to hear at all. The same hum she'd felt when she stepped off the ship, sharpened into melody by the silence of night.

Lore followed it.

The song rose as she walked, harmonies leading her on. Down the dirt road, almost to its end, a little hut set off from the others, right at the edge of the burnt woods. The song hit a crescendo, louder than it had been but still so soft.

She put her hand on the door.

The song fell away.

Lore pulled her makeshift lockpick from her boot, gave the door an experimental push to test the bolt's strength.

It opened.

Nerves bundled in her gut, Lore hesitated just before the threshold. What would Raihan do if she waltzed into his home with a rusty shiv? He didn't seem a neighborly sort; he'd barely said two full sentences on the ship. She didn't think they had any guns here, but barging into a man's home unannounced was sure a way to find out.

She peeked through the door.

Raihan was nowhere to be seen. But there were hundreds on hundreds of silver instruments, all whirring away. They were stacked on tables, arranged around piles of books in the corner, crowded before a door in the back wall. Weights swinging, pins spinning.

If she was quiet, darted in and took one and got out, maybe he wouldn't even notice.

Breath held, Lore stepped over the threshold.

As in the ship, the instruments whirled in her direction. The subtle noises of their movements stopped, and the resulting quiet was deafening.

Behind the door, something moved.

Not all of the instruments were frozen. A few of the silver tools still moved, swinging back and forth. Silently cursing, Lore grabbed one without looking to see whether it was still moving. If worse came to worst, she'd sneak in again tomorrow.

The door at the back of the hut opened.

She tried to run, then stumbled, her boot catching on a raised board in the rough floor. Lore didn't fall, but it was a close thing, and the momentary interruption of her flight was enough for Raihan to come through the door, for him to stare right at her. At the reaction of all his silver implements, pointing in her direction like tattling children.

"You," he murmured.

Chapter Eighteen

LORE

We will be known throughout the world, Our power
undeniable.

—The Book of Holy Law, Tract 21

They stared at each other. Then Lore bolted for the door.

"Wait!" He held up a hand, willing her to stop. "I'm not
going to hurt you; I just want to ask some questions!"

"Right," Lore snarled, gripping her lockpick so tightly it cut
into her palm, the weighted ball in her other fist as she raised her
hand to shove the door open. "You find me stealing, and you just
want to ask questions."

"You're welcome to steal that one."

Great. A fifty-fifty chance, and she'd ended up in the wrong
fifty.

"It's useless," Raihan continued. Now that he'd made her stop
her mad dash to escape, he seemed loath to move, still standing
in a semi-crouched position with a book in his hand as if afraid
he'd startle her into flight again. "Only Mount-mined silver can
find the lines. That one must have come from somewhere else.
There's barely any Mount-mined instruments around anymore,

but it seems like the ones still in existence are being used as Burnt Isles paperweights, so I make the prisoners bring me things just in case." He paused, studying her. Then, "You of all people should have been able to tell what was Mount-mined."

Her engagement ring was Mount-mined. That had to be what he was talking about; somehow, the Ferryman had found out who she was. Fear suffused her, then calculation. She could use that.

"I have a proposition for you," she said, placing the apparently useless instrument back on the table, where it swung twice and then came to a stop. "You give me one of these things that actually works, and I'll tell you whatever you want to know about life in the Citadel, the color of the Sainted King's chamber pot, any sordid detail you can think of."

Raihan furrowed his brow. "I'm sorry. The Citadel?"

"Isn't that what everyone wants to know?" There was a chair in the corner of the room, next to the pile of books; Lore collapsed into it. "It's not all that great, but I understand the curiosity."

"I don't think we're on the same page," Raihan said, finally completing the arc of motion she had interrupted and placing his book on the table with the silver weights. "I have no interest in the Citadel." He cocked his head, amended: "Well, no interest in the chamber pots, anyway. If you have any information on Church artifacts, however, I'd be all ears. The Mount-pointers that aren't on the Isles are probably there."

"Mount-pointers?"

The tips of his ears flushed. "That's what I call them. No reason to make up a flowery name when you can just call them what they are."

But Lore was less concerned with what he called his silver things than with what he'd said before. "Who do you think I am?"

The Ferryman shrugged, looking as confused by the turns of this conversation as she was. "I truly have no idea, other than that you must have recently come into contact with quite a lot of energy from the Fount, since you made all my instruments freeze up. I had my suspicions on the ship, and you just confirmed them."

Shit.

"I don't have any questions about the Citadel," Raihan continued, "but I'm more than willing to answer any questions you might have about the island and the lines, if you could help me out with a few experiments. I assume that you've drawn close to the Golden Mount recently."

That was a better answer than that she'd recently been the unwilling vessel of a goddess and still had the ability to channel god-power. If he'd known she was the Queen, he would have known she was magic. Letting him think she was nothing more than a courtier who'd angered the King was much easier.

"I can't imagine *how*, though, since you were a prisoner on the Second Isle." He gave her a quizzical look with deep-brown eyes. "Care to enlighten me?"

She might not have turned out to be a good spy, but Lore was a great liar. "Not the Mount," she said. "They opened up a new mine on the Second Isle. I guess the magic from the Godsfall was stronger in there." A flimsy story that wouldn't hold up to any scrutiny, if he decided to ask any new escapees. But with any luck, she'd be long gone by then.

If Raihan didn't buy it, his face was as good a liar as she was.

"Interesting," Raihan said. He gestured to the instruments on the table. "These are drawn to high concentrations of power from the Fount. As best I can tell, they point toward the Golden Mount when offshore, but I haven't actually tested the theory successfully. The few times I've gotten close—at least, I assume I have—they've start spinning again, like the entirety of the landscape around the Mount is infected with magic."

Infected. That was sure what it felt like.

Lore eyed the delicate instruments. It was incongruous to see them here, where everything was emblematic of living off an unhospitable land. "Where did you get them? Other than as payment; I assume you knew what they were before you started asking for them."

"Most of them were here when I arrived," Raihan said. "Nearly twenty years ago now. It was harder to get to the Harbor, then, and there were far fewer of us here. Someone was researching all this long before me. I've found some things on this island that made them stop, but never as intensely as they have for you. A few places deeper in the forest, where the scars from the Godsfall are more evident." He waved a hand at the books in the corner. "Those, too, though the effect has worn off."

Lore eyed the books next to her chair, not quite willing to touch them. Malcolm had her well trained at this point. "So they don't have... power-residue anymore?"

He seemed as unimpressed by her word choice as she was, though he was one to talk, with his *Mount-pointers*. He shrugged. "So it seems. These were brought to me when they were found in another hut, farther in the woods than our settlements have reached. It appeared they hadn't been touched since the Godsfall. Honestly, it's a miracle they're still intact." He went to the pile and chose a book from the top, opening it carefully and tipping it her direction. "Too bad no one can read them."

The text swam before her eyes. She recognized where she'd seen it before now. The prophecy under glass in the belly of the Church. The language Nyxara could read.

Well, fuck. This was probably helpful information, so of course it would be in a language she didn't know. Once again, she felt bereft at the loss of the goddess.

But she was still a receptacle for power. Spiritum, if not Mortem, not anymore.

Even without Nyxara's presence, she felt herself tugged backward in her mind, following instinct.

A flare in her vision, like she'd looked directly at the sun.

Flashes of golden thread, and black and blue and green and orange, as if she were seeing the underweave of the world, everything that made up everything.

A line in the book resolved, right at the top of the page. Quick and simple. Scrawled instructions.

Valley between two highest peaks. Burnt tree.

Then the language was incomprehensible again.

Lore gasped, bracing herself on the arm of the chair. Raihan stared at her, mouth agape.

All the silver instruments that had been pointing to her had moved, drawn into her gravity, spilling themselves on the ground as they drew close. They clustered around her feet like an advancing army.

"What, exactly, did you just do?" Raihan asked quietly.

She straightened, shaking, hands held like surrender. "I'm not entirely sure." Her mind worked quickly, fitting pieces together. "But I'll help you with whatever you want, if you give me one of these."

The Fount piece was here, on the island. She knew it like she knew the shape of Gabe's mouth, the feel of Bastian's skin. Intrinsic, second nature.

Raihan's forehead furrowed, his eyes narrowing. "I'll give you one," he said. "But whatever you're doing with it, you have to take me with you."

"Done." At this point, if he'd insisted she strip naked and do a court dance before taking one of the silver instruments, she would have asked which waltz he preferred. Lore grabbed one of the silver balances on the floor, the pin on top of the pyramid pointing directly at her even as she fumbled it into her hand. "Come on."

❦

Necessity made fast friends. Raihan gathered up a battered notebook and pen as he hurried after Lore, clearly planning to document whatever was about to happen. She should be concerned about that, maybe, but there was no time. This was the only chance she'd get at finding the piece of the Fount, and if he wanted to write about it, why should she care? It wasn't like his notes would get to anyone outside of the Harbor.

Valley, burnt tree. If she could find that, she could find the Fount piece. One step closer to making it whole and casting all this magic back where it belonged. The singing she'd heard earlier got louder as she walked, Raihan trailing behind. All she had to do was keep following instinct, let the power and the singing lead her.

They cast semi-suspicious looks at each other as they walked out of his hut and into the night-dark woods. Raihan had a lighter, the flicker of tiny flame just enough to illuminate their steps and keep them from breaking an ankle on the char-black tree roots. If the moon was shining somewhere, it was hidden behind the ash.

"If you're planning on murdering me," Lore said, the lockpick in her hand, "I would advise against it. I can defend myself quite handily."

"I don't doubt you can," Raihan said, raking a hand through dark curling hair. "I can't necessarily say the same, but hopefully you find me charming. Won't be the first time that's saved my hide."

"You're far more charming now than you were on the boat, at least. Talking will do that."

"Even with all the silver, navigating is a hard job. The lines change without warning sometimes, like currents. And I didn't want to talk to your friend, frankly. She's unpleasant."

"She's not my friend." Lore didn't comment on the *unpleasant* part. It was true, but a small part of her resented him for it anyway. This situation had chewed Dani up and spat her out, too.

"So are you one of those channelers from Auverraine, or something?" he asked. "The Mort?"

"Or something." Her voice was flat, a closed door to that line of questioning.

He didn't press. "I came from Kadmar to Auverraine to study Mortem channelers," he said. "Well, ostensibly. It was mostly to escape being impressed into the Kirythean army, once they took over. I graduated from the Kadmaran university with a degree in artifact study." He kicked aside a dead branch in their path. "The Empire was very interested in using my skills. I was very interested in not letting them."

"No one but the Church is allowed to handle any artifacts in Auverraine. I can't imagine you got very far in your research."

"No, but I got far enough from the Empire. For a time, at least." The lighter flickered in his hand, casting deep shadows across his face. "Kadmar—and everywhere else that's not Auverraine or Kirythea, really—has a more…loose relationship with religion. We see the gods as people making use of power, not necessarily divine beings worthy of worship." He shrugged. "At least, that's what it was like before Kirythea took over. Who knows what it's like now."

He said it flippantly, but pain lurked beneath his voice.

"So I assume Emperor Ouran caught you eventually?"

Raihan barked a laugh. "No. That was King August."

"Ah." Unwarranted embarrassment colored her cheeks. "That makes more sense."

"And it wasn't even because of my heretical line of work," Raihan said darkly. "He wasn't keen on anyone being in Auverraine without proper papers. Especially from a Kirythean-occupied country. Never mind that those were the people who most needed somewhere to go."

"Mercy was never his strong point."

"It's not a quality that Kings or Emperors hold in high regard."

Their path turned uphill, and neither of them spoke for a while in favor of breathing hard until it turned downward again.

Hunger clawed in Lore's middle; it'd been a long time since her last meal of dried meat on the Second Isle.

"So," Raihan began when they'd both caught their breath, "it sounds like you were in the Citadel before you ended up here. Were you a courtier, before you somehow got the ability to channel?"

Now it was her turn to bark a laugh. "Yeah. Sure."

Raihan didn't seem convinced, but he didn't ask again, like he thought she might go back on their tenuous bargain if he was too curious. Part of her felt bad; he'd been kind, all things considered. But the idea of having to explain everything made her feel like she might collapse in the middle of this path and not get up again.

The ground leveled, as much as she could tell in the scant light. On one side, the hill they'd just climbed down; on the other, another steep rise. "Looks like this is the valley."

"Indeed it is." Raihan gestured to her. "Is it moving?"

Lore produced the silver instrument she'd grabbed from her pocket. The pin swung a bit before pointing back at her. "No change."

"Hmm." He looked out over the dark trees. "What are you trying to do with it, exactly?"

"I need to find something. Something that should make this thing point like it's never pointed before."

Clearly, he wanted to ask her more about that, but Raihan just nodded. "Walk around with it. See if it starts to react."

"Very scientific of you."

"Science is little more than doing strange things and seeing what comes of them."

Lore balanced the instrument in her palm. *Burnt tree*, the book said. That didn't narrow it down much. Every tree on this damn island was some degree of burnt, scarred from the Godsfall. Still, Lore started forward, hoping she'd somehow draw close enough to the right place without stumbling and breaking a leg. The singing was nearly manic, but though it'd led her here, it didn't help with the specifics.

Slipping into channeling-space took less thought than breathing. It looked different now. There was the gold of Spiritum, but also snatches of blue. The occasional flash of orange and iridescent white; flickers of green, but those were harder to make out.

She'd grown used to finding tiny sparks of Spiritum in dead matter, the dregs of life still held deep in death. So the tree to her right caught her attention.

Black. Black all the way through, Mortem in every inch. Not one slash of gold or green. She couldn't use the power of death anymore, but she could still see it, still sense it.

There was something under all that dark. Channeling-space let her see through arbitrary barriers like dirt and rock, and down below the tree, tangled in its roots, was something shifting and prismatic. Something that shone every color and none at all.

The silver pin swung away from her, straining on its axis. The song crashed in a storm of harmony.

"Ah," Lore said.

She shook herself; the world organized back into light and color. "You didn't happen to bring a shovel, did you?"

"Weirdly enough," Raihan said, reaching into his pack and pulling out his notebook to grab something at the bottom, "I did."

Calling it a shovel was generous—it was a trowel if anything, perhaps even an overlarge spoon—but it did the job. Lore knelt on the ground before the tree, which out of channeling-space looked like any other tree in this forest, and dug into the earth. Behind her, she heard the telltale scratch of pen on paper. Raihan cataloging her movements, keeping a record.

The piece was buried deep and tangled in roots, a mark of how old the tree had been before having every bit of life sucked away to make an easy marker.

Easy for someone who could channel, anyway.

It took nearly an hour for Lore to extricate the piece from the ground. The song in her head picked up speed and volume, loud enough to make her grit her teeth. Raihan was silent as she worked, scribbling away in his notebook.

Nyxara had shown her almost all her memories, a first-person-point-of-view trip through becoming a god. But there were parts Lore hadn't had time to see—the Godsfall, its immediate aftermath. She could imagine Nyxara stumbling into the forest sometime during that long fight with Apollius as he slammed her into island after island, hiding the shard and covering this tree in Mortem. So that one day, someone could find it. One day, someone could bring this cycle to an end.

Gingerly, Lore disentangled the Fount piece from the roots. It was thick, a block of heavy stone with one smooth edge. She turned it over in her hands.

Carved on one side, a tiny crescent moon.

The thing looked dull, but her hands sparked to hold it, a frisson snaking down her limbs. She might be the avatar of a goddess, but this was bigger. A piece of the world's soul, hidden in the earth, waiting.

A storm came over her. That was the easiest way to describe it. The Fount piece almost fell from her suddenly numb hands, magic coursing like a lightning strike. It was hard to hold on, hard to keep her grip as power ripped through every vein, scouring her out. Searching her, making sure she was worthy. Lore's mouth wrenched into a silent cry, pain spearing through her, more intense than any she'd ever known. Her bones felt like they were slowly separating, pulled out of alignment; her muscles followed, the meat that made her body tugged in opposite directions to make room for something larger, something *more*.

As soon as it began, it stopped. Too quick for her to scream.

The song surged again, triumphant, and then settled back into a low hum.

"Did you find what you were looking for?" Raihan asked, oblivious to the trial she'd just endured.

Lore cradled the piece of the Fount to her chest. "Yes," she murmured. "Yes, I did."

🦋

"So you're a channeler."

"We established that."

"And this...rock...is something important for channeling?"

"Yes." Lore carried the piece of the Fount in her arms like a baby. Raihan had offered to put it in his pack, but she declined. She didn't want it far from her, even though holding it made her hands feel full of pins and needles, worse than she'd ever gotten from channeling Mortem.

He stopped ahead of her on the path, turned with narrowed eyes. "You expect me to buy that?"

Lore's fingers arched, the awareness of his Spiritum as concrete as her awareness of the dirt beneath her feet. She didn't want to kill Raihan, but she would if she had to.

She didn't wind the threads of his life around her fingers, didn't so much as give an experimental tug. But Raihan sighed anyway, shaking his head. "Look. Clearly, you're more than just a channeler. And clearly, that is more than just a rock. I helped you find it and didn't make a fuss about you trying to steal from me; the least you could do is be honest."

And it was true. Part of being a good liar was knowing how to give the barest glimmer of honesty; she could tell him what the shard was without compromising her mission. It wasn't like he'd tell Dani.

"This," Lore said, paradoxically holding the stone closer to her rather than offering it out as she spoke of it, "is a piece of the Fount."

He stared at her. He stared at the rock. Then he let out a quick, shocked laugh. "Seriously?"

"Seriously." Maybe he'd just think her mad. That was fine.

But for all his laughter, Raihan still looked curious. He stepped forward, as if he would examine it; Lore gripped it closer to her chest, fingers arching again, pulling a strand of Spiritum this time.

It was just enough to be a warning; Raihan didn't appear to know what she'd done, but he stopped anyway, hands held up. "I'm not going to take it from you, promise. I just want to see it."

Even if he tried, she could make his heart explode in seconds. Cautiously, Lore handed him the piece.

Raihan took it and immediately hissed in pain, fumbling his grip. It would have fallen to the ground had Lore not caught it.

Shaking his hands like he'd burned them, Raihan grimaced. "How do you stand to touch that thing?"

She shrugged.

He got out his notebook and flipped to a mostly unmarked page, gesturing for Lore to set the Fount shard in the middle. He studied it, writing down dimensions. "You know, I'm not entirely certain I believe you. But I saw the finder, so clearly, this is something having to do with the Fount." He carefully traced the shape of the piece, not touching the edges. "How did you know to look for it here? And what are you planning to do?"

She could probably get away with only answering one of those questions, so she chose the one less likely to reveal anything important. "I'm taking it back where it belongs."

He looked up, juggling his pen and his lighter. "Why?"

Lore shrugged, gave a reply that was as true as it was vague. "Because that's where it should be."

Raihan studied her for a moment. "You know," he said quietly, "you could just leave it with me."

She spun another strand of his Spiritum around her finger.

"I'll pay you for it, of course. You can have whatever you want."

"It's not for sale." Another strand of Spiritum. His heart sped up. "And you can't even touch it."

He pressed a hand to his chest but seemed to think the sudden uptick in his pulse was due to nerves. "This is exactly what I've been searching for. You don't understand the kind of advances something like this could make."

"I don't care." She could kill him right now. Burst his heart, sunder his veins. But she deeply, deeply didn't want to. She'd already killed so many.

And if she showed her hand with her power, there'd be no other option, if she wanted to keep him quiet.

So Lore reached into her boot and pulled out her makeshift shiv.

Raihan's eyes widened, his hands going from his chest to spread in surrender. "Fine, fine. You made your point."

She kept the shiv in her hand as she reached down and picked up the piece again.

He eyed her warily. "What do you think returning it to the Fount will do, anyway?"

"Fix things." The piece was too large to fit comfortably in her pocket, but Lore held it close to her chest, covering it from his view. "Make the world right."

"You have quite a lot of faith in a rock."

She shrugged again.

He pushed himself up off the forest floor, dusting char from his knees. "Maybe it can start fixing things," he said. "But I don't think that putting a fountain back together, even a magic one, is going to right every wrong in the world. People have to be involved in that particular evolution."

Lore wanted to ask what he meant by that, but she didn't. The sun was starting to rise; she needed to get back to Dani.

Notes taken, Raihan stood, slipping his book with its drawing back into his pack. "You never told me your name."

Another opportunity to lie, but Lore didn't take it. "It's Lore. Just Lore."

He nodded. "Well, Lore, I'll write your name down." He turned and started walking up the path. The sky was lightening, slowly, the sun rising behind the uncleared miasma of the Godsfall. "You can keep the Mount-finder if you promise to let me study that stone. Only in your presence, obviously. I'm not going to try stealing it from you." He gave her a sardonic look. "Not like you tried to steal from me."

"Done." Even though she didn't quite believe him.

When they reached Raihan's hut, he veered inside silently, raising his hand with a wave. Lore ambled down the path, fingers numb from holding the Fount piece. Behind the huts, the garden sprawled in low shadow, tenacious plants reaching for scraps of sunlight.

She stepped off the path, approaching the garden.

The crops were growing, but they could never be called *thriving*. Clearly, this was subsistence only, the Harbor community producing what they needed to survive and nothing else.

It made her think of the farmlands in Auverraine. The first time she and Bastian had channeled together, blissfully unaware of where it would lead.

Gently, Lore laid the stone on the ground, blood rushing painfully back into her hands. She shook them out as she knelt, sank her fingers into the soil.

So much death. The black of Mortem crowding out the thin golden threads of Spiritum. But they were there, shining in her reach.

She wanted to make a better world. Maybe she could start here.

Lore tugged at the threads of Spiritum in the earth, trying to strengthen them. But even though they came to her call, they refused to thicken, the leftover destruction of the Godsfall keeping them fragile. She channeled them through her body over and over, her will strong but slippery, unable to fix this centuries-old wrong on her own.

"Fuck it." She sighed, wiping dirt on her trousers. She picked up the Fount piece, defeat making it seem heavier than before, and trudged back to the path.

Dawn blushed the ash as she navigated her way to the empty cottage Sersha had given her and Dani. She breathed a sigh of relief when she saw that Dani was still asleep.

In the corner of the room was a worn leather backpack. Lore placed the Fount piece inside, then put the pack itself back where she'd found it, an unobtrusive bit of detritus from the countless people who'd come through this room.

When the time came to leave, she'd take this bag with her and trust that Dani wouldn't think too much of it. But she wouldn't tell her about the stone.

As if summoned by her thoughts, Dani stirred, stretching with a wide yawn. "Did you get it?"

Lore held out the silver instrument in answer, the key to navigating the ash-bound ocean. Dani leaned forward as if she would take it; Lore slipped it into her pocket.

A dark look crossed Dani's face, but she didn't press the issue. "Want breakfast? I'm sure it will involve fish somehow, but I'm too hungry to care." She pulled a face. "Let's try to avoid Sersha, though. I'm not keen on gardening."

Lore followed her out of the hut, only casting one glance over her shoulder at the bag in the corner. She could still feel the hum reverberating from the Fount piece, vibrating in her bones.

The song at the edge of her hearing flared again, another tide of melody, and then went silent.

CHAPTER NINETEEN

ALIE

We all must band together in heavy storms.
　　　　　　　　　　　–From a letter to the Balgian front lines

Alexis sent a note to her apartments the day after Apollius revealed Himself. *Please meet me in the Priest Exalted's office to discuss wedding preparations at noon.* They were acting as the Priest Exalted in enough capacities to allow the use of the office, apparently. She wondered why Apollius didn't go ahead and make it official. That line of thinking made her wonder what, exactly, the god's plans for the Church were. Alie stopped herself before she got too far along that road.

Honestly, the cover of the note was unnecessary. No one noticed Alie leaving her apartments, walking over the green toward the Wall, slipping out the storm drain. The guards were far too busy with the crowds.

Hundreds of people gathered just outside the Citadel Wall, waiting for another glimpse of Apollius. Word had spread fast, all of Dellaire knowing now that the day they'd been taught to pray for was finally here. Their god, in the flesh. Their god as King.

For such a large crowd, they were docile. A few enterprising folk had set up makeshift stalls, selling the same replicas of the sun-rayed crown that had been sold in the Wards on Bastian's Consecration day, touched up with gilt paint so the cheap metal below didn't show. Some murmured prayers or sang songs, broken melodies in rough voices. Others just stared at the Citadel doors, as if willing them to open and emit the Sainted King into the throng.

They'd probably get their wish soon. If there was one thing Alie had learned about Apollius, it was that He didn't often give up an opportunity to be worshipped.

There was no real reason for her to be out in Dellaire today. She had no meeting planned with Lilia, she was no longer plotting out an escape route for imminent use, and she could get to the Church through the Citadel green. Part of her was just...curious. Wanted to see how people would react to the news of gods, to the proof of them. Lereal's power thrummed beneath her flesh, urging her to grasp threads of wind, twist them to her will. It was oddly exhilarating, seeing people clasp their hands in prayer, seeing the tear tracks on their cheeks, and knowing the magic that so moved them reflected what she held.

She kept her hood up as she wove through the crowd. It extended into the South Sanctuary, the usually abandoned corridors now packed with the newly faithful. The hallway with the stained-glass windows of the pantheon was almost too full to walk down, penitents staring at the glowing panels as if it were their first time seeing them.

They looked fearful, gazing at the glass gods as if expecting Them to leap from the windows, to drag them screaming into a collection of hells.

Apollius had His scapegoats.

Thankfully, the guards hadn't let the congregation into the back hallways, where what remained of the Presque Mort did business. The staircase she'd climbed so many times before was empty, the nubby carpet warm from the light in the windows.

The statues were still there, one on every landing. Apollius Avenging, the moon-stone and sun-stone held in His hands. She stopped a moment, considering them, the obvious conclusion clicking into place in her head. Two of the pieces of the Fount. That was what they looked like.

And maybe...

Casting a surreptitious look behind her, Alie grabbed the stone held in Apollius's outstretched hand, the one with the sun. She pulled. It didn't come loose.

It wasn't the right one, anyway. She knew that as soon as she touched it. The power in her didn't leap, didn't recognize anything. This was just a rock.

"Worth a try," she muttered, and continued up the stairs.

Down the dark hall, to the familiar door. Alie pressed her eyes closed, just for a minute. Prayer had been a hard habit to break after a lifetime of being told she was blessed by birthright. That all she ever needed was to ask Apollius for what she wanted, and due to her station, He would be inclined to listen. It'd worked, sometimes. But now Alie knew the god had nothing to do with it. Answered prayers were just chance.

Still.

"Let them be all right," she muttered, thinking of Gabe and Malcolm in Caldien, Lore in the Isles.

She opened the door.

Alexis sat on the edge of the desk, nervously bouncing their knee. They stood when Alie entered. "You got my note. I wasn't sure it'd made it through the crowd."

But Alie wasn't listening. Alie was looking at the person seated at the desk behind them. "Lilia?"

"Excellent." Alexis ran a hand through their pale hair. "You've already met."

Lore's mother looked exhausted. The skin beneath her hazel eyes was bruised, and her white-gold hair frizzed around her temples. "We've met," she said shortly. "Alienor knows what we're looking for. She helped me get into the storeroom."

"Right," Alexis said. "Good. It's far less conspicuous for you to go with her than with me." They seemed extremely relieved not to have to explain everything. "Well then, we can—"

"Wait." Alie held up a hand, then waved it between the two of them. "How do *you* know each other?"

"We're colleagues, technically," Lilia said drily. "Alexis and I met when Gabe was drawing up the resolutions to reinstate the Buried Watch."

A resolution that had never made it all the way into law. It almost made Alie want to laugh, thinking about the mundanity of filled-out forms, how they'd once lived in a world where something so simple actually fixed anything.

"I got in contact with Lilia after all the Mortem disappeared from the catacombs," Alexis added.

"Under Gabe's orders?"

"Not exactly."

All of them conspiring without Bastian, the Presque Mort conspiring without Gabe. It made sense, she supposed. No one in the Citadel was an upstanding sort. "So I assume, if you two are working together, that you're no longer loyal to Apollius."

Blasphemy still felt strange on her tongue, and it still made Alexis flinch. "No," they said. "I'm not. This isn't how it's supposed to be."

They'd all been taught that whatever Apollius wanted was the way things were supposed to be, the morality of the world dictated by one god's desires. But they were far beyond that now.

Lilia had no patience for religious dithering. She sat forward in Gabe's chair and steepled her hands on the table. "Has Bastian managed to get a location for the Fount piece yet?"

"If he has, he hasn't had a chance to tell me." Alie snorted. "What with Apollius suddenly deciding that He wants to blow His own cover."

And kill Olivier to do it. Cecelia had shown up in court the next day, miraculously healed. At least Olivier had gotten his sister's health back through his bargain, though she couldn't forget the look on his face as Apollius raised him into the air, pumped his heart until his veins burst. He hadn't known he was going to die.

"I was afraid of that," Lilia murmured. "We need to move fast. Our contact in Caldien—"

"Your contact in *Caldien*?" Alie looked incredulously at Alexis. "Exactly how involved is this?"

They sighed, sitting once again on the corner of the desk. "Soon after the dock explosion, when I took the debris to Farramark, I met...someone." They didn't say who, and that annoyed Alie to no end, but she didn't press. "Someone who has been in and out of Auverraine, and has become a close companion to the Prime Minister. They're invested in making sure Caldien stays free of the Empire. And since Apollius has possessed our King and is using the Empire to make the Holy Kingdom..."

"That means they're working against Auverraine," Alie concluded. "So we're all traitors now."

"Thrilling," Lilia deadpanned.

"This contact claims that the Prime Minister knows where the piece of the Fount is," Alexis continued. "Apparently, Eoin is extremely interested in the elemental gods."

Dread shot from the top of her head to the pit of her stomach. "Does he know about Gabe and Malcolm?"

"He does," Alexis confirmed. "But that's a good thing in this scenario, I think. He'll keep them safe." They shifted on the desk. "As long as Gabe and Malcolm play along with what he wants."

Neither one of them said what they were thinking, though Alie was sure it was the same thing. Gabe had never been good at playing along when it didn't align with his moral compass. He held his convictions as close as he held his heart inside his ribs.

"Caldien was supposed to be in talks with Apollius," Alie said. "At least, that's what Jax told me."

If the implication of her being Jax's confidante fazed Alexis, they didn't show it. "I think," they said, "that in this particular case, no one is being exactly forthcoming with anyone else."

Lilia's eyes were sharp on Alie. "We need that location. Once the pieces start being found and brought to the Mount, Apollius will feel it. He'll know what's happening, and there is no length He won't go to in order to stop it."

"Good thing no one has the means to bring the pieces to the Mount yet," Alie said.

"Lore does," Lilia replied. "She's closer than anyone else. If she can find the piece on the Isles, that's at least a start."

"And according to certain myths, the Fount pieces can act as a compass," Alexis added. "Whoever has them can navigate to the Mount."

Lore was one of the people Alie couldn't quite break the habit of praying for, hoping she was as safe as she could be on the Burnt Isles, hoping she was holding on. "It seems presumptuous to think Lore is able to do much other than stay alive." She didn't mean to make it snap, but the words cracked like whips, and part of her hoped Lilia could feel the sting. "I told her that she needs to find the piece, but her schedule is full, what with the *mining.*"

Lilia's eyes, so like her daughter's, shuttered closed for a moment before opening again, lit with new resolve. "Lore is resourceful. If the piece is there, if she knows to look for it, she'll find it. And she'll find a way to get it to the Mount."

"You have quite a lot of faith in her."

"She's the only thing left worthy of faith," Lilia murmured.

"Even if Lore can do it, that's only one piece," Alie said. "How do we get the others there?"

Lilia gave Alie an arch look. "Sounds like you're cozy with Jax. You should work on getting cozy enough to ask for a boat."

Alie's cheeks heated. "We don't even have the piece yet."

"Doesn't hurt to be prepared."

Alexis sighed, standing up again to pace. "Alie, you need to try and speak with Bastian and see if he's found the location. We can't plan any further until we know that the pieces are within reach."

She arched a pale brow. "It's not quite as simple as inviting him over for tea."

"Of course not, but neither can you wait around and see if he calls for you." Alexis gnawed on their thumbnail. "We have to be proactive here."

"I repeat," Lilia said, "you can use Jax."

Alie's brow climbed higher. "I think you're overestimating—"

"Your hold on him? I'm not." Lilia shrugged. "If you didn't have influence over him, Alienor, he would have locked you in your room long ago, just to make sure you weren't doing exactly what you're doing."

The heat in her cheeks traveled to her hairline. Lilia was righter than she knew. Especially since Jax was aware of her Lereal problem.

"So use that," Lilia continued. "Tell him you want to set up a dinner with him and Apollius, long after sundown. Alexis will mastermind some sort of crisis that calls Jax away and gives you a moment alone."

It wasn't a bad plan, really. There was no reason for Alie to not go along with it. No reason for the idea of using Jax to be so unsettling.

She wouldn't go so far as to say Jax cared for her, but the beginnings of caring were there. It wasn't something she wanted to think about. It wasn't something she wanted to *use*.

But this was bigger than her wants. So she nodded. "I can do that. Probably tomorrow night, at the earliest. I'll let you know."

"Good." Lilia nodded. "You should be fostering closeness with him however you can. If Apollius decides to do something about you being Lereal's avatar, it could save your life."

Alexis's spine straightened, their eyes narrowing. "Lereal is *you?*"

Well, this was just getting better and better. Alie glared at Lilia. "Yes."

"And Apollius knows," Lilia said. "Once He decides to take action, having Jax as a shield will be beneficial."

"Maybe He won't do anything about it," Alie said, unable to banish a tiny filament of hope. "Maybe Bastian will kick Him out before He can."

Lilia's expression softened, almost pitying. She said nothing.

And that was the end of their meeting. Alie turned to go, leaving Alexis and Lilia in the shadows of Gabe's old office. She didn't say goodbye.

"Now, what exactly was this all for, Alie?"

Her shortened name coming from Apollius would always make her cringe. It sounded wrong, for all that His voice was Bastian's.

Across the table set up in Alie's sitting room, Apollius lounged with His elbow thrown over the back of His chair, the remains of a flaky pastry scattered on His plate. The last hour had been full of empty pleasantries, the kind of non-talk that Alie was used to as a Citadel courtier. But as dinner dwindled into dessert, and as the door to her suite remained closed with no interjection from Alexis, her conversational skills dried up.

Where in every hell *was* the acting Priest Exalted?

Though it wasn't like Jax was being obtrusive. He'd barely said two full sentences all evening, instead methodically draining glasses of wine as if they were water. He'd been fielding audience requests for Apollius from courtiers and commoners alike all day, and the strain was clear on his face.

The courtiers had mostly kept to themselves for the first days after the show of godhood, but now they were coming out of their apartments, waiting outside the Sainted King's chambers. He relented at least once a day, walking among them, soaking up their awe.

The requests for a royal audience had flooded beneath Alie's door, too, since she was still technically an adviser. She'd shoved them by the fistful into the fireplace, making her sitting room almost unbearably hot.

Thankfully, the fire had died down by now. Alie smiled and folded her hands in her lap. She could dither, ask if she needed a reason to treat her King and her future husband to a private dinner, but it wasn't in her nature. They'd expect to be here for a purpose, and she'd landed on one that would capture both of their attentions. "I wanted to talk to you about moving up the wedding."

Jax's pale eyes widened, his wineglass halting halfway to his mouth. Apollius's lips spread in a slow, cold smile.

"Moving it up?" He reached over and clapped Jax on the shoulder. "I didn't think you'd be so eager."

She'd thought often of what Lilia said in Gabe's office yesterday. How having Jax care for her could be helpful, how she should encourage it. And she'd come to the same conclusion. Even if it made her uncomfortable, like a fine film of dirt had settled over her skin and sunk so deep she couldn't wash it off.

Alie cast a fleeting glance at Jax, not having to fake the nerves or the blush rising to her cheeks. "It seems silly to put it off, when it could help bring some stability to the transfer of power. Especially now that You've revealed what You are."

Next to his god, Jax carefully set down his glass. "I don't want you to feel any pressure," he hedged. "We don't have to move too soon—"

"I think it's a splendid idea," Apollius interrupted. He crossed His legs carelessly, sitting back in His chair with a self-satisfied grin. "We can have everything ready two weeks from now, I think. Will that work?" He turned a wolfish grin on Jax. "Or is that still too far away?"

Jax looked like he'd swallowed a handful of rocks. His eyes swung from Apollius to Alie, almost beseeching, begging her to tell him this wasn't a joke. That she really wanted to marry him in two weeks.

Her heart knotted up in her chest.

"That should be fine," Jax said, his voice slightly strained. "Two weeks is more than enough time."

"Excellent." Apollius smiled at Alie, showing all His teeth. "What an auspicious beginning to our Holy Empire."

At that moment, a knock on the door. Finally.

"Come in," Alie called, trying not to sound relieved.

Alexis opened the door, their eyes going first to Alie, a quick flash of apology for their tardiness, before looking at Jax. "Your Majesty, a word? Lord Bartolmy has requested that you meet him in the North Sanctuary. Apparently, it is a matter of some urgency."

Jax turned to look at the acting Priest Exalted with his eyes narrowed. "Can it wait?"

"I wouldn't advise it, Your Majesty. He is...insistent."

Some courtiers had been pushier about divine audiences than others. A few of the more pious ones had resorted to standing in the North Sanctuary day in and day out, refusing to move until they had their moment with their god. Bartolmy was one of their number.

With a weary sigh, Jax stood. "I'll take care of this in short order, hopefully. If not..." He turned and looked at Alie, achingly earnest. "It has been a pleasure, my lady. I look forward to making our future plans."

"I'll bet you do," Apollius said with a grin.

Jax followed Alexis back out the door, the two of them speaking in low tones.

Showtime.

Apollius's smile grew sharper corners. "Clever," He said softly.

She refused to show Him fear, though that was the only thing running through her, cold as Lereal's wind. Alie said nothing, staring at Him, willing her friend forward. Willing her half brother to take control, if only for a moment.

A spasm in Apollius's fingers, still wrapped around a fork. A flicker of brown in His golden eyes.

"Fuck," Apollius hissed through His teeth. His hand lifted, the fork falling. His body cramped to the side, expression in flux between fury and fierce determination.

He fell over, nearly out of the chair, the spasm in His fingers traveling through the rest of Him, muscles twitching.

When He sat up, his eyes were dark, with no trace of gold.

Bastian.

Alie's hands fluttered in her lap, once again fighting back the instinct to run to him and make sure he was all right. But Bastian was strictly business; he knew their time was short.

"The ring," he said, his voice hoarse. "The one I gave Lore when we got engaged. It's a map. Or something like a map, anyway."

She nodded, no time for wondering how a piece of jewelry could be a map. "Where is it?"

He grimaced. "That's the thing. I don't—" His mouth pulled to the side, eyes flashing gold before going brown again. "It's hidden. Somewhere dark; that's all I know. You'll have to—"

Bastian's head wrenched to an alarming angle, every tendon in his throat standing out in sharp relief, his entire body quaking so hard, she thought he might break a bone.

It shook Alie from the staid, cold shell she'd built around herself for this dinner. Apollius wouldn't kill Bastian, not on purpose—He needed his body. But she couldn't imagine things would go well for Bastian if he pushed too far.

She jumped up from her chair and rushed to Bastian's side,

putting one hand on his forehead as if she could soothe Apollius out of him like a fever. "Bastian, don't strain too hard, it's all right…"

The tremors stopped, one last seize before Bastian's body went limp. Her heart and stomach changed places in the seconds it took him to breathe again, her pulse hitting so hard she felt it in the back of her tongue.

His neck slowly bent forward, overcoming the weight of His head in an unnatural roll. Apollius grinned at her, golden eyes bright, a gleam of sweat across His brow. "He put up quite a fight that time."

Alie backed away, wiping the hands that had touched Him on her bodice.

Apollius shook out His limbs as if Bastian were an irritating insect to banish. "That was a bold move, Alienor. I didn't think you had it in you." He chuckled. "You'll do an excellent job keeping Jax in line, if you stop pushing Me."

He should be raging at her. She would be less afraid if He was.

Completely unruffled, Apollius leaned forward in His seat, elbows braced on His knees, and gave her a sliver of a smile. It looked so much like one of Bastian's expressions, the one he had right before he eviscerated someone with his words. Seeing how they melted into each other made dread chew at the bottom of her spine.

"Do you think," He said softly, "that you are really that cunning, Alie?"

Alie schooled her face to impassivity and said nothing, nothing, though her hands fisted in her skirt hard enough that she felt threads breaking beneath her fingernails.

"I have kept you alive primarily as a mercy," Apollius said, as cool and collected as if they were discussing the weather. "There are easier ways than murder to get what I need from you, and I would much prefer them. I am not a brute, despite what My wife's mortal costume would have you believe." He sneered. "I can be infinitely reasonable. The fact is that you are more useful to Me alive than dead. Jax likes you, and I grow weary of jumping through his hoops. Having something to distract him makes My life much easier."

Her mind raced as more silken threads broke beneath her panicked grip. He knew. Of course He knew, just like Lilia said. But if He did, if there was a way to force her to give up Lereal's power, why wasn't He doing it? What did He gain from allowing her to keep it?

"All of this has more to do with free will than you think," Apollius said. He sat back, picked up His wine. "I could kill you to take what is rightfully Mine. But as I said, you are an asset. An Arceneaux, and we all know I'm particularly fond of those." A dainty sip, swirling His cup. "It makes much more sense for all of us if you decide to give Lereal's magic up on your own. I can wait. They were always the weakest of Us."

In the back of Alie's mind, a breeze, cold and biting, not gentle. The harbinger of a storm to come.

"And if I won't give it back?" she said quietly.

She'd grown up in proximity to power. Maybe that was why it had never occurred to her as something to want. But now that she had it, the idea of giving it up was hard to swallow.

He cocked His head, smile widening. "You will, Alienor. Hasn't watching your brother suffer been enough to convince you? Do you really want to surrender to a god that never should have existed? They may have been the weakest of Us, but They are still divine. Whatever kindness They show you now is temporary. The desire to live is stronger than any compassion." He snorted. "Lore is proof of that."

She stayed silent. So did Lereal.

"Now." Apollius finished His wine and set the goblet back on the table. "What were you and my host speaking of? I don't want to kill you, but I'm perfectly willing to alter my plans if necessary. I will get what I need regardless."

It was a relief to have to lie. Proof that Apollius couldn't look inside Bastian's mind and see what he did when he was in control.

It was also a relief that the bindings of honesty that let Gabe, Bastian, and Lore know when one was lying to the others did not extend to her.

"Lore," she said after a moment, putting a slump in her shoulders, a defeated undertone in her voice. "We were trying to find a way to rescue Lore."

"Her again." Apollius sighed. "I do wish Bastian would give her up. I'd be surprised if she even exists anymore. Now that she's close to the Fount, Nyxara has probably taken over."

Probably. So He didn't know. He wasn't omniscient. He was still just a man wielding stolen divinity.

There was something strange in the way He said it, though. Like He didn't quite want it to be true.

"Nyxara didn't want to take over," Alie said, warming to her role, wanting to keep Him on this subject. "She isn't like You."

"They are all like Me," He scoffed. "They're just better at hiding it. None of Them would allow this second chance at life to pass Them by. None of Them would let you go willingly."

Alie waited for a soft gust across the back of her thoughts, a reassurance. None came.

"That's the problem with all of you, really," Apollius continued. "You keep believing that I am the only threat. That I am uniquely evil, among all the gods. Among all of *you*." He shook His head. "But all of Them drank from the Fount. All of Them relished Their power. Sure, They gave it up eventually, but haven't you ever made a decision you regretted?" He pulled over the wine bottle and filled His glass again, all the way to the crystal rim. "And every single one of you mortal shells have done what you must for a measure of magic. To feel like you can turn back a tide." He stared into His wine, contemplative. "I'm not the worst of Us. I'm simply the most honest."

The door opened, Jax hurrying in, aristocratic features twisted in irritation. "I don't see why Alexis didn't turn him away," he said, seating himself once again. "Lord Bartolmy is convinced that You will bring down divine retribution if everyone in the court doesn't stop wearing dyed clothing. Something about a Tract interpretation."

"I don't give a shit about dyed clothing," Apollius said, grinning widely. "Honestly, the way you all have twisted around the Tracts is almost impressive."

Alie picked at her dessert, feeling Jax's gaze burn into her, willing her to look up.

She didn't.

Chapter Twenty

GABE

We* are there in your triumph and your defeat, in your stirring and your stillness.
                                    –The Book of Prayer, Tract 62

The tide washed over his feet in a steady beat, nearly matching his heart. The same beach, the same ocean, the same cliffs at his back. Maybe, if he stood here long enough, he'd see one of them again. Alie, with more news of what was happening in Auverraine.

Lore or Bastian.

His longing for one was the longing for the other, a fact that he couldn't quite wrap his head around even though his heart knew it. He and Bastian had been friends, then rivals, then bitter enemies, all of it suffused with a passion that raised his blood. He reacted to him in anger, always. But now, with the distance grown between them, he didn't know what he would do if he saw the man before him. Didn't know what he would say.

---

* Collective *we* only appears in first editions of the Tracts, later changed to singular *I*.

Something had changed. Or maybe it had always been this way, and he just refused to see it. At some point, the desire to punch Bastian Arceneaux square in the face had turned to a desire just to have him close.

And Lore—Bleeding God, it had always been Lore. Fierce desire had knocked him flat the moment he saw her in that alley, snarling and feral and Mortem-marked. She'd been the axis he and Bastian balanced on, the point to their triangle. The rope in their tug-of-war, as Lore herself had once so elegantly put it.

But maybe it was time to lay down the rope. Maybe that's what he'd really wanted all along.

"Gabe?"

He turned slowly, as if moving too quickly might banish her, a candle flame snuffed by a flash of movement. But no, there she was—Lore, standing up the beach, dressed in the same billowing white he wore. Her hazel eyes were wondering and her brown-gold hair streamed behind her, the scar on her temple only serving to add an edge to how soft she was. One of the most beautiful things he'd ever seen.

Lore looked scared to see him here, just a momentary flash of apprehension across her face. As if she wished he couldn't come, as if his arrival was the harbinger of something bigger.

Gabe didn't think. He just ran for her.

Whatever fear she'd felt was gone as soon as it'd come; she met him halfway, and his arms closed around her, lifting her up and crushing her against his chest; he was kissing her before the thought moved across his mind, her lips, her cheek, her forehead, whatever he could reach. Lore clung to him like someone drowning might hold fast to driftwood, something to keep them from slipping, something to keep them alive.

Even when Gabe put her down, he kept her in the circle of his arms, her forehead against his sternum. Lore was so *short*; not small, though, not petite. She was rounded and generous, and he wanted to keep touching her, never wanted to let her move too far away for him to feel.

She rested there, the beach silent except for their breathing, the waves making no sound at all. "I'd hoped that maybe we would all be here," she said softly. She didn't mean *all*, though; he knew that. She meant him and her and Bastian, the three points of their triangle.

He felt her tense as she said it, as if she hadn't meant to let the thought go. As if she were afraid he would take it as a wound, as her making a choice that he knew, now, she didn't want to make.

He didn't want to make it, either.

"Too much to hope for," he murmured into her hair.

Tension bled out of her, a softening relief. "I guess I should have learned my lesson with that one already."

Gabe twisted her hair in his hands. She sighed, leaning farther into him. Experimentally, he gave a tug.

Her sigh turned breathier, more of a gasp. Her chest heaved against him, and gods, he wanted her so badly.

Another gentle tug, guiding up her face. Gabe kissed her, tongue tracing against her lips. And for a moment, he thought this would finally happen, and everything in him turned liquid fire.

But then Lore flickered in his arms, going ghost before solidifying again. They didn't have much time.

Her heat-addled eyes cleared; defeat crossed her face.

"Soon," Gabe said, tightening his grip in her hair, strong on the back of her head.

She leaned into it. "Soon," she agreed.

Then Lore took a deep breath, looking up at him with a determined tilt to her chin. "I have something to tell you," she said. "Two somethings, really, and it seems like I need to hurry."

Gabe nodded. There was no time to be together physically, and no time to just *be*, either. He wanted that even more, really.

"First," Lore said, "you know what this place is, right? At least, why we're here?"

"Something to do with the gods in our heads, I'd imagine." The beach looked familiar, in a way. Not like he'd been there before, but like it was somewhere that had been described to him.

Though he had the fleeting feeling that he *had* been here before. Ephemeral and hard to hold on to, maybe a dream. The feeling of familiar fingers brushing his jaw.

"It's the Mount. Before the Godsfall." Lore looked over her shoulder, at the cliffs rising up to the blue sky. "It looks like what I saw in Nyxara's memories."

It should awe him to be here. But Gabe's capacity for awe was at its limits these days.

"We come here when we use our power," Lore continued. "At least, that's what Alie told me, when she and I showed up at the same time. And I only dream myself here on days that I've used quite a bit of Spiritum."

He arched a brow. "Not Mortem?"

Lore worried her lip between her teeth. Then, with a sigh, she held up her hand.

Gone were the charcoal-colored stars that had marred her palms that day after the explosion on the dock, when she knit the life back into nearly every courtier in the Citadel. Her skin was pale and unmarked, other than the eclipse carved into her hand.

Gabe took that hand, cradled it in his own. "What happened?"

"That's what I'd like to know." Her laugh was high, on the edge of hysterical. "I wished it away on the barge to the Isles. Said I never wanted it. And once I got to the Isle, my wish was granted." She closed her fingers. "At least, that's what Nyxara thought happened. The Fount took it back. I could hear Nyxara for a while afterward, even though I couldn't channel Mortem, but after... after I used a lot of Spiritum, She was gone, too."

She sounded almost bereft at that, but something like hope

leapt in Gabe's chest. "Would it be that easy for the rest of us to get rid of Them? Just wish it away?"

But Lore was already shaking her head. "On the Isles, maybe. Close to the Fount. But not far away. It isn't strong enough." She sighed. "Which brings me to my next point. The Fount is weak because It's broken."

"I know," Gabe said, then he told her about Eoin having the piece of the Fount in his Apollius Avenging statue. How he'd promised to give it to them, if they danced to his tune.

That part made her hold him closer, her hands fisted in the back of his shirt. She didn't speak, but the pitying look in her eyes said everything her mouth didn't. He was being used once again. At least this time he recognized it. At least this time it wasn't someone he'd once thought of as a father.

"Malcolm told me," she murmured. "About what Eoin was making you do." She paused. "About . . . hearing Them."

The source of that momentary fear, when she first saw him. Gabe nodded reluctantly.

"I should tell you to stop. To find another way to get the Fount piece." She closed her eyes and leaned into his chest. "But then I wouldn't see you."

"And I wouldn't listen," Gabe replied. "Because I have to see you."

Another sigh, humid against his skin. "So we know where the pieces are," she said after a moment. "At least, if Alie can find the one in the Citadel, and Eoin actually gives you the other. I found the one on the Isles."

"I'll do whatever I have to," he said, leaning his cheek on the top of her head. "Whatever Eoin asks."

So much for his dignity. He'd leave it in scraps. He'd burn himself alive if that's what Eoin wanted, just to see if the flames hurt.

"Bastian once told me I didn't realize when I was being used," Lore murmured. "He said that I was so used to it, I didn't recognize it, as long as it was done kindly." She moved back, looked up at him. "The time for kindness is over, I guess."

"It doesn't matter," Gabe reassured her, still stroking her hair. "As long as we can find the pieces and somehow get them to the Fount, it doesn't matter. We'll get our lives back."

"Will we?" She wiped her eyes. He hadn't realized she was crying. The sight of it set a deep ache in his heart; Lore hated crying, hated showing that weakness. "Seems more like we're trading one kind of puppetry for another."

His brow furrowed.

"One piece where I am, one where Alie is, one where you and Malcolm are." She huffed an angry sound. "Does that sound a bit too coincidental? Our strings are being pulled, still. You know how I found the piece? I heard singing. Something directing me where to look. It has to be the Fount. Interfering, but only sometimes. Calling to me now that I'm close enough." She shook her head. "Even if we win, we aren't free."

Gabe thumbed away a tear track. He didn't speak.

Here, in his dreams on the beach, his mind was solely his own. But he thought about those other dreams. Hestraon breaking off the flame carving, leaving it somewhere on the Mount. He should tell Lore about that.

But did it matter? They'd find it when they got there. There was no need to distress her further.

And it sounded like she might be thinking the same thoughts he'd been trying to banish. About power. About how giving it up wasn't so easy.

"The pantheon and Apollius might be gone," Lore continued, "but if we repair the Fount, It just takes Their place. Sure, It will be better. It will make the world act as it should." She rubbed the back of her wrist over her eyes again. "But we've seen how divinity works, Gabe. How everything is manipulated, even when it's benevolent. How do we go back now that we know?"

He didn't have an answer for her. In the deep of his mind, glowing embers, creeping flames.

The magic itself was not evil. It was what you did with it, how you shaped the tools given to your use. And who was to say the Fount was the best wielder of that tool?

Lore leaned back, her arms still around him, trusting him to anchor her. He couldn't read her expression, somewhere between afraid and determined. "There's something else. Something that will make you angry with me."

Gabe tucked a strand of hair behind her ear. "Honestly, I'm too happy to see you to be angry, but do your worst."

That was apparently the wrong thing to say; her eyes closed tight before opening again, though she looked into the middle distance over his shoulder instead of at his face. "I killed Anton."

For a moment, nothing. His mind ran clear as a mountain stream; his body had no reaction. Then, a crush, guilt and sorrow and horrible *relief* making him bow forward, now his turn to make her hold him up. It bent him nearly in half to bury his head in her shoulder, but he couldn't imagine letting go of Lore, couldn't imagine any other port in a storm.

She stroked the overgrown hair at the back of his head, a slight tremble in her fingers. "Do you want to know about it?" she whispered. "I can tell you, if you do. But you don't have to know."

Muffled, hidden in her hair. "Tell me."

So she did. How she sneaked into the greenhouse, that night after the tomb broke in the catacombs, after she gave Nyxara her first bodily death. How she cut off his head with the garden shears.

"He was in pain, Gabe," she murmured. "That wasn't any kind of life, not really. I was trying to be merciful. As merciful as I can be."

That was a kind of confession. Deep down, Lore was not a being disposed to mercy. Even without the Buried Goddess in her head, she was a dark and harsh thing, beautiful in the way a sharpened blade was beautiful.

"I know," Gabe said. He took a deep breath. "I know."

A pause on the silent beach. Time was slipping away from them. He could feel Lore going more diaphanous, melting into the air. Waking up.

"I should be grateful," Gabe said finally. "That you could do what I was too weak to."

"Not weak," Lore corrected, grabbing his jaw, making him look at her. "Too good."

But that wasn't right. If Lore was a dark and harsh thing, so was he, down in the bedrock of himself. Even if he'd tried so hard to scrub those stones clean.

She faded away, slowly. He stood there as it happened, until she was gone, until the circle of his arms was empty.

Gabe closed his eye.

❦

The scent of burning dough woke him—Val was probably trying to help with breakfast again. She'd taken it upon herself to be useful since they moved in a week or so ago.

Gabe forced himself out of bed, performed the barest hint of ablutions at the basin in the corner, picking up the straight razor meant for his face and turning in the spotted mirror to try shaving his head instead. He'd never kept it as short as Malcolm, shaven straight to the scalp, but it was probably all he could manage at the moment.

His fingers lingered on his hair, where Lore had run her hands through it in his not-dream. He put the razor down.

Downstairs, a cheery girl from the market was delivering milk and eggs to Mrs. Cavendish, the landlady. The delivery girl's name was Lucie, and before they'd moved in, she apparently only came by once a week. Ever since she saw Gabe, she'd been here every other day.

She sat on the edge of the table, eating a scone Mrs. Cavendish had provided—one that wasn't burnt, so probably not the responsibility of Val. "Oh, don't worry, I don't have more deliveries today!"

"Then we'd love for you to stay, dear," Mrs. Cavendish said.

Mari, seated at the table with coffee, looked at Gabe and hid a smirk behind her mug when she saw his grimace. He took a seat as far from Lucie as he could.

Oblivious, Lucie leaned conspiratorially close, nominally looking to Mari before turning back to Gabe so they were both included. "Did you hear about what happened?"

Gabe picked up a scone. "No."

Lucie seemed thrilled to be the one to impart the news. "The Sainted King in Auverraine is claiming to be Apollius reborn."

It wasn't news to Gabe, obviously, but he didn't have to feign his surprise. His pulse kicked in his wrists, and his breath hitched.

"Well, I never." Mrs. Cavendish shook her head at the oven. "It seems something dramatic is always happening in Auverraine."

"Quite a claim." Mari's smirk had fled the scene, her face grave. "Where'd you hear that?"

"Oh, everyone is talking about it." Lucie waved a hand. "I heard it from Matilda, who heard it from Grace, who learned it from her husband, who guards at the Rotunda in the evenings for a little extra pay. Between that and a new Arceneaux sister, it seems things are interesting in Dellaire." She grinned at Gabe. "Makes you glad to be here instead, right? I'm glad you are, anyway. Dangerous down there."

He was not one to be flirted with often—he didn't have the demeanor for it, and the Presque Mort tattoos on his palms put off anyone who might be brave enough to look beyond his glower—but Gabe knew Lucie was flirting with him.

She was very pretty. Logically, he knew that. Green eyes and bright-red hair the color of poppies, an easy smile. But he was spoken for. Spoken for twice over.

"Interesting," Mari said, when it became clear that Gabe wasn't going to give the verbal reaction Lucie wanted. She managed a wry smile. "It was always clear that the King thought highly of himself, but claiming to be a god is taking it to another level entirely."

Lucie laughed, sliding off the table. "Well, they say he's as handsome as a god, so I guess it went to his head. I've only seen portraits, myself. They're certainly godlike, though I think some artistic liberties were taken."

"No," Gabe murmured. "He really looks like that."

"Then that Queen of his he sent to the Isles must truly rue the day she killed his mistress," Lucie said, headed toward the door with her basket swinging on her arm. "A crime of passion, I know, but if I was marrying a King who looked like that, I would turn a blind eye to someone on the side."

Gabe swallowed down the harsh retort that rose to his tongue. It tasted bitter.

With a wave, Lucie was gone. He and Mari both waited until the sound of her footsteps had faded away and Mrs. Cavendish had bustled into the other room.

Then: "Fuck," Mari said, forehead in her hands, elbows braced on the table.

"Quite," Gabe replied.

Gabe left the house with his scone half eaten. The walls were starting feel like prison bars, and nervous energy kept building in his body, desperately needing an outlet. He gathered his cloak and walked out into the mist, planning to wander around the city until the exertion made him feel slightly less like screaming.

The citizens of Farramark walked fast, the weather not lending itself to lingering. But today there was a person standing in the pre-rain, wearing a hooded cloak, leaning up against the wall of the neighboring house, and smoking a cigarette. Gabe didn't think anything of it.

At least, not until the person pushed off the wall and started walking.

They stayed yards behind Gabe, ambling along the street. Entirely possible it was nothing.

But at this point, Gabe didn't count on that.

He took a side street at random, trying to look nonchalant. Moments later, the person with the cigarette was behind him. Another side street, headed left again; the person took that turn, too.

So he was being followed. Wonderful.

His plans for a long walk to pass the time soured. Gabe headed for the fighting barns. If Eoin was having him followed, maybe it was to protect his investment. Make sure Gabe didn't do anything that could compromise his safety, at least not before Eoin had seen him flick a flame in and out of existence at least a thousand more times.

All the way to the barn, the person followed, staying a few feet behind, never approaching any closer. When they were on the right street, the whoops of the crowd and crash of fists faint but audible, the person stopped next to another wall and lit another cigarette, within view of the door.

Gabe marched into the barn. He stayed at the back of the crowd, too far away from the ring to see anything. A crunch as a fist met a nose. Cheers and boos as a winner was called.

He stayed by the door and watched his follower smoke.

A minute. Two. Five. They flicked the ash to the ground, and then started up the street, apparently satisfied that Gabe was occupied.

When they were almost out of sight, Gabe slipped out into the mist. Turnaround was fair play.

The follower walked much faster now that they didn't have to worry about tipping Gabe off. It was obvious within two turns that they were headed to the Rotunda.

Gabe hung back, watching them approach the building and continue around the side, to the same entrance where they'd attended their first meeting of the Brotherhood. He walked slowly, keeping close to the sides of buildings, as they produced a key, unlocked the door, and slipped inside.

With a burst of near-silent speed, Gabe ran to the door, shoving his fingers into the gap before it closed all the way. He gently pushed it back open just enough to slip inside, then twisted the handle so it didn't make a sound as it closed.

The staircase was dark, but there was a dim glow down at the bottom. Someone was here.

He didn't press his luck by heading down the stairs. Gabe stood as close to the wall as he could manage, made his breath quiet.

"I'm honored you chose me, Eoin, don't get me wrong." That must be the man who'd followed him. "But I must say, it seems Finn would be the obvious choice, since his entire line of work is subterfuge."

The man sounded nervous. Whatever Eoin was doing down there, it wasn't something the delegates of the Brotherhood apparently wanted to take part in.

Rich men, comfortable men, who didn't like changes to those comforts. Even the ones who were fascinated by god-power didn't want to think of it as more than an academic exercise.

"I have my reasons." Eoin's voice, slightly strained. A clang of metal, something dropping to the floor. He hissed. "Damn, that's hard to hold on to."

"Seems an odd place to keep such a valuable thing."

"You say odd, I say safe."

"I suppose that's true," the other voice muttered. "Especially once you solder the door shut."

Eoin huffed a sound that wasn't quite a laugh. "Did you bring it?"

A ruffle of cloak fabric. Then a hiss. The smell of fire burned in Gabe's nose.

"A handy thing," Eoin said.

"My farrier uses it." The Brother's voice was strained, as if he was holding something heavy. "Helps direct heat. Apparently, they're used all over what used to be Myrosh."

Whatever Eoin was doing with the tool the Brother brought was quick work. The hiss shut off, and the burnt smell abated. "Excellent. That should stay secure until I'm ready to open it again."

"How exactly do you plan to do that?"

A grin in Eoin's tone, all teeth. "It shouldn't be a problem." A rustle of fabric. "This one, though, stays with me."

They mounted the stairs, boots on stone. The wall next to the staircase extended a few feet in either direction before hitting another; Gabe pressed himself into the far corner, where the dark was deepest, and pulled his hood over his head. He was fairly certain Eoin wouldn't harm him, even if he was found out, but he didn't want to test the theory.

The shadows were deep enough to give cover, and when Eoin and the unnamed Brother opened the door, the dim light from outside only served to deepen them. Eoin wore a pair of thick leather gloves, and he grimaced as he peeled them off, shaking his hands. "We'll have to come up with a solution for that. The tongs worked to get it off the statue, but we can't rely on them forever."

"At least the dagger doesn't give you trouble."

"Silver linings. Though Mount-mined metal used to be all over the continent; they couldn't charge such exorbitant prices for it if no one could touch it."

The other Brother cast an uneasy glance behind him. Gabe held his breath and pressed hard into the corner.

They left without seeing him.

Gabe counted to two hundred, slow, giving them time to get away. Then he crept down the stairs.

At first, he couldn't tell what was different. The same packed dirt floor, same false Fount, same stone walls.

Well. Almost the same.

In the corner, there was now a metal door. Or it would be a

door if it hadn't been melted shut at the edges. The copper bubbled, still hot from the fire Eoin had used, better than any lock.

Clearly, he'd hidden something here. And Gabe had a good idea of what.

He could melt the door off, take the Fount piece, and put the door back. No one would be the wiser.

His hands were already raised to channel fire when he heard footsteps at the top of the stairs.

Fuck.

There was no time to dart back to his dark corner, and the room was lit with sconces, all open with nowhere to hide. Desperation clawed at his gut, nowhere to go, cornered like a mouse with a damn cat—

Use it.

It wasn't a suggestion so much as a command.

And Gabe followed it, because he had no choice. One moment, he was solid and corporeal. The next, he was fire.

Not quite fire. The potential of it, every atom of heat in the atmosphere. It tore him apart, flung him out into composite pieces. If he'd still had a mouth, he would scream at the pain of it, the wrongness.

Because those spaces of himself were wide enough for something else to inhabit.

Every movement was an instinct rather than something thought through. Gabe traveled through the air, out the door, over the streets of Farramark, an invisible and unheard war. Hestraon was strong; Gabe grappled with Him, trying to hold on to the bits of himself with more desperation than he'd ever tried to do anything. He understood Malcolm's fear now, understood what it felt like to have yourself obliterated while something else tried to gather the scraps and turn them to another will.

We want the same things. Hestraon in his mind, Hestraon fighting forward. *I can do them better than you. Let Me.*

But he couldn't, he couldn't.

Fine. The god relented. *You'll come around.*

Gabe came back together like a thunderclap, the atmosphere rending to give him space where there'd been none before. It took him a moment to realize he was in the foyer of the boarding-house, slumped just inside the door. It took him another moment to realize Malcolm was staring at him, mouth agape, a cup of tea dangerously close to dropping from his hand.

"What in every hell happened to you?" he asked. Though the panic in his eyes and the wariness in his voice said he knew. Said he was waiting to see if he was still himself, or Hestraon.

"It's me," Gabe said. "And I think I know where Eoin is keeping the Fount piece."

He shared the news quickly: the Brother who'd followed him from the library, the odd door in the wall beneath the Rotunda soldered closed.

Malcolm was already rushing to find Val and Mari before Gabe finished speaking. "We have to go check our ship."

"What makes you think that?"

"If Eoin is having you followed to make sure you don't go any-where he doesn't want you to, do you really think he'd leave an open means of escape?"

Ten minutes, and they all were running to the dock.

Val was the first to realize something was wrong. She stopped, breath heaving, brows knit. "This is where we left it, right?"

Farramark harbor wasn't as extensive as the one in Dellaire. Only a handful of docks, and the one where they'd left the ship was decidedly empty.

Rage burned in Gabe's chest, in his palms. He turned to the low wooden fence dividing the harbor from the dunes and landed a punch square on one of the supports.

The whole thing went up in flames.

CHAPTER TWENTY-ONE

LORE

Do not let yourself be lulled: The first calm is the eye
of a storm, not its ending.
                        –From *Sailing Lessons* by George Merrou,
                            Auverrani naval captain, 465 AGF

It took Dani longer than either of them would have liked to find
a boat. They probably should have expected it—it wasn't like
there was much need for sailing vessels in the Harbor—but after a
day of compulsory gardening once Sersha found them, they were
even more on edge with each other than before.

When Lore was finished and caked in dirt, she went to
Raihan, fiddling with his silver instruments, carefully fielding
questions about her days in the Citadel. Despite the fact that
they'd each tried to steal from the other and that she'd threatened
his life, they were companionable. Raihan knew what it was like
to live on the run. Lore knew what it was like to be desperate for
answers that wouldn't come. They weren't friends, but a friendship could grow, given time.

So she felt incredibly stupid for not thinking of taking Raihan's
boat before Dani did.

On their second night in the Harbor, Lore crept into the hut after moonrise, hoping that maybe the other woman wasn't there. No such luck—she was pacing back and forth over the rough floor, and when she looked up, there was fire in her eyes. "So when were you going to tell me you'd gotten cozy with the Ferryman?"

"When I decided it was your business. So, never."

"You idiot," Dani hissed. "You let me spend a day looking for a damn boat when you could just convince him to let us take his?"

Her mouth opened for a poison retort, then closed again. It wasn't really a bad idea.

"You didn't think of that?" Dani tilted her head with a sneer. "It's really a wonder you survived in the Citadel for so long."

"He won't give it to us," Lore said. "He needs it for rescuing escapees." Part of the reason it hadn't occurred to her was because she knew Raihan would say no. They'd spoken of the work he did, how important it was to him to provide a way out of the Isles to those who wanted one.

"He does that maybe once every two months," Dani said, crossing her arms. "The rest of the time, it's just sitting there. Tell him we need it. To save the world, or some shit."

Which was why Lore was here again on their second morning in the Harbor, hoping Raihan would lend them his boat.

She didn't finesse the question. She just asked it outright, standing on his threshold with all his silver instruments pointing at her. "What would it take for you to let me borrow your boat?"

He looked up from his notebook, where he'd been scribbling in the margins of the page with his tracing of the Fount piece. Slowly, he closed it. "To get to the Fount?"

"No, to host a party." She rolled her eyes. "Yes, Raihan, to get to the Fount."

His mouth twisted to the side. "That would be less borrowing and more taking indefinitely."

Lore shifted on her feet. The rest of the thought hung unspoken—

if she took the boat, it meant no more ferrying prisoners from the Isles. "This is bigger than that," she said, as if he'd spoken it aloud. "This is..." She made a hoarse noise, not a laugh, and echoed Dani. "This is saving the world."

Raihan just looked at her, mouth still pursed, trying to fit something into language. "Is that what you think repairing the Fount will do? Save the world?"

She gave him a withering look. "I think it'd be a start."

"And what if I think the world is beyond saving?"

"Don't tell me you're a nihilist, too. I can only take one."

"Not a nihilist," Raihan said. "But I am of the opinion that the world can only be as good as the people in it."

Lore slumped into the chair by his piles of books. "The world is fucking doomed, then."

"Now you sound like the nihilist." Raihan poked at one of the sliver instruments, sending it spinning before it settled on Lore again. "Taking away a material good—a means for people to escape the mines—for something that might eventually be good, someday, seems like boarding up a well because you're hoping for rain."

Lore didn't have a rebuttal. She chewed her lip.

"You should fix the Fount," Raihan said after a stretch of quiet. "And maybe that will start the process of making things better. But as long as there are people on the earth, *fixing things* won't be a onetime occurrence."

"So it's pointless."

"Not pointless. But harder than fixing a Fount." He shrugged. "There are no absolutes, Lore. We won't ever reach some world-wide utopia where nothing bad happens again. Living is work. Goodness is work."

He was right, but she didn't like it. Didn't like the idea that she couldn't somehow fix everything and keep it that way. What was the point of power, if the universe couldn't be forced into goodness? If there wasn't a terminus that could be reached and maintained, damn the costs?

In the back of her mind, that place where Nyxara used to be, something nudged. The ghost of a glimmer, there and then gone.

"You can take the boat, if you want it," Raihan said finally. "It's still at the dock."

Lore looked up from the floor. "Come with us."

It hadn't occurred to her until this moment to ask, but now that she did, it made perfect sense. She could prove to Raihan that she could make the world be good. She needed someone to think she was capable of fixing something, that she alone could force the world to be what she wanted. She needed someone to believe in her.

A glimmer in her mind again, like sunlight cutting through clouds.

He looked at her with his brows drawn down, shadows cast over the planes of his face. The moment hung, expectant, a convict in the seconds before the gallows rope hauled them skyward.

"No," Raihan said.

She threw up her hands. "Why not? You're too smart to spend the rest of your life rotting away here. You said yourself that there's no way to safely navigate to the mainland; the Mountfinders only help on the Isles. So you're just going to stay here and breathe in ash until you die?"

"Everyone in the Harbor relies on one another. I have shifts to till the fields, turns to pull in the fish nets. I can't just abandon them." He paused, resting his elbows on the table. "And it doesn't...feel right, to leave. It feels like my place is here. For whatever comes next."

Lore didn't press him further. Intuition, that bitch, driving them all. Part of her wondered if Raihan felt like she had at the beginning of the summer, strung along on star-lines, played like a puppet by something bigger. She doubted he would tell her, even if she asked.

She also doubted she would see him again. Dani wouldn't want to linger, and Lore didn't, either. She wouldn't be able to fix the Fount until Alie and Gabe somehow found the other pieces, and somehow managed to get them to the Golden Mount. But surely, if she'd come this far, they would, too. Surely their puppet strings would play them in the right direction, bound like insects in spiderwebs.

"Thank you," she said. "For helping me."

Raihan nodded. He knew this was goodbye, too. "Good luck, Lore."

She left the hut as midday burned through the ash veil, casting shadows on the should-be-dead trees that had never recovered from the Godsfall. The village was awake, but no one spoke to her as she slipped through the streets, headed toward the tiny house Sersha had given her and Dani when they first arrived.

Dani was waiting, her nails dirty from garden work. She gave Lore a pointed look.

"It's done," Lore said, slumping into one of the chairs by the rough table. "He said we can take it."

"Then let's go." Dani brushed past her with barely a glance.

Lore stood with a sigh, gathering the bag with the Fount piece from the back of the room before following Dani out of the hut.

They were halfway down the dirt road before Dani turned back around, eyes narrowed. "What's in the bag?"

Dammit.

Lore kept her face impassive. "Food, mostly. Unless you wanted to keep eating jerky salty enough to pickle your insides for the entire journey? I also got us both a change of clothes. You smell."

It wasn't even a lie. Raihan had given her the food, and she'd found Sersha after gardening yesterday, asking for a pair of tunics and trousers in the loose, undyed linen that everyone in the Harbor wore. All of it was tucked carefully around the Fount piece.

Dani eyed her warily but didn't ask to see inside the bag. After a moment, she shrugged and kept going. Lore followed close behind.

The Harbor was bustling. The dirt road that housed both their hut and Raihan's was one of many, all spiraling out from the central green. Children played around the edges of the garden, the older ones helping harvest and till. Sersha was bent over, pulling potatoes from within a dark box she'd dug up.

A community. People helping one another. She was robbing the prisoners on the Isles of a chance at this, by taking Raihan's ship. The ash wouldn't let them go home, but they could make a home here.

Lore focused on her feet and tried not to think of that too much.

As they passed, Sersha raised her head. She didn't ask them where they were going, but she lifted her hand in a wave. Lore returned it. Dani didn't.

The beach itself was empty, Raihan's boat bumping against the dock with every swell of the waves. Lore eyed Dani's back. "I hope you know how to sail, because I sure don't."

"Relax." Dani clambered up the ship's side, then lowered the gangplank for Lore in an uncharacteristically thoughtful gesture. "I wasn't lying about having a lover at the shipyards, that day at Alie's tea. He taught me a few things."

Lore boarded the boat without a word.

"Now," Dani said, sitting the silver instrument on the deck. It spun, once, then pointed at Lore. "How do these things work?"

"Raihan told me." Lore gathered up the silver balance quickly, hoping Dani didn't notice how it reacted to her and the thing in her bag. "I have to take it below, set it up properly. Give me a second, and I'll tell you where to go."

For a moment long enough to make her stomach twist, Dani just stared at her. Lore twitched one finger, winding a thin thread of Spiritum. Just in case.

"Don't fuck with me," Dani said quietly.

"I'd never," Lore replied. "We are the very definition of mutually assured destruction."

Though was that really true now? Lore had no doubt that she could make her way to the Golden Mount using her own power. Steering the boat could be a problem, but even that she might be able to figure out, manipulate her magic in some way that made it unneeded. She could kill Dani right now, and it would barely interrupt her plans.

But...she didn't want to. So many deaths already piled on her heart, all the villages, Anton, Jean-Paul. She didn't want to add another unless there was no choice.

And she hadn't been lying, that day in the shipping office. She did feel for Dani. They were both only what impossible circumstances had made them, and what it had made them really wasn't so different, in the end.

Dani watched a minute more, eyes narrowed. Then she nodded.

Lore took the Mount-finder belowdeck.

The room where Raihan had kept the silver balances was cleared; he'd come back and packed them away at some point. Lore set hers in the middle of the table, warily watched the point of the pin like it was an accusing eye.

Well. Time to see what she could do.

Tucked into her bag, the Fount piece called out to her, singing its low song. With a glance at the door to make sure it was still closed, Lore pulled the carved stone from the tangle of spare clothes. The Mount-finder whipped around on its pin, pointing so directly it trembled.

Immediately, the world slipped into the grayscale of channeling-space.

Black threads of Mortem wound through the dead boards of the ship, wavering lines of pearlescence dancing with orange-red in the air. Every strand of the world, open to her senses.

A thick band of gold stretched out from the Fount piece in her hand, reaching forward. Through the ship, into the waves, like a gilded road. In her preternatural vision, she could see through the wooden walls, into the ocean beyond, that golden path leading into the depths of the sea.

The Fount piece was like a compass now that it was out here in the open ocean, close to its whole. Leading them to the source.

She didn't come all the way out of channeling-space as she left the room, staying far enough under for everything to still be black and white, to still hold the awareness of that ribbon of Spiritum emanating from the piece of the Fount.

On the deck, Dani waited, hands white-knuckled on the wheel of the ship, face all hard angles. Lore raised a hand, pointed in the direction of the golden road. "That way. It's a straight course to the Fount."

Dani spun the wheel.

The boat lurched in the proper direction, sent on its way by sails that Dani had apparently adjusted while Lore was below catching the breeze. When the Harbor was behind them, almost fully hidden in ash, Dani glanced Lore's direction. "I'm not sure how you feel about the whole only-channeling-Spiritum thing, but it's certainly an aesthetic improvement."

Lore knew what she looked like when she channeled Mortem. Opaque eyes, black veins. Her only reference for what she looked like now was what she'd seen on Bastian. The phosphorescence around his hands, the way he seemed to glow. She looked down at herself and saw the same, as if gold ran beneath her skin instead of blood, as if she'd swallowed the sun.

"It's an improvement all around," she said. Her voice sounded different. More resonant.

Dani gave her a sharp look.

Lore just gazed at her hands, glimmering softly, coated in a thin layer of light.

S omething was different.

The golden sea was shallower. Bastian wasn't sure how he knew that, since he seemed to float somewhere in the middle of it, continuously striving toward the surface. But after managing to dive to the bottom, to find that door that led out to the beach and the long corridor of memories, Bastian had a better feel for the parameters of his prison.

And they were shrinking.

It reminded him of a Mortem leak, a slow seeping of power from a godly body. *His* body, now, which was minorly concerning, even if he didn't have control of it most of the time.

Apollius's anxiety was a continuous static, a cloud that Bastian couldn't emerge from. There was still enough distance between them that he couldn't put an exact finger on its cause, other than assuming it had something to do with the shrinking he felt. But Apollius's worries didn't seem dire, necessarily. More like He was making a momentous decision. Like He'd reached a fork in the road, an unexpected turn in the path.

Bastian took advantage.

He dove down to that door in the bottom of his prison, stumbled across the now-empty beach, back into the corridor of memory. He remembered the approximate location of the door that held the recollection of the ring. He only needed a few seconds...

When he pulled the door open, the ring filled his vision, a first-person account of this moment. Bastian couldn't make Apollius in the past look at anything else, but he expanded his awareness, straining to take notice of the god's surroundings. A mostly dark room, though there, at the corner of his vision, was a cracked-open door.

Beyond, books.

He'd seen what he needed to see. Out of the corridor, back across the beach, back to the door and into the growing-shallow sea.

It wasn't smart to push his luck, maybe. But Bastian Arceneaux had always been more daring than smart.

He launched himself up, breached the surface, half expecting to be shoved back down—

CHAPTER TWENTY-TWO

BASTIAN

For all his faults, the boy has incredible strength of will.
—From the personal writings of August Arceneaux

No pain.

That, in itself, was remarkable. Every time he'd managed to wrest bodily control away from Apollius, it'd come with immense pain, his head aching like it would burst, every bone determined to twist the wrong way as the god fought him like an untrained rider on an unbroken horse.

Bastian twirled his wrists. He flexed his fingers. He bent his neck from side to side.

Then he grinned.

There was no real time to enjoy being back in his own body. It wouldn't last long. Already, the back of his mind was stirring, the place where Apollius waited, where he'd felt Him taking root right after the eclipse ritual, back before he knew what it was.

He had to find Alie.

He'd come to in his bedroom, blessedly empty—he could feel enough impressions of Apollius's emotions in the golden sea to know that was a rarity. For a being who'd been so singularly focused on making sure His wife had no other options but to stay by Him, Apollius had no issue with sleeping around.

The stray thought brought Lore to the forefront of his mind. Thinking of either of them—Lore, Gabe—and where they were, the dangers they could be facing, was enough to quicken his heartbeat.

No time for that. They could take care of themselves. Well, Gabe, anyway. He loved her dearly, but Lore's recklessness often got in the way of her common sense.

He had to hope she'd improved on that front.

Bastian threw on clothes and practically ran from his apartment. There was no guard outside the door; Apollius was in no danger from any mortal. Bastian kept to the shadows as he crept down the turret toward Alie's room, staying out of sight.

When he reached her door, he tried to keep his knock from sounding frantic. Apollius was fully awake, now, scrabbling at the back of Bastian's mind, trying to claw His way back into control. Bastian had practice keeping the god at bay, from those weeks when Lore was here and his affliction was mostly a secret, but it still wasn't pleasant. His head felt like it was being continually bashed with a hammer.

He could hold out now that he knew where the ring was.

Alie came to the door, brow creased. When she opened it, she flinched backward, made to slam it closed again.

"Alie, it's me." Bastian put out his hand, held it open. "It's me."

Her eyes searched his, closed in relief. Then she was all pragmatism. "How long do we have?"

"Not long. We have to go to the Church library."

She didn't question him. She just nodded and grabbed a shawl, wrapping it over her shoulders, toeing into slippers. "Let's go."

Miraculously, they didn't encounter any courtiers as they went out the Citadel doors—also unguarded, as if Apollius was daring someone to try something—and moved quickly across the southern green to the Church. The nobles that gathered there to try speaking with Apollius mostly kept to the North Sanctuary, and the majority of the others had already retired. Having a god among them had renewed their sense of propriety.

They didn't run into anyone until they reached the South Sanctuary.

It'd been stupid of Bastian to assume that there would be no one here, for all that it was the middle of the night. Honestly, it was lucky that tonight there was only one penitent, a young woman who couldn't be much older than he was, kneeling in the first pew.

A Presque Mort melted out of the shadows. Sophie, one of the monks he didn't know very well, a thick scar running over her forehead. "Holy One," she said with a deep bow, "I can escort You wherever You need to go, so that You aren't disturbed. I know You don't care to meet with anyone in this sanctuary." She glanced at Alie. "Should I send for the Emperor, as well?"

"No need." Apollius's voice sounded different from his own, brighter and more resonant, but Bastian didn't try to imitate it.

He thought he'd spoken quietly, but apparently it wasn't quietly enough. The woman at the front of the Sanctuary turned around.

Sophie moved in front of Bastian. "I'm sure You don't want to deal with this—"

"God?" the young woman asked, her voice raspy. Tear tracks gleamed on her cheeks.

He should leave. Their clock was ticking down; whispers of pain began in his head, his chest. But she looked so sad.

And so hopeful.

Bastian waved aside Sophie and started down the aisle. Behind him, Alie followed, silent.

The young woman couldn't decide if she should stand or kneel at his approach, getting halfway up before sitting down again. She finally landed on staying in her pew, her tear-shined eyes wide.

He didn't know what to do here. Apollius was a god; Bastian

wasn't. And the last thing he should want was to give anyone hope that Apollius was good, to sink them further into the delusion that this world was a just place, run by just gods.

But what would it accomplish, to stomp out hope?

He cleared his throat. "Why are you here?"

She clasped her hands in her lap, knuckles blanched. "It's my son," she murmured. "He's so ill. Has been since he was born. I've always prayed to You to make him well." She smiled, as if this were a good thing instead of a tragedy. "I thought perhaps You could hear my prayers better in here."

This was a bad idea. He could ask the woman to bring her son, try to heal him with Spiritum. But what were the odds that he'd be the one in control when she did? And what were the odds that, if he wasn't, Apollius would bother with healing one small peasant boy? If Bastian knew the god—and he did, intimately—it would be more likely for Apollius to make him sicker out of spite, to punish Bastian for these few moments of control.

So he'd better do it now.

"Bring him to me," he said, feeling Apollius grow stronger, feeling their clock wind down to zero. He gritted his teeth and held on. Just for a little bit longer.

Behind him, Alie's lips were a bloodless line.

The woman's eyes widened. She stood, bowing, a babble of thanks, and headed toward the door, out into the night.

Sophie watched her go. "Do you want me to lock it behind her, Holy One?"

"No," Bastian barked, one hand pressing against his temple. "I'll be back in a moment. Don't let her leave without me seeing the child." He stumbled out of the Sanctuary, down the hall, toward the Church library. Hurry. He had to hurry.

Alie caught up with him. "While I appreciate the show of magnanimity," she said, "that was probably not the best use of our time."

"Couldn't leave it." Reduced to fragments of sentences. "Can't choose what I do with it, most of the time. But I can right now."

She nodded in understanding.

The library was unlocked. They blundered in gracelessly, and Alie turned the bolt behind them. "Where is it?"

Bastian didn't try to speak, just headed toward the tiny alcove in the corner, the one where Malcolm had told him some prophecies were kept, the unimportant ones. This was what he'd seen in the memory, the sliver of light through that door just enough to tell him where Apollius and Gerard had been.

He pressed his palms against the wall.

The mechanism here was not magic, not like the doors Lore had opened with Mortem in the catacombs. Opening this door was just a matter of knowing where to place his hands, and though Bastian had never known about the secret chamber behind this wall, it was a fairly simple thing once you knew there was something to look for. He inched his hands over the wall until he found a place that stuck out, a stone not flush with the rest. He pressed down.

The door creaked open.

Beside him, Alie's eyes widened. "Myriad hells."

Had he not been preoccupied with the god trying to chew His way back into his brain, Bastian would have been stricken by the contents of the room. He was no stranger to obscene wealth, but the tangle of gold in here, the boxes of gems rough as if pulled straight from the Burnt Isles, was still mind boggling.

As was the state of the ring. It sat on top of a closed box, no case to speak of, as if it had been thrown there in a hurry.

Bastian guessed it had. He'd never stopped trying to fight his way free of Apollius; it seemed the god was warier of him succeeding than He'd let on. He must have tossed the ring in here right after taking it from Lore, before sending her to the Isles.

He picked up the ring and handed it to Alie. "Sunrise," he said

through gritted teeth. "Hold it up at an angle. Should show...
something."

She nodded, slipping the ring into her pocket. "Come on. You
don't have much time."

There was no energy left for speaking, every bit of him oriented
toward fighting off Apollius. Just long enough to heal the boy.
Just long enough to do one good thing.

He was there with his mother, small and bony, tired bruises
around his eyes that would be more at home on an old man than
a child. Bastian's vision was narrow, the sound in his ears soupy
and hard to suss out into individual words. He heard Alie's voice,
speaking softly to the mother. Sophie glowered at the end of the
aisle.

Bastian put a hand on the boy's forehead.

Like this, pushing so hard against Apollius he felt like he
might pass out, Spiritum and Mortem were easy to see. It was
something in the boy's lungs, the star-map of gold there marred
by a growing bruise of black threads, slowly alchemizing. It was
easy to channel that Mortem, turn it back to Spiritum.

Even though he could feel that the well of power was dwin-
dling. Being pulled away, somehow, a spool slowly spinning out.

But he'd done a good thing. The only one he was guaranteed.
He'd wasted so many opportunities for goodness, and damn him
if he'd let this one pass by, too.

"You're fine," he murmured. "You'll be fine."

His vision went black, then gold. Bastian went under.

CHAPTER TWENTY-THREE

ALIE

All that happens in the night eventually faces the light of day.

—Eroccan proverb

She knew when the change happened. When he turned from Bastian to Apollius, her brother drowned in the god who'd stolen him. His back straightened; His shoulders evened out. The line of His mouth went cruel. His eyes glimmered golden in the light of the Sanctuary candles.

"Well," He said, looking around. "What an interesting place to find Myself in the dead of night."

Alie clenched the ring in her dressing gown pocket, the prongs digging into the meat of her palm. Bastian had told her Apollius couldn't look into what he was doing while he had control of the body—the god had cut that cord when He fully took over. But that didn't mean He couldn't figure it out.

"Thank You." The woman with the sick son cared about nothing but the fact that he was healed, paying no mind to the Sainted King's slight changes in demeanor. Tears spilled down her cheeks as she hugged the child to her chest. "Thank You so much. We knew the world would become better, now that You're here. Everything will be made right, the earth a reflection of Your Shining Realm."

Something shuttered in Apollius's eyes at that. The sight of a god taken aback was an odd one.

But He clearly enjoyed the praise. He straightened and smiled, banishing the momentary unease that had flickered over His expression. "That's why I'm here," He said, ruffling the little boy's hair, the gesture stilted. "To make the world better."

The boy, for his part, mostly just seemed confused. His eyes kept swinging from his mother to the King, his pale brows drawn low and his hand fluttering around his chest, as if something was different there but he couldn't decide what.

"You got your miracle." Sophie didn't sound gruff, but she put on a stern expression as she stepped forward and waved toward the door. "The God of All Things is merciful."

"Oh, He is, He is." The woman bowed the whole way out the door, the endeavor taking much longer than it should as she kept turning around to do it. "I'll tell everyone of Your love and grace, my God, of Your goodness..."

Alie's grip on the ring tightened with every word.

When the woman and her son were finally gone, Sophie looked back at Apollius, questions that she wouldn't dare ask written clear across her face. After a moment, she went back to her post at the front of the Sanctuary in silence.

Beyond the stained-glass windows, the first fingers of dawn stretched into the sky.

It strengthened Apollius, made Him shake off the last dregs of Bastian. He tipped up His chin, closed His golden eyes, breathed deep. Then He vised His hand around Alie's wrist, and they marched out of the Church and onto the green.

"Now, Alienor," He said conversationally. "Care to tell Me why you and I were in the South Sanctuary in the middle of the night?"

Once again, Alie was desperately thankful that she was able to lie to Him. "I was praying."

Apollius scoffed. "You don't expect Me to believe *that*."

"It's customary for brides to pray nightly for the month before they're married." This part wasn't even a lie, though the tradition wasn't strictly upheld. Embroidering your lies with truth made them more believable. She'd learned that from Lore. "I might not be pious, nor feel that there is anything worth praying to, but it wasn't like I could sleep, anyway."

He smirked at her.

They passed Apollius's statue on the green, the empty plinths where the rest of the pantheon had stood now housing pots of roses. "He's stronger than I thought," the god mused softly.

"He wasn't here for long." Pointless to pretend that Bastian hadn't taken over at all. "He was confused, like he didn't know why he'd come to the Church. But he managed to heal the boy."

"Surprising that he would do anything to raise Me in public estimation."

"Bastian cares about people," Alie said. "He's not like You."

"You think too highly of him, but I appreciate your candor." Apollius grinned. "I see us having a fruitful partnership, if you finally come around to the fact that I've won."

If. She didn't want to think about what He'd do if she never came around. She doubted Jax could save her then.

Apollius headed back up the turret to the King's apartments. Alie lingered in the foyer, not wanting to obligate herself to walk with Him, nervously watching the sun creep over the horizon in the window. Part of her wanted to pull out the ring and try to decipher whatever map was hidden within it right here, but the chances of someone seeing were too high, even this early.

So she dawdled long enough to give Apollius plenty of head start, then bolted up the stairs.

As soon as her door closed, Alie pulled out the ring and hurried over to her window, throwing back the curtain. The sun was over halfway in the sky now, and Alie held up the ring so the morning light blazed through the heart of the gold-tinged diamond.

And...nothing.

The inside of the diamond glowed beautifully. She could see the facets where the stone had been cut and polished and nestled into its setting. But there was no map of any kind, and when she twisted it back and forth, no helpful beams of light shot out. There was nothing to suggest this was anything more than a normal, albeit very beautiful, piece of jewelry.

"Shit," Alie murmured.

Studying the diamond, turning it over in her hands with increasing desperation, made her think of Brigitte. Her friend who dabbled in jewelry, who'd been the first to notice that Lore's ring was Mount-mined.

And thinking of Brigitte made her remember that she was supposed to have breakfast with her this morning.

"Shit," she murmured again, and ran for her closet.

She and Brigitte had tried to be very intentional about their friendship, after what happened with Dani. Bri and Dani had always been closer than Alie and Dani were, so Bri took Dani's sentencing much harder. Alie knew that Brigitte still wasn't sure how to feel about her best friend being sent to the Burnt Isles. There was no way she could understand the necessity without knowing everything else. So many times, Alie had come close to telling her, but when it came down to it, she just didn't have the language to explain the nuances. And Brigitte had been brought up in the Church, just like Alie. Maybe she'd think that Lore should have died. Maybe she'd think Apollius was right.

Alie had so few people left. She couldn't risk that.

Her eyes were gummy and her throat felt scoured, her bed calling out to her. Alie ignored it, dressing herself and starting down the hall.

The apartment Bri shared with her parents and brother was one floor down from Alie, much larger than the one she lived in on her own. She'd always been equal parts jealous and confused by the close relationship Brigitte had with her family. Parents who loved each other and their children unconditionally were a foreign concept. She was ashamed of how it made her suspicious, but Alie had never experienced a familial love not fringed by enough strings to hang yourself with.

Bri opened the door when she knocked, her locs worn long down her back, a dressing gown closed over her chemise. She yawned, smiled. "Apologies for not being dressed. I didn't want to."

Alie laughed and hugged her friend. A small table was set up in the sitting room behind her, pastries and a pot of fragrant tea. Bruneau, Brigitte's brother, grabbed one of the cakes as he hurried across the room, throwing Alie a wave. He was in a similar state of undress and similarly unbothered by it, wearing only his chest binder and a pair of loose trousers.

They settled at the table, Bri pouring Alie tea. "Maybe I should send for coffee instead. You look exhausted."

"I'm not sleeping well."

Bri pressed her lips together, nervously playing with the end of one of her locs. "Wedding preparations?"

They'd only spoken of this once. Right after Lore was sent to the Burnt Isles, right after Alie's true parentage was revealed and she was betrothed to Jax. Brigitte had encouraged her to fight against it if this wasn't what she wanted. It'd made Alie want to laugh and cry at the same time. Her friend had no concept of being forced by family into things she didn't want.

So Alie lied. Alie made it sound like she'd come around to the idea of marrying Jax. Because unless they managed to somehow repair the Fount and banish Apollius from Bastian's body, she really had no choice, and she didn't have the energy to perform defiance.

Alie nodded over the rim of her mug. "The date has moved up. I requested it."

"From the King," Brigitte added. A doorway into another conversation, one that hung around the Citadel like fog on the morning ocean. "From Apollius."

As far as Alie knew, Brigitte's family wasn't any more religious than your average courtier, well-versed in the steps of piety without really believing. But people had reacted to Apollius's reveal in ways that weren't commensurate with Alie's knowledge of their devoutness. Avery Marmont, who had told her when they were children that he didn't think any of the gods actually existed, had been seen silently weeping in front of the statue on the green. Yvonne Gilliard, another childhood friend, had asked her if she wanted to be part of a prayer circle she was starting every morning at dawn in the North Sanctuary.

She had to tread lightly here. "Yes," she said quietly. "From Apollius."

Brigitte frowned down into her tea. "You know," she murmured, low as a secret, "I'm not sure if I believe it."

Alie gnawed her bottom lip.

With a sigh, Bri sat back, looking at the windows instead of Alie. "Maybe that's not the right way to put it. It's not that I don't believe He's Apollius—I mean, the alternative is that Bastian is pretending to be a god, and I don't see that happening. But I don't—" She tapped her lacquered nails on her teacup, searching for words. "I don't think this is . . . good."

Relief was a flood, so palpable Alie almost slumped over in her seat. Part of her wanted to tell Bri everything, try to explain the entire debacle, but she just settled on "Me neither."

That seemed to relieve Bri, too. She nodded enthusiastically. "All our lives, we were taught to believe that Apollius was coming back. That His return would bring a new, perfect world. And we never got specifics, I guess, but I assumed a perfect world would be one free of war. One where people weren't hungry." She shrugged self-consciously. "You know, I think most of this new-found piety is people being afraid. We have proof of the Shining Realm now. Everyone wants to be allowed in." She looked to Alie. "Does He talk about it? The Shining Realm?"

He didn't. Apollius had never mentioned it, not as a reward for those who were sufficiently worshipful, or as the place He'd bided time waiting for Bastian. Alie shook her head.

Bri glanced away again at the full light of morning in the windows. "I wish He would," she said softly.

They ate quietly. This was the gift of long friendships: the ability to be silent with each other and have it be comfortable. The way that simply the presence of the other person was a strut that could hold you up.

When Alie was finished, she stood, walked behind Bri's chair. She wrapped her arms around the other woman's shoulders and settled her chin into the notch beside her neck. Bri leaned into her embrace.

The comfortable silence probably would have persisted had Lore's ring not fallen out of Alie's pocket.

It bounced once on the marble floor in a way that made her wince, and came to a stop in a shaft of sun, gleaming.

She felt Bri straighten from her arms and had to fight against holding her still, trying to keep her from seeing. No such luck.

"Is that..." Bri breathed.

"Yes," Alie said, because what use was lying?

Their spell broke. Brigitte straightened fully, her lips working over questions that never gained sound. Alie nearly tripped trying to retrieve the ring, snatching it off the floor with so much haste that it almost went spinning away again.

When she turned around, Bri was standing, her delicate brows low. "Alie," she said, "why do you have the Queen's engagement ring?"

She'd gone about this all wrong. There might've been a way to salvage it, maybe saying that Apollius had given it to Jax to give to her, but now that she'd acted this way there was no chance Bri would believe her. She stood there in the light, her fist clenched tight around the Mount-mined diamond, and couldn't think of anything to say.

But she didn't need to. Another benefit of long friendships was not needing words to communicate, the other side of that comfortable silence.

"Come on," Bri said, turning to head toward the stairs that led to her room deeper in the apartment.

Alie had been in Bri's room thousands of times. She was messier than Alie, her clothes left in luxurious piles rather than put back into the closet, at least until maids came and rectified the situation. A small table was pushed in front of the window, strewn with tools that Alie didn't recognize but assumed had something to do with Bri's jewelry making. One of them, a metal tube with a disk of glass at one end, reminded her of a telescope.

Bri cleared a pair of slippers off a velvet chair for Alie, then sat on the bench in front of the table. "You stole it," she said. "And I know you have a reason. You've never been light-fingered."

You aren't going to believe me, Alie almost said, but that was a stupid thing to think at this point. They'd seen plenty of unbelievable things just this week.

"I need to find something," she said, hoping that Bri wouldn't pry too much, hoping the sixth sense of friendship would extend this far. "And apparently this ring can tell me where it is. But I can't figure out *how*." Now that she'd allowed herself to talk, her frustrations came in a flood. "The instructions were to hold it up to a window at sunrise, but I tried that, and it didn't show me anything."

"I've heard of this before," Bri said, an eager light in her eye. "Putting a message in a piece of jewelry, I mean. It's not the stone itself that's engraved, it's the setting."

"Then why would it matter if it was sunrise?"

"Any type of bright light will probably work." Bri turned to the desk and picked up the instrument that looked like a small telescope. "The stone needs to be illuminated to see the setting behind it." She held the tool up to her eye, twisted it to make some minor adjustment, then reached out and opened the curtains over the window. She held out her hand.

Despite everything—their long friendship, their love, their comfortable silence—Alie hesitated. The ring weighed in her pocket like a chain on an ankle.

She'd kept hope, but Alie knew the chances of this working out in her favor were slim. They were going up against a god, and even if they were all haunted by the ghosts of other gods, every possible step forward seemed like grasping at increasingly thin straws. If she handed over the ring, if she let Bri become part of this, was she damning her, too?

Bri read her thoughts. She twitched her fingers, quirked her mouth. "I won't ask any questions. Promise."

With a shaky breath, Alie dropped the ring into her palm.

The diamond sparkled as Bri turned it over in her hands. "You know," she said, almost to herself, "I figured something strange was going on when he gave her this. I couldn't have imagined just how strange, though."

"I don't think any of us could," Alie replied.

Bri snorted a laugh, fitting the ring into a metal mechanism that kept it upright, handling it gently. She cranked at a lever on the side of the machine, bringing the ring up to the center of the open window. Morning was in full glow, and the sun blazed through the golden stone, casting gem-faceted shadows on the walls. Bri fit the scope into her eye and leaned in close.

"Oh," she said. "There it is."

She offered the scope to Alie. Alie's hand nearly trembled as she took it.

"It's not a map, though," Bri said, frowning.

Alie put the tool to her eye. She stared into the diamond, peering through the golden depths to the symbol etched on the setting below, so small it was hard to read even with magnification.

A word.

Tomb.

CHAPTER TWENTY-FOUR

LORE

Be with us in the desolate places.
                              –The Book of Prayer, Tract 91

W e're here."

Her voice was scratchy. Lore didn't know how long it had been since she'd spoken, though it had to be hours, maybe even a full day. It wasn't easy to tell, here in the thick of the ash.

Lore stayed mostly at the prow through their near-silent voyage, occasionally going belowdeck to keep up the appearance of watching the silver instrument. Though she was pretty sure at this point her ruse was found out—if not that she had a piece of the Fount, at least that she didn't need Raihan's silver weight. Dani didn't mention it, though. Neither of them said anything to the other as they watched the horizon and ate dried meat, waiting in limbo for what would come next.

Dani narrowed her eyes at the sky. "Are you sure? I can't see shit."

Lore couldn't, either, at least not out of channeling-space. Sunk in magic, though, it was obvious. The path of Spiritum widened until it encompassed almost the entire ocean, a molten sea of gold guiding them on, growing stronger as the Fount piece got closer to the Mount.

The song in her head should have been reaching a fever pitch. But instead it stayed low and muffled, the Fount apparently confident she could find It without guidance.

A thump. They'd run aground. All around them, ash, as inscrutable as it'd been on the open water.

"Well," Dani said, releasing her death grip on the wheel. "I guess you were right." She waved a hand in front of her face and choked back a cough. "This place looks like the Godsfall happened five minutes ago."

Nyxara's memories were close at hand, the life She'd lived on this island, everything leading up to the fight that had changed the face of the world. Hope was a thin and ragged thing, but Lore still reached out in her mind, just to see. *Nyxara?*

Nothing.

Dani lowered the gangplank, the wood clattering onto sand they could barely see. The swirl of ash and fog revealed the island in flashes. A scrubby forest at the edge of the beach. The ground in the distance canting toward a peak. The top of it stayed covered, veiled in ruin. The few trees scraggling up the Mount were thin and blackened.

It'd been so vibrant, in Nyxara's memories. A paradise, burnt out but not allowed to die.

"Not much *golden* about it anymore." But there was an eagerness in Dani's voice, an anxious thread that belied her cool words. "Come on, then."

They walked down the gangplank onto the sand. The fog shifted as they headed in the vague direction of the forest, the ground littered with driftwood and shale. Here and there, a glimmer of gold, not Spiritum but the actual mineral, marking places where Apollius had been struck to the ground. It said something about the gravity of what they were doing that neither she nor Dani stopped to pick any of it up.

"We're going to break a leg if we don't take it slow," Lore said. She cleared her throat, but the persistent itch she'd gotten used to on the Second Isle was near-unbearable here. "No need to rush. It's not like the Fount is going anywhere."

Dani rolled her eyes. "I thought you'd be more eager, but sure. We'll go slow." She gestured upward, where the ash had peeled away momentarily. "Looks like the ash is cleared around the Fount. It'll be nice to finally take a deep breath. It's been months."

It was strange, the mundanity of it. Trudging through the fog, eyes aching and feet tired, and knowing she was headed to the birthplace of the pantheon. The home of the soul of the world. She'd had more exciting walks to the trash heaps in Dellaire.

Time seemed frozen here. Other than the few times the ash cleared, Lore's limited vision made it feel as if she were trapped in one place, endlessly walking and getting nowhere. Occasionally, the fog would shift, showing bare tree branches and the rubble of stone huts. Once, she saw a building she recognized—a tall spire, listing sideways, its foundation slowly eroding. Six names were written on the spire in faded gilt.

She wondered if they'd stumble into Nyxara's burnt grove.

After a while, they reached what looked like the remains of a village. The fog wasn't as thick here, dying off as they reached higher elevations, though the air was still gray and sooty on her tongue. The huts were in fairly good condition, slightly finer versions of the ones in the Harbor.

Lore stopped and sat down on a bench in front of one hut, leaning her head back against the wall.

"No." Dani shook her head. "We aren't stopping."

"I'm the one with the god-power," Lore said wearily, "and I say we stop."

Dani looked like she might dare Lore to use said god-power, her mouth pursed into a sour bud, but after a moment she rolled her eyes and sat down next to her. "You seem less than awed."

"I've seen all of this before," Lore said.

Dani's eyes burned with questions, but Lore didn't look at her. She suddenly very much wanted to be far away from the other woman.

There was nowhere else to go, so she stood and walked into the hut.

The inside was as ash-coated as the rest of this place. A cot stood in the corner, covered in rotting linens. A small table leaned against what had once been a hearth, choked with the remains of firewood. Everything on the table was coated in dust, almost too thick to make out what they were.

But Lore could, barely. They were books.

They looked just as old as Raihan's in the Harbor, possibly older. Lore half expected them to disintegrate as she gingerly took one from the top of the pile. Her fingers sank into the cover, made permeable by age and rot, but it mostly held together.

She thought of Malcolm, somewhere in Caldien, and could practically hear him screaming at her to get some gods-damned gloves. So she bundled her hand in the hem of her long shirt before gently prying the book open, separating pages stuck together with the wear of centuries.

A journal, it looked like. Not dated. The handwriting was faded and overly ornate, but she could make out enough of it to read, though some of the words were smudged.

I have been tasked by my god as the caretaker of His body, and to guard the Fount, that It may never be reassembled. To this task I commit my life, and my family's life, so Apollius may return and the world be made right.

H. Devereaux

It took a moment for the name to register. Devereaux. Dani's surname.

Her heart kicked into a frenzied beat in her ears.

Dani had known Apollius was alive, at least in a sense. Dani's older sister had been groomed to be His queen.

And Dani had been so confident they could get here.

Lore had never trusted Danielle Devereaux; their association was born of nothing but desperation. But she'd also never questioned whether or not Dani really wanted Apollius dead. She couldn't think of any other reason why Dani would want to come to the Golden Mount.

Unless her nihilism was a front, and she wanted to protect Him. To keep Lore from fixing the Fount.

The shard of It, golden-threaded and moon-carved, was still tucked into her pack, humming against her spine. She hadn't told Dani anything about the pieces of the Fount, but maybe she'd always known, one more detail given to her from Anton's cult. Dani hadn't acted like she thought anything of Lore suddenly carrying a bag from the Harbor, but she was sly, and if she knew about the pieces, it wouldn't be hard to put two and two together.

But then why help Lore at all?

Lore shook her head. The particulars wouldn't thread together quite yet, but they didn't have to. She could kill Dani with a thought, and the other woman knew it, even with the flimsy knife tucked into her boot, kept secret like she thought it could save her. If Dani planned on attacking, it would come quick and seemingly out of nowhere, her only hope the element of surprise. Lore had to be ready.

Part of her wondered if she should just take Dani out now. But the reluctance to kill lingered. They'd never been friends, but for the moment, they were still allies. At least, until Dani actually did something to change that.

And cowardly as it was, Lore didn't want to be alone on this island.

"Anything interesting?"

Dani hadn't entered the hut, just stuck in her head. Lore didn't act startled; didn't even try to hide what she'd been looking at. She closed the cover of the journal and shrugged. "Books, but I can't read them."

"Probably worth a fortune, if we could sell them to the Church." Dani jerked her chin. "But seeing as the Church would happily burn both of us, let's *move*."

They left the crumbling village behind, trudging along as the grade of the makeshift path slowly inched upward. Before too long, Lore's legs felt like they were on fire, her breath growing harsh. One would think that weeks of mining would have increased her stamina, but apparently not, and the air quality wasn't helping.

Slowly, the ash and fog cleared. When they passed a cliff—the same one where Nyxara had once thrown Her ring, Lore was sure of it—she could see the gray cloud of Godsfall debris roiling below them, a thunderstorm that never quite broke. It made the cliff seem not so high, like you could step off the edge and land in all that gray softness, walk over it right back to the mainland.

And then, after what felt like hours more of walking, there was the cathedral, a broken ruin. There was the courtyard, splintered wooden beams still lined in seams of gold.

And there was the Fount.

It looked like a well, small and gray and shining with a faint phosphorescence, as if the stones were threaded with captured starlight. The lip of it was jagged. The soul of the world, and it looked so humble. So small.

Once, there'd been tall spires, a building nearly as grand as the Citadel, though nowhere near as large. Lore recalled Nyxara's memories of this place, the tiles lining the ground around the Fount, a canopy of fine-woven linen billowing in the sea breeze. Most of that had gone, either blasted apart in the Godsfall or rotted out by time. The tiles were rubble, the canopy dirty fibers still clinging to some of the beams like a spiderweb. Only the courtyard around the Fount remained, and a few rooms Lore could see in the cathedral, open to the sky where the roof had fallen.

Dani stopped, breathing hard. Her eyes darted around the ruins. "Where do you think He is?"

Neither of them had much time for holy awe. Lore appreciated that Dani wanted to get right down to business, really. She shrugged. "Back in one of those rooms, maybe?"

"Could be." Dani glanced at her. "I'm going to look through the cathedral. You search out here."

Lore arched a brow. "Seems pretty clear He isn't out here."

"Check anyway." Dani waved a hand, dismissing her as she stalked through a crumbled archway. "Doesn't hurt to be thorough."

Then it was just Lore and the Fount.

The piece of It burned against her back, a pleasant heat like a fireplace after a cold day, a sip of whiskey on a sore throat. She could hear It singing on the breeze, light and harmonic, thrumming alongside her heartbeat.

Go on.

Not Nyxara's voice, not really a voice at all. Something different, something deeper.

Every thought she'd had about playing this close to the chest, not revealing the piece of the Fount, fled her mind. Everything in her pointed only to the heat and the song, to the reunification at her fingertips. Something she could finally make right.

She didn't notice stepping forward, didn't notice taking her pack from her shoulders and drawing out the piece, her hands immediately numbing. It fit perfectly into the notch in the side of the Fount, stone flush to stone as if it had never been broken at all.

Lore tried to step away, tried to take a moment to enjoy the foreign feeling of relief. But when she let go of the stone, it held her fast, sure as shackles, like her fingers were frozen to its surface.

The song in her head crescendoed, the melody vibrating her bones. A strangled cry left her throat, little more than a moan.

Her vision blurred. Went black.

A familiar feeling
drained
to the last
drop

Chapter Twenty-Five

LORE

Time is a vast ocean. Memory is a small boat.
  —Graffiti on the side of a Myroshan vessel, 67 AGF

*L*ore?

Nyxara's voice. Tired and languid, as if She'd just woken from a long sleep. Finally at rest, here in the Fount, finally able to speak again now that Lore was connected to It.

Lore didn't answer, couldn't figure out how. But when Nyxara's voice floated through her, it sounded like a smile. *Oh. You found it.*

Where are You? Lore managed to cobble words together, though it was a near thing, more emotion than language.

I'm not sure. Nyxara sounded slightly troubled, but it smoothed out quickly. *Resting. It's nice to be done. I wished it away for so long, but I'd already made My vow by then. When you wished it gone, it could be. You didn't take the drink. That wasn't on you.*

Wait. Lore felt like she was scrambling, lost in the dark, drowning without knowing which way was the surface. *I have questions—*

No, Nyxara said dreamily. *I'm done.*

"You can't be." That much, Lore managed to say aloud, her

voice echoing in the broken courtyard. "There's still so much to do, I still need Your help—"

You don't, Nyxara soothed. *You have everything you need, Lore.*

Something changed behind Lore's eyes. The black void gathering into a shape, one she recognized. One she'd lived in.

Nyxara smiled at her. It was a sad smile, a wholly human one. She carried no vestiges of the goddess she'd become, only the woman she'd been before the Fount, pale and dark-haired, a melancholy kind of beauty. She opened Her arms.

Lore didn't know how she managed to go into that embrace, how she was simultaneously tethered to the Fount and here with Nyxara. But she did, burying her head in the former goddess's shoulder, letting herself be held.

"You're stronger than I ever was," Nyxara whispered. Her voice sounded different than it had in Lore's mind, deeper and richer, not quite as exhausted. "Stronger, and better."

"I'm not," Lore murmured. "I'm not."

Nyxara tilted up her chin. "Then decide to be."

She didn't fade by slow degrees. One moment She was there, and the next She was gone.

And Lore was alone.

Let Her rest. The new voice, the not-voice.

"I don't understand," Lore said. Grief thickened her voice, grief that she didn't quite understand. Sadness where there should be joy. But the goddess was a piece of herself, a dark and hard-to-understand piece, and Lore mourned Her absence.

Nor can you. The voice—the Fount—didn't seem concerned. **It is not for you to understand everything. Only to fulfill the purpose you have been given.**

"And what is that?" Her voice echoed and broke, faded, sounded like many voices at once and nothing at all.

To become the vessel. To bring back all that is Ours. You have given Us one strand of magic; even now, you draw the rest,

the life and the water, the air and earth and fire. **You are Our lodestone. Our tributary.**

Her friends, her lovers, finding the pieces, drawn back here to where it all began.

Cycles and cycles.

We will be the only god once again, the Fount said. **We will take back Our power through you.**

"So you're using us, too," Lore murmured.

It is the nature of divinity.

She didn't like that. She didn't like that at all. "And then every-thing will be fixed? The world righted?"

A pause. **As long as there are mortals with mortal will and mortal hearts, the righting of the world cannot happen just once. It must happen over and over again.**

"So You aren't actually fixing anything."

The seasons will realign. The earth will balance, the Fount replied. **War, cruelty, injustice—We have no power over this. Only they do.**

They. Humanity. The Fount didn't count her as part of it, Lore noticed.

You were not shown everything, the Fount said. **When She gave you Her memories, you were interrupted.**

"Wait, I want to know—"

Lore was obliterated, the bits of herself she'd gathered blown apart and pulled back into something else, a memory that had never finished, a storm of blood and rage.

CHAPTER TWENTY-SIX

NYXARA

(I do not owe you scriptures.)

Her claws drew blood.

She'd drawn it before, when they were rough with one another, but that was in passion, never in anger. Now the sight of his gold-tinged ichor running down the black blades of her fingers brought a snarl to her lips, a howl to her teeth. Nyxara dove for Apollius, arms outstretched, wanting to rend him apart, leave him nothing but flayed ribbons.

Wings opened at his shoulders, gleaming pearlescent in the indigo night. Nyxara stumbled back, momentarily shocked. She'd known that he had kept changing, all of them had, but she'd never seen this. The Fount's power, twisting him further and further away from human, and he'd hidden its full extent from her.

Even as he stole from It, he became more beautiful. Beauty could never be trusted when coupled with power.

Nyxara screeched, lunging for him; he caught her by the hair and slung her away, lifting off the beach with a powerful beat of wings. She crouched on the ground, pained tears seeping from her eyes. They were ink-dark, they stained the sand.

"It doesn't have to be like this." His voice was resonant, all-consuming. It beat in her ears like a pulse. "I can take it away, beloved. If you don't want your power, the Fount will take it back. I'll take it back—"

"It's not just my power I don't want," Nyxara snarled. "It's *you*."

It was strange, to see pain on Apollius's face. She'd seen it before, of course, but not since they became this. Now he never showed anything so vulnerable, only rage, only pride, only contempt. But this, his golden eyes closing, his full mouth going limp, the line of his shoulders beneath those awful, beautiful wings slumping—it was pain, and in god-proportions, it was awful.

"That's one thing I can't give you," Apollius said, and he almost sounded sad about it.

She stood up, shaking, curling fingers that ended in sharp claws, narrowing eyes that had become voids of dark, scattered with stars. "Then kill me."

He heaved a breath that was nearly a sob. "I can't do that, either."

Knees bent, arms before her. Hestraon had taught her to fight, once. Taught her to brawl, because she asked him to, back when they were all friends with mortal bodies that only held one death. "You're going to have to try. Because I sure fucking am."

The memories blurred. A rush of violence—Apollius flying her up through the clouds, every beat of his wings bringing them high, only for him to slam her down again, a cataclysm of rock and tree and bursting, unimaginable agony. Her claws in his flesh, tearing into his cheek, his arm, blood in her mouth.

They fought through the sky, through the whole archipelago; white wings and black claws in a whirl of rage and curdled love. She burned down forests. She broke mountains. The earth shattered, spilling gold where Apollius's blood touched it, watering an infernal garden. Gems, where her tears fell, nothing about her human anymore, nothing about her natural. The penitents of the Church he'd built died in flames, crushed or burnt; some of them ran toward ships, some of them escaped, to tell stories of what they'd seen and the evil goddess who'd tried to defeat their god.

"Nyxara, *stop.*" He shouted it at her as he picked her up from the crater she'd made of an island, breaking the mantle so the sea crept in. "You can't end this. It doesn't end."

But it had to. He was defending himself. That was all, really. She kept trying to kill him, and he kept stopping her, but it had to *end*.

She rolled away from his next blow, turned to ribbons of moonlight. The only hope they had was the pieces, the secrets she'd held so closely that she barely even let herself think of them, banishing the memory as far as it could go. The pieces of the Fount that had broken when they drank. The one she'd managed to hide away before Apollius shipped off the rest, sent to the mainland with his faithful. How he'd raged, when he found it gone. How she'd soothed him, reassured him it was of no matter, that their power was absolute and unassailable.

There was only the hope that Braxtos had done as she asked, before leaving for good.

It'd hurt, telling him what to do. Apollius's bonds around her mind had nearly squeezed her out of consciousness, the vows he'd forced on her when they took their drink of the Fount making this weak plan against him all but impossible. She doubted she'd ever be able to speak of it again. Even thinking of it hurt.

Slipping through the weave of the world, knowing Apollius would follow, hoping she had enough time before he did. Reconstituting on one of the few islands they hadn't yet destroyed. Nyxara followed instinct, and when she saw the tree, grown lush and perfect, she could feel what was beneath it, hidden by Braxtos, tangled in centuries of roots.

She raised her hands. She pulled death from the rocks and the ground, pushed it all into the tree, crowding out every bit of life, snuffing it out completely. Marking it like a grave.

Apollius, crashing through the forest behind her. She turned to meet him with claws outstretched and teeth bared, knowing that there could be an end, maybe, someday.

It was back on the first island, the Golden Mount where he'd brought them and changed them, that she got her claws into his chest.

She could have stopped. Maybe she should have—he held her in the air, powerful beats of his wings keeping her aloft as he waited for her to see sense. But she wouldn't.

She could have stopped. He could have stopped her.

Nyxara's claws dug deep into holy flesh, past veins that ran gilded, past ivory bones. The meat of him was as red as anyone else's. When she closed her hand around his heart, she felt it thrum against her palm.

Her void-dark eyes looked into his, bright as the sun behind him. Time seemed to pause.

And she ripped the heart from his chest.

They tumbled to the earth, a blur of black and gold, plummeting to the ground and breaking through rock. Nyxara couldn't clearly see where they were, only that it was dark. She rolled away from him, blood sticky on her hands. In the distance, the Fount sang, a mournful melody, a dirge.

The momentary calm that had allowed Apollius to let her claw out his heart was gone. He lay on his back, panting, golden eyes panicked. Still alive, even without an organ, because they were gods and gods followed no rules. But she could see that he was fading.

"You don't understand." His voice was different, and she couldn't figure out what the difference was for a moment. It was his, unaltered, the way he'd sounded before all this. The same voice that told her he loved her for the first time. "Nyxara, I wanted to save us both. We can't die, we can but we *can't*, do you understand? I can't allow it. I can't let us go into the dark."

She didn't understand. His heart was still in her hand, still beating despite it all, weeping red and gold onto the stones. Nyxara crawled over to him, her cheeks wet with tears, trying to remember the bits of the book she'd read that he had written with the penitents. Harsh things, but beautiful things, too, truths she assumed he had seen that were kept from the rest of them. The answer to the question he'd first asked, the reason they were here.

"Don't be afraid," she murmured, stroking back his hair. "You'll go to the Shining Realm, see your family again…"

The noise he made was unlike anything she'd ever heard. Nyxara was familiar with agony, but if a sound could tear a soul out of a body, it'd be one like this. Not a scream; quieter, more visceral, the only thing left at the end of a world.

"It's a lie," he said. "It's a lie. There's nothing after this, Nyxara. Nothing. This is all there is."

One life, snuffed out like a candle, nothing left behind. Not even smoke.

It terrified her. It comforted her.

But Apollius…to know that his family was gone, and he would never see them again, and after that awful night there was nothing left. To look into that void, to find that answer, and live hundreds of lifetimes trying to outrun it.

Nyxara had made a friend of death. He never had.

And she still loved him. Her stupid heart still beat in time with the one in her bloody fist.

Wincing, all the pain catching up with her now that she was still, Nyxara got onto her knees next to Apollius. The hole of his chest made a *sucking* sound, his veins still trying to find blood that no longer had a muscle to move it. He watched her, eyes wide and tear-shining, breath shaking in and out of his lungs.

She didn't speak, because there was nothing to say. But she lowered his heart back into its cage of bones.

The hole didn't close, but the organ made the necessary attachments again. It'd never stopped beating.

"It will hold." He closed his eyes, swallowed. "It will hold long enough." He seemed to be speaking to himself rather than her. But when his eyes opened, they pinned her in place, sharp as a knife blade. "We can put this behind us, beloved."

They couldn't. She couldn't. What she wanted hadn't changed. Nyxara shook her head, slowly.

His face altered. The line of his mouth went stern, his eyes flinty. He sat up, still sheeting blood from the hole in his chest, looming over her.

Nyxara scrambled back until she met a wall and stone dug into her shoulder blades, until there was nowhere else to go.

Apollius reached down and tangled his hand in her hair, slowly tilted back her head. "If you won't agree now," he said, "perhaps you will later. You didn't kill me, but you shortened my time. I can make this work. I can do the same."

And he wrenched her head to the side.

And Nyxara didn't die, because the god of life wouldn't allow it. But she went away, wandering in the dark. Waiting for the continuation of a cycle she never wanted.

CHAPTER TWENTY-SEVEN
LORE

What do we do if the very foundations of our belief
are broken? How can anything built on them stand?
—From the writings of Margo Aveline*

The Fount let her go, finally. She'd been straining, even lost
in Nyxara's last memory; she stumbled back from the stones
with the force of someone winning in a tug-of-war, breathing in
sharp gasps, her hand on her own aching neck.

So there was the Godsfall. Nyxara, trying to kill Apollius and
then changing Her mind when She saw His fear. Apollius making sure She'd be in the same in-between space as He would be,
still technically clinging to both of the deaths the Fount had given
Them, because the truth was dark and terrible and inescapable.

After death came nothing.

Had she been asked a week ago, Lore wouldn't have been that
upset by the revelation. Life wore you out; having an afterlife
sounded tiring, when all you wanted was rest and reprieve. But

---

* Better known as the Night Witch.

now, with all the deaths she'd inadvertently caused fresh in her mind, it made her...empty. Hollow. Like a clock ticking down to nothing.

Apollius's anger made sense to her. His fear, His desperation. All of this, because one man didn't want to die. Because He couldn't bear to let the woman He loved die, either.

Loved. Owned. Lore had told Nyxara not to confuse them, that they weren't the same thing. And they still weren't. But the selfish part of her, the terrible part, understood how they might feel the same. That part of her could think of Gabe and Bastian and understand perfectly.

"I can't find Him."

Dani's voice made her jump. Instinctually, Lore moved in front of the Fount, hiding the piece she'd brought home. "What do you mean?"

"What do you think I mean?" Dani's face was blank, but the kind of blankness that came from exhaustion and defeat, not the absence of emotion. "He isn't fucking *here*."

In the memory of the Godsfall, Apollius and Nyxara had been somewhere dark, somewhere not the cathedral. Maybe He was still there. Lore almost wanted to curse the dead goddess for not having better memories of the place, but she couldn't quite bring herself to think of Nyxara with animosity yet.

Still hiding the Fount with her body, Lore stood. "Let's look again. Maybe you missed something." The dark place she'd seen could have been somewhere deep in the bowels of the cathedral, hidden beneath rubble.

"I'm telling you, He isn't in there." Dani threw up her hands. "But why not? Sure, let's take a second look. Maybe your magic will be useful."

She waited until the other woman had her back turned and was halfway into the shadows before following.

The remains of the cathedral were more extensive than they

looked from the outside. A labyrinth of empty rooms, open roofs, and broken walls, the crumbled leftovers of gilded stone and solid oak. Past the courtyard that held the Fount, there was a large open atrium, with rooms leading one into the other arranged around it.

The ceiling of the atrium had the largest hole, broken beams as sharp as bones. Lore's body remembered injuries she'd never suffered. Being thrown through this roof, her back hitting these tiles.

Dani led her deeper into the ruins, climbing over broken stone and fallen walls. The thick ash that blocked most of the sun kept plant life from flourishing, but some hardy moss blanketed parts of the floor, and a few night-blooming flowers that didn't mind the dark grew in the corners. Nightshade. Moonflower.

Lore kept an eye to the floor, looking for trapdoors or changes that might indicate a hidden staircase. She didn't see any, and most of the rubble was too heavy to move for a closer look. When they reached a room with surprisingly little damage other than a beam from a hole in the roof, she braced her hands on one end of it, just to check. "Help me move this."

To her credit, Dani didn't ask why. With a heave, they pulled the beam away from the floor and hauled it over to the wall.

Nothing beneath but broken tiles.

"If you're looking for a lower floor, I've already checked," Dani said. "There's none that I can find. Do you believe me now?"

"Yes." Lore's shoulders slumped. Apollius's body could be any-where on this damn island.

"We'll have to widen our scope." Dani propped her fists on her hips, looking at the cathedral like she could very happily set it aflame. "Divide up the island, search through a different part of it every day. Surely, He won't be that hard to find."

The words were false, a reassurance neither of them believed. If anything was going to be hard to find, it would be the body of a god who jealously hoarded His deaths.

"You're right." Lore sighed. "But it's getting dark. We'll have to start tomorrow, if we don't want to accidentally plummet off a cliff."

Dani nodded. "I'm sleeping on the boat. You coming?"

But Lore was already shaking her head. She'd stay here.

With a raised brow, the erstwhile noblewoman left the room.

Lore lingered a moment. All the awe she hadn't had time to feel when they first arrived washed over her now, not in worship but in dread. Here was the birthplace of the world's religion, and if she was successful, here would be its grave.

The Fount sang in her head, soft and lilting.

With another sigh, she clambered her way out of the cathedral.

In the courtyard, Dani crouched by the Fount. Right where Lore had replaced the stone.

Spiritum rushed to Lore's hands immediately, golden threads tethering her to the other woman. Dani tensed but didn't turn, continuing her examination of the moon-carved stone, careful not to touch.

"Do it, if you're going to." Her voice was low, but it carried here, where they were the only two living beings for miles.

She should. She didn't.

Though something in her, a glimmering nudge in that space where Nyxara used to be, raged at her for it.

By the Fount, Dani let out a quiet, humorless laugh. She stood and turned to face Lore, jerking a thumb at the moon-carved stone, nestled back into its place. "I was wondering if you'd found it."

More threads of gold gathered in Lore's fist. Dani stiffened, her face going a few shades paler.

"I know what you are," Lore said. "The journal was in the hut."

"Of course it was. A souvenir from my long-lost ancestor." Dani rolled her eyes. "Yes, Lore, my family was supposed to guard Apollius's body. We didn't do a very good job—the way to navigate to the Mount was forgotten a few generations back, I assume by those silver things being gambled away. There were some premature deaths before directions could be passed on, all the general ways a legacy is lost. But you're correct, this was supposed to be my job all along."

"*Your* job?" Lore stalked closer to Dani as she spoke, a hunter circling prey, spooling out Spiritum as she went. "Not your father's?"

Dani deflated a bit, the contemptuous smile losing its edge, something like genuine fear in her eyes. "He didn't last long once we got to the Isles. He wasn't made for this. Him, or my mother."

Lore didn't want to feel sorry for her. She shoved the feeling away. "So you used me to get here. To guard Him from me."

"No, you idiot," Dani spat. "I don't stand a chance against you. You can literally pull my life out of my body. You're doing it right now, even if you're too much of a coward to finish the job."

For that, Lore gave the Spiritum a tug. Dani's spine pulled straight, as if her life force were a rope lifting her from the ground. She rose to her toes.

"If I was going to work against you," she said, strained, "I would have done it by now, don't you think?"

A fair point. But Lore wound another strand of Spiritum around her fingers.

Dani's face paled further. "I know that you're trying to put the Fount back together," she said. "My family has known about the broken pieces for centuries, though we never knew where they were, other than the one in the catacombs."

It made sense. And after Nyxara's memory of the Godsfall, she knew why the goddess hadn't been able to tell her.

"Could you repay me for that tidbit with a looser grip?" Dani said.

At first, Lore tightened her hold again, just to make the other woman remember she could. Then she let one of the strands of Spiritum loose.

"Thank you," Dani said, her shoulders straightening. "Like I said, we know about the pieces. We were supposed to keep them from ever being reunited with the Fount, and find the other two wherever the pantheon hid them. I assume this one was at the Harbor?"

Lore didn't answer.

It didn't seem to faze Dani. "I don't know how many times I'm going to have to prove I am on your side, Lore. I want you to fix the Fount. I want Apollius dead."

The statement seemed unfinished, like something else should come after. Like this wasn't the sum of her goal, but it was all she'd share.

Lore nodded. Then she held out her hand. "Give me the dagger."

Dani didn't waste time pretending she didn't have one. "Seriously?"

A whole handful of threads, this time, enough to make Dani gasp.

"Fine," she wheezed, nearly collapsing as she bent over to root around in her boot. She pulled out the knife, useless against Lore's magic, but effective enough if she'd managed to catch her off guard.

Lore took it, slid it into her own boot. Then she let go her fist-ful of Dani's life.

Dani bent at the waist, pulling in great gasps of air. "That seems like overkill," she said between breaths.

"Maybe." Lore turned and walked back into the ruins again, intending to find somewhere to sleep. "But if you're going to stab me in the back, I'd like to return the favor."

CHAPTER TWENTY-EIGHT

GABE

Those who are strongest will rule over the weak. This
is how the world is structured; this is what pleases Me.
                                   –The Book of Holy Law, Tract 79

They fought about whether to go get the Fount piece. Mari tried
to be the voice of reason, reassuring them that even if Eoin had
taken their ship, they had a deal, and as long as they stuck to it, surely
he would give them the shard and help rescue Alie and Lore.

"Deals have much more weight with poison runners than politicians," Malcolm said, and Mari stayed quiet after that.

She was right in that Eoin taking the ship didn't automatically
mean he was going back on their agreement. But the whole thing
put a sour taste in Gabe's mouth, and his intuition—and the god
in his head—told him to run. He'd learned it was best to listen to
the one, even if he didn't really trust the other.

Gabe wanted to find the piece and leave right away, but Malcolm was more measured in his approach. Even if they managed
to take the piece and get out of the Rotunda without tripping
some alarm, now that Val's ship was gone, there was no way to
leave Caldien without stealing another.

"There's a way," Gabe growled, thinking of threads of fire and earth.

"No," Malcolm said, almost before he finished speaking. "No."

Bereft of other options, the plan now was to steal a ship. After the meeting of the Brotherhood tonight, Gabe and Malcolm would return to the boardinghouse, in case they were still being followed. Then they'd sneak out the back, return to the Rotunda, and steal the stone while Val, Mari, and Michal found something suitably small and unguarded in the harbor. Eoin would undoubtedly know who'd taken it, but hopefully they'd be halfway to the Mount before he discovered the Fount shard was gone.

So for now, they all pretended at business as usual.

Gossip between Auverraine and Caldien moved slowly, but not *that* slowly. The news of Alienor Bellegarde and Jax Aronicus's wedding being moved up was already making the rounds. Yet more gossip came in the form of Finn, tapping nervously at the table with his fingernails as he sat in front of a rapidly cooling cup of tea in the boardinghouse kitchen, an open letter before him.

Mrs. Cavendish had long since gone out to market, but she'd left a plate of biscuits on the counter. Gabe grabbed one and ate it without tasting, trying to decide if he was going to ask Finn what was wrong or not.

He narrowed his eye at the letter, reading it from a safe distance.

Then he dropped his biscuit.

"What does that say?" He knew what it said—he'd just read it. But he wanted to hear it confirmed.

Finn, for his part, didn't seem upset to find him peering over his shoulder. He shook himself, frowned at his tea. "Hells, this needs whiskey." Still, he drained the cup before answering. "Apparently, the Queen has escaped from the Second Isle. The Sainted King is sending all hands to capture her."

Alarm bells rang in Gabe's head, the smell of burning.

He'll take her, Hestraon murmured. *He'll take her again. They'll leave you alone.*

"How do you know it's true?" Gabe asked. "It's impossible to escape the Isles."

"Apparently your Hemlock Queen is quite resourceful." Finn cocked a brow. "I got the news from my contact in the Citadel. And they're the acting Priest Exalted, so they would know."

Alexis, then. They would certainly know.

"Fuck," Gabe seethed, marching into the hallway. "*Fuck.*"

He felt his edges wavering. Felt the outer reaches of himself going to light and heat.

Can You promise to let me go, after? Gabe asked. *Will You give me back to myself?*

The god waited a moment before answering. *I can make no promises.*

"Then leave me alone," Gabe snarled.

He rushed up the stairs to Malcolm's room, hammered on the door. It opened to reveal a sleepy-eyed Michal, a blanket drawn around his naked torso. "Gabe?"

Gabe pushed past him, into the room. Malcolm was already awake, similarly bare-chested at the small desk pushed against the wall. When Gabe stormed in, he turned around, brows furrowed. "You seem upset."

Astonishing deduction, but Gabe didn't snap at him. "Lore has escaped from the Isles. There's an order out for her capture. If Apollius gets to her before we do, it's over."

Malcolm blew out a slow breath. "We're leaving tonight. Once we get to the Mount—"

"We're leaving now."

"Gabriel. I understand your worry, but Lore can take care of herself—"

"She shouldn't have to." The words hissed between Gabe's

teeth. "I have to do something to save her. If He hurts her, if He uses Bastian to do it—"

"Bastian barely exists anymore, Gabe," Michal said gently, still standing by the wall. His expression was drawn and tired, someone who had given up hope and was pained to see another hold it. "Even if we put the whole Fount back together, we don't know what will remain of him."

Quick as called fire, Gabe was across the room, his hand vised around Michal's neck. Distantly, he heard Malcolm shout, but he wasn't listening. His mind was all jumping flame and ember-spark.

"He's in there," Gabe said. "And we will save him. We will save Lore."

Michal nodded, as much as he could against the hand on his neck.

Gabe let him go, slowly. When he turned around, Malcolm's fist met his nose.

It wasn't undeserved. Gabe knew that, now that the fire in his head was fizzling. He bent double, catching blood in his hand.

"Get a hold of yourself," Malcolm snarled, hands still in fists. "Do you understand me, Gabriel?"

A nod, blood streaming down to his lip. It tasted metallic, sickeningly warm.

You are soft, Hestraon said. *And you are a coward.*

Gabe didn't argue.

"We steal the piece tonight," Malcolm continued, his voice a strained kind of even. "We leave on whatever ship Val and Mari and Michal can nick from the harbor. We head to the Mount. The chances of Lore being caught between then and now are negligible." He sighed, fists loosening. "Just hold on for one more day, all right? We're doing all we can."

Not all.

But Gabe nodded. He left the room, went to his own. He sat

on his bed and stared at the wall, thinking of Lore and Bastian and Alie, all these people he loved and couldn't save.

❧

He stayed in his room until night began to fall, coating the window in veils of darkness. Through the wall, Gabe could faintly hear Malcolm and Michal whispering. He couldn't make out most of it, just a word here and there.

Unstable. Stronger. Worried.

Gabe *should* be worried. He knew that. He should be worried that he was hearing Hestraon, seeing the god's memories. He should be worried at how easily he'd taken to this power. How tempted he was by the idea of losing himself.

But his most prevalent feeling, when he thought of his magic, was a deep, awful satisfaction. For so long, he had toed every line, played by every rule. He still thought of that night in Lore's room, when they were just a monk and a poison runner. How he'd denied himself, denied her, for a mandate that no one else cared about.

He'd never thought himself worthy of love without caveats. In that, he and Hestraon were alike. But caging himself into being worthy had done nothing but keep him trapped.

Malcolm met him by the door, both of them already covered in their black cloaks. They didn't speak as they started toward the Rotunda.

It took him until the round building loomed into the sky to say something. "I'm sorry," Gabe breathed.

A nod. "Michal is the one who deserves an apology."

"Fair. He'll get one."

Malcolm sighed. "I understand. Truly, I do." He glanced sideways, expression soft. "But we can't be reckless with this. The stakes are too high. The whole damn world is in the balance here."

Gabe cared less and less about the world. Not if it would cost him Lore. Not if it would cost him Bastian.

Down in the belly of the Rotunda, the Brotherhood waited silently. Eoin's expression was eager, his hood the only one left down. Behind him, the copper door gleamed on the wall, fired shut and unassailable.

There was no preamble. Eoin already had the cup in his hand; he dipped it into the false Fount. Instead of passing it around the room, he drank the whole goblet dry.

Malcolm and Gabe shared a concerned look. Eoin was a fool, and these meetings were nothing but theater; still, the change in routine felt ominous.

Eoin dropped the goblet. It fell to the floor, rolled toward the Fount, clinked lightly against the side. Water streamed down his chin; he wiped it away, eyes strangely bright. "Something different tonight, friends," he said, turning to Gabe. Malcolm. "Instead of just showing us your power, I want you to walk us through it. Tell us exactly how it works, as if you were explaining the steps for use."

Gabe narrowed his eyes. "I'm not sure what you mean."

"Precisely what I said." Eoin wiped his mouth again. "Channel fire. Talk me through it, in detail, as if you were going to pass on the power to someone who needed to know the mechanics."

That was rather unsettling, especially with Eoin's eyes so bright, so eager. Especially with the door welded shut behind him, hiding the Fount piece.

But if Eoin had designs on Hestraon's power, he was destined to be disappointed. The only way it could pass through death was for a god to do the killing.

He didn't really need to close his eyes to call fire, but Gabe did, evening out his breathing, letting his body fall into channeling-space. He remembered doing this to channel Mortem, what felt like ages ago.

Calling fire felt different than calling death ever had. Death had never belonged to him.

"Block out all other distractions." This was bullshit, and Gabe had never been very good at bullshitting. Trying to explain how to channel to someone who couldn't was like trying to tell a rock how to make rain. "Concentrate on the atmosphere until it begins to break down into parts."

He'd opened his eyes, at some point, the world veiled in black and white. It made everything hard to see, indistinct shapes. Before, when he'd channeled fire, it had always been on instinct. Hells, his earliest experiences had been by accident, back when he didn't fully understand what was happening, when he would have done anything to stop it. He'd never taken the time to sink in, to feel the full weight of what he could do.

The world was dark and blurred, nothing clear except the strands of red-orange streaking through the air. Unfelt, unseen, but capable of cleansing destruction.

"You see what you want," Gabe said, not thinking through his words anymore. "The thread of the element, how it weaves into everything else. And you tease it out."

His finger twitched. One of those red filaments, a seed of fire, wound itself around his hand. Breached his skin and ran all through him.

"You let it into yourself," he said, "and you tell it what you want. And then you let it go."

He let the thread of fire burn itself to nothing, hovering in front of him, a spark and flame in the air that lasted only a handful of heartbeats.

"Excellent," Eoin said, his voice too close. "Doesn't sound too difficult at all."

Things happened fast then.

Gabe shook himself from channeling-space just in time to see the Prime Minister lunge for him, a dagger in his hand. Ornate, golden, old. Gabe feinted left, the point of the blade catching his shoulder rather than his throat.

The dagger was Mount-mined; he remembered the conversation he'd overheard, put the pieces together. Apparently, Eoin thought such a thing would allow him to steal god-power. But it was just a blade that stung like any other.

Gabe snarled, catching flame, turning it toward Eoin's cloak.

Or trying to—it was wet, soaking, and so was Eoin's skin, his hair. Wet footprints marked the ground between where they stood and the false Fount, filled only with common water. But water was enough; he'd bathed himself in it while Gabe was lost in channeling-space, made himself something that couldn't burn.

At least not for a moment, and a moment was all he needed. A Mount-mined blade wouldn't take his power, but it could take his life quite easily.

"You don't deserve it." Eoin sounded nonchalant as he lunged at Gabe again, the blade swiping for his throat and missing. He was barely trying; he knew there was nowhere for Gabe to go. "All this power that you worked against bringing back into the world. And what have you done with it? Nothing."

The other members of the Brotherhood stood at his back, blocking the stairs, holding plain steel daggers of their own. None of them advanced, letting their leader strike the killing blow. Three of them had Malcolm, two holding his arms, one with a blade to his neck.

Another halfhearted swipe of Eoin's dagger. He had Gabe cornered; he was in no hurry. He had never not gotten something he wanted.

They had to get that Fount piece. And then they'd have to kill their way out of here.

Even as the thought came, Gabe was already looking for another solution, already hoping he could reason Eoin away from this. He didn't want all those deaths on his conscience.

At least, he didn't *want* to want them.

"Why kill me?" Gabe stood, knees bent, hands held in loose

fists. Brawling came naturally to him; doing so with a man who held a knife wasn't smart, but Eoin's cloak would dry eventually. He kept testing the air, sparking dust motes into shooting stars that made the atmosphere glimmer, but Eoin's robe was still too wet to catch. No magical protection, just simple physics, and if that was what managed to get him stabbed, Gabe was going to scream all the way to his own personal hell. "It won't give you my power. It doesn't work like that."

"Doesn't it?" Eoin cocked his head. "I suppose we'll find out, once you're dead."

Another swipe of his dagger. It drew blood this time, a thin line across Gabe's chest.

"Take comfort in the fact that you would have made no differ-ence," Eoin said. "Your Queen is dead, your King is gone, and the Empire will be mine." He bared his teeth. "That's what you get for being too cowardly to use what you have."

Gabe's thoughts ignited, flames springing to life in his palms, burning out any shred of conscience, of doubt.

Eoin was covered in water, too wet to set afire.

But the other Brothers weren't.

A twitch of his fingers, red-orange threads.

The Brotherhood of the Waters burst into flames.

It took them a moment to realize what was happening. Then, chaos, some of them diving toward the Fount, others screaming and running up the stairs, trying to beat out the fire by ramming themselves against the walls.

With a roar, Gabe thrust his hands at the copper door in the wall. Fire blazed around it, lighting the metal bright orange, making it drip down the stone like scouring tears.

Eoin shrieked. But the sound wasn't anger; it was laughter, high and delighted. "Look at you!" He swiped out with the knife again. "How *useful* this will be when it's mine."

Embers crackled in the air, the fires burning everywhere finally drying the waters of the false Fount from Eoin's skin, his cloak and hair. Gabe twisted his fingers, drawing in flame—

"I get this one," a voice said from behind him.

A cloaked figure surged forward, familiar, holding a knife. A knife that he used to slice the Prime Minister's throat.

For such a powerful man, from such a powerful family, Eoin died easy. Gabe had seen enough powerful men die to know that it was never any different from anyone else, but it still surprised him, every time.

Eoin's killer turned, his hood thrown back.

"Now," Finn said. "To take care of you."

But Gabe was faster. He ran toward the copper door, gaping open like a death mouth. The flames didn't hurt as he shoved his arm through the opening, grabbing the piece of the Fount inside. It felt worse than the fire did, immediately making his arm numb to the shoulder. Pain rushed through him, enough to make him shout and almost drop the piece.

Finn came up behind him, struck the back of his head in the same perfect place Gabe had been taught as a child in the Presque Mort, and the pain flared out as his world went black.

CHAPTER TWENTY-NINE
ALIE

We remain vigilant, for buried does not mean dead.
—Vows of the Buried Watch

It was a miracle, really, that Brigitte didn't insist on coming.

In their shared childhood, Bri had been the friend up for anything, adventurous and charismatic, able to get them out of any scrape. She'd never been part of Gabe, Alie, and Bastian's trio, soldered together by unhappy mothers, but Alie had spent nearly as much time with Bri as she had with her boys. When Bri looked into Lore's erstwhile engagement ring and saw the word carved there, Alie braced herself for the questions, Bri's insistence on accompanying her into the tomb.

But Bri had put down her magnifying tool and held out the ring as if she didn't want to touch it anymore. Silence rang between them, its own kind of confession.

"Don't tell me anything," Bri finally whispered, her lips barely moving. "It makes me a coward, probably, but I don't want to know."

"It's all right," Alie murmured. "It's all right, Bri."

"It's not." Bri took a deep, shaky breath. "But I'm doing it anyway." She stood from her bench, gave Alie a tremulous smile. "I'll always be there for you. You know that. But this…it's too much."

And Alie didn't blame her at all.

So now, waiting for Lilia by a derelict house near the Harbor District under a sky blue-dark before dawn, Alie was alone.

The ring weighed heavy in her pocket; Alie spun it around in her fingers like a worry stone. There was no reason to bring it—it wasn't a map after all, just a clue, a one-word answer—but she didn't want to leave it in her room. The heft of it was somehow comforting, her nail skating along its facets a counterpoint to the thud of her heart.

Alie had never been this far into Dellaire. The southern Wards were a little larger than the northern ones, and this district was right at the edge, putting it nearly as far from the Citadel as you could get without leaving the city. She knew this was where Lore had lived before being caught by the Presque Mort; she supposed she understood the appeal.

This building was one of the outer entrances to the catacombs, according to Lilia. The house looked like it was barely holding together, like a stiff breeze might knock it over. Alie wasn't quite brave enough to venture in on her own, on the off chance the whole thing might collapse.

At least, not until she saw the bloodcoats.

They came around the corner of the street, torches outheld, the flames reflecting off the polished ends of bayonets. Patrols out here near the city limits were common, but Alie assumed she'd missed them, not thinking they would be so close to sunrise. Apparently, she was wrong, and she desperately didn't want them to see her.

She wore a cloak; she could just cower on the stoop, hope they mistook her for a beggar woman. But Alie had seen how bloodcoats treated beggar women. Best not to chance it.

With a curse in her teeth, she slipped into the house.

It didn't immediately crumble, so that was something. Alie pressed her back against one of the graffiti-covered walls, eyes canted sideways to watch the bloodcoats pass. They were loud, shouting to one another, obnoxious and vulgar and some clearly drunk. She wrinkled her nose. Dellaire's finest.

"Don't be afraid to show yourselves, whores!" one of them yelled. "Apollius *loves* whores! The gods are on your side!"

"Apollius said you should give us a discount!" another roared, and all of them laughed, sharp and brassy in the predawn.

Alie deeply hoped every working girl in the district was safe in their beds by this hour.

"You're one of them."

The voice was close, right in front of her. Alie swallowed a scream.

In the hallway before the door, stretched out on the floor and half hidden in shadow, was a revenant.

She'd heard of them. She was even sure that some of the courtiers would qualify, had they been born into different circumstances, with less money and less access to things that could hide their diminishment. More than one noble family had a relative who'd taken too much poison secreted in a faraway estate, haunting the halls as their mind wasted away just as their body had.

But she'd never seen one up close. Not one this far gone.

Poison had ravaged out all markers of sex or gender. The revenant looked like an animated skeleton more than anything, the sharp jut of bones hidden beneath a shapeless gray cloak. Their eyes were sunken pits, glittering at her in the dark.

"A breeze where she was a storm," the revenant said, with a dry chuckle like the rub of withered stalks. "The cloud to her coffin. All of them have awoken, then. I remember seeing her here, in this house. I remember sensing what she would become. Walk this close to death, and you recognize its queen." The revenant stirred, the sound of dry leaves in wind. "She met destiny that day. Thick as syrup in the air. A fate you could breathe in."

"Lore?" Alie asked quietly. "You've seen Lore?" Maybe her friend was more resourceful than she'd given her credit for. Maybe she'd somehow found a way off the Burnt Isles, away from the Golden Mount, back here to the city—

"Long ago," the revenant said. "Before she knew what would become of you all." The revenant sighed. "Being like this—thrown somewhere outside of mortality—makes time meld together. It's a shore, you see, and I linger at its edge."

"How does it end, then?" Alie whispered.

Another dry laugh. "It's a river, not an ocean," the revenant said. "There are many streams, many tributaries, and it flows ever on. The future is always changing. You could save the world or damn it, little breeze, and no one will know until the damning or the saving comes."

A rustle at the door. Lilia stepped over the threshold, covered in a dark cloak. She pulled back her hood and furrowed her brow. "Were you talking to someone?"

The revenant had turned their pale face back toward the wall, back into shadow. The low light made them invisible, one more forgotten thing in this falling-apart house, lingering between life and death.

"No," Alie said. "Let's move."

Lilia didn't look like she believed her, but there was no time to waste with interrogation. With a nod, Lore's mother started down the hall, picking her way over piles of trash and dust from the crumbling walls. At the hallway's end was a gaping hole, leading into nothing but darkness. Someone had painted a face on the wall next to it with *X*'s over the eyes.

"Is that a direction or a warning?" Alie asked.

"A bit of both." Lilia stopped at the lip of the hole. "Most people want to avoid the catacombs, but some—poison runners, mostly—use them to move undetected through the city. The rule that Presque Mort aren't allowed to enter without priestly dispensation comes in handy."

Alie had known that Lore's familiarity with the catacombs went deeper than being born there, even before she'd become Nyxara's avatar. It seemed she'd never managed to escape them.

Cool air blew from the hole, a dank scent of rock and deep places. The catacombs were safe now, no chance of leaking Mortem, but Alie still wasn't excited by the prospect of traipsing through them.

Lilia said nothing. Just gave her an arch look and disappeared into the hole.

With a bracing breath, Alie followed.

The shadows closed around her like water over sinking stone. A moment of panic, then the hiss of a spark; Lilia had clicked on a lighter, the tiny flame wavering to dispel the shadows.

"We'll come across torch supplies at some point," she said. "The poison runners leave them all over."

She turned, headed deeper into the catacombs. Alie stayed as close behind her as she could without stepping on the back of her boots.

It took hours. Alie should have expected that, probably—of course the lair of the Buried Watch and the tomb of the Buried Goddess would be far underground. Eventually, Lilia found the materials to make a torch, and the halo of light around them grew enough for Alie to stop feeling nervous and start feeling bored.

At least, until they came to the collapsed tunnel.

"Please tell me that's not the way to the tomb." Alie spun Lore's engagement ring around and around in her pocket.

"Unfortunately." Lilia stepped forward, put a hand on one of the stones. "I'm not sure when it happened. Sometime after I left."

Alie looked sidelong at the other woman. "Left the Watch, or left Dellaire?"

"The country," Lilia murmured. "I made it to Balgia before I felt guilty enough to turn back. I'd told her to leave a rose if she wanted my help. But I only waited a week to see if she would." Her fingers curled, then fell from the rocks. "I called her selfish, but she got it from me."

"You came back." Alie wasn't sure why she wanted to comfort Lore's mother. Maybe because she'd had few opportunities to comfort her own.

"I did, and it was too late." Lilia scoffed softly. "I can't make up for that. There's so much I can't make up for."

The sentence hung like something should come after it. Nothing did.

Lilia stepped away from the wreckage, surveying the rubble with a shrewd eye. "This should be fairly simple for you, I think."

"Maybe we can—" Alie stopped, shot an incredulous look at the former Night Priestess. "What do you mean, for me?"

"You're the one with god-power."

"So what are you suggesting I do? I have Lereal's power. Air. The weakest of the bunch." She hadn't known she thought of it that way until she said it. And she didn't like the way it filled her with...with *resentment*, as if this magic were something she wanted. As if she'd take more, if she could.

Lilia gave her a sidelong glance. "Subtlety is not weakness, Alienor. It's a strength all its own."

Alie straightened, flexing her hands in anticipation of weaving air threads. "This is ironic timing, certainly."

She closed her eyes, dropping down into what she'd heard Gabe call channeling-space before opening them again. This wasn't a necessity every time she used her magic—*Lereal's magic*, she reminded herself, *not yours*—and the one time she'd done something like this, stopping that statue from flattening her in the storage room, it had been instinct, not something she did on purpose. But for clearing the whole tunnel, she probably needed a bit more concentration.

The black-and-white world separated itself slowly, the weave of it widening as she focused. Tendrils of iridescence curled through the empty spaces around the rocks, even those that appeared to have no gaps between them. "I'm still not entirely sure what I'm supposed to do here."

"Have you ever seen a cannon fire without a ball?" Lilia asked. "At close range, it can still do quite a bit of damage, just from the force of the air."

Trying to mimic a cannon deep in the catacombs, whether loaded with a missile or not, didn't seem like a great idea. But Alie got the gist. If she harnessed enough air, made it go in the same direction, she could break the rocks apart enough for them to climb through.

With a twitch of her fingers, Alie coaxed the threads toward her, through her. It was never an unpleasant sensation, and that, too, was concerning. Channeling air and imbuing it with her will felt like stepping into cool water on a hot day, like a sky with the perfect balance of sun and breeze.

Her will was simple. *Forward* and *force* and *through*.

Alie pushed all those threads back out.

The sound made her want to slam her hands over her ears. The rocks broke with a grinding and squeal, like the teeth of an anxious giant, crumbling to the ground as a pattering of heavy raindrops. Instinctively, Alie covered her head.

But the tunnel itself remained intact. And when Alie shook herself out of channeling-space, a path through the tunnel was clear. Treacherous, maybe, and requiring more climbing than she'd prefer, but clear.

Next to her, Lilia took a deep breath and squared her shoulders. Then, without a word, she started forward.

Neither of them spoke as they made their way down into the catacombs, toward the home of the Buried Watch. Mostly because all their attention was spent on picking over the jagged pieces of rock on the ground, but Lilia's silence seemed heavier than simple concentration could explain. Alie supposed that was fair when you were venturing into the lair of the cult where you'd spent most of your life. The resting place of those who'd convinced her that the world needed her daughter dead.

But it was Lilia's home, too. And those people had been her family.

"What was it like?" Alie asked softly.

"Being part of the Buried Watch?" Lilia stopped on a patch of stone floor that wasn't littered with rock shards, staring into the dark. The flickering of her torch carved out the hollows of her face, made her look older. "When I first joined—when I had nowhere else to go—it was comforting. When I learned just how important our job was, just how badly things could go if we failed, it was awe inspiring." She swallowed. "And when I had Lore… when they told me what would become of her… it was terrifying."

She started forward again. Alie followed, not speaking.

"You have to understand that I thought I was saving her when I asked her to die," Lilia said, so quiet it was hard to hear even in the silence. "I know that's hard to understand, but I thought I was saving her from becoming something awful. I thought the world would end, were she allowed to go on, and she would be nothing but a puppet for the goddess. I had no way of knowing it wasn't true. At least, not the way I'd been told."

"I believe you," Alie said, because she sensed that was what Lilia wanted to hear. She didn't know if she meant it or not.

But it seemed Lore's mother was too deep in memory to hear, regardless of if she wanted to. "I couldn't do it, at first," Lilia continued. "When they marked her with the moon. I felt so selfish when I told her to run, but I couldn't bear to see her enter the tomb and be stripped out of herself, even though we all knew she was more dangerous than the Night Witch. It was wrong, and I regretted it; by letting her escape I'd consigned her to a worse fate.

But then we worked with the Church, found a way to fix my mistakes. To make Lore the end of the cycle, but not the world." She shrugged, limp and defeated. "I thought it was a good thing when the old Priest Exalted made plans to bring her in, right before her Consecration. To sharpen the powers of the chosen Arceneaux, to make Apollius return. It felt like righting a wrong." She paused, torch flickering. "I don't think any of us could fathom that it was Apollius who was wrong."

It was obvious when they reached the part of the catacombs that had housed the Buried Watch. The tunnels widened out. A soft glow emanated from plant life clinging to the walls, vines and mushrooms that Alie didn't recognize. She wanted to ask about them, but down here, near to where so much magic had been housed for so long, such things should be expected.

The bones, however, were a surprise.

Human, all of them, scattered around the tunnel, some broken from the collapsed rock, others whole. A shattered femur speared up from the center of the floor, sharp end ready to catch an unwary foot. A full rib cage lay on its side near where the tunnel began to widen.

She'd known that there were bones down here, left over from revenants crawling in to die, from those who couldn't afford a vault and didn't have anyone who cared enough to see them burned. But these bones didn't seem old, didn't seem like afterthoughts. They looked...new. Yellowed, still, not outside of a body long enough to bleach. The scent of rot married the mineral scent of the stone tunnels, the crisp and ozonic notes from channeled air, and she grimaced.

"Come on," Lilia said grimly.

She pushed forward. Alie didn't want to follow. But she wanted to be alone in the dark even less.

The tunnel widened into a cavern. Alie couldn't tell how large; the luminous plants only grew near the ground, and the dark seemed to eat the light from Lilia's torch, only letting it travel so far.

The former Night Priestess stepped carefully. There were more bones here, a maze of them across the floor. These had to be her friends, the other members of the Buried Watch, but Lilia showed no emotion other than a clenched jaw.

She didn't show any emotion even when she looked at the obsidian rubble of the tomb.

There had been many moments in the past few months when Alie had come face-to-face with something from a myth. She housed something mythical in her own mind, spun it with her hands. But still, the ruins of the tomb that had held Nyxara's dead body made her pause, made her breath leave in a gasp that might've been awed or terrified, and Alie couldn't tell which it was.

She also couldn't account for the empty feeling that sank her stomach, seeing that tomb blown apart.

"What in every hell happened here?" she asked, clutching her skirt in her hands so it didn't brush against bones.

"Lore happened," Lilia answered.

Even now, Lilia lingered at the side of the ruins, hesitant to step over the first lines of obsidian. Alie wasn't eager to, herself. In fact, she felt like crying.

"Shit." All her muscles hung slack around her bones; it was all she could do not to crumple. "If the tomb is gone, how are we supposed to find the shard?"

"The tomb isn't gone, it's just broken." Sucking in a sharp breath, Lilia stepped into the rubble. As she did, her spine softened, and she turned to arch a brow at Alie. "So we start looking through the broken pieces."

"Finding a broken piece in a million broken pieces." Alie sighed as she followed Lilia into the piles of jagged obsidian. "Brilliant."

And that was what they did. For hours, it felt like, though

there was no real way to tell time down here, nothing to mark its passing except the steadily worsening ache in her back. Alie thought her hell might be like this. Fruitlessly picking up shining chunks of black stone only to put them down again.

Some of the pieces of the tomb were larger than others. One of them was nearly as large as a mirror, and just as reflective. Alie stopped her searching and stared at herself, just for a moment. This body, the same one that had carried her through twenty-four years, now housing the power of a god.

But she liked how she looked with it. Her spine straighter, her eyes clearer. There was a faintness around her hands, making them look ghostly. As if they'd disappear when held to a light.

A light...

The bioluminescent plants didn't illuminate much, about the same as a full moon on a clear night. But over in the corner, a large group of them glowed brighter than the others.

Not quite a sunrise, but worth a try.

Alie fished the ring from her pocket. It buzzed against her skin. She picked over chunks of obsidian to the glowing plants and lifted the ring, expecting nothing.

A thin beam of light, like the tail of a shooting star, pointing to the middle of the rubble.

She glanced over her shoulder. Lilia had stopped her search, eyes narrowed at the ring. Alie jerked her chin to the beam of light. "I'd look there."

Lilia did. And it only took a moment to find the shard. She reached out to touch it and hissed, snatching her hand back. "Damn. That hurts like every hell."

Alie made her way over, cautiously bending down to the shard. Her hands buzzed, so much worse than touching the ring, but she gritted her teeth and closed her fingers on its edges.

Pain, scouring, like she'd been lit on fire. Alie's mouth opened, but all that came out was a harsh breath.

Then the pain was over, a half heartbeat of agony. It still made her hands numb, but Alie could lift it now. She hauled the piece up from the ground.

It was pale, seamed in gold. On the edge, a carved sun, a perfect match to the Arceneaux crown.

"How did it do that?" Lilia breathed.

"Something about magic, I'm sure." Alie tucked the ring back into her pocket. "The stone is Mount-mined. I guess things from the Golden Mount call to each other."

"And it doesn't hurt you to touch." Lilia shook her head. "A fail-safe, I supposed. So only gods can handle the pieces."

Something about that itched in the back of Alie's mind.

Above their heads, the cavern shuddered.

Lilia glanced up. "Did you hear that?"

Another shudder, dust clouding the air in the light from their torch.

Apollius had built the tomb, had put the Fount piece here. Had never wanted the Fount put back together again.

It made sense for Him to build in a defense mechanism.

Rocks pattered to the floor like rain, small enough not to cause undue injury, but large and sharp enough to hurt. One landed on Alie's arm, blooming a bruise. In the dark where their light didn't reach, the echoing sounds of grinding, falling, imminent collapse.

"Shit," Lilia hissed.

Alie's hand shot up, her fingers gathering in air. The iridescent lines flowed into her and then back out, weaving themselves into a shield over her and Lilia's heads. A rock, larger than the others so far, fell from the ceiling and bounced off. Alie winced. "We should run, probably."

As if her words tipped the scale, the ceiling of the cathedral crashed down.

This was no gentle warning, giving them time to escape—this was a full-measure assault, the magic woven into this place going after them like hunting dogs with the taste of blood. Stones twice as big as Alie crashed to the ground, bouncing from her shield— she kept from screaming, but only just, the impact reverberating through her outstretched arm. She and Lilia sprinted toward the mouth of the tunnel she had already cleared, tripping over bones.

And the collapsing didn't stop once they got free of the cathedral, of that first tunnel. The phosphorescence of the plant life slowly faded as Alie's fingers shook with the pressure of her air-woven shield. The Fount piece burned in her other hand, her fingers numb, the half of her concentration not spent on the shield focused completely on not dropping the stupid stone that was currently bringing the earth down on their heads.

"It'll collapse the whole damn catacombs!" Lilia shouted next to her, still barely audible over the screech of rock.

A light up ahead, after a churn of time that seemed both longer and shorter than the hours it had taken to hike down here. The hole in the derelict house, the place they'd entered. Alie had never run so fast in her life.

She pelted through the hole, Lilia at her back. They didn't stop, running through the house and out the door, into the street.

Shuddering, the groaning of old wood and old stone. The house's collapse was slow, not like the immediate destruction of the caverns below. And it was quiet, almost, as if the house's ghost was half given up already. The row houses were all crooked now, the foundations slipped from their moorings as the tunnel beneath them collapsed. They'd surely been unstable before, when the first tunnel Alie cleared had gone down. Now that the entire path up from Nyxara's tomb was rubble, the consequences were finally visible. A few people came out of the houses, frowning, trying to figure out what had happened. Alie pulled her hood over her head and turned away.

"So much for secrecy," Lilia said.

Alie hid the stone shard in the pocket of her cloak. It was too big to fit without bulging. As soon as her hand let it go, feeling started coming back to her fingers in painful waves. "No one pays attention to the houses out here," she said, hating that it was true, hating that she was using that to her advantage. "And most of them have been unstable for years. No one should immediately put together that it has anything to do with the tunnels."

"But they will eventually."

"Hopefully, by then we'll be long gone." The piece in her pocket seemed to...*tug*, almost, toward the shining line of the ocean beyond the row houses. A stream being drawn back to a river, a lodestone finding home.

Alie closed her hand around it, mindless of the pain.

CHAPTER THIRTY

LORE

The past is the easiest place to get lost.
                    —Taya Mireau, Auverrani poet

The island was thick with memory.

She and Dani had fallen into an uneasy routine in the days since they'd arrived. They'd divided up the island as best they could—Dani searched through the ruins of the villages, while Lore took the wild places, the idea being that she'd have an easier time navigating them, what with her god-affinity. Thus far, it both had and hadn't worked. Lore was able to explore the island without getting hopelessly lost, but neither of them had managed to find Apollius's body yet.

Last night, as they sat in front of a tiny fire that Dani had made with her lighter and some dead branches, she'd brought up the thing they'd both thought of but hadn't yet discussed. "What happens if we can't find Him?"

Lore had shifted on the ground, holding a half-eaten piece of dried meat in her hand. Their stores were running low, but she found she hadn't been very hungry since they arrived. As if the very air of this place sustained her. "He's here. We'll find Him."

Dani glared at her across the fire. "You can sense enough to be sure of that, but not enough to know where He is yet?"

Lore just looked at her. After a moment, Dani looked away. They hadn't spoken again, both bedding down for the night next to the Fount. Dani had given up sleeping on the ship, but neither of them were brave enough to sleep in the cathedral ruins. Lore knew enough not to believe in ghosts; still, Apollius's old church felt haunted.

The truth was that Lore *did* feel something. On the backside of the Mount, beneath the ash-cover, the mountain had a sheer rock face, as if something huge had slid down the earth. She kept finding herself drawn there, standing on a grassy outcropping that jutted out over the slice of stone, staring. This was where they should be looking.

She wasn't sure why she hadn't yet. Why the place seemed to both push her forward and draw her back. The place in her head where Nyxara had been seemed to tug her toward it, while the rest of her shied away.

But this had to come to an end, eventually.

Now she stood there again, the wind off the sea stirring the ash and feathering her hair against her face. She held on to the trunk of a burnt tree and leaned out, just a bit, looking down at that sheer face. If she fell, it wouldn't be immediate death. It'd be tumbling head over feet down this stone-slide, crashing against craggy handholds and pockmarks, until she hit the black water of the ocean.

And still, a glimmer. Calling her out onto that rock.

And if He was there? If she found Him, killed Him? What then?

It was a question she'd thought of before, but never with such immediacy. Apollius still had both deaths the Fount had given Him, one in body and one in spirit. So what happened when Lore finally killed His body? She didn't think Bastian would be as lucky as she was when she killed Nyxara. The goddess hadn't wanted a stronger hold in Lore's mind, but Apollius wanted all of

Bastian; giving Him one bodily death would only make His spirit dig in deeper claws. Especially now that she knew renouncing the gods was as simple as words said in the vicinity of the Fount, close enough for It to siphon back Its magic.

For Gabe and Malcolm and Alie, their plan could be enough. Gather back the pieces of the Fount, fit them to their proper places. Have them wish away their power as they stood close. But for Bastian, it would never be that simple. Apollius would never let him come here.

So they'd force Him, somehow. Drug Him, maim Him, do whatever they had to do to wrestle Him to the side of the Fount and hope Bastian was strong enough to fight forward. They'd come this far, impossibly. She refused to leave the job half done.

It is not the closeness alone that allowed Us to take Nyxara back.

The not-voice, the Fount speaking. It was fainter here than when she was in the courtyard, but still clear. Lore tipped up her chin to the sea breeze. "What is it, then?"

You renounced Her, and She desired to go.

Lore sighed. "So Bastian can't get rid of Apollius unless Apollius decides to leave?"

He cannot.

"This is all pointless, then. Apollius will never do that."

Not unless He thinks there is somewhere better to be.

"I repeat: pointless." It didn't make her angry, just filled her with a deep and abiding despair. The closer she got to an end, the further away it drew.

No, the Fount countered. **Not if you continue on your path. Not if you give Him somewhere else to be.**

A frustrated growl rumbled in her throat. "Whatever the fuck that means."

Her fingers tightened on the burnt bark. She leaned farther over the precipice, her center of gravity shifting.

He weakens, the Fount offered, as if it were a consolation. **His vessel has renounced Him and sometimes fights free. Each time the vessel is in control, a little more power is lost. Leaked back to Us.**

"But You can't hold it until You're put back together."

Not all of it, the Fount answered. **But some of it.**

Better than nothing, Lore supposed. Since the chances of Alie and Gabe and Malcolm being able to find their pieces of the Fount and get them here still seemed very slim, for all that her makeshift plan hinged on it. "So if Bastian manages to take over for long enough, Apollius will drain out? And You can hold all of Spiritum, at least, even if we don't manage to find all the pieces, and can't surrender all the magic?"

The Fount was quiet for a moment. **He will never be gone completely until He decides to leave.**

"That's really fucking unfair," Lore murmured.

For a moment longer, Lore hovered half on the knoll and half over the open air that led to the slick of rock. A wound left by the Godsfall; she knew that. If she closed her eyes, she could almost see the tumble of gods falling down the mountain as they fought, taking trees and growth with them, burning it or tearing it away as they rolled toward the sea. She could almost feel the dig of rock into her shoulders.

She could almost see the place where Nyxara had put Him, after it all. Where she'd brought His body, with the sucking hole in His chest, the barely tethered heart.

Lore straightened. Then she went to the grove.

The grove hadn't been hard to find. The second day they were here, the island divided into searchable quadrants, her feet had taken her here instinctually, something in her body knowing where to go. When she entered the trees, she knew exactly where she was.

It didn't look like her dreams anymore; didn't look like the forest she'd grown around her mind as paltry protection from the fate she couldn't escape. Didn't even look like the one in the goddess's memories. That forest had been green and brown and uniform, in a false blush of health. This one was burnt, the trees spindly corpses pointing up into the sky, the dead leftovers of something holy.

But it was Nyxara's grove. Her grove.

Her searching always brought her here by the end of the day, no matter how she tried to avoid it. Memory felt thick as hangman's rope, continually tightening, but Lore held it back, like she had every other time she came. She'd had enough of seeing a life that wasn't hers; her own was exhausting enough.

But today, the tide of memory was nearly too much to ignore, and it pulled her on, coaxing her to drown.

When Lore reached the grove, she went to the center, where the moss was still soft even if it was coated in ash. She lay down, shifting her head until she was comfortable. She closed her eyes and slipped into time's river, too tired to hold herself away.

It played out like it had when she'd touched Nyxara in the tomb—Lore looking out from Nyxara's eyes, experiencing Her memories as if they were her own. It was disorienting to be in the same place where they'd happened, five hundred years gone in a blink. One moment, the grove was gray and burnt, and the next it was vibrant, a sanctuary grown to keep her complacent.

She turned her head. Next to her, Hestraon, stretched naked on the moss, his eyes closed. He didn't look like Gabe, she knew that. But Gabe was all Lore could see.

"What are you thinking about?" He didn't open his eyes, but Hestraon reached out and grasped her hands. They were bound together with a ribbon at the wrist, and he stroked his finger along it, tender against her pulse.

Soreness between her legs; so that's what they'd been doing. Lore found herself disappointed this memory hadn't started half an hour earlier.

Nyxara rolled on her side and hooked her leg around Hestraon's, tugging him closer. "Nothing."

"Yes you are," he said softly. "You're thinking that you want to escape with us."

She looked away. The plan that would eventually lead to the Godsfall was in its infancy, but she knew that there was no way she could leave with the others. That he wouldn't let her. And she'd told them that it was fine, that she would be fine. Nyxara had a penchant for self-sacrifice that Lore couldn't relate to.

But Hestraon always knew.

"Nyxara." He cupped her cheek. "There has to be a way to escape him. I know you love him. I do, too. But you can't sacrifice yourself for his sake."

She closed her eyes. Huffed a short laugh. "Sometimes, I think that's the only escape I'll find."

"You don't mean that."

"I do." She opened her eyes. Looked not at him but at her hand tracing his side, his neck. "I think, sometimes, that the two of us together are too much for the world to take. That there can be nothing for me as long as he lives." She paused. "I'm tied to him so closely, sometimes I wonder if I would even exist, if he was gone."

"Then you'll both leave me," Hestraon murmured.

When Lore's eyes opened, the trees were burnt again.

The moss was comfortable. The island warmth and the futility of her mission pulled at her eyelids, made her body settle.

Lore didn't realize she'd fallen asleep until she saw the ocean.

She sat up, frowning.

The tide had washed in, warm as bathwater, soaking the filmy white dress she was always wearing here. Lore pulled her knees into her chest and rested her chin on them, staring out at the eternity of blue, the sky meeting the ocean.

If the Shining Realm had existed, it would probably look like this.

Gabe didn't call her name. Didn't do anything but come sit beside her. Like Hestraon in Nyxara's memory, he reached out and took her hand, staring out over the endless horizon.

"How are things going for you?" she asked softly.

"Shitty," he answered. "You?"

"About the same."

He glanced at her. "I heard you escaped."

"*Escaped* might be overselling it." Lore stroked her thumb along his. "But I'm off the Second Isle. I'm at the Mount."

He huffed a laugh. "I should have known you could do it."

Her wrist still itched with the ghost of that ribbon in Nyxara's memories. Her nerves tingled with the aftershocks of intimacy she hadn't experienced.

Lore was so gods-damned tired of waiting. Of existing in this stasis where every step forward came with a step back. Of losing herself in increments.

Once, she'd been a person who took what she wanted.

When she turned to Gabe, he was already looking at her. A question already in his eyes, a tenseness to his limbs, everything they had never allowed to happen crashing into this moment.

She leaned forward and answered the question.

Lore had thought before about how different it was, kissing Gabe versus kissing Bastian. How Bastian was a slow explosion, a discovery, while Gabe was all flash and fire. He proved it once again; there was no easing into this kiss, no steady build. They fell into each other like starving animals.

His mouth opened to hers like it was all he'd been thinking about. His tongue brushed along the side of her own, hungry and seeking. Her body, already warmed, went up like kindling to a spark.

Gabe pulled her onto his lap; Lore straddled his waist, hips already chasing friction. His hands were on the softness of her waist, pulling at the hem of her white robe, tossing it away into the surf.

He sat back, eyes glazed, taking her in. He didn't speak, didn't need to.

Another searing kiss, his hands rising from her waist to find her breasts—Lore threw her head back as his thumbs circled the gathered peaks, her gasp loud in the silence, without even the sound of the tide to blunt it.

As he kissed her neck, Lore took his hands, guided them behind her back. She put her wrists together like Nyxara's had been, pulling his fingers to circle them, bind them.

"Make me," she whispered. He'd know what she meant.

And he did. Gabe looked at her with glazed eyes and nodded.

Quick but still gentle, he flipped her over, back against the soft sand. He held her arms prone over her head so her body stretched out below him, helpless and writhing.

Bastian had wanted her in charge, that night. Wanted to give up control, wanted to know that their intimacy was only theirs. They might have the same wants as the gods who'd chosen them as vessels, but that didn't make those wants any less their own.

She wanted to be held down. Wanted to be denied, in an imitation of the way he'd denied her before. But this time, within her own parameters, and with the heated understanding that the denial was coming to an end.

Her body ached for him to touch her. Lore canted up her hips, trying to guide his hand that wasn't holding her arms over her head; Gabe gave her a tiny slap on the thigh. The sting of it made her jump, made her breath come ragged and all her nerves pull tight.

"Patience," he said, gently pushing her hair away from her face, touching her everywhere but the places she wanted. Lore turned her head, tried to capture his finger in her mouth; he pulled away with another light slap, this time right below her hips, and she arched into it.

"I've been patient." She pressed her thighs together, all but panting. "You could have had this at any time. All you had to do was say the word."

"I know," he said, skimming his hand lightly down her neck, between her breasts, but lifting it away before he went lower. "So I'm making up for lost time."

Because there was no way to know if this first time would also be the last.

As if he'd heard the thought, he kissed her again, tender and sweet, a counterpoint to the pressure he held on her wrists. And finally, his hand went where she wanted it.

Lore writhed on the sand while Gabe played her like a harp, bringing her over and over to a breaking point, then taking it away right before she went over the edge. She gasped and she cursed, quivering while he laughed, low and rumbling against her neck, kissing her there to make up for it.

"You asshole." Her voice came broken, every nerve in her body vibrating like glass about to shatter. "You're a monk, you shouldn't be so good at this."

He chuckled again against the shell of her ear, the sound going straight through her and making her legs clench around his hand. "I didn't always hold so close to my vows. I told you that."

She looked at him, something bittersweet spilling through her chest. "So why not with me?"

He looked at her a moment, all games gone, his eyes still heated but with a kind of sadness, too. He kissed her cheek. Not her forehead, like Bastian did, as if he knew that they each had a place with her and wouldn't overstep. "Because I knew I would love you, and I didn't know how to yet. It was too much."

It was all still too much. But she didn't want to think about that. She angled her chin so he would move his kiss to her mouth, and as it went deeper, as his hand worked at her just where she needed him to, she finally came with a hoarse scream.

Gabe swallowed it, let her ride it out, his palm pressed flat against her as she tremored through the aftershocks. When it was done, he let go of her wrists, gathered her close.

But Lore wasn't going to let that be it. She tugged at his hip bone, just like she had that night in her room, cold window glass at her back.

This time, he did what she wanted.

Lore sat on her knees on the sand as Gabe slowly stood, slowly took off his robe—a feat, since it was the same one she'd been wearing, but he managed to make it last. He was as meticulous with this as he was with everything else, folding it neatly, laying it flat on the ground.

"Gods," she rasped, "hurry the fuck up."

"Watch your pretty mouth," he said, looming over her still, grasping her chin in a firm but gentle hand, "unless you want something else to do with it."

"Maybe I do," she said, and proved it. He tasted like salt, and she licked along him, humming in approval when he tensed.

"Gods," Gabe murmured. "*Gods.*"

His head dropped back, his breathing ragged, and when she hummed, he jerked, one hand coming to her head and pushing her away. "That's enough, unless you want to wait at least fifteen more minutes."

"I've waited longer," Lore said, but she let him lay her down on the sand, let him brace himself above her. And when he surged into her, she kissed him again, and didn't stop until both of them came apart, the tide swelling around them.

They didn't untangle, even afterward. Gabe dropped his head into the crook of her shoulder, kissed it lightly. She ran her fingers through his hair.

The air around them shimmered. The dream, close to breaking.

"We found the piece of the Fount," Gabe said reluctantly into the crook of her neck. "But then we got captured by the Prime Minister's pirate lover. After he killed him."

"That was probably information you should have shared before we got started," she said, nuzzling into his neck.

"Probably," Gabe agreed, arching beneath her touch. "But for once, I did what I wanted to do first."

She couldn't blame him for that.

"You've had an exciting few days," Lore said. "What with a pirate lover."

"Believe me, it is more irritating than interesting." He shifted over her, running light fingers down her side. "In fact, I am currently passed out in what I believe he is using for a dungeon."

"You should be dealing with that instead of sleeping with me."

"On the contrary, I found it a welcome respite."

She tunneled her hand into his hair. "So what does he want?"

"Don't know yet." They were so used to strangeness at this point. So used to nothing going well. Gabe sighed and rolled off her, curling up by her side, his hand idly wandering down the line of her neck to her shoulder and back again. "But it will probably hinder our ability to bring the piece to the Mount."

Lore thought of Nyxara's memories of the pantheon's time on the Golden Mount. How They'd all moved through the threads of the atmosphere, the world allowing Them unnatural passage. "Maybe there's a way to get here besides taking a ship. The gods used to do that. Moving through the elements They had power over."

His gentle tracing paused. "I've done it. It didn't end well."

She sucked in a sharp breath. "I was afraid of that."

His hand started moving again, though it wasn't as steady. "Malcolm did it first, by accident. Told me that Braxtos came close to taking over when he did." He shook his head, churning sand. "I did it after—desperate times—and Hestraon almost had me. Malcolm was right." He looked at her. "But if it's our only option—"

"No." She pressed her palm against his jaw. "I can't handle that. I can't handle it happening to both of you."

Gabe and Bastian, both taken from her, eclipsed in godhood.

"We'll find another way." She said it with conviction, like she could make it true.

He closed his eye. He wore no patch over the other, something she just now noticed. The socket was healed cleanly. "If it saves us," he murmured, "it's a risk I'm willing to take."

She stroked her hand over his stubbled cheek.

A heartbeat, then Gabe looked away from her, out at the endless ocean, twisting a lock of her hair around his finger. "It's quite a lot of power we'll be giving up," he said. "Once we remake the Fount."

There was a question in his tone. Like maybe he didn't think that was the best plan after all.

And after her conversation with the Fount, that first day when she and Dani had arrived, Lore couldn't argue with him. "Yes," she said. "That's the current plan."

Current was doing a lot of heavy lifting.

Their thoughts traveled along the same lines, she knew. Maybe turning all this power back over to the Fount wasn't the right call. Maybe they could do more good trying to master it themselves.

But even though they were both thinking it, neither she nor Gabe said it.

The beach shimmered again, the atmosphere taking on a glassy, unreal quality. She turned in his arms, kissed him again, deep and long. "I love you. And if you see Bastian before I do, tell him I love him."

A question here, too. Gauging his reaction. Seeing how it landed.

Gabe sighed, cupping his hand against the side of her head. His thumb ran over the scar on her temple. "I didn't know I could do it," he murmured. "Love two people at once."

"Me either," she said. "I thought love would always come with choices, so I just refused to really make them. Even when I said I would marry Bastian, because I loved him, I loved you, too." She covered his hand with her own. "Love is bigger than we thought."

"Far bigger." Then, with another kiss to her cheek, Gabe was gone.

A blink, and she was back in the grove, awake on the Mount as it was now.

When Lore stood, she was pleasantly sore, her body languid and satiated.

She supposed she should be glad that Alie or Malcolm hadn't popped in while she and Gabe were busy, but she couldn't help but wish Bastian had. She'd never seen him on the beach; she assumed because Apollius had pushed him so far down in his own mind that simple dreaming wasn't a possibility.

The sky edged toward night. She'd slept the rest of the day away.

Lore made her way back to the Fount, wandering over the dead island. She'd been disturbed at first by the fact that nothing else lived here. No people, no animals or insects. Now it was nice to walk for miles and know you were almost completely alone, if you didn't count the woman who'd betrayed you and the god who should be dead.

It was almost beautiful, the way the moonlight filtered through the dead trees, made all the shadows stark. Especially after months without really seeing it, on the Second Isle where the smog was thick. It reflected on the cloud of ash below the peak, and on the water in the Fount.

Water that was shining gold.

Her brow furrowed. Slowly, Lore approached the Fount, as if It were a wild animal that might leap out at her. It had told her It could hold Spiritum, even broken as It was, gathering more every time Bastian fought free. Here was the proof.

The water in the Fount was still, always still. But as she watched, strands of gold twisted through the depths, just a slight shimmer. They were hard to see when she looked directly at them; Lore did better when she angled her eyes away.

Lore dropped herself into channeling-space.

The change from a colored world to grayscale wasn't that pronounced here, where everything was moonlit and burnt. The only thing that really changed was the water in the Fount.

Golden threads ran through it, as thick as they had been in the ocean, when Lore followed them to the Mount. A mass of black, too: the Mortem she'd given back. And shot through it all, flickers of blue.

Spiritum, and Mortem, and Caeliar's power, bits of it reclaimed from Apollius every time Bastian took control.

Lore settled herself against the side of the Fount—touching It didn't hurt like touching the piece had, as if that pain were an impetus to put it back where it belonged. She stared up at the moon, idly twisting Dani's dagger in her fingers, thinking about that solid wall of rock at the cliff face, and what she was almost sure was hidden behind it.

If she could only find a way in.

CHAPTER THIRTY-ONE

GABE

There is no dark that cannot be banished by a single
candle.*

        –A note in the Book of Prayer, Tract 3802

Gabe wasn't one for passing out, blows to the head notwithstanding. He'd been in plenty of situations where such a
reaction was warranted: Seeing unlikely survivors of horrible
accidents arriving to the Presque Mort. Having his eye pulled out.

But Gabe had always retained his consciousness.

Until now, anyway.

He came to in an underground room. At first, he thought they
were still under the Rotunda, still in the room with the false
Fount. But no; he'd burned that room. Burned the Brotherhood.

Maybe that was why he'd passed out. Using so much power.
Allowing his control to slip so dramatically.

You did what you had to.

---

* An addendum written by an unknown Malfouran monk, only appearing in
one Compendium circa 3 AGF.

He supposed that after such a show of power, he should be thankful that Hestraon was still only a voice in his head.

Slowly, his vision adjusted to the low light. A tiny room, four stone walls with a few empty shelves near the ceiling and nothing else. Malcolm lay next to one of the walls; a kick of panic in Gabe's chest made him reach over, hover his finger beneath his friend's nose. Still breathing.

Gods dead and dying, his head hurt. Gabe pulled himself to a sitting position against the wall and cradled it in his hands. He remembered Lore, the first time he'd ever met her, fierce and beautiful and cornered in that alley. He'd used chloroform to knock her out, bring her to the belly of the Church. Bring her to Anton. She'd complained of a headache then. He didn't think he'd been chloroformed, but if it felt anything like this, he needed to beg her forgiveness.

He needed to do that, anyway. Should have when he saw her just now. But there'd been other things to do.

Despite his dire circumstances, Gabe smiled into the dark.

"You're chipper."

Malcolm was awake. He pushed himself up, wincing, as if he felt the same headache Gabe did. "I hope that you're smiling because you already have an escape plan. I got up while you were sleeping; there's no way out of here."

He assumed Malcolm would not be amused by an account of what he'd done while he appeared to be asleep. "Unfortunately not."

"Fantastic." Malcolm slowly levered himself into a position that mimicked Gabe's. The room was small enough that their knees knocked together. "Do you know where we are?"

"No idea," Gabe said. "Though I can hazard a guess that wherever it is, Finn put us here."

Finn, who knew their power, who'd trapped them into telling the Prime Minister about it. Who'd killed Eoin.

"And we don't know what Finn wants." Malcolm nodded,

mouth a grim line. "This tracks, really. This is exactly the kind of luck we've had."

Gabe snorted.

"One good thing," Malcolm said. He reached into his pocket and pulled out the Fount piece. He must have taken it from Gabe, at some point, thinking the steward of the piece should be someone conscious. "We were right. This is it. Gives me pins and needles." As if to illustrate his point, he dropped it on the packed earth between them, not wanting to touch it for too long. "Finn undeniably knows what it is and why we have it, but he at least hasn't taken it from us."

The piece shone in the dark, seamed with gold. The smallest chip at the corner, where Hestraon had hacked off the flame carving, trying to be more like the gods He loved. "Yet."

"Yet," Malcolm agreed. "And there is still the question of how in every hell we're supposed to get it to the Mount. I doubt Finn is going to give us a ship."

Gabe gave him a level look, one that said everything he didn't have words for.

Malcolm gave a shuddering sigh. "I can't, Gabe."

"What if we don't have a choice?"

Malcolm shook his head. "Don't," he said quietly. "Gabriel, please."

Gabe's head fell back against the wall.

One small door was the only entrance or exit to their tiny cell, solid wood without even a barred window. It looked more like they were being kept in someone's cellar than a prison.

He rubbed at his temple again; something was odd about the feel of his skin there. It took him a moment to realize his eye patch was gone. He'd worn the thing for so long, he never even felt it anymore.

"You burned it," Malcolm said.

"What?"

"When you burned the Brotherhood," Malcolm said, "you went up in flames, too. But they didn't touch you. They burned off the patch, but the rest of your clothes were fine."

When he'd first lost his eye—first joined the Presque Mort—Gabe had been ashamed of it. Of all the wounds borne by the other monks, his well-healed missing eye was fairly tame, and only the infection that had set in made it a close enough brush with death to give him Mortem. But it was a reminder of his father's betrayal, a reminder of his own weakness, and he hated it. Long after it was healed, his empty socket sealed cleanly shut, he'd still worn the patch as if the scar was something to hide. Still ashamed, though he logically knew there was nothing for him to be ashamed of.

It made sense to him that he'd let the patch burn. He'd gotten rid of the thing that mitigated his fierceness, made him easier to look at.

Lore hadn't said a thing about it, as if she didn't even notice. Just like he'd barely noticed the scarring on her temple. Both of them marked, neither caring.

The door creaked open.

There wasn't enough room for Finn to stride in, but he still looked regal as he stepped over the threshold. "Good. You're awake."

Neither Gabe nor Malcolm spoke, both staring him down.

Finn sighed. "We aren't enemies. Just so you know."

"Locking us in a cellar sends a different message," Malcolm said.

"That's merely for convenience." Finn leaned his back against the door, kicked a boot up against the wood. "We're on the same side. We both want to stop the Sainted King from joining with the Kirythean Empire. Really, everything I've done has been for your benefit."

"Then why the prison?" Malcolm asked.

"You're gods," Finn said flatly. "One of you just burned alive half the ruling body of Caldien. Forgive me for taking precautions."

Here was where Gabe should feel some remorse, some horror at what he'd done. He didn't.

"You killed one yourself," Gabe said. "How does murdering the Prime Minister help prevent Auverraine from joining with the Empire? Seems more like that might speed things along."

His name made Finn's lip curl. "Eoin was useless," Finn spat. "He would have played cult leader up until the Empire was knocking down our door. I suppose I should have expected Eoin would try to take your power for himself, instead of doing anything to benefit Caldien. Idiot man."

There was no tenderness in his voice when he spoke of his former lover. Whatever care Finn had for Eoin had been gone long before he cut the other man's throat.

"So you decided to beat him to it?" Malcolm asked. He'd hidden the piece of the Fount, putting it in his pocket again, and now he was flexing his fingers back and forth, as if trying to get rid of the pins and needles.

"If I wanted to kill you," Finn said, "don't you think you'd be dead already?"

And that, at least, was one stroke of luck.

"And don't bother trying to hide that Fount piece," Finn continued. "The way Gabe took it wasn't exactly subtle." He leaned against the door, his nonchalant stance belied by the shrewd way he watched them, by the pistol glittering in his belt. "I could have taken it back. But that can be worked into our negotiations."

A look slid between Malcolm and Gabriel. Malcolm kept the shard in his pocket.

"So what do you want?" Gabe didn't mean to snarl, but his lip lifted with one anyway. Here they were, back at making bargains. "*Negotiations* makes me think you have a list."

His snarl didn't seem to faze Finn. "Exactly what you want. To stop the Empire, save the Queen."

"And what do you get out of it?"

"Remains to be seen." Finn shrugged. "A damn good story, for one."

There was no way in any hell that was the whole of it, but if he was offering help, Gabe didn't really care. "A pretender to the seat of the Prime Minister and his handful of rebels may have trouble ordering an army. This is a democracy, isn't it? You can't just take over his position because you killed him."

"It is a democracy, and had we time to wait until the people of Caldien could vote, they would have kicked Eoin out on his ass." Finn scoffed. "You think our operation is small? More than half of the Rotunda was tired of Eoin, and the rest of them are too craven to do anything but what a pistol tells them to. Most of the Brotherhood supported me."

"I suppose I shouldn't have burned them, then," Gabe said.

"No, you certainly should have. Even the ones who supported us only did so in secret. Cowards deserve to burn." Finn shrugged. "Your rampage helped my cause, really. The ones that are left now know we have a fighting chance of winning Auverraine."

Oh. *There* it was. Gabe's eye narrowed. "You're after the crown, then."

Finn smiled, a feral gleam of teeth, and didn't answer.

Malcolm sighed and tipped his head back against the wall. "It seems coups are catching."

"Do you want the Empire to go with it?" Gabe asked. "Or is the rule of two countries enough for you?"

"We'll cross that bridge when we come to it." Finn kicked off the wall. "I don't think I could do a worse job."

Brow arched, Malcolm rolled his head to look at him. "You know, I can't argue there."

"Thank you, Malcolm." Finn seemed sincere. "I'm after the greater good, really."

"And you managed to convince a sizable part of a governing body that risk for the greater good was better than complacency?" Gabe was honestly impressed, despite himself.

"Well." Finn shrugged. "Once they all knew what you could

do, they became rather easy to convince that we could win. Both the remaining members of the Rotunda, and my friends left in the navy—which has been ready to sail for weeks, by the way. And yes, sure, I'm positive I can expect some attempts at back-stabbing, especially if we actually manage to take over Auver-raine. But right now, they're in the palms of our hands."

Our hands. So he was dressing it up as allyship, but really, Gabe and Malcolm were the linchpins in his plan—the hinges it turned on. Gabe assumed they had been all along, that every shred of help the former pirate had offered was to lead them to this.

But that also meant they had the bargaining power.

Gabe stood, straightening to his full height. It made the top of his head nearly brush the ceiling. Malcolm followed his lead, but Finn didn't look cowed. He peered at them with a cocked brow, arms crossed over his chest expectantly.

"So you want us to join you," Gabe said. "To use magic to fight against the Auverrani army."

"Should be an easy task." Finn grinned. "You can burn the place to the ground or grow a huge tree through the middle of the Citadel, it makes little difference to me. And I'll let you keep the piece, do whatever you want with it. It rightfully belongs to you, really."

There was one hurdle passed. "You do realize that we'd be going up against a god?" Malcolm tried to look nonchalant, but anxiety thrummed beneath his voice. This was what they'd been working toward, but the prospect of being the front line was daunting.

"You're gods," Finn said simply, for the second time. "I don't think that will be much of an issue."

Gabe couldn't decide if he agreed. Couldn't decide if it was comforting.

Power changes things, Hestraon murmured. *Power moves mountains.*

"We need terms." Gabe had never been a good negotiator, but the conversation up to this point had been blunt enough that he didn't think Finn was much of one, either. "Auverraine may be taken over by hostile forces, but it's still our home. Its citizens cannot be collateral damage."

"I understand." Finn nodded, sobering. "Every attempt will be made to keep as many people alive as possible."

Which was probably as good as they were going to get.

Gabe looked to Malcolm. This was everything they'd hoped for—the promise that, maybe, they could stop the creep of the Empire, a Holy Kingdom spanning the globe under Apollius's thumb.

"We'll need a ship," Gabe said. "One of our own, when we leave."

"Just getting Val's back would be good," Malcolm said. "She's spitting mad about that, still."

"Can't give you one when we leave," Finn said, "but once the fighting is done, you can have whatever you want from the fleet."

So there was their passage to the Golden Mount. All it took was becoming weapons.

Malcolm's face was drawn into uneasy lines. His mouth worked a moment, then he gave Gabe a slight nod. If Gabe was in, so was he.

"We'll do it," Gabe said. "But we have some requests."

"Certainly." Finn waved a hand. "Whatever you want. Within reason."

"Our friends come with us." No way were they leaving Michal and Val and Mari behind. Lore's mothers would throttle him if he abandoned them in Caldien while he went closer to their daughter. "And we leave as soon as possible."

"Done." Finn turned toward the door. "Welcome to the Caldienan army, boys."

"Gods dead and dying," Malcolm cursed.

Gabe expected chaos in the streets, the citizens of Farramark reacting to the deposition of a Prime Minister who had seemed tolerated well enough. But when Finn led them from the room— a cellar in the bottom of some well-kept house near the Rotunda, a surprisingly genteel imprisonment—things seemed to be progressing as if nothing had happened at all. The roadways teemed with people on the way to their errands. The carriages they passed gave them slight nods of acknowledgment.

"This is the most peaceful takeover I've ever seen," Malcolm murmured, echoing Gabe's thoughts.

"It's because no one knows it happened," Finn said, ambling ahead of them. He twirled a finger in a circle by his head, indicating the whole of the city. "This is how it goes, when the government doesn't concern itself much with the people. Life here will continue on as it always has, regardless of who the Prime Minister is."

"Until we start the war," Gabe said.

"Well, yes. Until then."

Fire crackled in Gabe's fists, burned down his spine. War sounded good. War sounded perfect.

Next to him, Malcolm looked pensive. His hands opened and closed, his fingers flexing outward, as if he kept grabbing handfuls of something he didn't want to touch.

Finn led them to the boardinghouse, cheerily greeted Mrs. Cavendish. Mari was helping her in the kitchen, kneading the bread their landlady made every day. When Gabe and Malcolm entered behind Finn, her deep-brown eyes narrowed in suspicion.

"I would love fish for dinner, I think." Finn said it as if it were an idle thought. "Would that be possible, Mrs. Cavendish? I'm craving it something awful."

"Of course, dear." Mrs. Cavendish wiped her hands and set the cloth aside. "I was just about to go to market. It may take me a mite longer to go all the way to the harbor, but the walk will do me good."

Finn gave her a winning smile. Mari's eyes narrowed farther.

The poison runner didn't mince words once the landlady was out of the house. "I knew you were a snake."

"That's hurtful." But Finn's ease belied the statement as he turned around a chair and sat in it backward, resting his hands under his chin. "Especially when I'm giving you what you want."

Mari looked to Gabe and Malcolm, brow cocked. "Is he telling the truth, or is this a hostage situation?"

"A bit of both," Malcolm answered.

Finn's grin widened. "You wanted to march on Auverraine, right? Save your friends from a King unfortunately infected with godhood, save your daughter from the Burnt Isles?"

Mari's breath caught, one hand absently pressing against her chest before she forced it back into her lap.

"I find myself with the Caldienan naval fleet under my command, and the urge to make sure Kirythea doesn't even think about crossing the border," Finn continued. His grin went fierce. "Help me do that, and I'll do whatever I can to bring back your daughter."

Mari stood, the sudden softening that the mention of Lore had brought to her face washed into wariness. "Let me get Val."

"Right here, love." The other poison runner had daggers in her eyes, and one in her hand. The other rested on the hilt of a pistol always at her waist. For a smallish woman, Val certainly found lots of places to hide weapons. "Care to tell us how, exactly, one such as yourself is now the head of the naval division?"

"Easy." Finn shrugged. "I killed the Prime Minister, and all the Rotunda delegates who were in on it with me are too busy fighting over who gets his job or cowering in their giant houses to pay attention to who commands the fleet."

"That assumes the fleet will listen to you."

"They're mobilized and waiting for my word." The feigned nonchalance Finn had employed up to this point fell away, replaced with steely resolve. "They've been listening to me for years."

Val stared at him, expression granite. But she slipped the dagger back into its hidden sheath on her forearm, and her grip on the pistol relaxed. She looked at Gabe, then Malcolm. "And you two are in support of this, I imagine."

"I'm in support of anything that will save Lore," Gabe said. Bastian, too, though he didn't know yet how he could. He'd find a way. He'd save them both. Doing anything less was unfathomable.

Flame crept through his veins, his palms heated beneath the candle tattoos of a station he no longer held. When he blinked, the world was a tangle of red thread, fire waiting for a flint.

Val's lips pursed. She nodded. With a sigh, she waved her hand. "All I ask is that you give my ship back. It cost a fucking fortune."

The sea was shallow enough now that Bastian's head was almost always breaking the surface.

It was disorienting after so long being pushed down. He could see through his own eyes sometimes. Moving his own limbs still felt like a monumental effort, pushing hard against an immense weight, but he could do it occasionally. His moments of control were brief, nothing like the hour he'd snatched when he helped Alie find the ring, but they all felt like small miracles.

Apollius railed against him, screamed and cursed, but it was only so much white noise as that golden ocean gradually drained, a little every day. A steady decline of power, all of it siphoning... elsewhere. Lessening every time Bastian fought free.

Apollius knew what was happening. Of that, Bastian was certain. More than just the magic drain; He knew the why and the how, but He used every ounce of the power still available to Him to keep the knowledge from Bastian, to hold on to his body until... something.

All that Bastian could surmise was that a decision had been made—one that Apollius felt less than thrilled about, maybe, but also one that didn't feel wholly like a loss. The god was waiting.

So all Bastian had to do was wait, too.

CHAPTER THIRTY-TWO

ALIE

Never underestimate the loyalty of a once-kicked dog.
—Rouskan proverb

For two days after finding the Fount piece, Alie hid in her room.

It was a rather childish way to deal with it, she had to admit. The Fount piece and ring she hid in the very bottom of her unmentionables drawer, tucked into a corner behind a froth of lace. Apollius knew what had happened, certainly, and surely He would be able to figure out that she was the one who'd stolen the ring and found the broken piece. She knew that bloodcoats and builders had been dispatched to clear the area, to stabilize the street and make sure no other tunnels were in danger of caving in. Apollius had to know the reason, and now He would deal with her, kill her and wring out her power like water from laundry regardless of Jax's protection.

She'd considered leaving, chartering a carriage or stealing a horse. But the only landlocked direction to go if she wanted to stay out of the Empire was Caldien, and she'd be caught in no time, with the added complication of trying to come up with an excuse for why she'd run in the first place. Ratharc was an option, if she managed to steal onto a boat, but it would make the journey back to the Mount double. Bri's family's ship was on loan, apparently, expected back in three days, and then Bri assured her she could use it for whatever she needed.

Three days to hide, like a rabbit with a wolf at the door, and then she could escape, head to the Mount, follow the pull of the stone in her underthings drawer.

If Apollius would wait that long.

But as the hours ticked by, as Alie watched them go with a churning stomach and a cup of tea gone cold, the god in the body of the Sainted King never sent for her.

Jax did, though.

It was the evening of the second day when his letter arrived, slid neatly beneath her door, white paper and black ink written over in a strong, slashing hand.

We need to choose flowers, apparently. Meet me in the south gardens at sunset?

She could feign a headache, say she was too tired. But Alie's skin itched with the anticipation of being found out, and she dashed off a confirmation before she could talk herself out of it.

Maybe Apollius was too distracted to put the pieces together. Maybe He wasn't as smart as Alie gave Him credit for. Either way, the best strategy for casting off suspicion was not to act suspicious.

When the sun began to sink, Alie dressed and made her way down the turret, out toward the southern green.

The entire green was filled with flowers, really, but the eastern side—opposite the walled garden with the well that led into the catacombs—had the most variety. The Arceneauxs loved their roses, and most of the green was covered in them, but the southeastern corner was full of crocuses and lilies and ranunculus, nightshade and hemlock and hellebore. A delicate fence surrounded the flower garden, ostensibly to keep people away from the poisonous blooms, though Alie had never known the gate to be locked, and plenty of poison flowers grew unfettered inside the Citadel.

Jax stood just inside the gate, his shoulders tense and his hands clasped behind his back. He turned long before he could have seen her coming, as if listening closely to her footsteps, attuned to her movements.

Alie's palms were sweaty. She wiped them on her skirt. When she first came up with the plan to move their wedding date, it had been in abstract, something to occupy Apollius and make Him think she'd given up. Now that the new date loomed, she felt nearly dizzy with the weight of it, even though she planned to be gone as soon as Bri's ship was in the harbor.

All of this was theater, still. And she just had to keep acting.

Alexis stood with Jax, something that made her both immensely relieved and slightly worried. The new Priest Exalted gave her a pointed look as she unlatched the gate. They must have something to tell her.

She didn't hold out much hope for it being anything good.

Jax waved a hand at Alexis. "Repeat those suggestions for Alienor, if you don't mind."

"Of course." Alexis turned, walking through the garden, gesturing to flowers as they passed. "Auverrani weddings generally follow the language of flowers when choosing a bouquet. Lilies are popular, as they represent purity and fertility..."

Alie pulled a face.

"...and daffodils mean new beginnings, so they feature often..."

"I thought maybe it would make more sense the second time," Jax muttered.

Her lip tried to twitch upward. She fought it back down. Alie had thought that Jax's dour look meant something was happening with Bastian and Apollius, or that he knew she'd taken the shard. But it seemed like her betrothed was anxious over wedding flowers.

That shouldn't be endearing.

Alexis finished their brief lesson in a rush, then turned to Alie expectantly. "So what do you think, my lady?"

"Lilies," she said, mostly because it was the first thing they'd listed and therefore at the top of her mind. "Um, roses. Daffodils sound good, too." She looked to Jax. "Do you have any suggestions?"

"All of this is for you." There was a softness to his expression. "I'll do whatever you like."

A slight smile tugged at her mouth. She bit down, hard.

Alexis nodded, heading toward the gate. They gave Alie that pointed look again, and she nodded, slightly. She needed to stay in the garden long enough for Alexis to tell her whatever news they had.

She expected Jax to leave as soon as the business with the flowers was done. But he lingered, trepidation in his posture. Her anxiety swelled up again, the tide of it covering her like a shoreline.

"Once we're married, I'm sending you to Laerdas."

Of all the things she thought he might say, that one hadn't occurred to her. "What?"

"You'll be safer there." He spoke in a rush, like he wanted to get all of this out of his mouth before he was somehow overheard. "The situation here is...volatile. And I don't want you caught in it."

Alie gaped at him. "So you're just going to send me *countries* away?"

"I want to keep you with me." She wasn't prepared for that tenderness. It made heat rush to her face. "But I want to keep you safe more."

Bleeding God.

"Why?" She didn't look right at him, eyes on the lilies waving in the soft breeze instead. "You barely know me, why care so much about my safety? Because I'm the key to you having a legitimate claim on Auverraine? Because of my god-affliction?"

"No." He sounded slightly offended. "Because you'll be my wife. My responsibility." He paused. "Because I care about you."

Gods dead and *dying*.

Alie sighed. "Fine."

"Fine?" Clearly, he didn't expect her to capitulate so easily.

"Yes, fine." There was no point in arguing. She planned to be long gone before he could send her to Laerdas or anywhere else.

He nodded, relief clear on his normally stoic face. Jax lifted her hand and kissed her knuckles. "Good." Then he was gone, slipping through the gate, headed back to the Citadel.

Alie closed her eyes. Took a deep breath. Went to find Alexis.

The acting Priest Exalted hadn't gone far. They stood near the Citadel Wall, arms crossed and foot tapping. "Took you long enough."

"I have to act like I tolerate him." Alie chose not to interrogate why that brought a new wave of blood to her already-blushing face. "What happened?"

"War is coming," Alexis said simply.

She frowned. "We knew that—"

"Alie, the Caldienan navy is sailing on Auverraine as we speak." Alexis sounded dispassionate, but their pulse beat so hard Alie could see it in their neck. "I heard from my contact. Power in the Rotunda has changed hands. They're coming, and Gabe and Malcolm are coming with them, to get rid of Jax and stop the Empire."

Stop the Empire sounded good. *Get rid of Jax* made her stomach knot. Alie nodded, palms going sweaty again. "This is what we wanted."

"Yes." Alexis sounded as unsure as she felt.

Alie took her leave without saying goodbye.

But she didn't even make it into the Citadel before she was stopped again, this time by a bloodcoat she didn't recognize at the door. He angled his bayonet in front of her, blocking her entry.

"Excuse me?" She had no time for this.

The bloodcoat was unfazed by her rudeness. "You're to go to the royal apartments," he said. "King's orders."

As he spoke, two more bloodcoats approached from behind, boxing her in.

Here we go, Alie thought.

In the back of her mind, an anxious gust of chill wind.

They didn't lead her like a prisoner. That was reassuring, she supposed. The two bloodcoats casually walked her up the turret.

The bloodcoats opened Bastian's door. Alie stepped over the threshold. They didn't follow her, closing the door with a sound like a sepulcher. Leaving her alone with the god wearing her half brother's body, seated at the edge of the fountain in the middle of his solarium.

He looked...haggard. That was the best way to describe it. Still handsome, because it was apparently an impossibility for Bastian not to look handsome, but exhausted, as if he'd spent the time he should be sleeping running miles from some unknown assailant. For a moment, Alie thought maybe it really was Bastian, that his exhausted appearance meant he'd finally tamped down Apollius and regained control for good.

But when He looked up, His eyes were golden.

Alie stood as tall as she could, chin tipped up, hands in fists by her sides. "You called?"

A wine goblet was clutched in His hand. Apollius took a long drink, bloodshot eyes closing. He set the goblet down forcefully, swallowed hard. "Let's stop dancing around this."

Her clenched fists shook, just a little.

"You have something that belongs to Me."

"We've established that Lereal's power doesn't belong to You."

"Not that," Apollius sneered. "The shard, Alienor."

Her stomach bottomed out.

Apollius gave her a sardonic look. "Don't worry, I'm not going to kill you. Not unless you make Me."

"That's less than comforting," Alie murmured. "Not that You look strong enough for murder, frankly. What happened? Did Bastian make a break for it again?"

"I have the situation well in hand." And despite how awful He looked, Apollius smiled, and she believed Him. "Deepest apologies."

He was weak, but He was still in control. And it seemed He didn't mind the weakness.

It was almost more terrifying than if He'd been in full, resplendent power. That would at least make sense.

"I won't give it to You," Alie said. She didn't specify whether she spoke of Lereal's magic or the piece of the Fount. The statement covered both.

Apollius rolled His eyes. "You think you moved in secrecy? I knew you would look for the shard eventually. There is no one I trust enough to send after it, and even if you were to die in a trap of My making, I would get your power out of it. It was easier to let you find the piece and bring it to Me than it was to go Myself, what with certain ... difficulties."

Here was the plan, then. Why He'd kept her alive so long. But far from cowing her, the knowledge made Alie stand up straighter. "So Bastian is giving You a run for Your money."

The god narrowed His eyes and didn't respond to that. "We've found ourselves at the end of your overlong rope, *sister*. It's time to give them both up, the power and the piece. They'll do nothing for you."

"They don't have to," Alie snarled. "It's enough that You don't have them."

"Fierce little thing. Not like the Arceneauxs. They're cowards, you know. They were then, and they are now. Afraid of losing power, afraid of dying, afraid of what comes after."

"Bastian isn't afraid of You."

A sneering smile. "He should be. Something is coming that should scare him far worse than anything I've put him through so far."

Her heartbeat thrummed just a little faster.

Ponderously, Apollius stood, as if Bastian's bones had grown too brittle to support the weight of two souls fighting over one body. He lurched toward her on weak legs, still imposing even now, and Alie took a step back before she could stop herself.

"I grow tired of this, Alienor," Apollius said. She lurched backward as He came toward her, her fumbling hand finding the door. Locked from the outside, but still she tugged at it, calling threads of wind to pick at the mechanism. "You can give them up and live, or you can give them up and die. Whichever you choose has little consequence to Me."

He was close enough to touch her. Alie's wind threads unlatched something within the lock, and it gave with a click. She turned the knob without looking behind her, losing her balance.

But someone was standing at the door, working the lock from the other side, and strong arms caught her before she hit the tiles. Alie looked up into the furious face of Jax Andronicus.

"Jax," Apollius said, as if he were a friend dropping in to a tea party. "Nice of you to join us."

Jax helped her up gently. His hands left her as soon as Alie was upright. "Is there a reason You're intimidating my betrothed?" His voice was a low hiss.

Apollius waved a hand. Bastian's body was too tired to make it look carefree and nonchalant; it staggered through the air like something shot. "Your betrothed has something of Mine."

"You said there was a way to get it back without violence." Jax was just as tall as Bastian; Apollius couldn't loom over him quite as well as He could Alie. "You said she would be safe."

"And she will be," Apollius growled, "if she gives me back what is *fucking Mine*."

"It's not Yours," Alie said quietly. "Never was."

The god whirled on her, nearly stumbling on Bastian's tired legs. "I have been infinitely patient with you, Alienor, but now—"

His words cut off, strangled. Apollius lurched a step forward, then fell to His knees, gagging. Something spilled from His mouth.

A torrent of crystal-clear water, pooling on the floor, glimmering gold at the edges. Just for a moment, then it was gone, evanescing into the air.

And Apollius laughed. Booming and joyful, His head falling to the floor as if He'd finally laid down some heavy burden.

He looked up.

Not Apollius. Bastian.

Bastian, and his eyes were dark and wild, panic written across his face. "Something happened."

"I'd say." But Jax was arrested in motion, staring at where that pool of water had been.

"Lore is in danger," Bastian said. "Something happened, the sea is gone."

CHAPTER THIRTY-THREE

LORE

Fate will always find you.
    –Lyric from Malfouran tavern song, circa 365 AGF

S he was at the cliff again.

Lore held on to the same tree, leaned out over the edge of the knoll. The wind was high today, whipping her hair into her mouth, tugging at her loose Harbor-made clothes and raising goose bumps. The song of the Fount was faint within all that wind, a low melody she could almost ignore by now.

Today she was supposed to be searching the beaches, both the one they'd run aground on and the one on the other side of the island. The beach Caeliar had walked off, in Nyxara's memories, seeing how far She could get from the Mount. But when Lore woke, miraculously not sore after another night spent curled up next to the Fount, she hadn't hiked down to the beach. She'd come here, drawn once again to the sheer rock.

A tug at her hand, at her mind. Lore closed her eyes.

Slipping into memory on the island was like slipping beneath the surface of a still pool, comforting and easy. But this was something different. She wasn't in one of Nyxara's memories, fitting neatly into the goddess's skin. When she looked down, the angles were all wrong, taller and broader. The pain was exquisite, almost exhilarating, and concentrated in her chest.

Her open chest, a heart beating impossibly in a bloody hole.

This memory belonged to Apollius.

Lore tried to throw herself aside, somehow rip away, but it was useless. She was trapped here, inside the body of the god, until the memory let her go.

Apollius gasped. Lore felt Him try to channel Spiritum, try to weave together golden threads to heal Himself, but they scattered from His fingers. This wound was too great. It was a miracle He'd kept Himself going this long, three days after Nyxara had ripped the heart from His ribs, a literal expression of what She'd been doing incrementally for centuries.

A memory within a memory; He thought of what He'd done, after not-quite-killing Nyxara. Sent one of the monks who'd stayed through the chaos to the mainland, called in Gerard Arceneaux. Gave orders for Her body, then used His rapidly depleting strength to tell him everything He could think of, all the ways to preserve the world as something He could return to, something He could shape.

And He would return. One way or another. The darkness would not have Him forever, and that was the only thing keeping Him from complete, insensate terror.

With a painful beat of wings, Apollius rose in the air, settled on the side of the sheer rock face. He raised one god-fist, brought it down.

The cliff broke open. Behind it, a cavern.

He entered, the glow of His skin the first light this place had ever seen.

Apollius turned to face the open sky beyond the cavern He'd revealed. The strands of Spiritum that refused to heal Him would still follow His direction. He raised His hands, bent His fingers.

Rock was dead, but everything in this cliffside was not. He pulled life from the few remaining trees, the grass and moss, creatures in the miles-away sea. He wove it all together into a web of gold, a locked door against anyone who did not share His power.

This, too, was an instruction He'd given. The few monks still on the island were to come here and put the rocks back in place, rebuild what He'd broken, make this cliffside whole again. Then they were to fall into the sea, taking with them the secret of His resting place.

The net of gold shimmered, nothing visible beyond it. His vision faded, faded.

Apollius lay down. His vision went black. And His mind spun out into darkness, near the threshold of eternity but not beyond it. Ready to wait.

Lore's eyes opened.

She'd fallen to her knees at some point in the memory; her hands dug into the soft earth, grit thick enough under her nails to hurt. This was it, then. Here was His body, and here was the way to get to it.

Slowly, she stood, holding on to the tree until she was sure her legs could support her. With a firm nod, she made her way back to the Fount to get her bag and Dani's dagger. She hadn't been bringing it with her, unafraid of anything Dani could do. The other woman was smart enough not to try.

The Fount sang as she collected her pack. An anticipatory air to the melody now. A build before a big finish.

This is what We need, It said softly.

"No shit," Lore replied.

"What's going on?"

Dani wasn't supposed to be here. She was supposed to be on the other side of the island, looking through the ruined huts. "I could ask you the same question," Lore said.

"There's nothing in those villages." Dani leaned against a

mostly intact doorframe, arms crossed. "It's far more likely we're missing something in here."

"Hm." Lore turned away, headed back toward the path.

"You didn't answer my question."

There was a warning tone in Dani's voice, a fierceness.

"You found something," the other woman said.

Lore spun back around, mouth set in a thin line. "And if I did?"

Dani pushed off from the doorframe, stepped closer. "We're working together, Lore." She swallowed, a hint of emotion on her face that she tried to scrub away. Desire, blazing plain. "If you found Him, take me with you. Let me help."

A lie would do no good. Lore didn't know what it would take to kill Apollius's body; maybe she really would need Dani's help.

And what if it killed her? What if she tripped some mechanism, trying to open that Spiritum door, and killed herself falling down the cliff face before she could kill the god? Someone had to do it. They couldn't come all this way for nothing.

Lore jerked her chin, indicating for Dani to follow. Then she trekked back to the cliff.

Dani stayed quiet, even when Lore set down her pack, afraid the extra weight might overbalance her as she climbed out onto the rock. A handhold here, a foothold there; slowly, she made her way onto the slightly canted drop, painfully aware of the churning sea far below, the wind pushing at her body.

But she didn't fall.

Finally, she reached the middle of the cliff face, balanced on a tiny rock outcropping that she prayed with every breath wouldn't crumble. This was the place; she could see the seams between the stones, fit back together so perfectly that from far away, it looked unbroken. The monks had put it back like they were solving a puzzle before letting themselves fall into the ocean.

Lore leaned forward, placing her hands on the rocks, allowing them to take some of her weight so it all wasn't balanced between sky and sea. This close, she could feel Spiritum blazing behind the stones, as gold and strong as the day it'd been spun.

She dropped to channeling-space, blocking out everything but those sunshine threads behind the black of Mortem in the cliff.

It was similar to the door she'd opened in the vaults to find August's undead army, in the bowels of the Church to find the prophecy. Similar, but not the same. Those locks had only needed one piece tripped to be opened; this was a mess of magic, a tangled web that had to be unwoven strand by strand.

"Of fucking course," Lore muttered, and got to work.

Once she began, the threads came apart. Not easily, necessarily, but with a sense of purpose, of setting yourself to a task you were meant to accomplish. Lore didn't know how much time passed, her hands braced against the rocks and her vision grayscale, unpicking the lock Apollius had made.

But when it was done, the force of it knocked her backward.

A moment of empty air, her stomach recalibrating to the lack of solid ground, dropping and then floating up into her throat. There was no time to scream as she started to fall, but Lore still tried, a small, ridiculous sound more like a kittenish mew than a cry of horror.

It was replaced by an *oof* as something caught her hand.

Dani, standing inside the lip of the cavern she'd uncovered, bruised and bleeding from the fall of puzzle-piece rocks, from her scramble over the cliff face—she must have climbed over while Lore was untangling magic.

Lore's sweaty hand slipped in Dani's fist, pulling the smaller woman toward the edge. Every muscle in Dani's arm strained painfully, her mouth a twisted rictus. "You're going to have to help me here!"

Lore flailed in the air for ten seconds that felt like an hour before getting her feet on the cliff enough to push up and alleviate some of her weight from Dani's hold. She flopped herself over onto the newly made edge, sending Dani stumbling back. Lore pulled her feet in behind her and curled into a ball, panting in the sudden silence.

When her panic had calmed enough to move, she sat up slowly, peering at Dani in the shadows. "Thank you."

The other woman held her arm at an awkward angle, but it didn't look broken, though Lore had probably come close to pulling her shoulder from its socket. Dani held her elbow a moment before shaking it out. "You can't die yet."

And that was that.

Lore stood, her legs surprisingly steady. Dani had brought her pack, and she stuck her hand inside, bringing out the dagger. "He's in here somewhere." She marched into the dark.

They didn't have to go far. Inside the cavern, just deep enough for the sunlight not to penetrate, the God of Everything was stretched out on a shelf of stone.

Even in this strange not-quite-death, His body glowed, gold phosphorescence running beneath His skin. He was beautiful in the same shocking way Bastian was beautiful, only amplified by His otherworldliness: light-brown hair curling over His ears, a finely made face, strong nose and jaw. His wings spread out on either side of Him, gently draping over the stone that had become His plinth, the color of midnight snow no one had yet touched. A white loincloth covered Him from hip to mid-thigh, but other than that He was naked, all the wounds from His fight with Nyxara on display.

One, in particular.

The hole in His chest made a noise. A low, subtle sucking sound, like trying to drink from an empty cup. And there was the beat, a low murmur that echoed in the chamber, His heart thrumming long after it should have stopped.

Lore stepped closer, unable to tear her eyes away. His heart looked like a fist of congealed blood, the rim of the hole in His pale chest gummed with gold and scarlet. His ribs had broken around it perfectly, an ivory cage with sharp edges.

She reached in without a second thought.

His heart was warm. Even the blood that should have long since dried to flaking crust was liquid on her palm, coating her eclipse scar. Lore fit her hand around the organ, so small for such an important thing.

"If it didn't work the first time," Dani said behind her, "I doubt it will work the second."

It had worked, but Lore recalled her memory of the Godsfall, how Nyxara had replaced His heart once She'd torn it out. Lore didn't say that, though. She pulled her hand carefully from the nest of bones and wiped it on her thigh, hefting Dani's dagger in her hand.

"I don't think there's any special way to do it," Dani said, coming up beside her, almost uncomfortably close. She held a rock in her hand, as if she'd use it as backup if the knife didn't work.

"The sharp part goes in," Lore said.

The other woman raised a brow. "You've been slow with the stupid jokes since we got to the Mount. And here I thought being in a divine presence had made you magically mature."

A barb, not even a clever one, but it gave Lore pause. Dani was right. Since they'd arrived here, Lore had felt... disconnected from herself. Hollow, scooped out. She'd chalked it up to how lousy this place was with memory, how thin magic made barriers of time.

Maybe there was more to it than that.

This is good, the Fount soothed, Its voice quiet and distant.

Her most recent dream rose to the surface of her mind, never far from her thoughts. Gabe, the feel of him against her, inside her, panting breaths and slides of skin. That was the last time she remembered feeling something fully, not at a remove.

That conversation they'd had, afterward. The one they hadn't put words to, but each knew what the other was thinking anyway. Maybe they could do something better with this power than just give it up.

Lore tightened her grip on the knife. She had to kill Apollius. She had to—

—**take it**—

The song in her head resolved, not words, the not-voice. She nodded, considering, agreeing, there must b**e a vessel to bring it back**—

"Lore?"

Dani didn't sound concerned. She sounded eager. The rock turned nervously in her hand.

Lore shook her head. Tightened her sweaty grip on the hilt of the dagger again. Apollius's heart gleamed in His open chest, blood shining on barely moving muscle.

She took a breath. The song in her head paused.

She raised the dagger above her head, clenched in both hands.

She brought it down.

And as she did, Apollius opened His eyes.

He smiled.

Shock hammered through her, but her course was set, an arrow already fired. Lore gasped as the blade cut swiftly down into Apollius's open heart and slid in as smoothly as if the organ were the dagger's sheath. Lore tugged it out, sent it clattering behind her, gold-crimson blood torrenting from the wound.

Apollius pulled in a breath, His beautiful face a rictus of mingled pain and elation as He bowed up off the plinth, bent backward and nearly in half. All the atmosphere of the room seemed to pull in toward Him, a dying star eating the world. Lore braced her hands on the plinth to keep from falling forward, her face nearly touching the gaping hole of the god's chest.

His back settled against the stone again, as if it were a feather bed. His body was deteriorating, the same way Nyxara's had, becoming gilded ash as His heart pumped out. Distantly, she heard Dani scrambling, running back this direction.

His hand cupped her cheek just before all of Him winnowed away, sweet and gentle. "You're Mine."

And then Lore's mind was a storm.

A great rushing in, all the hollow places of her filling with something new. Spiritum, a crashing golden wave of it. Apollius, His second bodiless life strengthened by bodily death, rooting down into every hidden place He could find.

I told you, He said, His voice reverberating and echoing and all she could hear. *You were Mine, and are Mine, and will be Mine forever. This is a kind of being together, Lore. Nyxara. This is as close as We could ever be.*

The Fount said the only way Apollius would ever leave Bastian was if there was somewhere else He'd rather be. Inside her. Owning her, as fully as one could possibly be owned.

Lore tried to scream, but when she opened her mouth, it was His laughter.

She wasn't thrust to the back of her mind, not like Bastian was, not made a passenger like the time in the Church when she'd let Nyxara take over. Lore remained in charge of herself by half measures—able to move, to push herself back from the plinth where Apollius's body was now so much golden smoke. Able to claw at her ears to try to drown Him out.

Able to see Dani coming at her with the dagger she'd dropped. "Better than a rock."

Her eyes were wild, her smile wide—she swiped at Lore carelessly, clearly not anticipating much resistance. Her smile fell when Lore dodged clumsily out of the way, but not by much.

"You don't want it," she snarled. "All you talked about was how much you don't want your power, fucking whining all the time, wishing it away. So give it to me." Another swipe. Lore fell backward, her legs gummy and coltish with new power, the control of her body swapping rapidly back and forth between her and the god burrowing into her skull. "We both know you won't do anything good with it."

You can prove her wrong, Apollius whispered.

"It doesn't work like that," Lore rasped. "You have to be a god."

"I'm willing to try," Dani said, and lunged for her again. "I told you exactly what I wanted, Lore. That the world would have to be remade, every old thing passing. I knew it'd take someone with a parasitic god to kill Him." She swiped out, catching Lore's shirt, linen tearing. "But you? I'm pretty sure I can kill you all on my own."

Lore scrabbled back against the wall of the cavern, scraping her fingernails to bloody tatters. Dani stabbed forward at Lore again, and Lore threw up her hand.

The blade went straight through it, carving a hole in the center of her eclipse scar. She howled in pain, knees buckling.

Don't worry, Apollius soothed.

Lore didn't have the mental capacity to concentrate on channeling, on healing her hand—but she didn't need it. The god in her transcended the need for channeling mechanics, and the hole in her palm slowly closed, pushing the dagger blade out, like a rose slowly blooming from soil.

Gasping, Dani stumbled back, her expression gyring from disgust to awe. She rushed toward Lore again, gripping a sharp rock.

But Lore was ready. When the dagger was free of skin and sinew, Lore turned it around one-handed, in the same palm it had cut.

Make her pay.

She stabbed out, the blade sheathing into Dani's abdomen, right above her hip. She choked, falling inelegantly to her knees. "You don't want this," she spat, blood on her teeth. "You never did."

A lie, one Lore had stopped trying to believe about herself long before this moment. Maybe she'd never wanted the power she was given, but the concept of power in its entirety—that, she wanted.

"It's not just the power." Lore's voice, Apollius's voice, harmony from a single throat. "It's the chance to make a difference."

Dani sneered. "I can think of no one worse suited to becoming the God of Everything."

"You think you'd be better?" Just Lore's voice, now. They faded in and out of each other, her and the god.

"Better than you," Dani snarled, hands clenched over her stomach, her shirt becoming a mess of red. "Better than Them, and better than the Fount. That's all you're doing. Going back to something that never worked."

Like Raihan said. As long as there were mortals, as long as there was free will, there would be evil.

You can fix that.

"I can think of one way to make it better." Lore let the blade drop to the floor. "For me, at least."

She reached out. She pushed.

Dani didn't realize how close she was to the edge. She pinwheeled, trying to regain balance that was long since gone, and then she tumbled over the lip of the cliff. One scream, swiftly silenced by the first rocky outcropping, a meaty *thunk* as she hit it.

The rest of her tumble to the sea was quiet.

Lore's vision spun in and out, like looking through a constantly adjusting telescope. Sometimes, she saw herself as if gazing down from above; other times she looked out from her own eyes. It was disorienting, made her stumble. Her limbs felt too heavy and too light; she lurched over the ground when she tried to walk. Hit her knees, grit digging deep into the skin.

A glimmer of familiar feeling. Bastian. She couldn't see him, but she could feel him, his sudden panic. "Lore!" His voice wasn't audible, but she heard it anyway, echoing in her skull. "Lore, you have to fight Him off—"

You won.

Apollius's voice sounded so smug. So pleased.

You got Me out of Bastian. You lived when you should not have.

Lore stumbled from the cave but didn't fall. She didn't know how she made it to the grassy knoll, her body moving of its own accord as she fought to gather up the pieces of herself and knit them whole. Endless cycles, endings that began again. Apollius dug in like a snake to its nest, curled around the very foundations of her.

You averted the apocalypse.

So much blood on her hands. The villages, Anton, Jean-Paul, now Dani. She'd been the architect of so many small apocalypses.

She ran through the island, reeled back to the Fount, still singing. It sounded triumphant; why did It sound happy about this?

Apollius wasn't trying as hard with her. She knew that instinctually, knew that every movement of her own was only because He allowed it. Why? What made her different from Bastian?

You're smarter than him. You look out for yourself. You're far more like Me than he ever was.

"No," she moaned, crashing through underbrush, dead branches whipping at her face.

Yes, Apollius said. *You can make the world in your image. Better than your image. In a Holy Empire, there is no war. When everyone is brought under one rule, Our rule, they will be better for it.*

Lore fell to her knees again, this time on the mossy, broken stone of the courtyard. The voice of the Fount stopped singing and spoke instead.

Almost done.

Soothing, like a hand in her hair.

You've done well. We knew you would. It's been so long since We held power; We need a cup to pour from, in order to catch it all. Now give back what you have, wait for the others to bring you what remains. Then you can rest, Lore.

If Apollius could hear the Fount whispering to her, He gave no sign. He nestled into her mind, gold stringing through her limbs, gold all she could see when she blinked.

Lore staggered toward the Fount.

She nearly fell in; Lore braced her hands on the Fount's edge, her nails breaking further with the force of her grip.

Go on, Apollius said.

Go on, the Fount urged.

She knew how to give up power. She remembered the water flooding her mouth in the North Sanctuary after her impromptu wedding in chains, remembered its sweet, clear taste. Then, it had welled up from her easily, because she didn't want that particular magic, had never truly wanted it. It was foisted on her by a goddess looking for an end to an endless cycle.

Now her mouth stayed dry.

You know what It wants, Apollius said. *The only thing anyone has ever wanted from you.*

Her death. Her sacrifice. Lore and the greater good could not exist in the same world at the same time.

Be the savior, the Fount murmured. **Leave a legacy. Put the magic back where it is supposed to be.**

But who decided that? Who was the arbiter of what was supposed to be?

We are the same. She'd never heard Apollius sound genuine before. Every interaction she'd had with the god had been full of second meaning and innuendo, but now He spoke truth plainly. *You fear death just as much as I do.*

Nothing had defined Lore's life so much as a reckless determination to keep living it.

Below her, the ribbons of magic in the Fount swirled. She wasn't in channeling-space, but she saw the threads all the same; the deep well of Mortem that had all been called back, the dregs of Spiritum the Fount had managed to harvest from Bastian's brief moments of control, the blue strands of water that Apollius had stolen when Bastian killed Amelia.

Two choices here, and both required her to lower herself to the surface. Both required that she bring herself right to the edge of those waters that held everything, the seed from which the world had sprung. She dipped down, down, until the coolness of it brushed against her lips, until the sweet and mineral scent of it was all she could breathe.

"I will be better," Lore whispered, sending ripples over the surface of the world's soul.

And she drank deep.

CHAPTER THIRTY-FOUR

GABE

Guide us in our love and in our rage.
                        –The Book of Prayer, Tract 5433

He knew from their first voyage how long it should take to sail from Caldien to Auverraine, but that didn't stop Gabe from cursing the time. Flames sang in his fists, and he wondered more than once if he could make everyone work faster by setting something on fire. He'd decided against it, thus far, but the thought presented itself every time he saw someone pause.

"Calm down." Val bumped his shoulder. "They're going as fast as they can."

"I am calm." His voice was even.

"Like every hell." But Val didn't have it in her to admonish him too much. They both stood at the prow of Finn's ship, underneath the snapping emerald banner of Caldien, staring out at the horizon as if they could will it closer.

The navy was already mobilized and waiting for Finn. After gathering their meager belongings from the boardinghouse—Finn left a sizable pile of gold coins on the table for Mrs. Cavendish, since Eoin wasn't in a position to pay her anymore—the pirate had led them through the still-calm city and down to the harbor. People crawled over every ship on the docks, hoisting anchors and affixing Caldienan flags to the masts. Ships stretched out to the mouth of the harbor, casting shadows on the water as far as Gabe could see.

"Seems you were counting on us," Malcolm had said, squinting out at the assembled fleet.

"Men of a certain ilk recognize each other," Finn replied. "I knew you two had common sense."

"Common sense, and little choice," Gabe grumbled.

"That too." Finn had turned a scathing glance on Gabe. "Chin up, monk. You're getting everything you want."

Now, watching the current flow around them and waiting with his heart in his mouth for Auverraine to interrupt the endless line of sea and sky, Gabe knew Finn wasn't right. He wouldn't have everything he wanted until Bastian and Lore were safe.

Movement at his side. Michal, staring out at the open water, but in a manner that said it was only to avoid looking at Gabe. "So you and Lore."

He stiffened. He knew of Michal and Lore's history; jealousy was an emotion that came easily to him, but in this case, he didn't really feel it. Whatever Michal and Lore had was fleeting, a weed that never bothered putting down deep roots.

"You want to talk about this *now*?" Gabe rumbled.

"Not like we can make this boat go any faster by glowering," Michal said. "Though not for lack of trying on your part."

Gabe shifted, crossed his arms. "What about me and Lore?"

Michal sighed. "It's none of my business. Believe me, Malcolm has told me that over and over. But she's my friend. I care for her." Finally, he turned from the ocean to pin Gabe with his gaze. "And I want to know that you and Bastian are going to be kind to her. She deserves that, at least. Deserves some rest."

To hear the three of them lumped together so easily took Gabe aback. It was the same conclusion he'd come to—that he couldn't choose between them, and couldn't ask Lore to do it, either—but to hear it plain, not judged or questioned, made him soften in ways that felt dangerous when one was on one's way to battle.

And it was a glimmer of hope he hadn't known he needed, to hear the three of them surviving mentioned like fact. Like there was no other way this could go.

"I promise, Michal," Gabe said.

The other man nodded. "Good." He wandered away, off to find Malcolm.

Gabe stared at the current and thought about rest. Thought about how he could give it to Lore. Thought about the endless, exhausting pull of power.

"The captain wants you."

A sailor he didn't know stood behind him, hands clasped behind his back. "If you'll follow me."

It wasn't a request. Gabe turned from his contemplation of the water and followed the sailor to a door at the stern.

A war room, a large table lined with heavy chairs, the Caldienan flag hanging from the wall. But no one was in here but Finn.

The erstwhile pirate held a cigarette despite the close quarters, aiming his thin streams of smoke toward the tiny porthole. None of them quite made it, hanging around the room instead. "Sorry," he said, and sounded like he actually meant it, waving a hand to dispel the miasma. "It's what I do when I'm nervous."

Gabe crossed his arms as the sailor left, shutting the door behind him. "You're admitting to nerves?"

"You'd have to be an idiot not to be nervous on the eve of war. And I am neither an idiot nor fond of pretending to be one." Finn took one more drag before stubbing out his cigarette on the edge of the table, leaving a smear of ash. "I want to discuss what's going to happen when we arrive in Auverraine. Ideally, we would have done this before we ever stepped foot on a ship, but I believe I speak for both of us when I say time is of the essence."

"Get to Auverraine. March on the Citadel. Malcolm and I will go speak with Apollius." It wasn't much of a plan, but Gabe had to believe that Bastian was still somewhere in there. He had to believe he would fight his way out, and then they could find a way to the Mount with the piece and put everything to rest.

Is that what you want to do? Hestraon asked.

Finn looked at him like he'd been kicked in the head. "It's slightly more involved than *that*."

"What, then?" Gabe arched a brow. "I light the Citadel on fire, like you said before? Malcolm grows a tree through the middle of the North Sanctuary? I don't think either of those things will help us much."

"Neither will trying to convince the God of Everything to play nice."

Gabe ground his teeth.

"You can bet your ass that any attempt at diplomacy is going to go south," Finn said. He stood, matching Gabe's height. "We both know that's not how this is going to work."

"Why don't you enlighten me on how it will, then?"

"With your fire-god problem—and, hopefully, the element of surprise, given that you and the King were something like friends at one point—it will hopefully work fairly easily." Finn gave him a shrewd look. "It's probably best if you go in alone, actually."

"Go in alone to do what?" But he knew.

"Kill Bastian Arceneaux," Finn replied.

Fire feathering at the corners of his vision, crackling in his fingertips. Not anger this time, though. Closer to despair. "I can't."

"Sure you can." For all that he sounded flippant, there was sympathy in Finn's gaze. "I know you two have a history, Remaut. You and him and that girl who wove death. But he isn't that man anymore. He's the skin of a god. And that god is going to use him to do terrible things."

"You think I don't know that?" Gabe snarled. "You think that isn't all I've thought of for months?"

"Then surely you've come to the same conclusion." The sympathy was still there in Finn's face, but so was unflinching resolve. "There's no way to save him, Gabe."

He wanted to scoff at that. He couldn't.

"We're out of time." The kindness in the pirate's voice was worse than irritation would have been. "We have to make moves now. He surely knows we're on the way. So here's what we do: You sneak off once we get there, act like you've defected—"

The fire was not a conscious choice. Gabe did not recall the moment he slipped into channeling-space, did not mark the seconds he spent weaving red-orange threads around his fingers. But when he opened his hands, a tongue of flame licking from their inked counterpart on each palm, the terrified look on Finn's face was exactly what he wanted.

"I will not kill Bastian," he said, in a voice that roared like a house fire.

The pirate's terror lasted only a moment before he squared his shoulders, tipped up his chin. "You won't have a choice, if you want the support of this army."

"I'm stronger than your army." Not a boast, just simple fact.

Finn's eyes shot daggers. "Without the army, you don't have a ship."

But a ship wasn't necessary.

Gabe closed his hands. The fires in them didn't wink out, not like before. Instead they wreathed his fists, shining gloves of flame. Then he turned and left the cabin, making his own plans, apologizing to Lore in his head.

Knowing that once he came back from this, it wouldn't be solely as himself.

Malcolm was back up on the deck, talking quietly with Mari. He turned when he saw Gabe approach, eyes going wide at the fire around his hands. "Gabe, what are you—"

"We're going." Gabe's voice sounded alien to his own ears, popping like wet wood in a furnace. "Now."

"Gabriel." Malcolm eyed the flames with trepidation, but the hand he laid on his shoulder was gentle. "We'll get there soon."

"No." His mind was blazing, the burning storm of Hestraon urging him forward. The god wasn't strong enough to take over, but Gabe could sense that He wanted to. That he was flirting with fire, about to throw himself into the inferno. "We're taking the other way."

By the railing, Mari's wide eyes tracked between Malcolm and Gabe, her mouth working around words that she discarded before giving them sound. "Now, let's be calm about this."

But the time for calm was over. The time for cowardice was gone. "I have to try," Gabe said, staring beseechingly at Malcolm. He could see his reflection in his friend's gaze. See how the white of that one eye he had left was now a blazing, bloody red. "Malcolm, I have to try to save him, and this is the only way."

And then he was gone.

He felt it like he felt a stretch in the morning, elongating all his muscles from where they'd cramped in uneasy sleep. He felt it like a yawn after a day of exhaustion. One moment, Gabe was corporeal on the deck of a Caldienan warship, and the next he was air, diffused into every particle of heat in the atmosphere that could ever become fire.

He lingered, just for a moment. Long enough for Mari to let loose a startled cry, long enough for Malcolm to curse and pound a fist on the rail. "*Dammit*, Gabe!"

But then Malcolm was gone, too. Using his power to dive deep, through the ship's hull, through the miles of water beneath, finding the deep roots of sea-dwelling plants winding beneath the sand and following along.

Gabe became fire, knowing Malcolm would follow deep within earth, and the fire took him all the way to the shores of Auverraine.

All the way to Bastian.

CHAPTER THIRTY-FIVE

BASTIAN

Matters of the heart can be easy, if you let them.
—Fragment of poem found in Myroshan monastery

It had been so long since Bastian was in total control of his body, and he found himself out of practice. He stumbled when he tried to get up, falling off knees that creaked onto legs that felt jellied. The only upside was that this sent him careening right into Jax, which made the other man get his hands off Alie.

Bastian made it look like he'd done it on purpose, not straightening to his full height until the Emperor was knocked backward. He glowered. It'd been a long time since he got to glower. Apollius preferred sharp smiles. Bastian used to, but now, he felt like he would transition into glowering.

"You," he seethed at Jax. "I should have you executed. No, fuck that—I should kill you myself, right now."

The Emperor was too shocked to look afraid. Bastian could use that. He lifted his hand, twitching his fingers.

"No, Bastian." Alie, his sister, always one to advocate for diplomacy. Wide-eyed, she stepped between them, one hand outflung to either man. "Now isn't the time."

Which was just as well. Because when Bastian reached for Spiritum, nothing was there.

Lore and Gabe called it channeling-space, that grayscale place he slipped into right before calling magic. That seemed a bit over-wrought to him, so he'd just never referred to it at all. But now he couldn't find that invisible door in the aether that let him through, couldn't veil the colors away so that the threads of the world shone bright. There was no magic anymore, not for him.

He should be upset by that. Instead, Bastian felt the lifting of an incredible weight.

"Well," he said, lowering his hand. "If I want to kill him, I suppose it will have to be bloody."

Jax breathed in a way that didn't quite show relief. Alie bit her lip.

Bastian sat down slowly on one of his spindly wrought-iron chairs and looked at Alie, his every muscle feeling like a wrung-out rag. "Apollius is gone."

"Good." Despite the circumstances, a sunny smile broke across her face. Her hands came together at her chest, as if she would clap them like a pleased child, but she just gripped them there like the moment was something to cling to. "Thank all the gods."

"Or don't. As it were."

"Figure of speech. Those are harder to get rid of than I thought." Alie rushed forward, Jax forgotten by the door, tipping Bastian's head up and turning it this way and that, like she was afraid Apollius might be hiding somewhere instead of banished. "How did you do it?"

"That's the thing." Fear wasn't a new feeling, but to have it suffuse his whole body like this, to know it was his and not shared by a god, nearly made him weak-kneed. "I didn't."

Alie's dark-green eyes narrowed. "You mean..."

"He just went away," Bastian said. "And I don't know where He went. But I can imagine that it isn't back to the Shining Realm. Not when everything He wanted was right in His grasp."

"No," Alie agreed, stepping back and letting her hands fall away, convinced now that the god was gone. "No, that seems unlikely. If He went elsewhere, it's because wherever He went was closer to His goal."

"Into someone closer to His goal," Bastian amended. "Since His body wouldn't hold."

As if they'd both had the same thought, Bastian and Alie turned slowly to Jax.

It took a moment for the Emperor to figure out what their gazes implied. When he did, he stepped back, hands held up. "It isn't me." Bastian didn't know the man well, but he knew that this uncertainty, this wide-eyed guilelessness, was unlike him. "Alie, I swear to you—"

"Stop." Alie held up a hand. Bastian noticed, distantly, that it trembled. "I know it isn't. If Apollius could have you, He would have taken you in the first place."

There was something in her tone when she spoke to the Emperor. Something soft that Bastian didn't like.

He arched a brow at the other man. "But that doesn't mean I shouldn't lock you up. It sounds like war is coming; no further reason for diplomacy, is there?"

"That would be fair of you." Jax had regained his regal air, recovered from the moment he let it slip, when he thought it might affect Alienor. Even now, when Bastian was threatening him with imprisonment and bodily harm, his eyes kept going to his betrothed. "But I propose a compromise."

"I've broken the habit of compromising with Emperors," Bastian said.

"I want to help you, Bastian." But Jax was still looking at Alie. "The idea of a Holy Empire...I thought it was a good one. I thought it was a way to bring peace. But that was foolish; I understand now."

"Convenient, to understand under the shadow of a noose."

"Nothing I say will convince you," Jax said. "So let me show you. I have a private ship currently docked in your harbor, crewed by men who know how to keep their mouths shut. It can be ready in an hour to sail to the Burnt Isles."

That got Bastian's attention away from nooses. Lore. Seeing her. Saving her. The last memory he had of himself in his own body was lying beside her that night she left. Knowing, somehow, that the beginning they'd just had was also an inevitable end.

And now Apollius was gone. Now, Bastian was almost certain, Lore was in even more danger than she had been before.

"That's a start," he said, after a moment of quiet. "But you'll be on it, where I can keep an eye on you."

"I will be, too." Alie crossed her arms.

But Bastian was already shaking his head. "Absolutely not. The last thing we need is—"

The door burst open. On the other side, Sophie, one of the Presque Mort, her eyes wild. "Report," she wheezed, catching her breath from what appeared to be a dead run up the stairs. "Caldienan ships on the horizon."

Well. So much for war coming; it was here.

Sophie closed the door as soon as she'd made her pronouncement, rushing back to Alexis. Bastian, Jax, and Alie stood in shocked silence, until Bastian broke it with a harsh laugh. "How much do you want to bet Gabe is on that ship? Impeccable timing."

A shimmer in the air. Bastian's spine and stomach momentarily felt like they were trying to change places, a sucking gravity pulling him toward the center of the room, then pushing him away hard enough to bow his back.

A spark of light, embers in the air. The sharp scent of green.

Gabe and Malcolm stood in front of the fountain.

So not on the ship, then.

The way they'd arrived, in a sudden drift of magic, let them bypass any defenses. Not that any would have held them back, Bastian was nearly certain. Malcolm stumbled, tipped forward. The hands that stabilized him on the floor before his nose smashed into marble had tiny leaves growing from the nailbeds. The same small leaves sprouted from the corners of his eyes, closed now against what looked like a splitting headache.

And Gabe...gods, he was magnificent.

The eye patch was gone, so nothing covered his face, nothing to hide how beautiful and terrible he was. The white of his eye glowed red-orange around the bright-blue iris, like a beacon on a stormy shoreline. A flame hovered in each outstretched palm, shivering above inked candles. Char lines tracked from his wrists to his elbows, like he'd dipped his hands in ash.

But there was more different about him than just his appearance. This man wasn't the one who'd escaped on that ship to Caldien a month ago.

He was more.

"Remaut." Bastian's mouth was dry. "Gabriel."

"Is it you?" His voice sounded different. Softer, strangely, with an underhiss of ember.

"It's me," Bastian said. "He's gone."

The blue-and-red eye closed, both in relief and, strangely, in sorrow.

They moved toward each other, cautious, the space between them volatile in a different way than it ever had been before. No, that wasn't right. Things between them had always hovered around this want, this desire, but they'd never allowed themselves to acknowledge it. Not until Lore was in that space, too, the magnet drawing them both.

Bastian stepped toward Gabe, and already his hands rose with the want of him. Something softened in Gabe's never-soft face, despite the fire in his eye.

But then Gabe saw Jax.

Even lost in his struggle with Apollius, Bastian had found ways to keep Gabe away from the Emperor. His care was that deeply rooted, that he would refuse to let Gabe get hurt, even with the god in his head and the enmity that his love had twisted into at first. He'd thought that perhaps it was overkill. That it'd been so long ago, maybe Gabe wouldn't recognize Jax even if he was right in front of him.

Stupid thing to think.

That almost-softness fled, set on fire and burned away in seconds. Gabe still moved forward, but not toward Bastian—he all but pushed him out of the way, his other hand rising, that tongue of flame growing tall and unflickering, and Gabe brought up his flat palm like he'd throw the fire directly in the Emperor's face.

He would have. And Bastian would not have stopped him.

But Alie did.

"Gabriel!" She darted in front of Jax, hands up. Wind whipped at Bastian's hair, but he couldn't see the threads she wove. "Stop!"

He wasn't cowed by her magic, but his name in her mouth gave him pause. Gabe didn't close his fist and dispel the flame, but he lowered his hand, brows drawing together. "What are you doing, Alie?"

He said her name like he had to think about it. Like another had come first to his tongue.

"Stopping you from committing murder." She drew in a shaky breath, standing at her full height. "And creating an international incident."

"Too late for that one," Bastian said. He wanted to interfere here, wanted to pull Alie aside and let Gabe finish the job. But he restrained himself. Mostly because he still felt weak in the knees and couldn't bear the idea of losing a potential fistfight to his half sister.

"Too late indeed." Gabe's mouth was a snarl, his eye fixed on Jax beyond Alie's shoulder. "War is here. Killing him won't make it come any faster."

"But it won't stop it, either," Alie said.

"I'm not so sure about that."

"I am." Malcolm had recovered, mostly. He sat on the lip of Bastian's marble fountain, eyeing them all wearily. "Finn told us he wants Auverraine, Gabe. If Jax is gone, he's still coming after Bastian."

The subtle difference in Gabe wasn't present in Malcolm. The other man seemed fully himself, even laced in leaves.

Gabe's eye fixed on Bastian. He took a breath.

Then he closed his fist, smothering the flame. "Do not think this is lenience," Gabe said, his gaze swinging from Bastian to Jax. "Do not think that just because I am not dealing with you now doesn't mean I won't."

Throughout this drama, the Emperor had remained still and silent, watching the proceedings as if he couldn't quite believe how much his luck had turned. But now that it was clear he'd live for at least a few more hours, he straightened, lifted his chin. "Gabriel. I need to apo—"

"Don't." Alie glanced at her betrothed over her shoulder, shook her head. "Just don't."

"In fact, Jax," Bastian said, "you should probably go prepare that ship you promised. I want to be on it as soon as possible."

◆

Jax left. Malcolm and Alie did, too, muttering excuses about getting things together for the imminent voyage to the Burnt Isles. Gabe half mentioned getting there in the same way they'd just left, though he didn't list specifics; before he could finish speaking, Malcolm's eyes had arrowed to him, sharp as pins, fury flattening his mouth.

"No," he said. "I am never, ever doing that again."

Gabe blinked, his hand raising to fall again. "Malcolm..."

"Do you have any idea how close it was?" Malcolm didn't raise his voice. But every line of him was held tense, something that could snap with the slightest pressure. "How hard I had to fight so that He didn't take over?" He glared at Gabe. "Harder than you fought, apparently. I thought you didn't want this."

Gabe swallowed. Said nothing.

"And Michal is still there," Malcolm continued. "Michal, and Val, and Mari. If anything happens to them, Gabriel, I will never forgive you. Know that."

Then he left.

Then it was just Gabe and Bastian.

They stared at each other across the solarium. The orange-red in Gabe's eye hadn't faded, the pupil blown wide as he looked at Bastian.

It was down to him to break the moment. Always was. Gabe was much better at holding silence than Bastian had ever been.

"It's not just you in there." How could it sound so nonchalant when this was the last thing Bastian had ever wanted for him, for any of them?

Gabe shook his head.

Bastian's exhale tremored. "Fuck, Gabe, why would you do that?"

"Because there was no other way." The voice that wasn't entirely his sounded reluctant. "Not if I wanted to save you both."

"Gods." He wanted to cry, but Bastian Arceneaux did everything he could to keep from crying in front of other people. "Gabe…"

Gabe studied his closed fist. "When we came here—moved through the magic—I felt Him. Hestraon. I'd done it before, I knew if I did it again, He would…not take over entirely, but be more present." He opened his fingers, inspected the char marks. "We want the same things."

"As long as I finally have you back." Bastian's breath shook. "I'm willing to put up with just about anything, Remaut, as long as I have you back."

Gabe shuddered, a long movement down his long body. The air between them was thick, expectant.

Neither one of them knew how to navigate this. The new realization of what they were to each other, what it meant, lay like a shroud over the room, and neither of them knew how to rip it off.

Who was he kidding? Of course he did.

Bastian strode across the floor and kissed him.

He'd thought often about how the monk would kiss. Considered asking Lore a couple times. All in all, it was exactly as he'd imagined—Gabe was surprised, at first, and then hungry, his mouth pressing down hard to open his own, his hands coming up to tangle in Bastian's long hair. Bastian gripped his jaw hard enough to leave fingerprints, to feel the press of bone under skin. Nothing about this was gentle; they kept their gentleness for Lore. This was their own.

Even with the god of fire in Gabe's head.

Gabe pulled away, his forehead tilted down against Bastian's, his breathing ragged. "Every day," he murmured into the humid space between their mouths. "Every day, I worried about you, you absolute bastard. Every day I prayed you could fight your way out."

Ironic, considering what he'd done to himself, but Bastian didn't say that. "Praying probably wasn't the best move." He reached up and tugged Gabe's hair, making his chin tip so his lips brushed Bastian's again. "I like the grown-out look on you, by the way."

With a groan, Gabe batted away his hand, then grabbed it and caged it on his chest instead. "I never should have doubted that you could annoy your way out of being possessed by a corrupt god."

"That's the thing." Bastian stepped back, just enough to look Gabe full in the face. "I didn't get out on my own. Through annoyance or otherwise."

Concern drew down Gabe's brows, wrinkled the healed flesh over his empty eye socket. "So that means..."

"That means Apollius decided to vacate the premises," Bastian finished. "And I can't imagine He went somewhere convenient for us."

"The Mount," Gabe breathed. His hand, still holding Bastian's against his chest, squeezed hard.

"I'm leaving for the Isles as soon as Jax gets the ship." Bastian curled his palm around Gabe's jaw, gave his cheekbone one swipe with his thumb, and let his hands fall away. "If I can find Lore, get the piece to the Fount—"

"We," Gabe said. "If we can find Lore."

"You aren't coming, Remaut. Especially not now."

"Like every *hell*—"

"I won't risk losing you both." Bastian's hands cupped Gabe's face again, though now they were stern rather than tender, making the monk look at him. "Do you understand? I've gotten close once. I didn't care for it."

"You think you're the only one who's worried?" Gabe's teeth flashed, and Bastian wanted to kiss him again, if only to make him shut up. "You've been possessed for at least half a year, Bastian. It's all I've been able to think about. You trapped by Apollius, and Lore trapped on those damn islands."

"So you allowed the same thing to happen to you?"

"I did what I had to."

"That's the trouble with you. Always thinking that the thing you have to do is the thing that hurts you most."

"I won't let—"

"Please." Punctuated by a hand in his grown-out hair, another scrape of his thumb over the stubble on his jaw, a burning desperation in his gut. "I have a bad feeling about it, Gabriel. And you know that means something." He paused. "I have had very few people to love. Don't make me lose both of them."

Gabe didn't answer. But his teeth clenched tight, and after a moment, he sighed, leaned his forehead against Bastian's again. His skin was warm, too warm.

"Ready."

If Alie was surprised to see the two of them so close, she didn't show it. In fact, she looked almost relieved that they were in a posture of romance instead of violence, for once. A leather bag was slung on her back, clearly meant for traveling.

Bastian rolled his eyes. "Not you, too."

"No, Alienor." This from Jax, slipping into the room. Staying near the wall, away from Bastian and Gabriel. "This will be far too dangerous."

"For once," Bastian sneered, "you and I are in agreement."

Gabe didn't voice the same, though his eye cut toward the Emperor with a hint of begrudging respect somewhere in all that hatred.

It had no effect on Alie, who glared at them all with equal frost. "I welcome any of you to try to stop me."

None of them had the chance, because at that moment, the door opened again, emitting three more figures into this hellish charade of a rescue.

Malcolm. Alexis. And a woman whom Bastian didn't immediately recognize, long pale hair and a slender frame, though her hazel eyes looked familiar...

For a moment, he forgot that Spiritum was no longer in his grasp, that he couldn't reach out and grab her life and rip it out like a crooked seam. His fingers still twitched as he lunged toward Lore's mother, and when no magic came to them, he prepared to settle for his nails.

A whoosh, a snap of smoke. The flame was back in Gabe's hand, hovering right over his palm. "You," he seethed.

Bastian curled his hands into fists. He could let Gabe take this one.

The woman—Lore's mother, the Night Priestess—didn't seem surprised by their reactions, though her expression was slightly perplexed at the way Bastian yielded to Gabe. "I guess you got Him out?"

"I did," Bastian said with a poisonous smile. "So you'll get both of us doing our level best to make you pay for what you did to her."

The flame in Gabe's hand grew. "I go first."

"Hold on." Alie dropped her bag, coming once again to stand between Bastian and Gabe and a brawl waiting to happen. "Lilia has been helping me. She wants to kill Apollius, free us all, and bring Lore home."

"Fancy that," Bastian said. "A bit like a child changing teams every time it seems the other may be winning."

"Fair assessment." The threat of flame didn't cow Lilia. She gazed at them both with a shrewd eye, much in the way any mother would weigh suitors who came calling for her daughter. It was a new sensation for Bastian, to be measured up with the possibility of failure by anyone other than his father. Galling, too, when she was the one who'd tried to murder Lore.

Gabe gave his thoughts voice. "Wonderful to hear that you've changed your tune," he snarled, "but sins have their consequence."

"That's a Tract, isn't it?" Lilia cocked her head. "I don't know my scripture as well as I should, considering."

The flame in Gabe's hand shrank, just a bit. A confused look crossed his face, as if he hadn't meant to quote anything holy.

Lilia's expression softened. "You have every right to hate me. Both of you. But Alie is telling the truth. I want to help."

"And what kind of help can you be?" Bastian asked.

She looked at them shrewdly, weighing her words. "The kind you will need," she said finally. "If things have gone truly fucked."

Vague, but time was ticking down. If they were leaving imminently, there were kingly things he had to see to.

"Alexis," Bastian said, straightening, clasping his hands behind his back. Authority had never been something he came into naturally; he had to put it on like a costume. "You're in charge while I'm gone."

Alexis's eyes widened. "Majesty—"

"There's no one else in this damn city I trust," Bastian said, interrupting their protestations. "I'd love to avoid a battle with Caldien, but if it's inevitable, the navy knows what to do. They've had orders for this for ages. You just have to give them permission to do it." He paused. "And if they make it on land, order all the citizens of Dellaire to enter the Citadel. We aren't well equipped for siege, but it'll be safer than the rest of the city."

Part of him was reluctant to leave his people like this, in the hands of another. Bastian had never relished being king, but it came with a level of responsibility that he felt deeply.

Though in honesty, the people of Auverraine were probably in better hands with Alexis.

With a dry swallow, Alexis nodded. Then they chuckled. "So I'm acting as King and as Priest Exalted. Guess Anton finally got what he wanted."

Gabe did not laugh. Neither did anyone else.

Sensing their joke was not well-thought-out, Alexis sobered, nodded. "I'll do what is needed."

"Excellent." Bastian swept his hand toward the door. "Then let's go."

Malcolm fell into step beside him as they all marched out. He put his hand on Bastian's arm, wordlessly asking him to slow. Bastian did, letting Gabe take the lead, his char-marked hands clenched to fists.

"Watch him," Malcolm said quietly, when everyone else was far enough ahead of them not to hear. "I'm worried."

"About Hestraon?"

"About all of it."

CHAPTER THIRTY-SIX

ALIE

Sometimes the heart is wrong.
    –From a letter archived in Farramark University

Jax's ship wasn't the opulent affair she expected. Alie's experience with sea voyages began and ended with parties she'd attended on docked vessels owned by fellow nobles, parties where the hosts had been smart enough not to set sail when the alcohol and poison would be plentiful. Compared with those ships, essentially floating Citadel apartments, Jax's personal vessel was sparse, and his crew worked silently, their loyalty to the Emperor crowding out any curiosity.

She stood at the stern, watching Auverraine recede. Night had fallen, covering their actions, though there really wasn't anyone to hide from near the harbor. Most of Dellaire's population was up near the walls, still looking for a glimpse of their god.

Despite that, they'd managed to get out of the Citadel fairly easily, once again making their way through the storm drain. "Almost nostalgic, isn't it?" Bastian had said. No one laughed.

Outside, they all stayed in the shadows of the walls while Malcolm fetched a carriage, and Gabe drove them down to the dock at a breakneck pace. Bastian wanted to sit up front with him, loath to let the other man out of his sight, but Alie convinced him otherwise. "Do you want to risk someone recognizing you and making you listen to their prayer list? No? Then get in the carriage."

The Fount piece hidden in her cloak buzzed against her thigh, intensifying the closer they got to the water. Pulling them on, guiding them, urging them toward the Mount. At least they wouldn't have any trouble navigating.

They disembarked from the carriage and hurried onto the ship, she and Bastian and Gabe, Malcolm and Lilia. And Jax, the Emperor of Kirythea, who was staring right at her from his place near the wheel, watched closely by a glowering Gabe.

Alie didn't return his gaze. She looked at the water, turning to watch the oncoming open ocean. The sky over the Sapphire Sea was only clear for so far before the stars were choked by the ash shrouding the Burnt Isles. She didn't know much about other oceans, but she'd read about them. Endless horizons that seemed to stretch forever, without the detritus of a holy war blocking it out. She was used to gazing over what should seem infinite and having it strangled.

So when she saw the light, it took Alie a moment to understand.

An explosion. That's what it looked like, at first.

A ball of light in the distance, as if the sun had come home to roost, dimming itself to something only a little brighter than the moon. It grew as Alie watched, its golden glow drawing in ribbons of blue, of black, a swirling cosmos of impossible color on the horizon.

Then, with a resounding boom, it was gone, taking the ash with it.

And the horizon, for once, looked endless.

Endless, other than the misshapen forms of islands in the distance.

Lilia, who'd been silent since they boarded, stood at the railing on the starboard side. Her face was unreadable, expression blank, but there was sheer terror in her eyes.

"What was that?" Gabe's voice, close to the prow. But his tone said he knew.

"The smog," Alie murmured, staring out over a star-strewn, unmarred sky. "It was burned away, by...something."

"We all know what that something is." Bastian's jaw was a pale line in the moonlight, the shadows carving his face into a picture of exhaustion. He didn't say what they were all thinking.

Apollius.

Gabe put a hand on his shoulder. "We'll get to her before He does."

Bastian reached up and covered the other man's hand with his own. He didn't say anything.

Alie stared up at the stars and tamped down her instinct to pray.

With the ash and fog gone, it was a clear shot to the Burnt Isles, and presumably to the Golden Mount. Malcolm estimated they should be there in a day. While sailing to the cradle of godhood was a significant historical event, they had all lived through quite a few significant historical events in the past year and found their patience for another lacking.

So Alie was in bed, tucked into a bunk belowdeck. Not sleeping, though.

Malcolm and Jax were still above, Jax to keep an eye on the crew, and Malcolm to keep an eye on Jax. Lilia was at the other end of the cabin. Gabe and Bastian were pressed into one bunk a few feet away, Bastian's head on Gabe's bare shoulder. Both of them snored. Alie hoped Lore was prepared to deal with that.

Alie hoped Lore was in a position to, when all this was over.

Between her own anxieties and the symphony of snores, there was no way in any hell she'd be sleeping. With a sigh, Alie got up and rubbed at her eyes. She'd stuffed a robe in her pack; she pulled it on and belted it tight.

Then she went back up to the deck.

A lone sailor stood in the bow, manning the wheel to direct them toward the Isles. Alie went to the stern, watching the gas lamp glow of Auverraine get smaller and smaller. If she concentrated on the water, she could see the thin steel lines the prison barges used to navigate from Auverraine's shore, bobbing gently below the surface.

Idly, she wondered what the prisoners had made of the ash's sudden clearing. Whether it was taken as a sign of salvation or doom.

"You couldn't sleep, either?"

His voice pricked down every vertebra of her spine.

Jax came up beside her, close but careful not to touch. He looked nearly as haggard as Bastian did, his cheeks hollow, his eyes fever-bright. He sighed, resting his forearms on the railing. "I've tried. But having the plans that you've spent your entire lifetime working toward completely upended isn't conducive to rest."

"I'm not going to say I'm sorry," Alie said quietly. "I try not to lie, when I can help it."

He laughed, a rueful huff deep in his throat. "I would expect nothing less."

They stood in silence. It wasn't as comfortable as it had been before, strangely. Everything that should stand between them—his Empire, his plans—had all been expunged, burned out by Bastian finally getting rid of Apollius.

But there was still something in the way.

He felt it, too. After a moment, Jax turned to look at her, and she could feel his gaze like a hand on her cheek. "Alienor. We should talk about what comes next."

All Alie's insides were opposing magnets, repelling and drawing her in equal measure. She didn't know what she wanted.

From the corner of her eye, she saw his hand lift. Twitch. Hide in his coat pocket. "I..." He ran a hand over his face. "I still want to marry you. Apollius may be...wherever He's gone...and my feelings on Him may be different. But I still think our partnership would be beneficial."

Now it was her turn to bark a laugh. "Our *partnership*? I suppose this is a business deal, in the end. Might as well talk about it like one."

"Alie." His hand did rise, this time, and settle on her arm. "That's not what I mean."

She should have shaken him off, but she didn't. Instead she whirled to him, snarling up into his face. "Then tell me what you mean without making it sound like an entry in your ledger."

He didn't match her snarl. He looked at her with such infuriating tenderness, when she was trying to be fierce, as if he didn't believe someone who looked as soft as she did was capable of being sharp.

And he kissed her.

Alie had been kissed plenty of times. But it had always been for fun, half a joke, with no meaning behind it other than a good time. She didn't know how to categorize this kiss. Protecting and owning. Gentle but unyielding. He turned so his back was pressed against the railing and pulled her close, shielding her from the wind that seemed to come from all directions, a bite of winter chill.

And there were no gods to help her, and she kissed him back.

When they broke apart, she rested her head on Jax's chest. Warm, and his heart thumping, steady and even while her own felt like it'd run right out of her ribs.

"I care for you," Jax murmured, rumbling against her ear. "Could you bring yourself to care for me?"

"It depends," Alie whispered, because the fact that she did still felt like a weakness.

He nodded, as if he'd expected nothing less. "I still want to send you to Laerdas. Even after all this business with Apollius is over, there will still be war. We'll have to regroup, but the Empire will—"

"The Empire?" She picked up her head, leaned back to look at him. "What do you mean?"

"Our plans have changed." Just like he'd said before, but she'd convinced herself that *changed* meant *ended*. The lights of Auverraine behind him looked like fireflies in his sea-swept hair. "I'm not sure yet how Apollius will figure into our conquering of Caldien, but still, the news of Bastian being Apollius will have traveled, and we can use that to our advantage. No one has to know that he is no longer a god. And there are ways to subtly alter the narrative. Maybe we can say that Apollius has left again, and we must build His Holy Kingdom before He returns." His eyes were far away as he put plans together, though his arms were still around her. "Yes, that could work nicely."

"You still want to conquer the continent," Alie murmured. "You still want to make the Holy Kingdom. Even now that you know Apollius is a fraud."

"I don't want to make it for Him." Jax tipped a finger beneath her chin, brought her closer. "I want to make it for us, Alienor. For our children. The whole world will be at their feet. *They* will be the gods." He smiled. "I will make an Empire in your name, instead of Apollius's."

The growing warmth she'd felt for him, slowly cultivated over months, snuffed out in a second. This was the man who'd pulled out Gabe's eye. This was the man who had trampled all of the southern continent, left devastation in his wake as he flattened nation after nation and stripped everything from them to build his own power, the power of his family. This was the man who saw people like pawns, who only acknowledged the humanity of a few and thought everyone else little better than livestock.

This was the man who'd been kind to her, yes. The man who was handsome and promised to treat her well.

But just because his hands were gentle with her didn't make them any less bloodstained.

"So you're still making an Empire," Alie said. "That hasn't changed. None of this has made that change."

"Of course not." Apparently Jax couldn't read the complex thoughts behind her eyes, didn't feel the way she stiffened in his arms. "The Kirythean Empire is the work of generations. I can't throw all that away just because our religion is different than we once supposed." He gave her a soft grin. "I won't throw it away. Not when I can give it to you instead."

"And if I don't want it?" Alie whispered, her voice hoarse. Her resolve strengthening, as threads of wind wove themselves between her fingers.

"Someday, you will," Jax replied. "That kind of power...that kind of comfort...is nearly impossible to give up, Alienor. You'll see."

"I do," she said.

And Alie pushed him.

It was quick, but to Alie, it seemed to happen in slow motion. She pushed at his chest at the same moment she stepped out of his arms; if he'd been expecting it, even a little bit, she wouldn't have been strong enough to send him past the edge. But he was surprised, and so was she. He overbalanced quickly, tipping over, falling into the ocean. She didn't even need to use the magic threaded through her fists.

There was barely a splash, though there was a hollow sound, as if something had hit the hull.

Alie stared at the waves, thinking he would claw onto one of the steel barge-lines, enraged and screaming, all his tenderness erased by what she'd done in the same way hers had been struck by his enduring plans for the Empire. But the water was placid. He didn't resurface.

She thought of that hollow sound. His head hitting the ship, maybe. She'd meant to kill him—obviously—but for some reason, the thought of his neck breaking on the way down was worse than the thought of him drowning.

A moment at the railing, waiting for tears. But Alie had none. She wasn't sad, she was just cold. In the back of her head, wind whipped and howled.

It felt anticlimactic. Like there should be fanfare, a rush of either congratulation or condemnation, a hole in the world. But maybe death always felt like this. Something there, then something gone, and everything around it quickly filling the gap, going on as it always had.

A small sound behind her.

She turned. One of the crew, his eyes wide, his hand reaching for a pistol at his belt.

Alie grabbed threads of air. Tightened them around his throat. "This ship is full of gods," she said, her voice tired. "Do you really want to face them?"

He gasped, eyes bulging. He shook his head.

Her fingers loosened their grip; air went back into his lungs. Good; she was only up for killing one person tonight. "Tell the others."

The crewman scampered away.

Alie went below in a fog. She climbed back into her bunk, not realizing just how hard she was shaking until she heard the faint rattle of the headboard against the wall.

When she fell asleep, it was not dreamless.

Here was the beach, sun shining on blue water and white sand. Here was the island, the Golden Mount, as it used to be. As it might be again, now that the ash and fog were gone. Who knew what Apollius had managed to do, now that He'd left Bastian? She had no idea where He was, what form He'd taken. It was almost worse. At least when He'd possessed Bastian, they all knew what to expect.

Alie stood at the edge of the water and let it run up over her feet, waiting for guilt. It never came, at least not in a pure form. It was tangled with relief, with resolve. Reassurance that she'd done the right thing, rash as it may have been.

Jax would lie to the world to bring it beneath his rule. And just because he'd cared for Alie, that didn't absolve him.

She could do better.

Movement, up the beach. Alie turned.

It was Lore.

Just for a split second. A moment of her friend's shape, there and gone in the space of a breath.

"Lore!" Alie ran to where she'd been, wondering if maybe Lore was just going in and out of sleep, her rest fitful. She had to tell her they were coming, warn her that Apollius was planning something they had no context for, no real way to stop.

Another flash. Lore, again, diaphanous as a ghost, gone in a blink.

"Shit," Alie groaned. "This would be the time you can't fall asleep—"

The rest of her thought cut off, because the next time Lore appeared, it was for more than a second. Two, maybe.

Long enough for Alie to see that she was soundlessly screaming.

S he could hear everything, and everything was so loud.

She didn't hold all the world's soul—only half of it, the half that had been contained in the still-broken Fount, death and life and water—but even that was enough to drown in. Not everything should have sound, have a song, but it did. Life was the trill of high voices, death the rasp of someone singing from deep in their throat, water a sinuous weave of harmony between it all. The melody of the universe, clamoring through her, vibrating her bones.

This is good, beloved. Apollius, in her head, sounding almost lascivious. *This is so good.*

Her vision gyred in and out, too unstable for her to move in any significant way. She lay on the broken tiles beside the Fount, panting from a mouth that still tasted like cool, sweet water.

She'd won. Apollius was here, she held all His power, trapped Him within herself. Bastian was free. Soon her friends would be, too. Once they came here, once they gave her the magic they'd unwittingly stolen. She would have everything, and she would be better.

She'd won, hadn't she?

You did, you did, Apollius murmured, soothing. *And now, there are things to do.*

It was so dark, choked with fog, with ash. She was tired of it; He was, too. Lore stretched out her hand, fingers spread. The fog was water, the ash was death, and she spun them both into herself and tucked them away, her body made reliquary.

The sun shone bright on every inch of the Golden Mount for the first time in five hundred years.

But there was no time to revel in it, to lose herself in the sensations of the present and those of memory, the way the island had been and the way it was now. Lore was a kaleidoscope, becoming someone different with every slight movement. Seeing the island through her own eyes, Apollius's.

Her vision split. Not the way it had been, scoping in and out from looking down at herself to looking out of her own staring eyes—wider, expanding, the Mount growing small as her consciousness raced over the waves.

Until it came to a stop in front of warships.

A fleet of them, covering the ocean as far as she could see. Lore drifted high above, the masts pointing at her like accusing fingers, emerald pennants with the golden flute of Caldien snapping in the wind. A blink, and she was in the water below, the hulls slipping past her like the bodies of slick beasts.

An army, headed not for Auverraine, but for the Isles.

And Gabe and Malcolm weren't on these ships. She knew that like she knew the catacombs, the lines on her own palms, the curves of her eclipse scar. They'd been here, but now they were gone, leaving only faint scents of their power—a snap of green, a lick of smoke. There was enmity here in their places, anger at them brewing somewhere within this fleet. She could feel that, too, the thrum of life gone hot with rage.

They're coming for you, Apollius whispered. *Coming for them. War is in your fist, beloved. How will you twist it?*

So many ways she could. The world was shredded to ribbons, and she could tie them in so many knots.

But there was one power she knew better than all the others.

Lore reached out and grasped the black threads on the bottom of the ocean, Mortem once again coming when she called. So much life down here, but so much death, too. Forgotten people, those thrown away, rotting down in the sand.

But with Mortem, with Spiritum, she could put them back together just enough.

Lore gathered the threads of death from every drowned body she could reach. She wound life through her fingers, wove them together.

And she pulled.

CHAPTER THIRTY-SEVEN

GABE

If you are to be paired, strive to be known in your fullness, to find your perfect match.
—The Book of Mortal Law, Tract 3469

When he woke, he spent a few minutes just looking at Bastian.

It was very hard for him to believe that they were here. Here, on a ship headed toward the Golden Mount, but also here, together in this bunk, sleep-sweaty and pressed together, Bastian's morning breath hitting him full in the face. The Sainted King slept like the dead, so much so that Gabe had tightened his grip on him more than once in the night, just to feel him breathing.

They are not alike.

Hestraon sounded contemplative, looking out from Gabe's eyes. When Gabe's hand rose again, it was under the god's direction, not his own. Hestraon gently brushed Bastian's hair from his forehead.

Not in appearance, and not in heart, Hestraon said. *This one is softer. More yielding. More willing to admit love, not seeing it as weakness.* A pause. *He sees you as an equal, not a possession. Not ranked by your power.*

Gabe pushed at the fire god, tried to tuck Him back into his mind.

But there is no way to know if that will hold.

"Get the fuck out," Gabe growled.

Hestraon didn't go, but He did cede bodily control. Sweat dotted Gabe's brow.

He extracted himself from under Bastian slowly, trying not to wake him up. A moot point; it seemed like Bastian would sleep the whole day away, were he allowed. Gabe would physically fight anyone who tried to rouse him.

With a kiss on Bastian's stubble-rough cheek, he was up, pulling the same shirt he'd worn yesterday over his head. He hadn't had time to pack anything, not when leaving Caldien, not when leaving Auverraine. He supposed he should be grateful that his clothes didn't disintegrate when he left Finn's ship, reducing himself down to ribbons of flame, seeping into the atmosphere to rush to the Citadel.

He'd known what would happen if he did that again. Weighed the consequences and decided he could live with them. Even now, Hestraon's presence didn't incite fear. Just wariness and an expanding of consciousness, every facet of the world standing out in brilliant detail.

Jax's ship was unexpectedly utilitarian. There was only one cabin space, filled with more bunks than they needed. All of them that had been occupied last night were rumpled to the point where Gabe couldn't tell if someone was in them or not. Gabe had specifically chosen one in the middle, so he could be between all of them.

He'd thought Bastian would sleep in the one nearest his head, before the other man made it clear he planned to sleep as close to Gabe as humanly possible. Lilia slept in the one at his feet, pale hair spilling over the side, so unlike Lore's.

He didn't know what to make of Lore's mother. He'd thought

of her as a ghost story, a heretic, a villain. She was all of those things, certainly. He didn't trust her.

But she was here. And he respected that. Even if he wouldn't hesitate to light her on fire at the barest hint that she would bring harm to Lore.

The sun had fully risen, beating down on the deck. Gabe hadn't noticed just how much the ash of the Burnt Isles had shielded them before. Now that it was gone, he felt his skin reddening the moment he stepped out of the shade.

Malcolm stood at the prow, yawning. A crewman steered the ship, hands held stiffly. He kept looking at them, almost fearful.

Gabe glowered. He didn't mind being feared.

"Where's Jax?" Gabe asked as he approaching the railing. He hadn't seen him in the hold, and he didn't like not keeping a constant visual on the Emperor.

Malcolm shrugged, still yawning. He eyed Gabe warily, as if searching for the god in his form. "Figured he was still asleep."

"He isn't down there." Unease prickled along his shoulder blades. "Is Alie awake?"

Malcolm jerked a thumb behind him. "I don't know how long she's been up. Had to be early, though."

Frowning, Gabe turned away and headed toward his former betrothed.

Alie was still as a ghost and just as quiet. Dressed in the same gown she'd worn yesterday, she shivered next to the railing, not touching it, just staring out at the waves.

He came up beside her. Cleared his throat. "Alie."

She nodded. That was the only acknowledgment of his presence.

"Are you all right?" he asked inanely, after heartbeats of silence. She scoffed. "No."

Gabe wasn't sure how to move here. He cared for Alie—always had, always would—and that caring had gone through many iterations, fluid and changing. Though there was no romance there, he still didn't like the idea of her with Jax. And she hadn't done a very good job of trying to hide her growing affection for him.

Still, who Alie decided to be with wasn't his call. But if Jax had hurt her, he would set the bastard on fire.

That seemed to be the solution presenting itself for every problem, lately.

He gripped the rail with both hands. "Alie, we all just want you to be happy. And if that happiness is with...him...then I will try to find a way to live with it." He paused, then added a caveat. "Provided that he stops, you know, trying to conquer the known world."

She didn't look at him, and when she spoke, it was almost lost to the wind. "I killed him."

The words didn't register at first, just sounds that wouldn't quite resolve. When they did, Gabe took an involuntary step back. "Wait..."

"Threw him over the side." A tremble began in Alie's hands. "He wasn't going to change. He was still set on creating the Empire, maintaining it with lies. So I pushed him."

Gabe's fingers flexed in and out, unsure of what to do. Finally, he settled his hand on her shoulder. She tensed but didn't move away. "Alie..."

"Don't. I can't...just don't." A tangle of negations, thick in her throat. She swallowed, forcing them back down. "You did what you had to do, and so did I. I daresay I got the better time of it, since my solution didn't involve inviting the god in my head to take over further."

Gabe stared at his hands, still char-marked.

Alie sighed, squared her shoulders, putting the matter to rest. She turned to him. "I saw Lore."

Despite the impossible situation she'd just thrown him in the middle of, Gabe's heart jerked in his chest. "On the beach? Was she all right? Did she say—"

"I think it's safe to say she's not all right," Alie interrupted. "She was flickering in and out, not all there. And Gabe, she was...she was screaming."

So was Gabe, internally, everything in him feeling like it was about to burst into flame. "We need to go faster." He whirled around, as if there were something he could do to make that happen, like he could direct his own nervous energy into the ship somehow. "We have to get there *now...*"

"I'm working on it." And for the first time, he felt the wind, stiffer and more solid than it should be, pressing his shirt against his body and filling the sails. Alie's fingers twitched, a tremble running through her from both pent-up emotion and the channeling of air magic.

"I'm trying to be careful," she said, a line of concentration between her brows. "I don't want to accidentally capsize the damn thing. But we're making progress. We should be there in an hour or two, I think."

He glanced toward the prow. The vague shapes of the islands were closer than they'd seemed even moments ago.

"I..." He trailed off, peering out over the ocean, toward the Burnt Isles. Surely, he was seeing things, his perspective warped by having one less eye than average. "Is that..."

Alie's eyes narrowed at the small shapes on the water, dark and spiking against the morning sun. "Warships."

The shapes were hard to make out, still too far away to be much more than smudges on the horizon. They'd moved fast.

"Caldien," Gabe breathed.

"I thought they were sailing on Auverraine?"

"They were until Malcolm and I defected." Finn must have altered course moments after Gabe and Malcolm left, knowing where they would go, and gotten far enough ahead while they planned in the Citadel to keep from being seen until morning light. "I have to go tell Bastian."

"They might help us," Alie said uncertainly.

"I admire your optimism." Gabe disappeared below.

🦋

Bastian was still asleep. Gabe hated to wake him, but between Alie's news about Lore and the fleet led by an angry pirate, he didn't see a way around it. Gently, he smoothed back the tangle of Bastian's dark hair. "Bastian."

He'd been sound asleep, but his name in Gabe's mouth was enough to wake him without any further prodding. Bastian grinned, dark eyes sleepy, and took hold of Gabe's hand, bringing his lips to the tattooed candle on his palm. "Do we finally have the brig to ourselves?"

"The brig is something different. This is the hold, I think."

"Whatever you want to call it." Bastian stretched languidly, tugging at Gabe's hand.

And there was no time, but he let himself be pulled atop Bastian, their chests pressed together. Kissed him slow and easy, like they had hours instead of minutes, like the world wasn't falling down.

Bastian reached for his belt, and for a moment, Gabe let him. But then he sighed, rested his head against Bastian's forehead, and moved away.

Gabe sat on the edge of the bed as Bastian sighed dramatically. "Should have known we wouldn't get lucky."

"I have news," Gabe said. "Alie saw Lore in her dreams."

Like it had for Gabe, Lore's name seemed to snap something in the King to attention. He sat up, suddenly wide awake. "She's alive, then. We have to move fast."

"Alie is pushing us as fast as we can feasibly go. But that might bring another problem, because the Caldienan fleet is up ahead."

A moment of wide eyes, a flicker of hopelessness before

Bastian banished it. Even Gabe wasn't allowed to see him hopeless. "Dammit. All right; we can salvage this. Caldien is on our side. If we tell them that I'm no longer Apollius, they'll help us reach Lore. We'll have to explain Jax…"

"Not a problem anymore," Gabe murmured. He considered telling Bastian exactly why but held the information close. It was more of a discussion than he wanted to have at the moment.

Bastian's brow furrowed, but he raced on. "If they still want a war, the navy is under orders to give them one. After your show of power, I don't think they'll try to stop us." He glanced at Gabe. "You never told me why you and Malcolm opted to use magic—to great effect, by the way—to come to the Citadel instead of staying with the fleet. Unless you wanted to see me *that* much."

Despite his tone, a sadness lurked beneath his voice. Gabe had given up control of mind and body to get to the Citadel faster, and he knew that Bastian would always blame himself for that.

"Because," Gabe said, tangling a hand in Bastian's hair, "they want to kill you and take your crown."

"Ah." Bastian sighed. "That does complicate things."

"I could burn the fleet," Gabe said, his hand dropping. "That would take care of it."

The Presque Mort didn't teach pacifism—far from it—but Gabe still knew it was unusual for him to sound so ready to commit several murders.

Bastian arched a brow. "As much as I love you bloodthirsty, dearest, I don't think that's the right way to go about this."

"We've surpassed caring about that." His palms crackled, fire dancing in the corners of his vision.

The thump of running feet up above, someone sprinting across the deck. Malcolm's face appeared in the square of sunlight that made up the hatch. "The Caldienan fleet is up ahead," he said, unnecessarily, "and there's a skiff on its way to us."

"Well," Bastian said, "at least they're being diplomatic."

CHAPTER THIRTY-EIGHT

BASTIAN

Much of power comes down to acting like you already have it. Behave as one who should be listened to, and people will listen.

—From *Comportment,* by Yvonne Angier

Bastian wasn't surprised to see Val and Mari, once the skiff got close enough that he could make out their faces. Still, relief hit him like a glass of wine on an empty stomach. Lore would kill him if he let something happen to her mothers. It wasn't much of a surprise to see Michal, either, though the sight of his old boxing nemesis brought a sort of painful nostalgia—he'd heard that the other man had taken up with Malcolm and been part of the escape to Caldien, but the sight of him was still something from before his life spiraled completely out of control.

The fourth person on the skiff, though, was unfamiliar.

Not unfamiliar to Gabe, apparently. His monk's tattooed hand closed around Bastian's shoulder, trying to maneuver in front of him.

Bastian brushed him off. "Touched as I am by your protectiveness, Mort, I am capable of holding my own."

Gabe crossed his arms with a scowl.

"You seem to recognize their fourth passenger," Bastian remarked.

"You could say that." Gabe's scowl carved itself even deeper into his face. "That is the acting leader of Caldien, now that Eoin is dead. The leader of the navy, at least, which puts him in a more powerful position than anyone left in the Rotunda."

His heady relief turned colder. "Eoin is dead?"

"Lots of people are dead," Gabe replied, in a tone that made it sound like he didn't think any of them a great loss.

Worry closed a fist in Bastian's gut.

From behind a mast, Lilia crept into the sunlight, her lips pressed together. She stayed quiet, though when she saw Val and Mari, she wrapped her arms around herself, as if guarding against her own collapse.

Bastian and Gabe both glanced at her, their heads pulled by the same string. Then they looked at each other. Neither of them had yet had a chance to speak much with Lore's birth mother. Bastian, for his part, didn't know what to say to the woman. She'd birthed Lore into a cult, but it'd been out of desperation. She'd told her to run, then tried to catch her again. Now she was here, sailing to what could easily be an apocalyptic battle with the god she was supposed to serve.

He of all people knew that love was complicated, but he couldn't make head or tail of Lilia's.

"Before you send us on our way because of the company we keep," Val yelled up from the tiny skiff as it bumped against the hull, "please know that we didn't want to bring him."

Mari gave her wife a put-upon look. "But we thought it would be best if we could discuss everything at once."

"I," Bastian muttered, "have had enough discussions to last a lifetime, frankly."

Malcolm rushed from the prow. The crewman glanced backward, then quickly turned away again when he saw Alie.

She must have put the fear of all the gods in them somehow. Good for her.

Michal climbed up the rope as quickly as he could, reaching for Malcolm before he was fully on the ship. They fell together in a messy kiss, and when they pulled away, Michal shook Malcolm by the shoulders. "I don't know what kind of god-fuckery that was, but do not *ever* do it again, you hear me?"

"Never." Malcolm kissed him again. "Never."

"Listen," Val huffed as she came up the ladder, "Finn told us what set you off, Gabriel, and I assume you've learned better since you're here and the King is...oh."

"The King is what?" Bastian gave Val a level stare.

The grizzled poison runner studied him a moment. Then, she smiled. "Doing better than anticipated, apparently."

Mari said nothing once she was up the ladder, though her eyes narrowed at Bastian and her hand hovered in the vicinity of the dagger at her waist. Val glanced at her wife, gave her head a tiny shake. Mari didn't seem completely convinced, but she dropped her hand.

Finally, their fourth passenger ascended, hopping out onto the deck. He was handsome, though Bastian as a general rule didn't go for dark-haired men, with green eyes and a scar over his cheekbone.

Bastian gave him a dazzling smile. "I hear you're after my crown."

Finn returned the smile. "It's a topic for discussion."

"Is this *really* the time for that?" Mari looked witheringly between Bastian and Finn. "Please hold your coups until after the apocalypse."

Finn stretched out his hands, gold rings glinting. "I only try to make the best of every situation." He looked at Bastian again, still perplexed. "Though this one seems more complicated than I anticipated."

"You aren't alone," Malcolm muttered, his hands still held tight in Michal's.

"Aren't you supposed to be possessed?" Finn asked, peering at Bastian.

"I got better," Bastian answered.

"Just like that?" Val frowned, her hand hovering by the grip of her pistol. So prone to violence, were Lore's mothers.

"A bit more complex, but just how complex remains to be seen." Bastian turned a level eye on Finn. "However, this situation actually seems fairly simple, if we're talking coups."

"Notice that I came without backup," Finn said sardonically. "I'm trying for diplomacy here."

Gabe put himself in front of Bastian again, his one eye dark. Finn held up his hands. "No coups. We're putting a pin in the coups."

"Excellent." Bastian patted Gabe's shoulder. "Down, Mort. You don't have to hover."

"I'll hover all I please," Gabe growled, but when Bastian reached out and grabbed his wrist, he let him. Idly, Bastian entwined their fingers. Gabe slid his thumb in a half-moon over his knuckles.

Gabe's hand was unnaturally warm. Orange still shone in the white of his eye.

He didn't know what to make of these glimmers of Hestraon. Bastian didn't have a real sense of what this all was like, for the others. His own possession had been fierce and total, blocking him completely out of his own mind. He didn't think it was exactly the same for Gabe, but he still didn't like it.

Especially since it felt like his fault.

Alie stepped up, chin held high, and faced Finn. "Truce. The last thing we need right now is to be fighting you and Apollius at the same time."

Finn glanced at her dismissively, looked away, then glanced back, a double take as blatant as if they were in some seedy tavern.

His eyes didn't travel up and down her form, but only just, remaining on her face and very appreciative. "And who might you be?"

"My sister," Bastian answered, warning in his tone. "And very, very far out of your league."

Understanding dawned on Finn's face. "So you're the one marrying the Emperor. The one that the erstwhile fire god here was so intent on saving, along with the Queen." He waved a hand at Gabe, brow quirking as he noted his and Bastian's clasped hands. "I figured it was because he held a candle for you, but it seems I attributed that candle to the wrong person. And where is the Emperor?"

"Dead," Alie said evenly. "So tread lightly."

Bastian's hand jerked in Gabe's, shock moving through him like a lightning strike. He turned to Alie, mouth open with a thousand questions poised behind it, but Gabe squeezed his fingers. "Later."

Were the pirate captain of the Caldienan fleet not right in front of them, Bastian would say fuck you to that *later*. As it stood, he swallowed his half-formed questions.

The appreciative light in Finn's eyes only got brighter. "I see." With one last look at Alie, he turned to Bastian. "Now, what's this about Apollius being gone? That seems to solve nearly all of our problems, doesn't it?"

"He's not in me anymore, but He's not gone." Bastian jerked a thumb toward the Burnt Isles on the horizon, his brain still spinning around the fact that Alie had apparently killed Jax. There was a tremor in his sister's hands, a wavering behind the steely resolve in her face, but there was no time to address it now. "We have reason to believe He's there. What with the sudden clearing of a smog that lasted centuries."

"Fair assumption," Finn said. "And your plan to deal with that is..."

"Kill Him," Gabe answered, low and pointed. "However we have to."

Low fire in his voice. Unease sat uncomfortably in Bastian's middle, like the morning after too much wine.

Movement behind him. Bastian glanced back. Lilia was still next to the mast, and still silent. Her hazel eyes were wide, staring at Val and Mari, her pale hands working over each other, worrying at her nails. She hovered there, caught between moving forward and hiding herself away.

"Fine by me." Finn looked back over the water, toward where his fleet waited. "Getting to the Golden Mount shouldn't be terribly difficult. And that's still where you want to go, right?"

"What happened to your plans on my crown?"

"Like I said, a pin in the coups." Finn grinned. "We can discuss proper repayment for my help after the apocalypse is averted. Not much point in ruling a world where the God of Everything is trying to do the same. Fairly certain I'd lose."

"Even if we can't find where Apollius has gone, we can still restore the Fount," Malcolm said. "That has to count for something."

"There's our plan, then." Bastian nodded. "Go to the Mount, find Lore, restore the Fount." He gave Finn a shrewd look. "Business between us can be resolved at a later date."

"The pin in the coups can be removed then." Mari's eyes were flinty.

Finn didn't respond, just gave Bastian a wolfish grin. "Well then, that's settled. We'll head back to..."

His words staggered, faded out; his expression changed to one of guarded puzzlement. Finn cocked his head toward the fleet. "Am I the only one who hears that?"

He wasn't. Bastian heard it, too.

Screaming.

"Myriad hells." Val leaned out over the railing, shielding her eyes as if shade could make her see farther. "What's happening over there?"

"Maybe your crew decided to hold a coup of their own," Gabe said darkly.

But then the sound of distant screaming was undercut by the slap of something hitting the hull, and a scream much closer than the waiting fleet.

Bastian half expected the ship to capsize, assuming that the slapping sound was some great beast of the sea. But when he turned toward the sound, back at the stern, there was no massive fin, no toothed snout.

There was a hand, rotting. Closed around the ankle of a crewman. It pulled him inexorably toward the side of the ship as he clawed at the planks, gouging runnels with his broken fingernails.

Gabe acted fast, running to the crewman, trying to haul him backward. Bastian went to help, but whatever pulled at him was too strong. With a tearing cry, the crewman went overboard.

Another hand slapped onto the deck.

Drowned bodies, eyes black and mouths yawning open, pulling themselves up out of the sea.

Looking just like the bodies Lore had raised in the catacombs, what seemed like lifetimes ago.

"Mortem." Gabe seemed more horrified by how the corpses had been animated than by the fact that they were clearly attacking. More horrified by the implications. "Those were made with Mortem."

Well, shit.

Reaching for Spiritum was instinct, trying to slip into channeling-space. But Bastian's hands remained empty of golden threads, and his vision stayed in stubborn color. He had no magic, no way to sever the ties of Mortem animating the drowned bodies. He had nothing but the knife in his shoe.

Which he pulled and used, hacking at the hand still straining against the hull, trying to haul the rest of its bloated body up onto the deck. The hand came off easily at the wrist, the rest of the corpse dropping back into the ocean with a wet plop. The fingers kept wriggling. Bastian kicked it over the side.

When he whirled around, Finn was staring, a ring of white visible around the entirety of his irises. "What in every fucking hell is that?"

"Dead bodies that my wife is somehow reanimating." Bastian looked to Gabe. "Either our girl has gone rogue, or Apollius made her do it."

Gabe had looked right next to rage before, but now he was made of it. His hands spread open at his sides, flames poised in each palm. "I've got the next one."

"There might not be a next one." Val was leaning over the railing, staring into the water. "The dead don't seem concerned with us, your now-handless fellow notwithstanding. Pity about that crewman."

"What?" Bastian crossed to her, peered over the railing.

The dead were a school of fish, arrowing through the water, corpses slipping graceful as mermaids beneath the waves. All of them headed for the horizon, for the Isles. For the Caldienan fleet.

"Looks like they're only going after Caldien," Val said.

"Not quite," Malcolm said grimly.

Bastian looked up from the macabre parade beneath the sea's surface. More ships appearing on the horizon line, sapphire pennants snapping. Kirythea. All the ships that had been patrolling the sea around the Isles for the past year, now gathered up and headed their way.

And approaching from the north, barely large enough to see— more ships, with a sliver of purple waving from splinter-thin masts. Auverraine. Alexis must have gotten reports of Kirytheans on the move, given the word.

"Well," Bastian said. "Now it's a party."

Excellent, beloved.

The dead came to her calling, easier than ever before. They unearthed themselves from centuries of sand, their bodies barely held together by magic. She directed them like a symphony, steering them toward the Caldienan vessels, the Kirythean fleet, the Auverrani warships just encroaching on the horizon. She was god and she knew no loyalty but to herself.

And to Me.

One ship she left alone, after a single mistake at the beginning of her raising, when power was heady and hard to steer. That one ship seemed to glow in her mind, a map to it like she used to feel the map of the catacombs. Her body had always been a compass.

Everyone she loved—used to love, still did, love that had grown and festered through ages—in one place. One fast ship, steered by threads of wind, bringing close those reliquaries of power that she would take.

Her body was changing. She could feel it, pain but pleasure, too. Growing larger, shining like a miniature sun. Lifting off the ground, hovering above the Fount. The skin of her back went taut, then burst, a gout of white feathers and golden blood, wings that spread from one edge of the isle to the other.

"I will be better," Lore murmured to herself, quiet in her metamorphosis. "They'll see."

They will, Apollius soothed. *They will.*

CHAPTER THIRTY-NINE

BASTIAN

War is where true leaders prove themselves.
 —From a letter written by Emperor Ouran to
 his son before the death of the Duke of Balgia

Alie didn't ask before speeding up their ship, and it nearly sent Bastian pitching over the edge. The railing dug into his gut, the prow almost lifting from the water as Alie spun threads of wind, puffing up the sails near to bursting.

A fist in his shirt, Gabe hauling him backward. They landed in a tangle on the deck, just in time for Bastian to see Lilia grab Mari's arm and pull her away from the rail, too.

"Thanks." Mari's voice was unsteady, from either the sudden speed or the sight of the restless sea-dead or both. She stood, brushing herself off, giving Val her hand to pull her up from the deck. "I'm Mari. I don't think we were introduced."

"I know who you are," Lilia said quietly.

Next to Bastian, Gabe moved to stand, his jaw clenched and the white of his eye in flame colors, fixed on Lore's birth mother. Bastian put a warning hand on his shoulder. He had no warm feelings for Lilia, either, but he didn't want to interrupt her right now. Better to keep watch, to make sure Lore's true mothers were safe with the one who'd wanted their daughter sacrificed.

For a moment, Mari looked confused. Then the confusion cleared, her brown eyes going armored. "You."

Val, standing steady as a rock despite their racing over the waves, edged between Lilia and Mari. "I hope you have a very, very good reason for being here," she said, low and dangerous. "And it better not involve any mention of how my daughter should be dead."

Lilia's eyes flickered closed, then open again. "No," she said, quiet but vehement. "I want to help. I am only here to help."

"You understand why we have a hard time believing that." Mari put a hand on her wife's arm, maneuvered her back so she had a clear line of sight to the former Night Priestess. "After the way you showed up when she was fourteen. Barely a year free of you, and you already regretted the one moment of kindness you'd shown her."

Gabe gave him a puzzled look. Bastian returned it, just as confused. As far as he knew, Lore had never had any contact with her birth mother since escaping the catacombs at thirteen, not until the eclipse ritual. Anton had been watching her the whole time, letting her live as he made his plans right under August's nose for Bastian's ascension, not bringing her into the Citadel until everything was in place.

"We never told her that you still wanted her dead," Val seethed. "We never told her that you came back. Because she was a child, and you were her mother, and she didn't deserve to know that. She deserved to think that you loved her, as much as a thing like you could."

Mari didn't stop her wife's vitriol. She watched Lilia like one hungry dog watches another, wary and ready for attack.

But Lilia wasn't up for that. Lilia closed her eyes again, sagging, like her skin hung too heavy on her spine. No tears, though, as if all of them had been wrung from her long ago. "You're right," she said, so quiet it could barely be heard. The backdrop of sound was whipping wind, the skip of the hull over the waves, the growing clamor of screams as the dead attacked the Caldienan ships. But Bastian was listening intently, crowding out everything that didn't have to do with Lore, and he heard her just fine. "I haven't been her mother. I was just the person who gave birth to her. But I want her to have a life. The world must be saved from her, but I want to save her, too."

Val and Mari slid their eyes toward each other, still with that wariness. After a moment, Mari nodded. "We'll be watching."

It was good enough for Bastian. But when he looked over at Gabe, the other man still wore a mask of violence.

Gabe helped Bastian to his feet. His hands lingered on Bastian's shoulders, so warm they nearly burned. "When we get there," he said, "I need you to stay away from Him."

Bastian bared his teeth. "I understand why you'd want that, Gabriel, but that is not a promise I'm making. I don't know what form He's in, now that He's out of my head, but if it has a face I want to punch it."

Gabe's fingers tightened on his shoulder, one hand coming up to cup Bastian's cheek, equal parts gentle and gripping. "I have to keep both of you safe." And there was no hyperbole in his voice; he sounded like such a thing was integral to his own survival. "I don't know what He's become. I don't know what He's done to her. But I will free her, whatever I have to do. And I don't need you getting in my way. I have the most to atone for, I served Him—"

"Shut up." He didn't want to hear those lies, poison dripped by Anton into Gabe's ear. And just in case the words weren't enough, Bastian clapped his hand over Gabe's mouth. "Just shut the fuck up, Mort. All three of us are getting out of this, do you hear me? I won't accept anything else."

Gabe frowned, heat building against Bastian's palm. The screams from the Caldienan ships were getting louder, the firing of pistols, the smack of dead flesh hauling itself onto wooden decks.

Bastian removed his hand just long enough to replace it with his mouth. Gabe's was unyielding, clearly not wanting to stop this argument, but they were nearly in the thick of the fleet now and Bastian wasn't interested in hearing all the ways Gabe thought he had failed. "Use some of that firepower for good, love. I don't think bayonets work against the dead."

With one more burning look, Gabe backed away, hands at his sides again, balancing his flames. The Caldienan fleet surrounded them, now, the crewman at the wheel cursing as he pulled this way and that to keep from slicing right through another ship, steering against Alie's breakneck pace. Even at their speed, the fleet was huge, and they were stuck right in the middle, the Isles visible beyond the thicket of masts. The Kirythean ships were here, too, though they were too preoccupied with fighting corpses to fight Caldien. The sailors kept shooting at the endless hordes of ocean-dead, but all the bullets did was send flecks of rot spattering the decking, slowing the corpses down but not stopping them. They were eerily silent, their mouths yawning open, no sound coming from all that black.

Gabe closed his eye, as if feeling out his targets. Then, with a roar, he thrust his hands outward.

The corpses went up like bonfires, dotting the ships in spots of flame, Hestraon's magic now strong enough to bypass things like waterlogging. Gabe's fire was tactical, igniting only the dead, but the bodies flailed and so did the sailors near them, human screams of agony joining those of fear, rigging catching fire. The smell was terrible enough to make Bastian's eyes water, burning flesh and salt.

At the stern, Alie made the wind pick up, manipulating threads so the ship went ever faster. They approached the first ships and passed them in a heartbeat.

"Gabriel!" Malcolm, yelling from the prow, his hands white-knuckled on the railing. Michal stood next to him, hand on his pistol, though his wide eyes said he knew it'd do no good. "Could you try not to burn the entire fleet while we're in the middle of them, please!"

Gabe didn't seem to care. He was single-minded, hands ablaze, thrusting flame out into the air and letting it catch where it would. In moments, the ship they sailed on was the only one not somehow on fire, a dot of calm in a burning sea.

If killing that many people affected Gabe, he didn't show it.

"My lady, could you please slow down!" The Kirythean crewman at the wheel spun it just in time to avoid a burning ship.

"No." Alie was deceptively calm. The same calm that she'd had since this morning; apparently, since she'd tossed Jax overboard. Now was decidedly not the time to address that, but it was a thing that would need to be addressed at some point. Bastian couldn't get a read on whether his sister was proud of herself or regretful. Maybe she didn't know, either.

A *boom*, shuddering through the ship, through the ocean it sailed on. At first, Bastian thought Gabe had lit up a corpse too near a store of gunpowder, but no—the sound had come from above. From right over the Isles.

And something was blocking out the sun.

Only for a moment, though, a momentary rush of dark. Then blinding light, blazing from the sky, so bright it cast harsh noonday shadows despite the early hour. Bastian threw up his arm, shielding his eyes, trying to get a look at whatever was casting that light through his fingers.

Whatever it was, it had wings.

Fuck.

"Well," he said, his voice hoarse in his dry throat. "I think we found Apollius."

CHAPTER FORTY

GABE

I sing of Hestraon, god of fire and forge, whose every feeling burned.

—Auverrani hymn, outlawed in 2 AGF

Gabe burned and burned and burned. Seeing that shape, white wings that spanned the whole of the island below, made Hestraon surge forward in his head, a storm of sorrow and longing and deep anger.

That's Him, Hestraon said in Gabe's skull, echoing like the hiss of flame. *That's Him.*

He let loose another gout of fire, roaring, heedless of Bastian's voice yelling at him to stop. The dead were still coming, still climbing up from the depths to attack Caldienan and Kirythean and Auverrani alike, but those ships were well behind them now, left in their wind-sped wake.

Up ahead, the Burnt Isles.

It was strange to pass them, these islands that had been talked of like one of the myriad hells for as long as Gabe could remember. The two closest ones, first, where the mines were, carving out the riches that Apollius and Nyxara had rained on the earth as

They tried to kill each other so long ago. They were near enough to the shore to see people on it, a horde of inmates that looked nearly as numerous as the dead, staring at them, shouting, trying to figure out what was happening. He wondered, idly, how many of the dead in the sea had been prisoners first.

Then they were past the prison islands, urged to impossible speed by Alie's winds. They skipped past beaches that had been hidden in ash for five hundred years. Another with people on the shore, all dressed in the same pale fabric, half of them staring at the passing ship and the battle on the horizon, the other half looking fearfully up into the sky, to the god hovering there, white wings and gold and horrible light. More islands, uninhabited, burned out and dead.

And finally, the Golden Mount.

Alie's now-gentling winds pulled them right to the beach where he'd slept with Lore, the same sands he'd kissed her on. The trees were just as dried out as on any of the other islands, but the sand was pristine in the shadow of the looming mountain. The shadow of those wings.

Gabe didn't wait for the gangplank. He jumped off the side of the ship, his knees protesting the landing, but he barely felt the pain. "Malcolm, I need that piece."

"Wait, Gabriel." Bastian, jumping after him. "We have to—"

"He's up there," Gabe snarled, throwing his hand in the air, to the shining winged thing that could only be Apollius. "He's up there, and He's done something to Lore, and He possessed you. I am going to make Him pay for it."

"I'm on board with that," Bastian snarled back, "but we have to have a *plan*."

Apparently, all of them were forgoing the gangplank; Alie climbed down, dazed from channeling so much magic. There was a strange ghostliness about her hands, making them almost translucent. Lilia was behind her, and Val and Mari had already jumped into the surf, eyeing the god in the sky with expressions that vacillated between curiosity and awe and terror.

Malcolm clambered to the beach behind Bastian, the piece in his hand. He hissed as if it burned his fingers. "I assume the Fount is probably exactly where He is? Because of course It would be."

Lilia's eyes narrowed at the sky, her face blanched in fear and resignation. The resignation seemed odd to Gabe, but not enough to make him stop and consider it. He grabbed the shard from Malcolm, his hand going numb to the elbow. That only made him hold it tighter as he whirled toward Alie. "Give me the other one."

But she was eyeing the god hanging above them with nearly the same trepidation as Lilia, a more personal kind of horror seeping into her expression. "Gabe, shouldn't we—"

"Give it to me." His voice crackled like kindling. The flames at the corners of his vision were constant, an endless flicker distorting everything.

The Fount piece shone in Alie's hand, retrieved from a pocket, bright against the copper-brown of her skin. She turned it nervously. "You shouldn't go alone."

"He won't," Bastian said, at the same time that Gabe said, "I won't let any of you get hurt."

They looked at each other, brows lowered in twin expressions of wariness. Bastian would stay here. Apollius had hurt him enough. Gabe would fight tooth and claw before he gave the motherfucker another opportunity.

Even if it meant he had to fight Bastian first.

And it looked like Bastian knew it. His dark eyes went flinty, something in them calcifying. "My love," he said quietly, "don't make me do that."

Gabe said nothing, still holding his hand out for Alie's shard.

She hesitated, still, turning the thing over and over in her hands. Finally, with one more look at the god above them—the god that was barely moving, other than the occasional beat of those giant wings, as if something else held the majority of His attention—she let the stone drop into Gabe's palm.

Gold opened before him, a gilded road in the air leading straight up the Mount.

Just as the masts of ships appeared on the horizon.

Whatever lead Alie's wind had given them was gone—the rest of the fleets were fast approaching the Golden Mount, Kirythea and Auverraine chasing Caldien, some still ablaze, others snuffed out. Gabe wasn't sure if it was on purpose, or if they were just trying to escape the dead.

The distant sounds of screams and gunshots said that even if they hadn't brought the dead with them, they had certainly brought the war.

He turned, his edges already fading to ember-shimmer, prepared to phase through every iota of heat in the atmosphere to get to the top of the Mount. A hand on his arm stopped him just before he disappeared into a shower of sparks.

Gabe whirled, expecting Bastian, but it was Malcolm standing there. Malcolm, a determined clench in his jaw, his hand outstretched. The tiny leaves that had flecked his nail beds and the corners of his eyes were withered and brown, falling away.

"Take it," he said.

At first, Gabe thought he meant the shard, that he'd somehow forgotten already handing it over. But then, shining in Malcolm's palm—a pool of clear water.

Malcolm was unsteady on his feet, but he looked better than he had in months. Gabe hadn't noticed just how drawn his face was, how stooped his posture, until he stood here unencumbered. He held the power of Braxtos in his hand, the sip of the Fount that had given him magic and damned him, and he offered it to Gabe.

Alie's eyes kept flickering from Malcolm's hand to Apollius hovering above, as if expecting the god to swoop down and take the offered water. But if Apollius was aware of what was happening right below Him, He didn't show it. Bastian, too, was peering up at the god, looking almost puzzled.

The shouts from the ships drew closer, more appearing on the distant sea. Pennants in blue and purple and green, the cloud and boom of cannons.

"I never wanted this," Malcolm said. A tremor ran through him, rippling the mirrorlike surface of the water in his palm. Dead leaves shed from his hand. "And I don't know how this is going to go, but even if it doesn't work out the way we want, I have to be free of it. I can't live with it anymore."

Not exactly a vote of confidence, but Gabe understood. He said nothing, just lifted his friend's hand to his mouth and drank.

It tasted like starlight, at first, impossibly cold and clear. Then the grit of dirt, earthy green. Gabe could feel every dying tree on this island, every run of roots that had gone dry and desiccated in the burned-out ground. He took a shuddering breath, the power of earth melding with fire in his veins, his vision a dancing tangle of green and orange.

Another whispering voice in his head, not as loud or as close as Hestraon, but with the same unearthly resonance. *This is a dangerous game.*

Braxtos said nothing more. Or, if He did, it was lost in the rush of magic, drowned by the waters of the Fount making a home in Gabe. Washing him out and settling into the hollows.

One last voice. Not-voice, low, a register nearly too deep to recognize.

Another way, perhaps.

Alie stepped up while Gabe shuddered. When he opened his eyes—flames still flickering in the corners, but with a green tinge over everything now—she stood before him with her chin tilted and her eyes shining.

"Alie." Warning in Bastian's tone, but a lost kind, as if he couldn't quite figure out what he was warning against.

She shook her head. Brought her hand to her mouth. Spat, as if the magic within her was a sickness. Then she held out her mouthful of the Fount, the skin of her forearms looking more opaque, somehow, a strange ghostliness gone. "I can't fight a god, but maybe you can."

Something in the way she said *you*. Gabe was different now from the boy she'd grown up with, the man she'd known. Something stronger, something stranger.

But he took her hand and drank down her power, the starlight-cold this time giving way to a light and airy taste, almost bitter. He stood and shuddered through the change, shaking as all that magic swirled, carving through him like a river making a way through a mountain. No words from Lereal, just a fleeting sense of worry before They were washed under.

Half the Fount in him. Half in Apollius.

In his mind, grouped with the other gods, Hestraon shimmered with impossible heat. A lurch of god-thought, hidden behind his own.

There is still one more piece. But now You have half of the world's soul. Maybe He will love Us now.

Gabe grew taller. His eyes were fire, his hands were translucent, tiny leaves pricked from his nailbeds. The apex of heresy.

So much magic made it hard to know which element to dissolve into, so he turned and started toward the burned-out trees, toward the golden path that tugged him on from the Fount pieces in his hands. Memories torrented through him, none his own. The Mount as it had once been, his vision wavering between a burnt forest and a lush one, his ears hearing peaceful stillness for a split second before going back to screams and gunfire.

"Wait, you asshole." Bastian, though it took him a moment to put a name to the face, the feeling. He was something the gods in his head had no concept of, someone entirely Gabe's own.

And he was *furious*, his teeth bared as he made Gabe turn

around, shoving his face so close that his mouth nearly collided with his cheekbone. He'd punched him, once, broken his nose all over the wallpaper and then healed it just as fast. It looked like he wanted to do it again.

"You are not going up there alone." Every word punctuated by a shake, their chests pressed together like they had been this morning in that tiny bunk, a different kind of passion. "You don't know what you'll find, what you'll have to do, and you will not do it alone."

On the beach behind him, the ships were close enough to the shore for sailors to start jumping down, making their way to the island. What they'd taken as the sounds of fighting among three armies was instead those three armies taking on a common enemy—the dead were still rising, the dead were still coming, the dead were here.

Still, this was a safer place than the Fount would be.

They stood in the cover of burnt trees. The dead seemed only interested in the sailors, in keeping those on the beach from coming any farther onto the shore.

Bastian would be safe here, in the remains of the forest.

Gabe knew just where to press on a neck to steal away consciousness. Even now, with so much magic and so many voices tangling through him, he remembered being a Presque Mort. So he reached up, as if he would embrace this man he loved. And he did, for a moment, kissing him like he'd never get the chance to again, because there was just no way to know. Bastian kissed him back the same, their mouths opening like they could swallow the other down and keep them safe that way.

When Gabe stepped out of Bastian's arms, they were limp. He caught his King, gently lowered him to the ground, hidden in the dry remains of underbrush.

Finally, Hestraon said as Gabe made his way up the Mount. *I've waited for this for so long.*

CHAPTER FORTY-ONE

ALIE

In every trial, You are with us. You are as inescapable as the sun.

—The Book of Prayer, Tract 54

She had no weapon. Not that it would help her much if she did; Alie didn't know how to use a dagger or a pistol, had never been taught the finer points of self-defense. And now she didn't even have her magic. Had that been a mistake? She couldn't decide if she thought so or not. It felt both awful and necessary, a decision that wasn't really a decision at all.

The ships were in the shallows; sailors stumbled into the water, fighting off the attacking dead. Alie wondered if they'd come to the same conclusions about who the winged being in the sky was, if they thought that reaching the shadows of those wings would somehow save them.

She envied anyone whose thinking could remain that simple.

"Here." Val, always ready for a fight, had already turned toward the water in a half crouch, waiting for the first onslaught to hit the shore. She took a knife from her boot and tossed it to Alie, who nearly sliced her hand open trying to catch the hilt instead of the blade. "Looks like a gun won't do you much good against living corpses."

"Not unless you have lots of bullets and very, very good aim." Mari pulled her own pistol from her belt, running her hands briefly over the fully stocked bandolier she wore on one shoulder.

"We should follow Gabe." Even though she knew that would be no safer. Alie looked up again, at Apollius in the sky. At least, she thought it was Apollius, didn't know how it could be anyone else. But there was a familiarity about the form she could see so clearly outlined in all that harsh light, a softness that didn't seem like the god...

Lilia, next to her with her own dagger in her fist, also stared up at the winged creature. "We should," she said quietly.

But at the moment Alie turned to run toward the forest, to hide from the horror on the ocean, something grabbed her ankle.

A corpse, bloated and rotting, seeping dirty water out of every orifice to stain the white sand. Its mouth hung open, a yawning void of stinking black dropped all the way to its chest, chin resting on exposed ribs. The hand gripping her ankle was the only one it had, the other arm ending at the elbow, dripping fluid.

Her vision went white with terror. Alie didn't know whether any of the screams she heard were her own, though she tried; her voice seemed unable to free itself from her throat as she stabbed wildly at the undead thing's fingers, horrifically strong, nicking her own skin in her desperation so that fresh blood mixed with fetid salt water. Alie didn't feel it, driven only by the instinct to go get away escape *run*.

The instinct was so strong that it took her a moment to realize the corpse wasn't trying to hurt her. Just stop her.

The corpse that had tried to climb up onto the ship had been silent, and she'd heard nothing but screams through the sound-screen of her winds as Jax's ship flew through the tangle of fleets to get to the Mount. But now, closer, the dead body was speaking.

Not speaking, no—whispering, sound leaking from it as surely as water and rot, though the stretched-open mouth didn't move.

"Keep away." The words were stilted, as if the beginnings and endings had been shaved down, even this uncanny speech too much for a long-dead, unmoving tongue. "Keep away."

And every corpse, all of them littering the shoreline and climbing over the railings of the ships, whispered the same thing. It was a low susurrus beneath the clamor of fighting, not so much a sound as a drumbeat in her ears, barely heard but undeniably there.

With another plunge of Val's knife, Alie managed to finally sever the thing's wrist. The fingers still wrapped her ankle, but the rest of the corpse fell away, flailing in the surf as she scrambled up the beach, ripping at her skin in her desperation to get the gripping fingers off her. They let go, finally, leaving brackish prints. The hand convulsed on the white sand, still grasping at empty air.

The horrible strength of the dead things was evident all around her. While Alie was trying to free herself from one raised corpse, sailors had stumbled up onto the beach, bringing the hordes of dead with them. A Kirythean soldier fell to his knees only a yard away, hacking at a corpse clinging to his back as if in a macabre wrestling match. The soldier bled profusely from his shoulder, his laurel-embroidered tunic clotted with red. Desperately, he pulled a pistol from his waist, barely bothered to aim. He hit the reanimated corpse, but he also hit the Auverrani sailor behind him, trying desperately to run for the burnt forest. The Auverrani soldier went down; the corpse did not. Alie could see the horizon line through the hole in its head.

Another soldier, in Caldienan emerald, flailed in the shallows, trying to scream and swallowing mouthfuls of sea. He choked, but it was due more to the corpse squeezing rotting hands around his neck than to drowning. Another corpse held his legs, tugging him back into the surf anytime he almost clawed his way to shore.

The two corpses pulled the man in opposite directions. Alie knew what would happen, her brain putting together the puzzle of their opposing forces and their unnatural strength, but she found herself unable to look away. Things fell to slow motion, her mouth opening in a soundless, maddening shriek that mirrored the sailor's as the dead things pulled, and pulled, as his torso began to stretch—

Scratchy fabric against her cheek, smelling of gunpowder and blood. Darkness over her eyes, a hand pushing her face into a muscled, unfamiliar chest, hiding her away from the evisceration she could still hear, even muffled by this palm.

"Don't look." Finn. It took her a moment to place his voice, the musical lilt of his accent. "Don't look. Run."

Then he was gone, pelting down the beach with his pistol in one hand and a sword in the other, dripping salty gore. He hacked apart another corpse as he went, dismembering it in violent, wild strokes.

Run, he'd said, and what else could Alie do? She stumbled up on numb legs, still gripping her completely useless dagger, and lurched toward the tree line.

Malcolm was close to it but not trying to enter the woods. Michal stood behind him, facing the shore, blood spattered across his face. Pieces of corpses littered the sand around him, horrific confetti; his eyes were wild as he spun, looking for more. Alie ran to them, mostly because they were familiar, and she felt safer with another living person by her side.

"Go!" she yelled as she ran, waving a hand at the spindly forest, the trees nothing more than skeletons sucked dry by the long-ago apocalypse, standing watch as this new one began. "Get in the woods!" Surely the Mount was safer than this, even with Apollius looming in the sky like a sickened sun.

But Malcolm shook his head, eyes wide and unseeing. He gestured toward the woods, too, not wildly like she had, but with an air of resignation.

When Alie reached his side, she saw why.

A barricade of the dead, just inside the tree line. Stretching as far as she could see, from one end of the island to the other, guarding the path to the Mount. All of them dripped, summoned from the sea, though Alie didn't know when they'd managed to creep up here, to make a wall of corpses against anyone who might try to reach the Fount.

"Keep away." Said at all different times, a twisted round. "Keep away."

Whether the order had been given to them, or they were ordering the living, the result was the same. Every living thing on the island that wasn't already on the path to the Mount was trapped here to be pulled apart by the living dead.

The god didn't want an audience.

"Fuck." Alie whirled away, a sob rising in her chest. "Fuck!"

The beach was a horror. The broken remains of sailors littered the sand, clotted and black with blood, sharp spires of bone poking through skin. The dead went about their business dispassionately, breaking the living apart, still droning their imperative in that low, sonorous dirge.

The line of corpses in the trees didn't move. Malcolm grasped her hand, his own slick with cold sweat. "Gabe must have made it to the path before they blocked it. That, or he burned his way through." He kept his hand on Michal, as if afraid the other man would fall into the clutches of the dead if he didn't keep touching him. "If we don't try to go up to the Mount, maybe they'll leave us alone."

"They weren't trying to go to the Mount." Alie's voice was a saw in her throat, her hand cutting back to the beach to indicate the fallen soldiers. "And the dead certainly didn't leave them alone."

Michal looked up at the winged shape in the sky, still motionless, still blazing with all the light of the sun. "It isn't moving," he murmured. "Why isn't it moving?"

The shoreline was too full of ships to let others wash up onto the sand; from out on the water came the sounds of battle, still, both against the dead and against one another. Nearly every sailor on the beach was torn apart by inhuman strength. Thankfully, none showed signs of reanimating, Apollius keeping His army only to the sea-dead, old bones and rotted flesh. Some of the Mortem-raised corpses slipped back into the ocean, their job here done, mortals kept away from the Fount. They headed toward the ships and the other living people they had been divinely told were enemies.

Finn stood at the tide line, salt water frothing red washing up over his boots. He looked behind him once, made eye contact with Alie. With a nod, he waded out into the ocean, climbed up onto his ship.

Val ran up the beach, blood both fresh and rotted staining her shirt, though none of it appeared to be hers. Mari came behind her, a gory handprint on her leg the only sign of any trouble. Lilia was farther away, her face and hair streaked in slimy sea-leavings, a hacked-apart corpse at her feet.

Everyone accounted for, except Bastian. The last Alie had seen him, he was following Gabe into the trees, insisting on going to the Mount. He'd gotten into the forest before the dead took their places; hopefully, that had kept him safe.

She looked up at the sky again. As safe as any of them could be.

"What in every hell?" Val stopped short, breathing hard, staring at the line of corpses.

"Apollius doesn't want anyone but Gabe getting to the Golden Mount," Alie said.

"Fuck what Apollius wants." Val started toward the tree line. "If my daughter is up there, I'm going, too."

"Love—" Mari started, holding out her hand. But she was too late.

As soon as Val set foot in the forest, the dead dove. One of them grabbed her arm, another her leg, all of them latching like leeches, pushing her backward. Val spat and cursed, hacking at them with her blood-gummed dagger, still fighting toward the trees.

Mari screamed, a feral sound that hit Alie's ears like an ice pick. She jumped in after her wife, firing off shots that miraculously didn't hit Val, so many that some of the dead's limbs were shot to pieces. The two of them fought four of the dead, the rest of the corpses staying in their line, as if they knew more wouldn't be needed.

Alie didn't have the conscious thought to join in. But she did, and so did Malcolm and Lilia and Michal, all of them grappling to try to free Val, who still pushed for the path to the Fount with single-minded determination. Alie cut herself again hacking at a corpse's arm; she didn't feel it. It didn't matter.

They were going to lose.

A horrible popping sound, a sickening tear. Val's arm came off in the grip of one of the dead, spurting blood, the bone of her shoulder an ivory island in a sea of raw meat.

And finally, at the same time as her visceral, throat-tearing scream, the god in the sky moved.

Not just moved—*roared*, a sound to break an eardrum, to end a world. The stark shadows on the ground cut sideways as those wings folded inward, then thrust out, and the god dove downward, back to the Fount.

Gabe must have arrived.

At the moment Apollius dove, all the dead collapsed, as if they were puppets and He'd been holding their strings. The gaping mouths closed, the whispers stopped; they were nothing but bone and meat and rot again, shuddering to the burnt forest floor. Some of them oozed apart, the magic that had held them together gone.

When the god moved, He took the light with him. Never mind burning like a second sun; it seemed He *was* the sun, like

He'd swallowed its light and kept it to Himself, and when He wasn't in the sky the world couldn't have it. The island plunged into darkness, amplifying the sounds of Val's blood hitting the ground, her pained breaths hissing through her teeth.

"We have to cauterize it." Mari, her voice dazed. She held her dagger in her hand, searched around on the ground as if she might find a ready-made fire. "We have to right now."

Michal nodded, pulling a flint from his pocket with shaking hands. He gathered up a small pile of deadfall and sparked the starter, the dry twigs smoking as he blew on them to fan the flames. Mari handed over her dagger, her eyes flat as some hunted thing.

"I'll do it," Malcolm said quietly. "I know some doctoring."

Val's chest shuddered.

Alie looked away, wincing at all the blood, glancing toward the trees instead.

The way to the Mount was clear.

"Go." Malcolm, still heating the knife, his form nebulous in the sudden dark. "I have to stay and take care of Val. But if you want to go, you should."

Val was alive, for now. Mari wouldn't leave her, pressing an already-soaked cloth to the stump of her shoulder, lips white and thin. Michal knelt beside them, giving whispered instructions, as Malcolm twisted the orange-glowing knife in his hand and approached with his jaw clenched.

That only left Lilia.

Alie turned in a wide circle, searching. But Lore's mother was gone.

CHAPTER FORTY-TWO

BASTIAN

There comes a point when hope is lost, but you can't acknowledge it. You have to keep pretending hope is there.

—A letter from the Rouskan front lines, pre-Kirythean-takeover, author unknown

His head throbbed like someone had kicked it in. Bastian put a hand to his temple, half expecting it to come away bloody. But he was whole, apparently, no worse for wear other than scratches down his arms from the burnt brambles he lay under.

Burnt brambles Gabe had pushed him under.

With a curse, he sat up, mindless of the new scratches scoring his skin as he fought free of the underbrush. He expected screams, the sounds of battle from the ships they'd all known would land here eventually, the war finally come to pass.

But he heard no screaming. More worrisome: Everything was dark.

He craned his neck, peering upward. The winged being in the sky was gone; it seemed Apollius had taken all the light with Him. The island was dark, and he was alone, and somewhere Lore and Gabe were fighting against the God of Everything without him.

"Fuck that," Bastian sneered.

A hand on his arm; his muscles still remembered the boxing ring. Feint left, slip his arm from that grip, slide out a foot to catch an ankle. Whoever it was hit the ground before he realized that the hand was familiar, that the body was much smaller than his own.

"Dammit, Bastian!" Alie's voice, indignant, but shaking leaf-light. Something had scared her, and she still wasn't over it. Probably the hordes of the dead. "It's me!"

"Sorry." He offered her his hand, pulled her up. His eyes had adjusted to the dark quickly; he took in her ripped gown, clotted with rot, her wild eyes and mussed hair. "How bad was it?"

Her lip wobbled. "Bad. Val lost her arm. Malcolm is tending to her now; before I came to find you, they were about to cauterize the wound with Mari's dagger. I think she'll live."

"Is that the only one of ours hurt?"

"I think so," Alie answered. "Lilia is gone, but I don't think she's dead. I think she followed Gabe up the mountain."

"Then I guess I'll see her up there," Bastian said, turning away, already tensing to run.

"I'm coming with you."

He stopped, glanced back at his sister. "No, you're not."

"You might be the King, but we're way past this—"

"Alienor, you've done enough." He put both his hands on her shoulders, like he could hold her in place. "You found the piece. You navigated a court completely under Apollius's thumb, helped plot a resistance against a god. You gave Gabe your power. You killed your betrothed because he was still a tyrant, and don't pretend that didn't hurt, because I know you, and I know you aren't built for killing."

Her lip wobbled again, the movement harder to hide this

time. She clamped down on it, took a staccato breath that sawed through her teeth.

"I think I could have loved him," she said, like some shameful confession. "If I'd let myself forget what he was. If I let myself only see the face he showed me, and didn't think about what he was to the rest of the world. That's why I did it. Not because I didn't care. Because I did."

"Because you are better than I could ever dream of being," Bastian said.

"Oh, hush." A tear broke from her lash line. She scrubbed it away, then put her hand on top of Bastian's. "That has nothing to do with it."

It did, but he didn't argue. Bastian knew about loving monsters. About sacrificing the world on the altar of those who held his heart.

Her hand tensed on his. "I can't let you do this alone."

This. Neither one of them knew what waited up at the Fount, but they both knew that the possibility of it being good was next to none.

"You'll have to," Bastian said, almost apologetically. "Please, Alienor, one of us has to survive."

Her eyes widened. "Don't talk like that."

Bastian shrugged. "Just being pragmatic."

Alie swung her gaze from him to the path, winding up through the burnt forest, the ruins of long-ago settlements of faithful.

"Someone has to be here to take the crown," Bastian said. "Just in case."

"I don't want it," Alie murmured.

"Neither did I, and yet." He let his hands fall from her shoulders. "If something happens to me, there should be an Arceneaux to give it away. Or burn it, whatever. Make one of those democracies Caldien is always banging on about. But you and I both know that if neither of us make it back, it will be chaos."

It was deliberate, this shift into logistics. And Alie's eyes said she knew exactly what he was doing, but she let herself be led anyway. "You're right." She sighed. "I can think of at least three people who would say the throne is rightfully theirs, and four more who would try to make their own principalities."

"Can't have that," Bastian said. "Or maybe we can. But either way, one of us has to be there to help." He snorted. "To usher in whatever world comes next, because this one might be ending."

"Changing, at least," Alie said, looking up at the darkened sky again. When she spoke again, she kept her eyes there. "Go on. Don't make me watch you run."

And he did, taking off with a rush; he couldn't phase into light and flame, but he could do this, run so hard he left everything else behind. His heart thrummed, pulling him toward Gabe and Lore, toward whatever waited for the three of them, here at the end.

Bastian fled into the dark, and hoped with everything he had left that he wasn't too late. For what, he wasn't sure.

CHAPTER FORTY-THREE

GABE

HESTRAON

Those who are united in rage become one in their determination.
—The Book of Mortal Law, Tract 890

He remembered all of this. His vision fractured and spun as he ran through the burnt forest, through the ruins of settlements the early Church had built. Now rubble, now new and shining, centuries vacillating in front of his eyes. He was Gabriel Remaut, but he was also Hestraon, Hestraon as He'd never been before, as He'd always secretly wanted to be, in the most shameless depths of Himself—imbued with more power than just fire, holding half of the world's soul.

He'd never wanted to be the only god. Not like Apollius. But He'd wanted to be more than He was. Wanted to be someone who could bring Them all three together, finally, Him and Apollius and Nyxara all made equal. Someone who could fight through the layers of possessiveness and jealousy that kept Apollius away from Him. Hestraon loved Apollius, but He hated Him in equal measure. Apollius had wanted to keep them all caged; was what Hestraon wanted so different? To make Him be good. To change Him. To use this power They'd taken to leave the world better than They'd found it.

And Gabe wanted that, too. But he also wanted Apollius dead.

We can reason with Him.

"Fuck that," Gabe growled as he ran on legs that knew no human weariness. "He dies today."

There's another way.

The path to the Fount was a shining golden road, but beside it, visible in this magic-sheen, was another. Thin and wavering, following the curves and dips, leading not just to the Fount but to the final piece of It.

When you put It back together, you can leave that part out, Hestraon said. *You don't have to wish it away. You can hold on. Make Him see reason now that We're equal.*

Gabe didn't answer.

The world flashed by. He'd phased into fire when he left Bastian and recalibrated to new magic, then back out halfway up the mountain, driven by some instinct that told him to conserve his energy. He also wanted to look for Lore—he assumed she was probably at the Fount with Apollius, her power somehow strung out into the god's control so He could rule the dead, but there was always a chance she was elsewhere on the island. He couldn't feel her as he ran past the ruins of temples faster than any mortal could go. Couldn't even feel the dregs of her, traces of where she might have once been.

And when he finally reached the Fount—the broken columns framing the broken well, the collapsing cathedral—he saw why.

There was Lore. Not Lore, at least not fully. But her form, stretched large, her skin gleaming with all the flame of the sun, the only light on the island. Her eyes were like lighthouse beacons, piercing him;

wings spread from her back, huge and unwieldy, white seamed in gold. The sound of mournful singing was everywhere, seeming to come from the Fount.

Lore looked at him with those lighthouse eyes, tears leaking from their corners. Her expression twitched, changing emotions with tiny movements, going from triumphant to terrified.

"I did it," she said, and it was her voice, but also not. More resonance behind it, the same kind that had been in Bastian's. "I drank the soul of the world. Half of it. I stopped a war."

In a way; she'd stopped the armies from fighting one another by tearing them apart with the dead, some twisted victory. Gabe edged closer, his hands up to show his candle-inked palms. In his head, Hestraon was silent. Waiting to see what he would do.

"Lore," Gabe murmured. "Apollius."

"Both of us." That wasn't her voice; that was His. Her expression changed again, not just triumphant, but gloating. "You become one, in a marriage. Finally, we've done it. She's mine in every way she possibly could be."

Gabe lunged forward, calling fire from the air and sending it toward Him in a furious torrent.

And not just fire—earth, too, and air, an onslaught of every power he had. Not to kill, because at this point to kill Apollius would be to kill Lore, but to do *something*. Roots tangled around the god's ankles, a gust pushed at those monstrous wings.

The god laughed, and it was Lore's laugh, free and loud but with a low, menacing undercurrent. A wave of her hand; the roots severed, the wind stopped. But the fire caught on her wings, adding more horrible light, and she raised them as they burned, though Gabe could see them blistering and knew it had to hurt.

"You could never compete with Me." Her eyes matched her burning wings for intensity, blazing in her face, all gold with no iris. "Did You think breaking that rock would change it? That You'd become just as strong?" She grinned. "I know all about what You did, Hestraon, even if the others never noticed that the stone was broken. It changed nothing."

"It wasn't to be strong," Hestraon answered with Gabe's mouth. "It was to be something You could love like You loved Her."

"Idiot," Apollius sneered. "Both of You were tools, in the end. I just cared for one more than the other."

It wasn't Lore. Gabe knew that. Lore loved him and Bastian both, just like he loved both of them.

But how can you know? Hestraon asked, the question just in his mind, for Gabe alone. *How can you know, when they were so much more powerful? When you could never compare to a King and a Queen?*

Gabe just called more fire. He roared as he sent it out, knowing it would do nothing.

"So we'll fight, then?" Lore's voice and Apollius's, braided together. "Do you think that's wise, Gabriel?"

A sudden storm, surrounding her in clouds that filled immediately with rain; the fire on her wings was doused, leaving the scent of burnt skin and feathers, and then the storm was gone.

"This is what she is now." Addressed to Gabe and Hestraon both, a pronouncement of ownership. "She is this, and she is Mine, and there is nothing that you can do about it. You were never more than a diversion."

"No," Gabe said, and he didn't know if he was protesting on his own account or Hestraon's.

Gabe dove forward, aiming for the god's legs; he was easily sidestepped, and it felt like something grabbed the heart in his chest as he was slammed into the ground, his lungs seizing, organs momentarily paused in their workings. His Spiritum, held in Lore's fist. Apollius's fist.

A stutter in movement. Lore's hazel eyes, momentarily surfacing from gold, brightness fading. "Hestraon." Horror twisted her face as she saw the truth through threads of Spiritum, even as she made Apollius loosen his hold. "Gabe, what did you do?"

Apollius, again, golden-eyed, Lore's mouth bent in a cruel smile. "Yes, beloved. He's here. We can finally have this out."

Gabe struck again in the seconds she'd granted him, more useless fire, more grasping vines. Desperate to somehow unhook Apollius from Lore, to untangle the chimera they made. Laughter, the god easily avoiding every move. Lore burned like the sun, all the light in the world packed down into her form; she cast such long shadows. Apollius taunted, but Gabe wasn't even listening, concentrated only on the fight he could not win, the prize that could not be secured. Fighting wouldn't bring Lore back to him, but it might buy him time.

The thin golden road to the last Fount piece led to Its broken side. The last piece, his piece, and the rest burning in his pocket, making his legs numb.

He could see where they fit into the jagged lip of the Fount. All he had to do was get them there. Gabe crawled forward.

The razor tip of a shining wing, spearing toward him in the unnatural night. Gabe tried to duck out of the way, but it caught him in the chest, sent him flying. He landed in a crumpled heap by the Fount, ears ringing, bones that should be broken aching all the more for still being whole. His power did not heal him, not like Spiritum had healed Bastian; it only made him linger in the hurt.

Lore fought free, one shake of her head. "You can't win," she said, but the last word was strangled out, her neck wrenching as Apollius came to the fore again, her voice changing mid-sentence. "Gabe, you can't win, it's pointless to try—"

The god crouched, eyes beaming like searchlights. "I want to hurt you so much worse, but she fights hard against it. Because she loves you, still. She loves you, and that is why she wants you to succumb to this." The shining hand rose, touched Gabe's face. It burned, not like fire but like acid. "This is the better way, Gabriel. Hestraon. I was trying to save you all along. We could never be equal, but we could be something."

His vision was all flames, and when words came, they weren't his own. Hestraon, using Gabe's mouth. "It doesn't have to be like this."

"Of course it does." The hand that had caressed him back-handed Gabe across the face, sent him skittering sideways in a cloud of embers. He coughed, dirt in his teeth, futilely calling up more fire that the god sidestepped. "I'm keeping Her safe, don't you understand? I could keep You safe, too. Isn't that what You wanted? Me to care for You the same?"

Another backhand, belying the earnestness of the words. The only thing holding Apollius back was Lore. Fierce, beautiful Lore, who never knew a love that didn't end in violence.

"I am what You are," Hestraon said, the words making Gabe recoil even as his mouth moved. "Half the world's soul. It can be the three of Us."

"You," Apollius said, casually kicking him in the ribs, "will never be what I am."

Despite the pain, Gabe scrambled forward, fumbling the shards of the broken Fount even as Hestraon tried to take over his fingers and make them fall, convinced He could somehow win Apollius over. One, carved with leaf and wind and wave, slotted into place. The other, marked with a sun, settled beside it.

Gabe scrabbled in the dirt, following the wavering golden path. No bigger than a pebble, the flame-carved shard winked from the ground. When he picked it up, his hand felt like it was made of stone.

It's a mistake. Even now, Hestraon couldn't admit defeat. Couldn't bear the thought of hurting Apollius. *They'll never love you like you need. Isn't this proof enough?*

The fear of it threatened to pull him under. Gabe was not someone who trusted in love. Nothing in his life had taught him it was safe. If Lore had never known a love not colored with violence, he'd never known one that didn't end in betrayal. His father. Anton.

But if he had to have faith in anything, it was Lore and Bastian.

And even though he was afraid—even though he relished the feeling of power singing down his veins, the security of a magic that had made a home in him—that faith was enough. He was enough. They'd shown him that.

He thought of what he'd said to Bastian on the ship. That he had the most to atone for. Part of him still believed that, but love cast out fear. He would be loved, no matter his past, no matter his magic or lack of it. Just as himself, he would be loved.

I am not You, he said to the god in his head. *And Lore is not Nyxara, and Bastian is not Apollius. We are our own.*

He fit the flame-carved piece into the lip of the Fount.

The Fount glowed golden. The song swelled.

Nothing else happened.

Lore glanced at the newly whole Fount dismissively. "Well done," she said. "But you're too late, and too wrong. Without the waters, the Fount is nothing. And It never fixed anything. She knows that now. Why go back to the way things were, when a new world is possible?"

His mouth was bleeding. Pain splintered through his abdomen with each heartbeat. All of Gabe was one pulsing ache, a worse hurt than having his eye pulled out, a worse hurt than anything he'd ever endured.

The thing Lore had become spread her hands wide, the light-house shine of her eyes beseeching. "I got My answer, Hestraon. I know what happens after death."

Gabe wiped blood from his lip. He didn't try to rise, staring at the god, chest heaving. Keeping his energy, knowing this fight would just keep going and going.

Maybe not, Hestraon said in Gabe's head. He didn't sound anguished anymore. He sounded thoughtful, and so tired. *Maybe not.*

I'm not giving her up, Gabe snarled.

I'm not asking you to, Hestraon replied. *I am asking you to think of a different way.* A pause. *Be better than Us. You already are.*

Lore slumped. The expression on her face now was familiar, even if the dimensions were made alien by divinity—defeat. Utter, trampled defeat. And hadn't they both known it would come to that? Hadn't they both known that when you go against gods, your chances are paper-thin?

When she spoke again, it was her voice. "There's nothing after death, Gabe. Nothing. No personal hell, no Shining Realm. Just darkness."

And he wished he could be surprised. His whole life, he'd labored in anticipation of the Shining Realm, and now he knew it didn't exist, and he wished he could be surprised.

Apollius's voice, now, Lore's only there in under-rhythm. "There is no world beyond this world. You pass into nothing. Something the Fount could form, but chose not to. I tried, out there in all that dark. It would not yield to Me. I couldn't make it anything but a void."

Fear in His voice. God-size and all-consuming.

The god straightened. Held out a gold-seamed hand. "So give Me Your power. Become one with Me, that We may become something that can outlast any death. Not two deaths, but none at all." He paused. "I'm giving You what You want, Hestraon."

The golden hand beamed the light of the stolen sun. Lore's voice now, unsure and wavering. "All you have to do is give up the magic, Gabe, and we can all be together still. You, and Bastian, and me, just a different Me. There has to be something new. We can't keep doing the same thing over and over again."

And this, too, was something they'd both known, a conclusion reached together on that beach, still slicked with the other's sweat. The same thing as before would not save them. Not the Fount, left here all alone, untended and unrevered, inhuman in Its decisions. Not the gods, stealing divinity to assuage Their own fears. Not the religions built around Them both, scaffoldings of superstition to make death seem kinder, to try to force it to be kinder.

You cannot make a thing be good, he thought at Hestraon. *You cannot make gods respect human feeling, or ask compassion from something that has forgotten it. You cannot force love from something incapable.*

I know, the god mourned. *But I have to try. All I ever did was try.*

So when the god urged him to stand, foreign consciousness tugging at Gabe's muscles, he followed that leading.

Vision spangling, bifurcating into looking at Lore and looking at a woman with claws and dark hair, looking at a blue sky and a shining cathedral and then ruins in a god-shaped shadow, Gabe held out his arms. Lore had moved so the Fount stood between them; cautiously, she crept to Its lip, staring at him across Its emptiness.

"This can't happen, Lore," Gabe said quietly, addressing only the woman he loved. "It's too much. No one can hold it, only the Fount." He laughed, a humorless bark of sound. "Even if It is an unfeeling, alien thing. It seems most gods are." His arms stretched farther, making himself a target, showing the depth of his love in full surrender. "I know you're in there. I know you're stronger than He is. Come to me, and we'll fix it. Come home."

She crept closer, again, making her slow way around the Fount. Her beacon eyes were soft; tears still spilled down her cheeks. Step by step, Lore approached him, until she stood directly by his side. This close, the monstrous, godly changes were even more evident—she was taller than him, a miraculous first, and every vein in her skin ran gold.

Gabe turned to her, his posture one of surrender. "We can make a different way," he whispered, his voice, Hestraon's. "You and me and Bastian. A new way all our own, with no gods in it."

Her hand came up. Caressed his cheek, still that acid burn, but Gabe leaned into it, because it was her.

"Give it to Me," Lore murmured, and it was her voice but Apollius's desire, the two of them so muddled together now. "Gabe, just give Me the magic. Someone has to hold it, and I will be better than the Fount. I remember being human. I remember how to be kind."

He wanted to believe her. He couldn't.

She brought her lips close; her breath smelled of sunshine and blood-salt. "Once all the power is Mine, I can make you something undying. All three of us."

He was tempted. Of course he was. It was Lore who always said to fuck the greater good, but he hadn't quite lost his grip on it. It had only grown loose.

But it was enough, for now. To think of the world and not just of himself was enough. He was thankful for Lore's selfishness, thankful for all the ways it had saved her. But that wasn't him.

He shook his head. "We can find another way."

"There is no other way," she whispered, Apollius's voice, hers a scream beneath it.

And then Gabe's neck snapped.

N^{o.} Her brain was one shout, almost enough to drown out Apollius. Lore tried to fall to her knees, but her movements weren't up to her alone, and the god kept her upright, refusing to bend at His final victory.

Yes, He murmured, soothing her interior screams, the two meeting in some macabre harmony. *This is what has to happen, beloved.*

"He would have given it up." Her words were broken, serrated with sobs as all the magic washed through her, every scrap that had ever been stolen from the Fount. She finally won the fight against her body and managed to kneel next to Gabe's lifeless form, cradling his head in her too-large hands. It lolled, awful, a broken toy. She could hear the crunch of vertebrae when she tried to move it, so she stopped, as if he could still be hurt. "He would have come around, would have given the powers to us, You didn't have to do that—"

Pain.

It was so sudden, so intense, that Lore couldn't scream. All she could do was tense, curl herself as small as her divine form would allow, wait for it to be over.

But it would never be over, would it?

I will do what I please. A whisper, worse than a roar. *I gave him a choice, did I not? And he chose the world over you. Over us. All Hestraon's talk of wanting it to be the three of us, wanting to be equal, and when He got the chance, He didn't take it.*

Lore shuddered and shuddered, the pain continuing even though He'd already gotten her attention. He'd made it sound like they would be partners in this, that day when she killed His body and killed Dani and drank half the world's soul down. But that had never been the plan, and she was stupid, so stupid to think it had been.

Mari had told her once that half of love was being afraid. Not of the person, of course not—but being afraid of how that love could ruin you, how it could feel like handing over part of your soul to be trampled. Not a fear of what the one you loved might do to you, but a fear of what the world could, when you let part of your heart walk around outside your body.

She felt for Nyxara. She could see how someone starving for love might mistake those kinds of fear for each other. How power could feel like safety, how a want for good could be twisted so thoroughly.

Now she was god. Harbinger of the apocalypse, and finally, the apocalypse was here.

No.

Not a scream this time. A simple statement of fact.

She could deal with pain. She'd done it her whole life, her body made sepulchral by the magic it carried. She could push through it.

Lore closed her eyes, took a shuddering breath. Sharing her mind with Apollius was being knee-deep in brackish water, a current tugging at her that she'd never felt when it was just Nyxara. Like the river of time she'd stepped out of to save everyone, once, stretching out a second. This was the same idea. She was stuck in her head because she allowed herself to be, drowning in a sea of magic.

But all she had to do was step out. Feel the pain, and forget it, and step out.

No. From Apollius, this time. *You stupid thing, don't—*

Lore stepped.

CHAPTER FORTY-FOUR

LORE

Every ending is just a pause.

— Jorach Birham, Eroccan poet

Someone was running up the path. Lore could hear it, in that moment she took control again, the sounds of the world drowning out the screams in her head. Someone was running up the path, and she should care about that, but at the moment all she could bring herself to do was sit here and cradle Gabe in her hands. He didn't wear his eye patch anymore, something she hadn't noticed before. She stroked her fingers over the exposed skin of his temple, the faint red line where it had been for so many years.

Deep in her head, she could hear Apollius screaming, screaming. The pain was exquisite, but she floated somewhere above it, above that churning magic sea, grief buoying her to a place where it was abstract fact rather than concrete experience. Her body changed, shrinking down to the size she should be, her unnatural golden glow dimming so she was more moon than sun. Fitting.

Eventually, Apollius would battle His way back into control. She wasn't strong enough to keep Him at bay forever; her mind would break under the pressure if her body didn't first. A mad god would be worse than a selfish one.

But she wouldn't think of that now. Wouldn't think of the solution presenting itself, the one she'd run from for so long. She cleared her thoughts as best she could, smoothed her hand over Gabe's hair.

She could bring him back. The soul of the universe swam beneath her skin; she could bring him back. But it wouldn't be *him*, really; she knew that. It wasn't like the docks when that ship exploded, settling everyone's lives back in place before they'd crossed the threshold. Not even like when she'd tried killing herself and Bastian to banish the gods from their minds. Death could be delayed, but it could not be cheated, and once you'd entered eternity there was no real return.

So she sat here, and cradled him, and waited for whoever was coming up the path to see what she had done.

Of course it was Bastian, his dark hair matted with sweat, his face scratched and bleeding. He panted as he came to the top of the path, the only one of them left with no god-magic to make living hurt less.

His eyes widened. Sheened, then closed. "Oh, love," he murmured, the lines of him going crooked. "Oh, love, what happened?"

Lore didn't know how to answer. When she opened her mouth, a broken sound came out.

Bastian walked like weights were tied to his legs, collapsing next to them in a heap. A ring of white showed all the way around his irises as he stared at Gabe's body. Lore didn't expect him to rage, she knew he wasn't like that. But neither was she expecting him to put his arms around her shoulders, draw her in close. "You didn't mean to," he murmured into her gold-glowing hair. "I know you didn't mean to."

And she meant to say of course she didn't, meant to say she

loved him and loved Gabe both, but it was Apollius's voice that seized her tongue. "Of course I did, imbecile."

Bastian's arm stiffened around her, like he could squeeze the god out.

Lore clapped her hands over her mouth, locked every muscle, but His voice came still. "I offered him immortality. To give over his power, let Me become God of Everything, and I would make him something undying. But he wouldn't, so I killed him, and I became God of Everything anyway."

It was a horrible feeling, to stretch your lips in a smile you didn't want. When all you wanted was to sob.

But Bastian didn't let her go, even as she felt herself slipping, felt Apollius clawing His way forward. And it was awful, horrible, to see him pulled apart like this. Love for her, love for Gabe, grief and terror and rage all mangled together and inextricable.

Three of them, the triangle, the whole that was more than halves. She'd thought maybe there would be peace for them at the end of all this, now that they knew what they were to one another. Lore hadn't had real peace, ever. It evaded her at every turn.

But it was something she could give Bastian, maybe. Give everyone else still in this world, both those that knew it had almost ended and those who never would.

She tried to pull out of Bastian's grasp; he wouldn't let go. "I have to do it, Bastian. It's the only way; it's always been the only way."

He pretended not to hear her.

The Fount still sang, music on the very edge of her ear. Its song had been mournful after she drank It dry, taking everything It held within Its waters. The timbre of the song was changing, now, lifting out of minor keys. Hope. Hope that this could be over, that the cycle was finished and could never restart. The magic was deep in her; it was no longer a matter of just spitting it back into the Fount. It'd changed her, utterly.

She was death walking, she was the seed of the apocalypse, she was the fire that let the forest grow anew.

For that to happen, she had to burn out.

"Listen to me." She seized Bastian's chin, looked into his eyes, reveled in the way they were only brown with no fleck of gold. "I love you. I loved him." She swallowed. "There's nothing after, but if I manage to find him in all the nothing, maybe I can send him back."

"Stop, Lore." He covered her mouth with his palm; she saw him wince, like her skin still burned. "Stop. You aren't dying."

The word made Apollius flare, her vision bypassing gold light to completely white out. Her control slipped, fell away as she sank back into that internal sea, her body contorting back into god-proportions.

Lore's hand smacked Bastian aside; she rose up, up, her feet leaving the ground, wings outstretched. "I will never die!" she screamed, Apollius's voice seizing her own vocal cords, the tone of her own lost in His fury. "Do you not understand? The world is new, I am its new sun, and I will *never fucking die*! The nothing will not have Me!"

Fear, again. Not the kind that came from love. The kind that was concerned only with yourself.

Movement by the path, but Lore was too far gone to pay attention, too busy trying to fight free of Apollius. Too busy trying to give her life away, after all these years working to save it.

Gods dead and dying, this was unfair.

Lore fought to gain control of her unwieldy body, at least enough to make herself step forward. She did, but it was lurching, her legs too long, her fractured mind unused to directing such bulk. The shine of her own eyes was blinding, beamed back at her by the gold-seamed stone of the Fount. If she could get there, throw herself inside, manage to claw through Apollius's increasingly desperate hold...

Something blocking her path, illuminated in her eyelight. Long, pale hair. Hazel eyes. A body taller and slimmer than her own, but somehow still similar.

Her mother.

A familiar and indescribable pain, one so different and so much heavier than anything the gods in her body could ever inflict. Her knees went weak; Lore stumbled, bowing toward the ground. Apollius fought for control of her jaw, her tongue, but her grief was too strong. How awful, that when her mother finally came, it was too late. How terrible, that her mother only saw her when she was monstrous.

"Mama," Lore murmured, quiet and raw and asking for something she knew couldn't happen, because that was the magic of mothers. Even when you knew better, part of you expected them to do the impossible. "Help."

"I'm here, baby." Her mother's voice was thick with the strain of running, with unshed tears. "I'm here. I can help. But you have to do what I say, even if it seems hard. You're so strong. You're so brave. You can do it."

Lore did not feel strong. Lore did not feel brave. But she nodded. "I'm sorry. I was stupid, I let Him convince me that I could make things better—"

"Don't apologize for wanting better." Even in the catacombs, when their relationship was odd and strained at best, her mother had never spoken to her like a mother would, either in love or in admonishment. It felt nice, almost, to be scolded now. "Do not apologize for having your want for better turned against you, Lore. That's all any of this is, really. For the people who truly believe, the people who haven't used faith only for power. Compassion, and a want for better, and even if it's all a lie in the end: Those things are good. Those things are true."

Next to her, by the Fount, Bastian still cradled Gabe's body, running his fingers over and over through the other man's hair.

He didn't try to approach Lilia, as if he knew his part in this was paused for now.

A sob broke in Lore's throat. It gave Him an opening. "You stupid buried whore," the god snarled at her mother, "you know nothing of divinity—"

Lore clamped her teeth into her lip until she felt the skin break, not letting His voice out.

"Listen, my baby," Lilia said. "You have to give it to me."

The song of the Fount reached a crescendo, resolving once again into words. **Yes**, It sang, **yes, a vessel, one to bring it all back.**

Lilia was not the avatar of a god. But maybe it only took divinity to steal power, not to have it given. Lore was the God of Everything, and there was nothing beyond her grasp.

In her head, Apollius shrieked. He battered at her insides like her bones were prison bars; the pressure in her head crept close to bursting.

"You'll die," Lore said simply, an argument stripped bare. "Bringing it to the Fount will kill you, it's too much to give back any other way."

"I know," her mother soothed. She stepped forward, cupped Lore's monster-proportioned face in her hands. "I know. I'm ready for that."

"What if I'm not?" Lore whispered.

She'd never had Lilia as a mother, not really. Even in those first thirteen years, she'd been held at arm's length. And now, here: proof of her love, proof it had always been there, and the final proving was that one of them had to die, and Lilia would not let it be her child.

Tears fell freely from Lilia's eyes, twin to Lore's own. She leaned her head forward, resting her forehead against her daughter's, clearing Lore's own tears away with gentle fingers.

"You," Lilia said, "are the only good thing I have ever done.

Making you run that day tore me in half. It was my one good deed." She took a deep, shaking breath. "Let me atone, my baby, my heart. Let me finally make a world you can live in."

Lore fell forward, into her birth mother's arms. Her sobs were artless, racking things. Lilia held up against them, her hands soothing, sweet in a way they had never been allowed before.

Apollius was still screaming, His cries going from wheedling to begging to raging, telling her all the ways He'd make her suffer for even considering this. But Lore, here in her mother's arms, surrounded by her mother's love, could ignore it. Her mother had come to save her.

And Lore would let her.

The waters of the Fount imbued every part of her body; not a swallow so much as a reservoir. And when Lore let it go—fully relinquishing every bit of herself that had ever wished for this power, rejecting every bit of awful divinity—it didn't feel like it had in the North Sanctuary after marrying Bastian, when her sip came back to her mouth. It fled from every pore of her, seeping out like a wrung rag.

Seeping into her mother, instead.

But there was a moment in all that rush, just a heartbeat, when they were both human-shaped, right when the magic left Lore, right before it entered Lilia. When they could just be a mother and a daughter embracing, for the first and last time.

Lilia pushed Lore away with golden-shining hands. Her hazel eyes were wide and bright; she gasped, and Lore knew she was hearing Apollius, that the god was hurling every kind of abuse He could, knowing His second death approached.

Lore's mother looked at her. Smiled. "Love you."

Then she threw herself backward, into the Fount.

It erupted, the power It had once held returning in a flare, almost as if It had forgotten how to hold it. Or maybe in celebration.

A storm of golden light and deepest dark twined together over the lip of the Fount, obscured in a gout of clear, sparkling water. It threw itself on the canvas of the world, marring the sky. Blackness, swirling, an infinite void framed in molten gold, as if the Fount had spilled forth eternity.

Lore had been there, on that threshold. She'd seen this yawning star-filled door. And now she knew that nothing lay beyond it. That her mother was gone, gone completely, and even though that was rest, a sob still broke in her throat.

The hum in the air intensified. The open door into eternity grew slowly as she watched, like a flower in bloom. The very atmosphere seemed strained, bending forward, everything pulled toward that threshold.

The threads of the world flashed around her, as if the seams had been cut. A new dread chewed at the bottom of her stomach. Lore made herself look up, head heavy with grief. "What's happening?"

The Fount didn't answer her. The humming continued, the pull, the void in the sky opening, opening.

"This world has not done well," the Fount said finally, speaking aloud rather than in her head, a low boom of sound. **"It's time to make another."**

The words didn't register at first. When they did, Lore slammed her hands on the ground with a frustrated scream. "No! I did what You wanted! You have Your power back!"

In the corners of Lore's vision, threads of magic disentangled themselves from stone and leaf, water and wind; the world unraveling back down to composite pieces. **"We have Our power back,"** the Fount agreed. **"And We are using it."**

She'd had many instances when she thought she felt despair, but none of them compared to this. Lore slumped on the broken tiles of the Fount's courtyard, her scarred palms limp in her lap. All this, and still, the world ending. All this, and still, she'd begun the apocalypse.

"It is too great a rip to mend," the Fount continued. "A god-imbued soul tearing their way into eternity. The only thing that can sew it back is another death, another who has held divinity. It would close the doorway." It paused, and when It spoke again, there was a suggestion of thoughtfulness, and admonishment. "But you are not willing to die."

Of course. Of course.

"What if I did?" Lore asked.

"Our way is cleaner," the Fount replied. "Easier."

She huffed a laugh. She and the Fount, united in this: They both always wanted the easy way out. If you were captured, take the deal the corrupt King offered you. If the world you'd made wasn't up to snuff, tear it down and try again.

It'd caught up to her, finally.

Lore didn't have it in her to curse. She barely had it in her to sob. She just let herself fall forward, her head slumped to the broken tiles, taking one last moment to feel her breath, feel her heart.

Feel that hand in her hair, caressing, familiar.

Bastian.

"Well," he murmured. "We've come to my part, at last."

CHAPTER FORTY-FIVE

BASTIAN

Behold, You always make a way.
—The Book of Prayer, Tract 8645 (the last
Tract in the Compendium)

It had occurred to him while he sat with Gabe—Gabe's body, but he refused to think of him like that, as just a corpse—and watched Lore embrace her mother that he was probably going to die tonight.

The thought wasn't *new*, of course. There had been part of him entertaining the possibility pretty much since Apollius vacated his body, since he boarded Jax's ship bound for the Golden Mount. He should have been worried over the political implications of suddenly going against Kirythea's plans, how he would deal with his court's newfound religious fervor. But those things had been far from Bastian's thoughts, and not just because he was, when you came right down to it, not a very good King. It was because he'd known, somehow, that those things would not be his problem. That they would be left to better-suited minds than his own.

Because this was his part. Dying for Lore. For the rest of the world, too. But mostly for her.

He watched her slump, after her mother was gone, swollen with magic then swallowed by the Fount. There'd been surprise in Lore's face, when Lilia disappeared and the star-void materialized in her place, erupting from the Fount like a geyser of black-and-gold water. He'd had no such surprise. He knew something more was coming.

There was always something more.

But Bastian took his time, even as Lore railed at the Fount, as he felt the world going to threads around him. There was time, because he was going to die, and his dying would end it. A cork in the wine bottle of eternity, sealing it closed.

Gabe's eye was open, glassy; Lore hadn't had a chance to close it, full of shock and god. Bastian did it for her, gently closing Gabe's lid over the shining blue iris. He ran his hand over the stubble on Gabe's chin, raked his fingers through that red-gold hair until he'd broken up most of the dried blood, brushed the flakes away. He kissed him, one last time, though he could hardly stand to do it when Gabe's mouth was stiff and cold. For a man who always tried to *appear* stiff and cold, he'd never, ever kissed like it. Bastian had only experienced those kisses a handful of times, but he was confident in his assertion. Gabriel Remaut had always kissed like fire.

Then Bastian stood up and walked over to his other love.

There were no tears left in Lore. He knew that feeling. She lay limp in the ruined courtyard, utterly defeated as the Fount began the process of unspinning the universe, trying to work up the courage to die. Gently, Bastian reached out and tangled his hand in her hair, a gentle pressure.

She didn't understand at first, when he said they'd come to his part. Bastian's fault; his flair for the dramatic dictated that he not just say *Never mind all that, I'll die for you instead*, especially when it seemed that he would not get many more opportunities to be dramatic. But when she did, those perfect eyes blew wide, her jaw went tight, and her chin came up, a picture of defiance as familiar to him as the scar on his palm.

"No," she said simply. No cursing, no fighting, just simple negation. "I won't allow it. Please, Bastian, I can't lose you both."

"It seems one of us is going to have to lose the other two, or the world will end. How's that for fairness?" He smoothed back her hair, and she leaned into his touch, so tired. "Lore, dearest, there could be a life for you beyond this. Let me do this for you." He knelt next to her, pulled her forward so his lips brushed her forehead. "Let me be the hero, just once."

"I never wanted you to be a hero," she murmured. "Either one of you. I didn't need that."

"Of course not." He smiled against her skin. "I would say you wanted to be your own hero, but that's not quite right, either. We just didn't need heroes, any of us. I'd like to try, all the same."

Her grip on him tightened. All around them, the Fount sang, eternity hummed, and the void in the air slowly, slowly grew.

"Please, Bastian." She didn't know what she was pleading for, not really. The words were just the shape her desperation took. "Please, I can't do this."

"You can, though." He brought her hands to his lips, kissed her rough knuckles. "You've fought so hard to live, Lore. You've survived things no one else should, and there has to be a reason for that. Let me let you keep it." He spoke against her fingers, hushed. "Let me be your hero."

"You were, anyway," she murmured, tears sheeting down her cheeks. She did nothing to stop them, so he did, instead, wiping them away. "Both of you were better than I deserved, for however long I had you."

"Hush." He kissed her forehead. His own throat was a saw-blade, but damn him if he'd let her see, if he'd let her know just how afraid he was. All that yawning black, and the thought of that door leading to Apollius's memories, that endless void. "We were for one another. All three of us. So I'm going to be for you now, all right?"

"I won't let you." She stood on unsteady legs, hobbled toward the Fount and the yawning void above It. "I finally have something worth sacrificing myself for—"

He grabbed her arm, and she fought him, and even though she was weak it was still a struggle. Bastian pinioned her arms against her sides and hugged her to him, hard. "I'll knock you out if I have to," he whispered into her hair. "I know the exact place on the back of your head to press. Watching Gabe so closely paid off there."

Lore shook her head. He enclosed it tenderly between his palms to stop her, his eclipse scar rough against the one on her temple. "I'm not afraid," he lied. "You said maybe you could find him in all that nothing. Maybe I can, too."

Bastian hadn't been one to pray, even when he thought there was something to pray to. Now he knew there wasn't, but his words had a talismanic quality anyway, full of hope. As if by saying them, he could will them true.

She was sobbing now, his Lore, his dearest. He wished there were a way out of this that didn't cause her pain. But there wasn't, and if there had still been gods to curse for that, anything but the unfeeling Fount, he would have done it.

He held her close until the sobs subsided, as much as they were going to. He wiped at her cheeks. "Take a breath, love, you look a mess."

One sob turned to half laughter. Lore buried her face in his chest. "Is that how you'll remember me, if you're . . . if remembering is something you can do?"

"No." He cradled her jaw in his hands. "Do you recall that first night at the boxing ring? When I devised a very clever trap to catch you? I do. I looked across the ring, when I knew Michal was coming, when I knew he would see you. And you had this look on your face. Surprised, your mouth open—delectable, might I add—and your hair wild, and your eyes bright. You looked like you could kill me, and I would have let you. And there was our

Mort beside you, so noble, ready to jump to your aid, but watching me move like a starving man all the same. That's how I'll remember you. Both of you. Fierce, and beautiful, and at a beginning rather than an end."

She sobbed again, choked it back. Relaxed her hold on him, gradually, until he could ease away. It felt wrong not to touch her, but this couldn't be put off any longer. Bastian thought of it as any other duty he didn't care for, as he turned to the humming void, the doorway into eternity that would eat the world if it wasn't closed. One more task, then he could rest.

"I love you," he called to Lore. Casual, the same way he'd say it when leaving breakfast. "Remember that. We both loved you up until the very end, and whatever is left of us will love you long beyond that."

He stood in front of the hole into eternity, giving it the same unimpressed look he'd give a courtier he didn't like. "Well," he called to the Fount. "It seems You need an erstwhile god to die, and I am applying for the position."

"**You would suffice.**" The Fount sounded bored. The making and unmaking of worlds was nothing to It. "**You would mend the seams.**"

"And the world will go on?" He didn't want to be fearful, but it crept into his voice all the same.

"**We will go on as We always have.**" Waters splashed against the side of the Fount. "**It will be interesting to watch, at least.**"

"At least," Bastian agreed. He turned to look at Lore again. No more words; he'd said them all. But he raised his hand, kissed his scar. Lifted it in the same wave he'd give her if he were only leaving for a meeting, as if he'd see her again soon.

Willing it true, with every scrap in him, every piece that had once held power.

Then he stepped through the door, into the dark and stars and molten gold, to whatever waited next.

Chapter Forty-Six

LORE

In the end, the making of a god is a simple matter:
It is someone deciding that the world is not as they
want it, and letting nothing stand in their way. It is
someone defying every destiny with no regard for
consequences.

—From *Divine Destinies: The Making of the Pantheon*, by
Argus Snow (outlawed 15 AGF, only surviving
copies found in Farramark University)

She didn't remember the walk down the mountain. Lore was
already leaving the courtyard of the Fount before the doorway even closed, wanting her last memory of Bastian to be of him
whole and steady and moving forward, rather than disappearing
into the stars. The humming died away, zipped up like a mouth
suddenly closed. The singing of the Fount crescendoed, triumphant, jubilant.

The apocalypse averted. It had only cost her everything.

The sun came back at some point in her trip back down to the
beach, seeping light over the burnt forest, the ash-free sky. Idly,
she wondered what Raihan's silver instruments were doing now,

if they were still or wildly spinning. She wondered what the world she'd made would be like.

She crossed the tree line, silent. There were more people on the beach than she'd anticipated; some ships, Auverrani and Caldienan and Kirythean, but the soldiers didn't appear to be fighting one another. The suddenly avoided end of everything brought people together, apparently.

There were other boats, too. Rough-hewn things, made from lashed-together logs, crewed by an odd assortment of people in pale fabric. The escaped prisoners from the Harbor—it seemed they'd made more vessels after Lore took Raihan's boat. Maybe now they could finally find their way home.

One of the pale-clad people was near a familiar shape on the beach near the tree line, binding someone's shoulder. Raihan. Helping Val, who looked to be missing an arm. Lore shuffled over to them, moving on instinct. She wouldn't allow real thoughts in her head, not yet. They hurt too much.

Malcolm saw her first. His expression cycled through shock, then fear, landed on concern. "Oh, Lore."

At her name, the others turned. Alie, Val, Mari. Mari rushed for her, Alie not far behind. Val tried, but she moved slowly.

Mari enveloped her in a crushing embrace; Lore wanted to return it, but her limbs felt full of stones.

"Mouse," her mother breathed into her hair. "Oh, gods, I thought you were gone."

She had been, for a time. But Lore didn't say that, just rested her head in the crook of her mother's shoulder. As she did, her eyes connected with Alie's. A knowing look passed between them. Alie pulled in a sharp breath.

Lore went to Val, gingerly touching her gore-caked shoulder. "I'm so sorry, Ma."

"Wasn't you." Her smile was a strained thing, but it was there. "One of those pesky corpses."

"More than one," Mari said softly.

"But it was me." She wanted to cry, but she didn't. Her emotions felt too far away to affect her, like she'd fallen down a dark hole. "I told them to keep everyone away."

"I forgive you," Val said simply, bringing up her remaining arm to pull her close. "You weren't yourself. And I suppose I could have taken the hint. At least it wasn't my shooting arm."

Lore closed her eyes.

Alie waited until her mothers had released her before she stepped any closer. She approached slowly, as if Lore might startle away, placed a hand on her arm. "Are they..."

The words wouldn't come. So Lore just nodded.

Alie's breath caught. She pressed the back of her wrist against her mouth, sobbed once. Closed her eyes. When she opened them, they shone with purpose. "Well," she said. "I guess that means I'm the Queen of Auverraine. Dammit."

Her voice broke on the last word. Lore bundled Alie up in her arms, the smaller woman's sobs racking her entire frame. Lore held her until it was through, damp-eyed but keeping it together. Her grief was too deep to show anyone, a feral animal that hid from the light. It would only emerge when she was alone, and Lore wasn't entirely sure if she'd survive when it did.

Malcolm approached with the same cautious air Alie had. He didn't ask questions, just enclosed both of them in strong arms. Michal followed him but hung back. He raised a hand and placed it between Lore's shoulder blades, one comforting touch.

When their holds on one another relaxed, the worst of it past, Malcolm tried to crack a smile. "I'll make sure there are books about them," he said, with a quiet, strong conviction. "Gabe would hate that, probably, but Bastian would love it."

"As long as everything in them is true," Lore said softly. Thinking. She looked at Raihan, then back up at the Mount.

Raihan walked over cautiously. Curiosity shone in his eyes, and a little bit of shame at that curiosity, though not enough to blunt it. "We saw the fog break, and then we saw the ships," he said, answering the question on Lore's face. "And when all my instruments started spinning as if to break apart, Sersha said we should come investigate. Wasn't as comfortable as sailing my boat, but the skiffs we made were serviceable."

"I'm sorry about the boat," Lore said. "It's here somewhere."

He nodded. "If the dead didn't tear it apart. Seems we just missed them; they all slipped back into the sea while we were sailing."

"I must've let them go when Gabe made it to the Mount," she murmured, piecing it together. "Right before I killed him."

She hadn't meant to say that. A flinch shuddered through every person in their small group, but none of them moved away from her. Alie reached out and grabbed her hand. Malcolm put a shaking palm on her shoulder.

Raihan's eyes widened. He nodded but said nothing.

Alie sniffed again, once, then dashed her hand across her face. "So it's over, then," she said. "The Fount has all the power. The world will right itself."

"Some of it," Lore said quietly, still feeling her gaze drawn upward, toward the Golden Mount. "Some things are on us. A higher power can't fix everything." She snorted, lightly. "It doesn't *want* to. It isn't human. It can just make another world, reuse the bits of this one to create something else. But this is the only world we have, and we're the only ones who can make it good. Who can prove it's worth something."

Val sighed. "I'm about past believing in the goodness of humanity, frankly."

Lore pressed her lips together.

"It could happen again," Malcolm murmured. "Someone coming here. Taking part of the Fount. It wouldn't be exactly the same cycle, but close enough."

They stood in silence. There should be a feeling of victory here. A crisis surmounted. But there was no triumph. Just something that felt like waiting.

Mari shook it off first. She turned to Lore with a smile that was only slightly strained. "Let's go, mouse. We need to get Alie back to Dellaire; Finn has agreed to escort us. There will be plenty to do once we arrive, I'm sure, but first you'll need to rest..."

She trailed off slowly, timed to Lore's shaking head. "I can't," Lore said, not realizing what she meant to say until it was already out of her mouth. "I have to stay."

"Don't be ridiculous," Val snapped, the same tone she took with poison runners who'd fucked up a drop, though there was less vitriol and more fear behind it. "There's nothing here, Lore. It's done."

"But it's not," Lore said. "At least, not forever. Malcolm is right; this could all start over again, so easily. Someone has to make sure it doesn't. Someone has to make sure the cycle doesn't begin again."

"But it doesn't have to be you." Mari's dark eyes shone; her hand on Lore's arm was gentle and pleading. "You've done enough. Let someone else do this part."

She couldn't, though, because this part was hers. Gabe had been the catalyst, rushing in to save her like always, freeing her from Apollius but only through the worst circumstances. And Bastian had been the consequence, a sacrifice to close a cosmic door.

And Lore was, as always, the end.

So she just shook her head. Smiled at her mothers, at Alie and Malcolm and Michal. "I have to," she said simply. Then she turned, headed back toward the Fount. Behind her, she heard the scuffle of Val wanting to follow, of Mari doing the same. The low murmur of Alie, of Malcolm. They both understood. The ghosts of divinity made these kinds of things clear.

Before Lore crossed the tree line again, she turned around. Looked at Raihan. "Come with me."

He startled back, brows furrowed. "Why?"

"Because things should be written down, and I know you have a notebook." She pushed through the burnt trees. "We need to make sure it's only the truth, this time. The truth and nothing else."

🦋

Quickly, quickly; back up the mountain, past the broken settlements, back to the made-whole Fount, gold and shining and singing. Raihan walked with his mouth agape, peering at everything as if he wanted to memorize it, but Lore stalked into the courtyard with the same stance as she'd once stalked into a boxing ring, hands on her hips and feet planted.

"I have a bone to pick with you," she said to the Fount.

The singing didn't stop, but it softened, became a buzz of background noise. The Fount's voice moved sinuous through the air, allowing Itself to be heard. **"And what is it that you want?"**

"What I want is my men back," she said, "but I'm willing to talk terms. You need me, still."

From the corner of her eye, she saw Raihan wrestling a notebook of his pocket, hurriedly finding a pen. He looked around for somewhere to sit and write, then decided on the ground.

She let him get settled before continuing. There needed to be a record of this.

"You grow arrogant," the Fount said. It wasn't cajoling anymore, not now that It had what It needed from her. Ridiculous to think of a magic fountain as sounding irritated, but at this point Lore was used to ridiculousness. It was rather rude, though, all things considered. **"You are not a god, to demand things of Us."**

"I mean, I was up until a few hours ago, by Your insistence. You needed me to bring You back the magic You lost. The magic You let Yourself lose." Lore crossed her arms. "And that really brings us nicely to the crux of my argument: This can happen again."

Water sloshed thoughtfully. "**What do you mean?**"

"You know what I mean," Lore said. "I saw Nyxara's memories. They stole from You, but You let them—gave terms, gave second deaths, allowed Them to become what They did. You could have stopped Them, and You didn't. Why?"

The waters churned, threads of magic tangling and coming apart as the Fount thought. "**We did not *want* Them to take from Us, you understand**," It finally said. "**But as it was happening, We thought . . . it was something new. A new world. And new worlds are Our business.**"

"So it was just a diversion for You," Lore said. "You didn't think of the consequences. How like a god."

The Fount frothed but didn't dispute her.

Lore glanced sideways at Raihan, writing so furiously he'd nearly worn holes through the paper. Good. He was getting all of it.

"And that," Lore replied, turning back to the Fount, "is why You can't be trusted."

The waters churned faster now, nearly breaching the sides of the Fount's walls. "**Insolent child. We are not your petty gods, with human wants. We are older. We are unknowable.**"

"Yeah, that's the problem," Lore said. "And it's true. You have nothing human in You. This world is of little consequence, since You can just make another. You can spin new existences into possibility on a whim—at least, You can when You have all Your power. You were going to let this world dissolve like . . . like a child destroying a toy it doesn't want to play with anymore!"

Glowing waters sloshed in the Fount, but that was Its only reply.

"There is so much You don't understand," Lore continued, calmer now, "and I think that's why You allowed the gods to take from You. You wanted to see what would happen, when the world was governed by human hearts. We are all an experiment." She cocked her head, trying to sound less furious than she felt. "And the experiment went wrong, and then it was up to us to fix it. So now You have Your power back. But what happens when someone else comes here, centuries from now, and wants a piece of it? What if, by that point, You're curious again?"

The Fount bubbled. "**We do not make the same mistake twice.**"

"Respectfully, I don't believe You."

"**What are you suggesting?**"

"I'm suggesting that You need a guard," Lore said. "Someone to stay here and make sure no one else gets it in their head to try on godhood. Someone with a human heart to keep You from making inhuman decisions."

"**Someone for them to worship,**" the Fount said derisively.

Lore's nose wrinkled. "I deeply hope not."

Raihan looked up from his scribbling, eyes narrowed even as his hand kept moving. "What are you playing at, Lore?"

"I'm done playing," she said simply. "And I won't let the game start again."

The Fount burbled some more, as if beginning to boil, the weight of Its thought hanging heavy in the air. "**You mortals only last so long. Who will take your place?**"

"Seeing as I don't really trust anyone else," Lore answered, "I think it would be in both of our best interests if You did something to combat that mortality. Not get rid of it, mind You, I know that's impossible. Just extend my time." She arched a brow. "Maybe You'll learn something by then."

"**So you are doing the same thing He did,**" the Fount said, as contemptuous as a magic fountain could sound. "**Looking for a way out of dying.**"

"Not at all," Lore murmured, thinking of Gabe, thinking of Bastian. "I'd love to die."

The Fount had no reply for that. **"You said you wished to talk terms,"** It said finally. **"We suppose you will want repayment."**

"Give them back to me," Lore said simply, her voice a wound.

"They are far gone. Death cannot be cheated." It paused. **"But it can be . . . abbreviated."**

"How abbreviated?" Her heart slammed against the base of her throat.

"Five hundred years," the Fount said. **"The time from the Godsfall to now. Then you can have them back. But they will die again, you understand this? Immortality is not an option."**

"We don't want it," Lore said. "We just want a life together. It already began, and we want a different ending."

"We accept your terms." The waters of the Fount splashed lightly, washing up the sides of the golden stone. A small wave lapped over the edge, collecting in a shallow basin made from a broken tile. **"Drink. There is no power in it, only longevity."** Its not-voice went wry. **"We *have* learned things."**

Lore knelt. Then she sat, crossing her legs beneath her; a less comfortable position, but she didn't want any posture of worship for this. She cupped her hands, scooped up the water, and drank.

It washed through her, shining and cold, stringing stars through her bones and minor harmonies around her organs. Lore gasped and opened her eyes. She felt no different, not really. But the world looked a little brighter.

She stood, making sure her legs were steady, then walked over to Raihan. He'd stopped writing, pen hanging limp in his fingers. "Well," he said as she approached. "That was . . . something."

"Did you get all of it?" She sat beside him, glanced at his notebook. Messy scrawl covered the pages.

"Every bit," he said.

"Good." Lore closed her eyes, sighed. "We need to make sure only the truth is shared this time. There will still be opportunities to twist it, but if we can make sure the truth is out there, it will make a difference. Surely."

"Surely," Raihan repeated. A moment of silence. "What do you need from me, Lore?"

"Just to stay," she murmured. "Just to write the truth."

He nodded. Then he stood, walking toward the path. "I'll start now," he said. "Sharing the truth, I mean."

Lore watched him go. Then she was alone with the Fount. She looked at It with her eyebrow cocked. "You're stuck with me, now. For five hundred years, at least."

"An interesting five hundred years, We are sure," the Fount burbled.

"Undoubtedly." Lore flexed her fingers back and forth. "Now there's something we should fix."

The Isles were still burnt. The dregs of the Godsfall still poisoned them. The Fount couldn't fix everything—she couldn't fix everything—but she could fix this.

Lore settled her hands on the lip of the Fount, right over the pieces they'd found and brought back. It buzzed like It had before but didn't make her go numb. She was something that could withstand It. She and the Fount, of the same nature.

Lore looked deep into the waters. A swirl of color, but right now she needed gold and green.

They rose to the surface, then spun away in lazy spirals. She watched them, grabbed them, pulled them into herself. Imbued them with her will, easy as taking her next breath.

The power flowed through her, and then into the earth.

Buds sprouted on long-dead trees, blooming green, the bark going from char-black to deep-brown. Grass unfurled like a carpet. Wildflowers opened in colorful swaths up and down the path to the Mount.

The green and gold settled back down into the Fount, replaced by air and water and fire.

These, too, she channeled easily, funneling them up into the air, recalibrating the atmosphere. Seasons realigned, weather stabilized. The sharp gust of an autumn breeze ruffled her hair.

The magic resettled. The waters of the Fount spun. **That's nice,** It said contemplatively, Its voice only in her head again. **Nice to feel like things are back as they should be.**

"It's a start, at least." Lore sighed, exhaustion filtering through every muscle. "Not so bad, being helpful, huh?"

The waters swirled in thought. **You have carved a beginning, daughter of the dark, when your nature was always an end.**

"I am nothing if not contrary," Lore replied, and settled her back against the stones to watch the sun set over the ocean.

EPILOGUE

THE GODDESS OF WAITING

1–100 AFA (after Fount's ascension)

The first one hundred years were the hardest.

She lived like a mortal for them, and that was probably why. That, and everyone she knew dying.

Alie came to visit her sometimes, when her duties allowed. After some convincing, she'd held on to her throne, but she legislated away most of its power to the newly wrought delegate system. It worked well, apparently. Astonishing what people could accomplish when they chose their own leaders.

Finn was one of the elected, after renouncing his Caldienan citizenship so he could marry Alie. Lore found that she wasn't really surprised when she heard that bit of news. Good for Alie, tying down a pirate.

Still, it took time to dissolve the Empire, to break it back into composite parts. Things didn't always go smoothly—it was hard to get everyone to agree on how to deal with the Empire breaking up, and there were a few who wanted to try conquering the newly sovereign nations. Alie shut that down quick and hard. "The last thing I want to do," she said, sitting on the lip of the Fount with Lore during one of her visits, "is accidentally make another Empire."

Her eyes had been far away when she said it. Like she was thinking of Jax.

Her mothers had stayed with Lore for the first five years or so, but when Alie reached out to them and asked if they'd help with some scientific studies at the university—poison no longer allowed anyone to extend their life or reach for Mortem, but researchers were still interested in how they could use it for pain mitigation—Lore convinced them to go.

"We don't want to leave you all alone, mouse," Val had said, chewing at her lip. Her shoulder had healed cleanly, with only the red mark of the cauterization scar and the loss of the limb to mark it.

You aren't alone, the Fount said, indignant. **You have Us.**

The Fount only spoke in Lore's head now, so she didn't do anything but smile, small and tentative, but there. "The world is only as good as we make it," Lore said, pushing back her mother's hair. It was gray all the way through. "So go make it."

Alie married Finn soon after, and one day, she came up the path to the Mount heavy with child.

Ten years since the Fount, give or take. It was hard for Lore to count time anymore, the years of her penance blurring together. But all that time came rushing to her when she saw her friend, swollen to at least eight months out of the nine. Lore had never wanted children, had never even considered the possibility, other than that one fleeting moment when she thought about how being an Arceneaux Queen would necessitate heirs. Still, there was an ache in her when she saw Alie. She wondered if the child would look like her or like Finn.

She wondered what kind of fathers Gabe and Bastian would have been.

Alie sat cumbersomely on the lip of the Fount. "So," she said. "when are you going to come back?"

Lore arched a brow.

"The Empire is dissolved," Alie said. "The continent is at peace. The weather and the seasons are back in order. What else do you have to do?"

"Keep watch," Lore said.

We would not make the same mistake twice, the Fount burbled grumpily.

"Just in case," Lore added. "I need to serve my time."

Because this was a prison sentence, as surely as her time on the Burnt Isles had been. All that death on her hands. Everything she'd done possessed by Apollius, yes, but the things she'd done on her own, too.

"Come on." Alie tried to sound playful, but there was a note of desperation there. "You've more than atoned. It will be five hundred years before they come back; you just plan to sit here that long?"

"I have to guard the Fount," she replied. "That was the deal."

A deal that sat so heavy, most days. But those were the days that made her feel better, more human. The scary days were the ones she could barely feel passing. When her burden was light, as if this was a weight she'd always been meant to shoulder.

The Fount bubbled but said nothing.

Alie sighed, tossing a corkscrew curl up onto her forehead. "I know, but..." She stopped. Huffed a laugh. "It's so odd, seeing your friend become a god. I mean, we've already done it once, but to see it happen again, like this..." She trailed off again, the sentence one that wound through weeds. "I just didn't want this for you, is all. You deserved a life."

"I'll have one," Lore said. "I just have to wait for them first."

Alie took her hand.

After her daughter was born—one she named Loria, a combination of two names that made Lore want to cry, hers and her mother's—Alie mostly just sent letters. Lore understood.

Her mothers came back at least once a year after taking the

research positions, but when age made traveling difficult, they resigned and settled back on the island. It felt like a blink of an eye to Lore, and then they were dying.

She was with them when they did, holding their wrinkled hands in her still-young ones as they breathed their last, as the bright Spiritum in them turned to Mortem. Lore saw the threads, weaving in and through everything. Sometimes the world appeared more like a tapestry than something living, something real. It scared her a bit, to see it like that, to feel herself becoming less and less a part of it.

Val went first, forty years after Lore had become the guardian of the Fount. Mari went soon after. It was peaceful for them both.

"Will you be all right, mouse?" Mari asked. Her voice was thin with age but still warm.

Lore put her mother's hand on her cheek. "Of course," she lied.

Mari closed her eyes. "None of us wanted this for you. But I suppose the world had other plans." Her eyes opened, already clouded at the edges, knowing the next time they closed would be the last. "Remember to live, Lore. I know you have to wait. But when the time comes, when you're free, do everything you ever wanted. You saved this world; don't let your years go by without seeing all of it."

She buried them next to the cliff where Nyxara had once thrown her wedding ring. They'd liked the view. When she sat back, her hands caked in dirt, she allowed herself to cry.

Is it like this for everyone? the Fount asked softly. **Such a deep wound?**

"Usually," Lore said, cleaning her palms on her trousers and wiping her eyes.

The Fount took a moment, considering this. **We are ... sorry.** The word sounded strange, coming from It. **We see now why there is so much to fear.**

"That's what makes life worth it, though." Lore stood, stretching out muscles that should have been sore from such labor, but weren't. "You have to appreciate everything, because it ends."

Raihan didn't last much longer than her mothers. He came to the island once a month or so, meticulously interviewing her about her day-to-day—she never had much to tell him. He had far more to tell her about the world beyond, now that he'd returned to Kadmar and led the university there.

"Things are better," he said the last time he came, his voice creaking with age. "More countries are trying a delegate system, letting the people rule themselves. They send aid when needed, food and supplies. People are kinder to one another."

Lore smiled tremulously. "So people are better now."

"And thus the world is," he said.

The Fount didn't respond. But she could feel It thinking, churning over Itself.

When Raihan died, he left behind neatly bound stacks of manuscripts detailing what had happened the day she made her deal, everything that transpired afterward, the true nature of the Fount and of divinity. At first, Lore didn't want to do anything with them, wanted to continue her quiet existence where she was nothing but a rumor, the stories of her all true but not widely shared. She knew how religions worked and wanted no part in making one.

It was Malcolm who changed her mind.

He didn't come as frequently as Alie—he and Michal settled in Caldien, and the journey was hard as he got older—but he came sometimes, Michal in tow, and once brought their children with them, who gamboled around the Fount like It were a plaything. Lore let them. The Fount bubbled contentedly, as if It enjoyed their presence.

One day, Malcolm came up the mountain alone.

"He died in his sleep," he murmured, settling beside her on the lip of the Fount, wincing as he did. His hair was still cropped short, snowy now, and his kind eyes were surrounded with wrinkles. "Our children were with him. It was painless. I don't think I'm far behind." He cracked his neck. "Hopefully not, anyway. Who knew I'd be the one to live so gods-damned long? I'm fucking tired."

He stayed with her longer, that time, the two of them enjoying the other's company mostly in silence. It was a special grief, to have lost the people you shared a life with, and they both were intimately familiar with it.

Before Malcolm left, he went into the ruins of the cathedral and came out with his hands full of Raihan's manuscripts. Lore was already shaking her head when he placed them on the broken tiles of the courtyard with an air of finality.

"I understand," Malcolm said, not giving her a moment to voice her displeasure. "But they deserve the truth, Lore. What was the point of having him write everything down if you aren't going to share them?"

What indeed? the Fount asked.

She sat on Its lip, watching the waters within churn and gyre, the glowing threads tangle. "I don't want to be worshipped, Malcolm."

It's nice, sometimes, the Fount offered. **But We do not blame you.**

"I'm not saying you have to be." Malcolm came to sit next to her, moving slow. "But didn't you do all this so that anything known about the Fount would be purely truth?"

"There can never be pure truth so long as humans are the ones interpreting it," she said.

He sighed. She could tell he wanted to call that out, her use of *humans* as if she wasn't among their number. But she wasn't, and they both knew that. A hundred years, nearly, and she was exactly the same.

People are better, Raihan had said. *The world is better.*

"The fact is," Malcolm said finally, "that a religion is going to spring up around this. It's inevitable. People look for things to believe in." He held up Raihan's books. "You can't control what they end up thinking about you. Hells, I feel like the time is coming when you won't really be able to keep them away from your island. But you can give them the truth. You can try to trust them." He paused. "Lore, isn't the whole point trying to make the world something you can trust?"

It felt strange to hear her name. She hadn't thought of herself by it since her mothers died. She wasn't really Lore anymore, she just...was.

The Fount bubbled, thinking.

She hunched forward, arms crossed on her bent knees. "I don't want to make the same mistakes," she whispered. "I'm so fallible, Malcolm. It would be so easy."

"You won't," he said.

You won't, the Fount agreed.

"You were never one for belief, Lore. But if you have to believe in something, let it be yourself."

He took the books with him.

100–200 AFA

In the next century, people started coming to the island. She could have stopped them. She didn't.

They mostly left her alone. They never even approached the top of the mountain. They knew she was here, and clearly they believed in what she was, in the story Raihan had meticulously written down. But if they worshipped her, they kept it quiet and left her out of it. For that, Lore was grateful.

You could go to them, the Fount said. **If you are lonely.**

"How can I be lonely with You yammering in my head all the time?"

It splashed at her.

One day, after the pilgrims had been on the island long enough to revitalize the villages and build more of their own, a girl came up to the courtyard of the Fount, all curiosity and big eyes.

"You're a goddess," she said simply. "And you're waiting."

"I am," she replied. There was no reason to quibble over it. She knew what she'd become.

The girl cautiously came closer. Sat on the broken tiles in front of the Fount. Lore had never repaired them, never repaired the cathedral. There were some paths whose ruin needed minding.

"My great-grandmother knew you," the girl said. "Rosie. You were on the Burnt Isles together, before the Liberation."

Rosie, who'd covered for her that night when she and Dani met Raihan. Such a small thing, a tiny moment in her too-long string of them, but Lore remembered, and she smiled. "I remember Rosie."

The girl smiled back, small and trepidatious but genuine. "Will you tell me the story? I've read it," she hedged. "Everyone on the island has read the Book of Waiting."

So that's what they called it.

"But I would like to hear it from you," the girl continued. "The whole story."

And Lore told her.

The Fount listened, and churned, and thought.

200–300 AFA

The tradition started there. Every one hundred years, the people on the islands would pick a girl, usually young, and send her up to the Fount and Its guardian, to ask the story and write down the truth. A truth that had already been written, many times over. But honesty needed renewing all the time. History needed a recounting.

The Goddess of Waiting knew it wasn't necessarily an accurate way to get a picture of the world, but everyone they sent was infallibly kind. The villagers took care of one another. No one ever went cold or hungry.

The goddess told the same story every time someone came. It became the way in which she counted time, this century-marking storytelling. It reminded her of who she had been, as her unnaturally long life and proximity to magic changed her—not utterly, not like when she held the world's soul, but she didn't look human anymore. Her hands were seamed like the Fount's stones to the elbow, her skin cracked rock with gold waiting beneath. Her eyes shone gentle light.

The goddess remembered what she looked like when she used to channel Mortem. The white eyes and black veins. She wasn't sure which version of herself she preferred.

Every time she told the story, the Fount listened as if it were the first time.

300–400 AFA

She told the story for the fourth time. It was nearly rote at this point, but for this telling, she let herself feel it all. Her eyes pricked with tears, and when the story was done, she bowed in on herself and sobbed.

Oh, little goddess, the Fount murmured. **We are sorry, We are sorry.**

The girl they'd sent to hear the story stood carefully, approached as if the goddess were a loaded gun. She put her hand on her shoulder. "How much longer do you have to wait?"

"One hundred years," the goddess said, and the weight of every single one of them settled so heavy.

The girl's hand trembled on her shoulder. "You should rest," she said quietly. "You're almost done."

She hadn't slept since she made her bargain with the Fount. Her body didn't need it. Every day melted into the next, sunset to sunrise again, and she'd watched them all.

But the girl was right. She did need rest. It was almost done, almost finished, and she was so tired.

The goddess stood when the girl was gone.

Go on, the Fount whispered, like a mother sending a sleepy child to bed. **We'll wake you if We need you.**

She went to the cave where the god before her had waited. The irony was not lost.

You've done well, the Fount soothed. **Guarding Us all these centuries.**

She smiled listlessly at the ceiling, tear tracks drying salty on her cheeks. "And have You learned anything?"

Already, she was drifting into sleep. But she heard the Fount when It answered.

Many things.

500 AFA

Little goddess.

A gentle nudge. A quiet song.

It is time to tell the tale again. Softer, almost sad: **And then your waiting will be done.**

Finally. Finally.

The goddess rose. She went to the Fount.

The girl chosen to write down the story this last time was a pretty young thing, maybe twenty, all green eyes and red hair. The goddess knew that the world beyond the island had changed, but she didn't know how, and no one told her. They dressed the same, in trousers and shirts and boots. They wrote with pens, in notebooks, and though they looked slightly different from century to century, they didn't change all that much.

When she approached, the girl stood. She smiled eagerly. "I begged them to let it be me. I've wanted to hear this."

The goddess arched a brow and settled on the lip of the Fount. She began her story, once again, for the last time. Anxiety thrummed through her as she spoke. The world seemed to bend, to rush her on.

We see, the Fount said, running beneath her thoughts. **We have heard this so many times, and We see now.**

The girl wrote dutifully, asking questions. The goddess tried not to be annoyed when she was interrupted. She wanted to get this done. She had things to do.

This girl peered up from her notes, eyes narrowed. "Which one was your favorite?"

The Goddess of Waiting laughed. It was an unexpected thing. She hadn't laughed in so long, and it felt so good, that she did it again, louder. Something seemed to fall away, a shroud that she hadn't realized she'd spun around herself. She'd been in stasis for so long, as if her waiting had enclosed her in a cocoon, the goddess-self a mask she'd drawn over her real face.

But this was the fifth time she'd told this story, this was her five hundred years, and the life she'd waited for was so close, she could taste it. Her debt was nearly paid. There was a hum in the air, building as she told this story, making all the hairs on her arms stand up. The waters of the Fount sloshed forward to gently touch her hand.

"Neither," she told the girl. "I loved them both equally, wanted them both the same. Gabriel kissed like fire. Bastian wanted me in control. They were so different, and so perfect, and I loved them both so much I've been waiting on this damn rock for five hundred years for them to come back."

The girl's eyes went wide, and so did her smile, her pen moving fast over her notebook.

Lore—that was her name, her name was Lore, and yeah, she

was technically a goddess, but hopefully that particular trial would be over soon—leaned forward. "What's your name?"

"Kenna." The girl's eyes were saucer-wide. The goddess did not often ask for names.

"Well, Kenna," Lore said, "you'll be the last to hear this story."

Yes, the Fount said. **Yes.**

Kenna's eyes were going to fall right out of her head if she widened them any more. "I . . . are you sure?"

"Very sure." Lore stood. "I have plans."

Kenna left in a dreamy haze.

Lore's time was up. She could leave. But before she did, she turned to the Fount.

"So You said You've learned something."

The waters bubbled and frothed. **We have, hearing the story. Watching you.**

Her brows climbed. "Watching me?"

For five hundred years, you have waited for love. For five hundred years, you have treated your friends with kindness, as they go and make the world kinder in turn. The water splashed up, wetting the hem of her skirt. **We are not human. We will never be. But We have learned human kindness, and it is something worth saving. This world is worth saving, because people like you are in it.**

She smiled, her eyes wet. Strange, how easily she could cry now. "Proud of You."

The Fount sloshed at her again. **Now go. Like you said, you have things to do. People to meet.**

Her heartbeat kicked up in her chest, anticipatory sweat on her palms. "I'll be keeping an eye on You. As long as I'm able."

Live your life, little goddess, the Fount said. **Make it full and beautiful and kind, Lore. We will keep this world, and watch it become better.**

Lore put her hand on the lip of the Fount, over those pieces that had once been broken. Then she turned away.

Moss furred the floor of the cathedral, grown up around the fallen beams. It made the ruins look softer. She supposed years would do that. They had certainly softened her.

On the other side of the ruins was another cliff, one she'd discovered in her long imprisonment here. It was hidden from view, only reached if you climbed through the underbrush, the now-blooming trees and vines that crowded the back of the once-grand structure Apollius had built. Only the stones stood now, everything else long rotted away. Lore climbed through it, the hum in the air intensifying, every nerve in her body alight. And as she did, the vestiges of godhood fell away like a shed snake-skin. The cracks in her hands healed over, hiding the gold. Her eyes dimmed down to hazel.

They stood on that cliff. They looked exactly the same. Bastian and Gabe, both here and both hers, holding hands.

She fell into them.

They all sank to the ground, and she didn't realize she was sob-bing until Gabe brushed a tear off her cheek, until Bastian pulled her close and kissed her forehead. "There, dearest," he murmured. "Compose yourself."

She laughed, the feeling still odd, burrowed into his shoulder. Gabe laid his head in her lap, and she ran her hands through his hair, across his neck.

"I'm sorry," she murmured. "I'm so sorry."

He caught her hand, kissed it. "Don't be. It's in the past." He chuckled. "Long past."

"So what..." She didn't really know how to ask, didn't know what she *wanted* to ask. She looked between them, her monk and her prince, at a loss for words. "How...was it?"

A moment of silence before they all burst out laughing, col-lapsing into one another again. When they quieted, Gabe's hand on her cheek and Bastian's running through her hair, Bastian sighed. "Good news," he said. "Apollius was lying."

She sat up from where she'd reclined against his chest. "He what?"

"Not lying, I don't think." Gabe ran a hand down her arm, like he had to keep touching her, his head still in her lap. "But His experience of the afterlife wasn't everyone's."

"He made His own hell," Bastian continued, picking up the strings of Gabe's conversation like they were of one mind. "And it was a dark void where He was powerless."

"So where did you two end up?" She almost didn't want to know. Didn't want to imagine them locked in hells of their own making.

"Not sure," Gabe said, smiling. "But I think it was the Shining Realm."

She'd accepted the former god's word as fact, made her peace with this life being all there was, and after only darkness. But apparently she hadn't bought into that quite as fully as she thought, because some heavy weight on her heart lifted, with a flood of intense relief. "What was it like?"

"Oh, you know." Bastian shrugged. "Endless wine, perfect weather, the sound of singing all the time." He looked at her, soft-eyed. "They're all there, Lore."

Her family, her friends. People she'd see again, waiting beyond that starry doorway.

But first, a life. Here, with them.

Bastian read the thought on her face, gently kissed her brow. "But as of right now, I am more concerned about this world than that one." Bastian stood, held out a hand. Lore took it. Gabe took her other one and planted a kiss on it, then her cheek. "We've kept our lady love waiting long enough, I think. Let's go see the world Lore saved."

The Goddess of Waiting ended. Lore began.

ACKNOWLEDGMENTS

It's still bonkers to me that I wrote a whole trilogy. When I first started writing, I saw myself as a standalone author; the idea of having to come up with a story that spanned multiple books, and sustain all that worldbuilding, made me incredibly nervous. But this story needed more than one book, and this last one in particular might be my favorite I have ever written.

Thanks as always to Whitney Ross, my powerhouse of an agent, who never lets me off the hook and always has the most incredible edits—and is always a listening ear for my myriad anxieties. Working with you is a dream.

Thanks to Brit Hvide, who has ushered every single one of my books into the world with such impeccable guidance and true friendship. I am so thankful to work with you, but also just to know you.

Huge thanks to the entire team at Orbit, especially Ellen Wright—the devil works hard but y'all work harder, and I am endlessly grateful.

To the Pod—would not be here without you.

To Erin A. Craig—you are one of my favorite people in the whole world.

To the group chat, you know who you are—for years, you have

kept me grounded and sane and made me laugh and cry and held me through everything. I love you more than words can say.

To my husband, and our perfect feral children—my life is worth living because you are in it.

It's obvious to anyone who read this book (or really, any of my books) that my feelings on religion and spirituality are incredibly complicated. They still are, but this trilogy gave me the space to write about that complication, to sift through all the broken pieces and hold them to the light and see which ones still shine. I'm writing this in December of 2024, and the world is a terrifying, grief-stricken place. It's scary and getting scarier, and all we have is one another. All we have is the hope.

The ways that religions—Christianity in particular—have been twisted to justify hate and violence is a despicable thing that wounds me deeply every time I think about it. I know there are many like me, who grew up in church and are faced with the task of figuring out how to live with a broken belief system, one that taught loving your neighbor and taking care of people and yet often seems to be used for the opposite. People who can no longer stomach the institution, but still long to hold on to the good things it gave you, the radical love that it should be. But even when the systems are so broken, the foundations—compassion, and a want for better—those things are good.

Those things are true.

The hope is what hurts, but the hope is all we have.

Hold one another close. Because better is possible, and we have to make it.